Flames of LOVE

The Remingtons

Love in Bloom Series

Melissa Foster

ISBN-13: 978-0-9910468-9-8
ISBN-10: 0991046897

This is a work of fiction. The events and characters described herein are imaginary and are not intended to refer to specific places or living persons. The opinions expressed in this manuscript are solely the opinions of the author and do not represent the opinions or thoughts of the publisher. The author has represented and warranted full ownership and/or legal right to publish all the materials in this book.

FLAMES OF LOVE
All Rights Reserved.
Copyright © 2018 Melissa Foster
V2.0

This book may not be reproduced, transmitted, or stored in whole or in part by any means, including graphic, electronic, or mechanical without the express written consent of the publisher except in the case of brief quotations embodied in critical articles and reviews.

Cover Design: Elizabeth Mackey Designs

WORLD LITERARY PRESS
PRINTED IN THE UNITED STATES OF AMERICA

A Note to Readers

I have been excited to write about Siena Remington since I first met her in *Bursting with Love* (The Bradens). She is such a sassy and confident character. I wondered if I'd find any vulnerabilities, and I also wondered just what type of man could handle such a strong woman. The deeper I dug, the more I discovered, and her vulnerabilities made me love her even more. When I met Cash Ryder, who is equally as challenging, I knew they were the perfect match. I hope you love Siena and Cash as much as I do!

The best way to keep up to date with new releases, sales, and exclusive content is to sign up for my newsletter or to download my free app.

www.MelissaFoster.com/news
www.MelissaFoster.com/app

About the Love in Bloom Big-Family Romance Collection

The Remingtons are just one of the series in the Love in Bloom big-family romance collection. Each Love in Bloom book is written to be enjoyed as a stand-alone novel or as part of the larger series. There are no cliffhangers or unresolved issues. Characters from each series make appearances in future books, so you never miss an engagement, wedding, or birth.

For free downloadable Love in Bloom family trees, publication schedules, series checklists, and more, please visit my special Reader Goodies page.
www.MelissaFoster.com/RG

Sign up for my newsletter to be notified of my next Love in Bloom release.
www.MelissaFoster.com/Newsletter

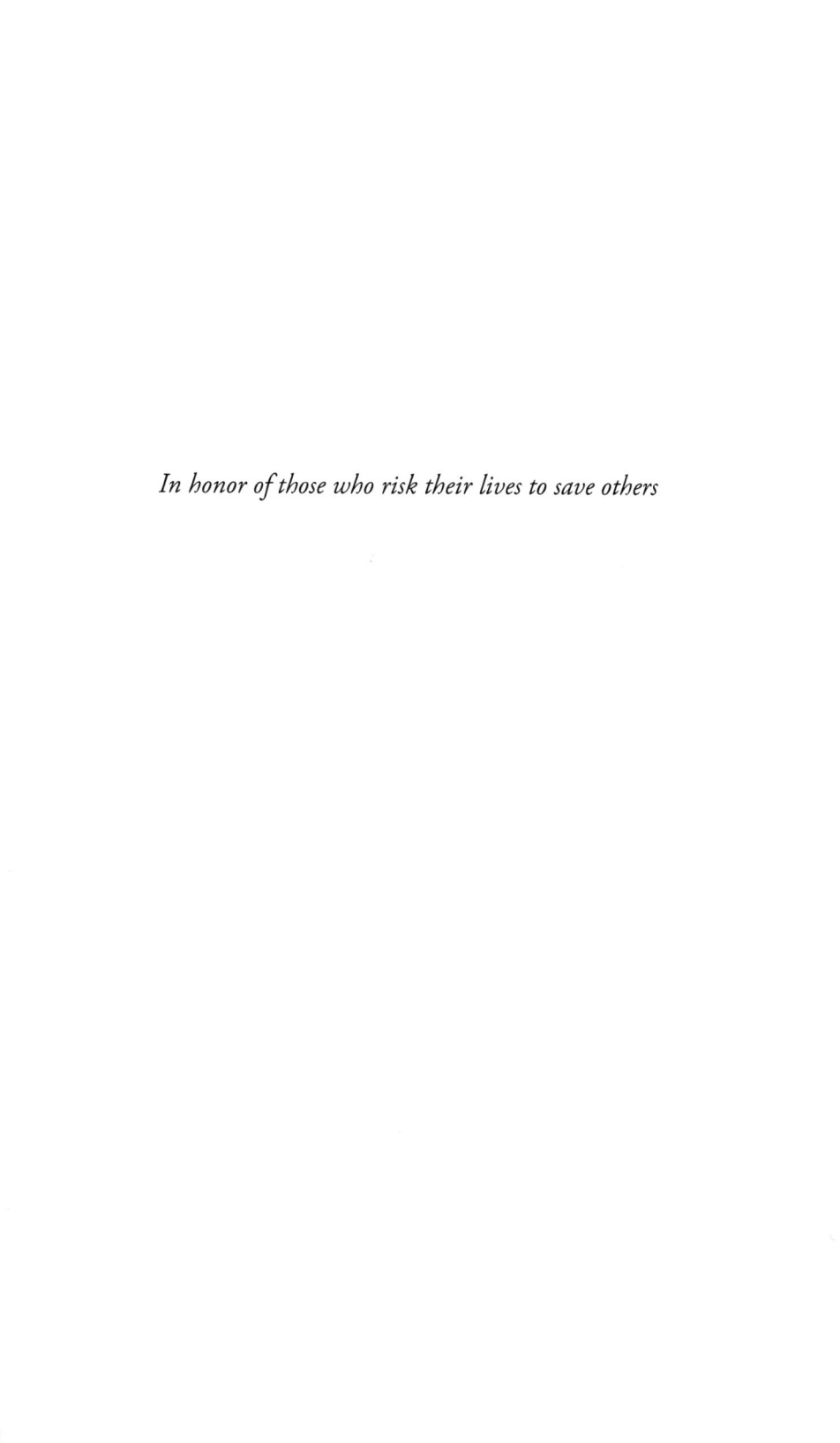

In honor of those who risk their lives to save others

Praise for Melissa Foster

"Contemporary romance at its hottest. Each Braden sibling left me craving the next. Sensual, sexy, and satisfying, the Braden series is a captivating blend of the dance between lust, love, and life."
—Bestselling author Keri Nola, LMHC

"[LOVERS AT HEART] Foster's tale of stubborn yet persistent love takes us on a heartbreaking and soul-searing journey."
—Reader's Favorite

"Smart, uplifting, and beautifully layered. I couldn't put it down!"
—National bestselling author Jane Porter (on SISTERS IN LOVE)

"Steamy love scenes, emotionally charged drama, and a family-driven story make this the perfect story for any romance reader."
—Midwest Book Review (on SISTERS IN BLOOM)

"HAVE NO SHAME is a powerful testimony to love and the progressive, logical evolution of social consciousness, with an outcome that readers will find engrossing, unexpected, and ultimately eye-opening."
—Midwest Book Review

"TRACES OF KARA is psychological suspense at its best, weaving a tight-knit plot, unrelenting action, and tense moments that don't let up and ending in a fiery, unpredictable revelation."
—*Midwest Book Review*

"[MEGAN'S WAY] A wonderful, warm, and thought-provoking story…a deep and moving book that speaks to men as well as women, and I urge you all to put it on your reading list."
—*Mensa Bulletin*

"[CHASING AMANDA] Secrets make this tale outstanding."
—*Hagerstown* magazine

"COME BACK TO ME is a hauntingly beautiful love story set against the backdrop of betrayal in a broken world."
—*Bestselling author Sue Harrison*

Chapter One

SIX INCHES OF fresh snow covered the roads. Even with the windshield wipers set to high, Cash Ryder could barely see a few feet in front of the all-terrain vehicle he'd borrowed from his buddy Tommy. The roads appeared empty, but he knew that in a storm like this one, there could be fifty cars just outside his range of visibility. It was as if New York had been swallowed by snow, and Cash wondered how many accidents the local fire department would have to deal with. As a firefighter, he'd seen it all, from overconfident teens skidding into trees to truckers unable to stop their massive rigs from rumbling over the tops of cars that had collided on black ice. Cash was headed to his eldest brother Duke's house, just outside of New York City, and the storm had come out of nowhere. He needed a break from the city. Hell, he needed a break from life. Visiting his brother for the evening had seemed like the perfect escape. He hadn't seen him for a few weeks, and the last time they'd been together, Cash's emotions had been raw. He'd laid into Duke—and everyone else who was in his path—with a venomous rage that even he hadn't known he possessed. Luckily, Duke wasn't a grudge holder. He understood that even the most prepared person could be knocked sideways on occasion, and Cash knew that Duke would always be there for him.

He gritted his teeth as memories of the tragic day that completely fucked with his mind played through his head like a bad rerun. His pulse quickened, chased by full-body chills. Sweat beaded his brow despite the cold. *Shit. I couldn't get to the guy.* He tried to comfort himself with the last, and most difficult, reminder the therapist his chief had told him to speak with had given him. The one she felt was the most important—and the one that he could barely stomach. *It wasn't my fault.*

Skid marks across the fresh snow pulled him from the painful thoughts. Not just skid marks, but thick trails, as if a car had skidded sideways. He eased up on the gas and craned his neck, squinting into the storm. *Shit. Definitely recent. Definitely over the edge of the mountain.* He pulled onto the shoulder, cursing under his breath. Pulling his woolen balaclava over his head, he zipped his parka, and reported the accident to 911. Then he put on his gloves, grabbed the emergency bag that contained a first-aid kit, a glass-breaking tool, and other rescue items he never left home without, and headed into the storm.

SIENA REMINGTON'S TEETH chattered as she struggled against the airbag pressed against her chest. *Okay. Okay. Calm down.* Wasn't that the key to surviving? Remaining calm? Her heart slammed against her ribs, which ached from the impact of the accident. She tried to get her bearings, but all she could see was white. The car leaned to the right, and she had no way of knowing if she was on the edge of a precipice or on solid ground. She hadn't seen anyone on the roads, and she'd skidded off the pavement ten minutes ago. She hadn't even told her friend Willow that she'd left the city and was on her way. *Oh God.* Her cell phone rang. She scanned the floor. *Goddamn phone.* She hadn't even reached for it when it rang as she was driving. She'd glanced at it—for a second, maybe two—and then *wham!* Her car was skidding off the road toward the edge of the mountain. Now the frigging phone was nowhere in sight. *And I'm going to die out here in bum-fuck New York. Shit. Shit. Shit.*

"Hey, you all right in there?"

A man's deep voice broke through her worry. "Yes! Help me. Please!" *Oh, thank God.* "Hurry. Please hurry." She grabbed her hat from her pocket and pulled it down low over her head, debating braving the conditions and getting out of her car. She couldn't remember ever being so cold.

A gloved hand cleared the snow from her window; then a set of eyes pressed close, one hand shielding them as the window fogged from his breath. Siena gasped a breath before realizing that any sane person would be covered up in this weather. Her heartbeat picked up as she stared at the mask that covered everything but a swatch of skin around serious, dark eyes. *Sexy dark eyes, filled with serious concern. Jesus, what am I thinking?*

"Please help me." She struggled with her seat belt.

"Are you hurt? Injured in any way?"

Siena moved her legs and arms. "No. I don't think so."

"Good. Your car is sideways." His voice was muffled behind the mask and the window. "It's stable, but when I open this door, it could jostle it into a slide, so I want to get you out as fast as possible. Can you get out of your seat belt?"

She pulled at the buckle. "Yes. Yes, I think I can." *Oh God. Please get me out. Sideways?* "A slide? Like I could slide off the mountain?" Tears pressed at her eyes.

He looked away, then back through the window. "I don't think so. You're on a pretty flat spot. Got the seat belt off?"

"Yes. Wait. You don't *think* so? What if the car slides? Am I near a big drop? Jesus, I don't want to die."

His eyes narrowed. "Calm down," he commanded.

Siena clenched her chattering teeth.

"I'm a firefighter. I can get you out, but you have to remain calm. Can you do that?"

She nodded. *A firefighter. Thank God. Hurry. Hurry.*

He didn't seem to struggle with the door. He opened it slowly, and his powerful arm circled her shoulder. "I've got you. Now slide your legs over and out of the car. You sure you're not injured?"

She felt safer just knowing she wasn't alone, but as she stepped from the car onto the steep incline, she slipped and reached for the first thing she could hang on to—him. She clung to the man's thick parka as he pulled her away from the car, his arms circling her. Her legs began to shake. Or maybe they'd been shaking the whole time and she just hadn't realized it.

"You're okay. I've got you." His voice soothed her.

He did have her. His body was so big, it practically consumed her. She opened her mouth to speak, but her jaw was shaking too much to form any words. She nodded again, looking down to keep the snow from her eyes.

"I've gotta get you up there." He pointed to the road. "The emergency crew should be here soon, but I want to get you into my truck and get you warmed up."

It was snowing so hard she could barely make out the road at the top of the hill. Her cute Burberry coat did nothing to warm her from the cold that was quickly settling into her bones.

His masculine scent permeated her fear as he pressed his body against her, and the combination of being safe in his arms and his warm, earthy scent comforted her. She climbed up the bank, still within his grasp. Every time she lost her footing, he held her up.

"You've got it. That's it."

She clung to his encouragement like a lifeline.

"That's it. Take your time. I'm right here."

Back on the road, she focused on the headlights from his vehicle. *Safe. I'm safe.*

"Let's get you into the truck."

The tracks from her car were almost completely buried beneath fresh snow. If he hadn't come along, she would probably still be down there.

"Th-thank…you," she managed. He'd spoken with such care, so different from the men she socialized with. They'd never brave a blizzard to rescue her. She was sick of those kinds of men. They treated her like she was stupid and easy just because she was pretty. She wanted to be loved and cherished, romanced, not taken out to dinner with the expectation of sex. She didn't want to be wined and dined with diamonds on every finger. She wanted a man who would look at her the way her brothers looked at their girlfriends and fiancées. Her brothers would go to the ends of the earth to rescue her or their girlfriends, no matter what the risk. *Romance. Yes, that's what I want.* How much more romantic could things get than being rescued by a mysterious stranger in the middle of a snowstorm? She allowed herself to fantasize about it for a moment, giving herself something to focus on besides the fact that she'd just slid fifty feet down an embankment and had nearly frozen to death. As if the accident might have almost been worth it. As if fate had a hand in it.

The man settled Siena into the passenger seat, and she saw his eyes darken, growing more serious. Then he climbed into the driver's seat, sighed, and cranked the heat.

She took off her thin leather gloves and put her bare hands in front of the heater. "Ahh. That's so much better." Her shaking calmed to a mild tremble. "Thank you for helping me."

He shifted his eyes to hers. "I have to go back for my bag. I called 911, so the emergency crew should be here soon. Stay here, okay?" He climbed from the truck, leaving Siena to nod after him.

Now that she was out of danger, reality came rushing back to her. She was supposed to be at her friend Willow's parents' house over an hour ago. *Damn it.* She needed to call Willow. She waited for her rescuer to return, thankful for the warmth. Twenty minutes later, she wondered what was taking him so long. She could probably climb down and get her phone herself instead of making him do everything for her and, she realized, she also needed to retrieve her purse. She wasn't hurt, and now that she knew she wasn't going to die, she wasn't as frightened. Siena put her gloves back on and trudged through the thick snow to the edge of the road, shivering and regretting her decision. She peered over the edge of the mountain but didn't see the guy anywhere.

"I told you to wait in the truck." His stern voice came from nowhere. "Visibility is near zero. If a car comes by, you could be killed."

She strained to see him through the falling snow.

"I'm right here." He climbed up over the edge of the road with a bag strapped to his back. "Don't you get how dangerous these conditions are?" He grabbed her arm and dragged her back toward the truck.

Too fucking sexy, even without being able to see his face, and a big-ass chip on his shoulder. Fantasy dead. Moving on. Except her heart wasn't moving on. It hammered against her chest.

Siena pulled her arm from his grasp. "I have to get my purse."

"I'll get it."

"I need my phone."

He opened the truck door and shoved her in, then pinned her to the seat with his dark, sexy stare. "Use mine."

She looked down at his thick gloves, one on her thigh, one on her arm, keeping her from leaving the truck. A flash of fear shot through her. She didn't know him, and she was no match for his strength. What if he wasn't a firefighter at all? She took a deep breath. If he wasn't there to help, why had he left her alone in the truck? Wouldn't he have taken her off to some kind of rape-and-pillage shack in the woods somewhere?

I'm being stupid. Of course he's here to help.

She pushed aside the thoughts and followed her gut instinct. Something in his eyes made her feel he was trustworthy, although she definitely wasn't used to being told what to do. Siena was one of New York's top fashion models. Men lavished her with gifts and went to great lengths to get her attention. She didn't even like being lavished by the wealthy suitors who pursued her, but she definitely preferred that to the attitude-ridden rescuer before her. She dropped her eyes to his broad shoulders, square as the day was long, and she could almost hear the hot-man-on-the-premises warning bells go off in her head.

There's one hell of a body beneath that parka. She trembled again, but she couldn't tell if it was from the cold or the thought.

She narrowed her eyes, scrutinizing his goddamn sexy eyes again. *Look away. Just look away.*

His eyebrows drew together and scanned her face as intently as she had been scrutinizing his. The concern she'd seen earlier had vanished, replaced with something harder. Colder.

"What's your name?" His voice was gruff.

She tugged off her hat, challenging him with a hard stare. "Siena Remington." *That's right.* The *Siena Remington*. Her snooty thought was wasted. By the look in his eyes, it was clear that he had no idea who Siena Remington was.

"Well, Siena Remington, I'm Cash Ryder. Didn't it occur to you to put chains on your tires? Or maybe to skip your evening drive altogether?" He pulled his hat off, sending his dirty-blond hair tumbling down over his forehead. It brushed his lashes, softening his look as he raked his eyes down her trembling body.

Her heartbeat sped up again. He needed a trim and a shave, and she wished he'd put his hat back on. It was a lot easier matching his attitude when she didn't know for sure how hot he was.

"Or maybe you couldn't wait to show off your new designer jacket?" He smirked.

She pulled her hat back on, anger brewing in her belly. "It's a rental car." No way did she just almost die miles from home and then get rescued by a guy who looked like Bradley Cooper and had a chip on his shoulder as big as Charlie Sheen's.

"Why are *you* out in this mess?" She was shivering inside the truck and he was solid as a rock outside, snow piling up on his shoulders. *Of course he is. All that anger in his blood must keep him warm.*

He narrowed his eyes again. "Visiting my brother." He

shook his head. "Didn't you think twice when you saw the snow?"

"I didn't know it was going to be this bad. It wasn't this bad in the city." She slid from the truck to her feet and stood in front of him. Jesus, he was tall. And so damn close to her that she could feel his thighs pressing against hers.

He shot her a look. "Where are you going?"

"Walking."

He grabbed her arm. "Oh no, you're not. I didn't just save your ass to have you die of hypothermia or get run over by a car." He wrapped a powerful arm around her waist and lifted her back into the truck. "Close"—he locked eyes with her—"the door."

"No."

"Do you *want* to die in the cold?"

She pressed her lips together. "I'm not going to be the damsel in distress for some cocky firefighter to brag about rescuing." She wiped the snow from her jeans where it had blown in through the open door. Damn, it was cold. And he was so damn hot, and such an ass, that she wanted to kiss him and smack him in equal measure.

He leaned in to the truck, his face an inch from hers. His eyes darkened to nearly black, and a grin spread across his lips.

Siena could barely breathe. She tried to blink away the heat that rolled off him in waves.

"I'm shutting the door," he said in a seductive tone, as if he'd said, *I can't wait to lick every inch of you.*

Her whole body shuddered, and she wished her teeth would stop chattering, though she had a feeling it was nerves more than the cold causing it. "I'll…call…" *Shit. Who can I call?* "One of my brothers to get me."

"I already called 911, but I guess they're overwhelmed with calls tonight." He pressed his gorgeous mouth into a tight line, then leaned in close again. "You would make someone else come out in these conditions and risk their life when I'm already here, wouldn't you?"

Yes! No! Shit, how did you make me sound so selfish? She slammed her back against the seat and stared straight ahead, steeling herself for what was sure to be the ride from hell back to her apartment.

Chapter Two

WHERE THE HELL is the emergency crew? The last thing Cash wanted to do was babysit Siena Remington for the next hour. Goddamn city girls were never prepared, and it pissed him off. Cash was always prepared—ready for anything. He had great instincts and lightning-fast reflexes. Neither of which did a damn thing for him a month ago when he couldn't get to the third floor of an apartment building that was engulfed in flames because of some careless tenant who'd left a newspaper too close to the stove.

Even through his parka he'd felt the curves of Siena's body when she clung to him like he was her only hope of survival and looked at him like he was Superman. She felt damn good, and he was far from Superman. The combative emotions slammed together and rattled his nerves. She was so damn bullheaded that in less than five minutes she'd already made him crazy, and despite that, he was drawn to her like a kid to candy. He was too damn attracted to her. He had to get away from that truck. *Anything to break the connection.*

He opened the door and stepped out of the truck. "I've gotta get your stuff. Promise me you'll stay put. It's too dangerous out here for you to be traipsing along the road."

Siena stared out the window. "Fine."

He glanced at her profile. She had a perky nose, high cheekbones, and almond-shaped eyes that were narrow and angry at the moment, but when he'd first pulled her from the car he'd seen them full of vulnerability and something more—determination? Hope? He wondered what they looked like when they were in the throes of passion. *Christ. What am I doing?* As he made his way through the thick snow and back down the embankment, he couldn't shake the feeling that he'd seen her before. He couldn't place where, and he was too frustrated to think about it. His mind drifted to when he'd leaned in close to her. She smelled fresh and clean, and her skin looked so damn soft that he'd had the urge to stroke her cheek and to kiss her and he had no fucking idea why. Jesus, he needed to get laid. He'd been out of the game for too long, but even as the thought entered his mind, he cringed. That would have been his go-to fix for any frustration a year ago, but lately, getting laid wasn't anywhere near his agenda.

Cash pushed his thoughts aside as he slid down the last ten feet of the embankment to her car. He had to get his arms around whatever was driving him to think of kissing Siena Remington. The last thing she—or any other woman—needed was a firefighter who took unnecessary risks on the job. *Jesus. I've turned into the kind of guy I hate.*

Pathetic.

When he returned to the truck, Siena was staring straight ahead. She didn't turn when he placed her bags in the back or even when he handed over her purse.

"Thank you," she said curtly.

After contacting the emergency dispatcher and updating them on the situation, Cash focused on getting back on the dangerous highway and navigating the snowy conditions as they headed toward the city rather than making an effort to ease the tension that had thickened between them. Visibility was poor, and even in the city, cars were moving at a snail's pace. *What was she thinking going out in this?* By the time he pulled down Siena's street, he thought the smoke had finally stopped steaming from her ears. He'd tried not to eavesdrop when she'd called her friend Willow. *Willow?* But how could he tune her out completely in such a confined space? She hadn't mentioned him by name. *Someone driving by stopped to help me.* She made no mention of dealing with her car or getting checked out by a doctor.

"You should call someone to get your car."

"You think?"

Her sarcasm didn't escape him. "And maybe get checked out by a doctor."

"I'm fine."

"When people are in emergency situations, their muscles tighten up. You could have jarred a shoulder, or your elbow or wrist."

He threw the truck into park and opened his door.

"You don't have to get out. I'm fine," Siena said as she climbed out.

"Let me get your bags." He reached behind him as Siena opened the back door and reached in, dragging her bags from his grasp.

"Thanks for rescuing me," she said without even looking at him; then she closed the door and he watched her walk inside.

Cash drove to the firehouse with the radio blaring, trying to get Siena out of his mind. He was ready for a beer, and he knew that not only would there be no beer, but that Tommy was working, so he wouldn't have anyone to join him out at a bar.

"Tom?" Cash called as he walked through the firehouse door. It smelled like chili, and he heard the guys talking in the other room. He went to the kitchen and grabbed a soda from the fridge, wishing it were something stronger to erase the sting of the evening.

"Hey, man, that was a quick visit." Tommy Burke, Cash's closest buddy for the last ten years, came into the kitchen and smacked him on the back. At six four, Cash had an inch and about twenty pounds of muscle on Tommy. Tommy grabbed an apple and bit into it. His thick, dark hair curled up at the edges, which Cash knew meant he'd spent enough time outside to get soaking wet. "Crazy out there tonight. We've already been on three calls."

"Yeah? All end okay?" Cash pulled off his parka and hung it over a chair at the table.

"Yeah, man. It's always okay."

Cash narrowed his eyes. They both knew that wasn't *always* the case.

Tommy slapped him on the back again. "I know, man. I know. C'mon. There's a John Wayne movie on. Some Western shit."

Tommy knew Cash hated television, just as Tommy knew Cash hated walnuts, didn't prefer blondes, could kick his ass in ice hockey, and thought sports figures were overpaid losers who played games for a living and reaped enormous salaries while firefighters scraped by on pennies. Tommy also knew that Cash had been taking too many risks since he dragged Cash away from that goddamn apartment fire. The rescue that changed everything Cash believed in and had turned his behavior upside down for the past three weeks. They'd met when Cash had first come to New York ten years earlier. At twenty-two, he'd graduated college with a degree in fire protection engineering and zero interest in doing anything except fighting fires. They'd gone through training together, pulled each other through the shit and laughed at the ridiculous. Tommy was like a brother to Cash, as were many of the guys. But he was closest to Tommy and their buddy Boyd Hudson, who was away for training. Most people thought Cash had four brothers and a sister, but in his mind, *brotherhood* ran deeper than bloodlines.

"How was Duke?" Tommy asked as he settled onto the worn brown couch in front of the television.

Cash sighed and lowered himself onto a recliner. "Never got there."

"No?"

Cash shook his head and picked up a magazine from the coffee table. "Rescued some woman from the side of the road." He shook his head again, wondering what would possess anyone to get behind the wheel unprepared for the weather.

"Bad?" Tommy asked.

"Nah. Slid off the road and over the embankment. The car didn't roll." He flipped through the pages, not paying attention to either the television or the magazine. "Where's Kelly tonight?"

"I can't seem to get anywhere with that woman." Tommy threw his head back, and his thick dark hair fell away from his face. He closed his eyes and groaned.

"You still haven't made any headway with her?" Cash asked.

"Well, I wouldn't say that. We're great friends."

"Dude, the friend zone? You gotta cut that shit. Nip it in the bud. Let her know how you feel. You've been playing this game with her for years."

"It's not a game, and I have." Tommy grabbed a can of soda from the table beside the couch and took a drink. "I don't want to talk about Kelly." He leaned forward and rested his elbows on his knees. "When are you gonna stop being a hotshot and get your shit together?"

Cash shifted his eyes away from him.

"Cash, you gotta rein in that shit." Tommy spoke just above a whisper. "The chief's not going to let it go on forever and the guys?" He shook his head. "Man, they're pissed."

Cash ran his hand through his hair, listening to the other guys in the hall. "I'll figure it out, Tom. Back off."

"Hey, I'm trying to save your ass. Chief Weber will put you on the desk, and you know it. You can't take risks in the field. Shit, you used to be the one to drill that into the rookies' heads. You don't even use your breathing pack."

Cash stood and paced. "Jesus, I came here to escape this bullshit."

"Hey, whatever, man. I just want to help." Tommy finished his soda and crushed the can in his palm. "You can live in your guilt-ridden place for as long as you want, but I can't imagine the chief is going to let you risk our lives long before you're on desk duty."

Cash slid him a look, and Tommy raised his hands in surrender.

He flipped a page in the magazine and froze. *Holy hell. No freaking way.* He squinted at the gorgeous, nearly naked body covering the entire page. The model's eyes were closed, her right arm covered the center of her right breast, the angle of her body covered the left, and she had nothing on but a silky pair of pink, lacy panties. He tore his eyes from the panties and back up to her face. Siena Remington's face.

"You might want to wash your hands after touching that page. Joey had that mag in the bathroom with him for way too long this afternoon." Tommy laughed.

Cash couldn't take his eyes off of her.

"Did you even notice the Johnnie Walker bottle?"

Cash shook his head. "What?" He blinked several times, trying to clear his head. *She's a model. A smoking-hot model.*

Tommy leaned forward and pointed to the bottom of the page. "The ad's for Johnnie Walker." He laughed again. "That magazine's made the rounds, and I have no idea where it even came from."

"I bet it has." Cash rolled up the magazine and headed for his locker.

"Hey, don't get the pages sticky."

He'd make sure no one got the pages sticky. He shoved the magazine into the top of his locker and went to take a shower. A cold fucking shower.

Chapter Three

FROM THE SIXTH-floor window of Siena's agent's office, the city looked crisp and beautiful. With the thick window between Siena and the noise below, the streets even looked peaceful, despite the number of cars shuffling along, bumper to bumper. She loved the feeling of being separate from the noise almost as much as she loved being part of it. Between the sun and the plows, the streets were once again black, mounds of snow piled along the edges, and despite the people hurrying down the sidewalks, the snow looked peaceful and pretty rather than scary and chaos inducing as it had the night before. Siena loved living in the city, and unlike her older brothers Sage and Jack, who longed to live in the woods somewhere, she wouldn't trade city life for anything. She and her twin, Dex, were alike in that way, while her other older brother Kurt, a writer, never left his home office. She thought he could probably live anywhere and be happy, as long as he had access to a keyboard.

"Siena, you look lovely." Jewel Wells had been Siena's agent since Siena turned eighteen, when the agent who had represented her as a child referred her to Jewel. As Jewel air-kissed each cheek, Siena was glad she'd opted for Chanel instead of her jeans.

"Thank you." She lowered herself into a chair across from Jewel's desk wondering why Jewel had requested the meeting. "Your message said there was something important you wanted to discuss?"

Jewel ran her hand along the side of her needle-straight blond hair, which swung in a blunt cut just above her pearl earrings. "Yes." She inched her chair closer to the desk and clasped her hands together. "Siena, honey, you know how important image is in this business."

"Yes." *Oh God. Image is everything.* Siena held her breath and quickly went through her memory of the last few days. She hadn't been seen with anyone inappropriate; she hadn't gotten drunk and made an ass of herself. She hadn't gotten a DUI. *Oh God. The accident.* "If this is about the accident—"

"Accident? Should it be about an accident?" Jewel arched a slim brow.

"No. I was going to meet Willow at her parents' house outside the city last night and I ran off the road." *And met a hot asshole firefighter that I can't stop thinking about.*

"I'm sorry. I'm glad you're okay."

"Yeah, me too. I was driving a rental, and it was towed last night. Apparently, it wasn't totaled, so that was good."

Jewel nodded. "Yes, that is good. Siena, in the past eight years, I've never steered you wrong, have I?"

Siena sat up straighter at the seriousness of her tone. "No."

"And I've led you to elite model status and guided you to a secure seven-figure income, which I think you enjoy."

Shit. Where is this going? Siena's stomach tensed. "Yes."

"I've been thinking about this a lot, and I know how you feel about some of the men we've encouraged you to go out with in the past, but I think it's time to up your exposure."

Jewel lowered her chin and smiled, a look that Siena recognized to mean *Take this very seriously.*

"But I'm one of the top models at the agency. My exposure is high." Siena sat up straighter. "What exactly do you mean by *upping my exposure?*"

"We've been following the careers of Kristi Samington and Chloe Terlson, and since they began dating athletes, they're in almost every magazine on the planet on a consistent basis, which translates into more deals, higher offers, and greater longevity." Jewel's eyes widened as she spoke, and excitement surrounded her words.

Siena shook her head. "So…you want me to date an athlete? Like a football player or something?"

"Well, we've chosen a few for you. And you don't have to really date them, but we'd like you to be seen with them enough for the press to speculate." She pushed four head shots across her desk.

Siena picked up the photographs and leafed through them. Four thick-necked athletes stared back at her. *Muscle-head clones.* She was so tired of being told whom she should date that she really didn't feel like dating at all.

"But if the press thinks I'm dating one of them, then what happens if I actually go on a date with someone else?"

Not that there was a chance in hell of that happening. She'd basically sworn off men. Until she found a guy who knew what romance meant—holding hands, thinking about the other person's hopes and dreams before their own, laughing at stupid things even if it made them look silly—she was very happy sitting at home reading at night, or hanging out with Willow, or going dancing and *then* going home alone. Anything other than poking at a salad while the guy across the table undressed her with his eyes. *Is it too much to want a guy who pays attention to more than my looks? Who picks up on the little things? Unsaid things?*

A smile spread across Jewel's coral lips. "Well, then, that just raises the controversy, doesn't it?"

She winked, and Siena's stomach clenched. "Jewel, how vital is this? I mean, if I choose not to do it…"

"Well, let's just say that we wouldn't want to see your next contract go to Kristi or Chloe, now, would we? Oh, and, Siena, you know how these things work. You can't tell a soul that you're not really dating them. We can't take a chance of the press disbelieving their own eyes. We want them to eat the stories we feed them." Jewel rose to her feet. "By the way, don't forget the annual calendar shoot tomorrow at three. Willow will be there, of course, and Trey is excited to make this year's calendar a little racier."

"Great." Siena forced her best smile and pushed the photographs across the desk.

"Let me know by the end of the day which one of these guys you want to go out with and I'll arrange it. And of course, I'll tip off the paparazzi, too."

The idea of going out with an athlete turned her stomach, but not as much as knowing that Jewel, whom she trusted with her career, was the one pushing for the date. Jewel had never made dating the men she suggested feel so critical before. She'd never tied it in as blatantly to Siena's future success. She valued their relationship, and she believed that Jewel had always been looking out for her best interests, but now? She wasn't so sure. "You pick and let me know."

CASH STOOD OUTSIDE Vetta Miller's apartment with a bouquet of daisies and a fresh bowl of spaghetti with meatballs, one of the few dishes Cash knew how to cook. He adjusted his long-sleeve shirt and cleared his throat before knocking. He listened for Vetta's slow shuffle, heard the click of the dead bolt, the slide of the chain, and the click of the second dead bolt. The door opened slowly, and Cash waited for Vetta to lift her gray eyes and meet his gaze.

"Cash," she said with a smile.

Always with a smile, which tugged at his heart and tightened the noose of guilt that hung heavily around his neck at all times. Her silver hair was twisted into a loose bun. Her deeply wrinkled round cheeks trembled a little with her smile. Vetta shuffled to the side of the doorway in her slippers, allowing Cash to enter the small apartment.

"Come in, sweetie. You look so handsome today."

"Thank you, Vetta." He leaned down and kissed her cheek as he walked into the apartment. Cash had been visiting Vetta for the past few weeks, and he still couldn't nail down the smell in her apartment. It was a cross between mothballs and chicken soup. Every surface in the small living room was covered with doilies. Much of what Vetta owned had been lost in the fire, and though she was now living in a different apartment, the sofa, upholstered chair, and coffee table looked like new teeth in an old mouth.

Cash looked away as he passed the black-and-white photographs of Vetta and Samuel hanging on the wall in the living room.

"I've brought you spaghetti and meatballs. Would you like me to put it in the kitchen? Heat it up for you?"

Vetta settled into a thickly upholstered chair beside a reading light. "How lovely. Thank you, but I'm not very hungry. Perhaps you could just put it in the fridge for me?" She made a little humming sound as he opened the fridge and put the dish inside. He noticed that there weren't many groceries in the fridge.

"Do you need me to make a run to the grocery store for you?" He returned to the living room and sat on the couch, feeling Samuel's eyes on him from his perch on the wall. He lifted his gaze to the old man's portrait. Samuel was ninety-two years old when he perished in the fire that would haunt Cash forever. He swallowed against the lump in his throat.

"Aren't you a dear for offering, but no, thank you. I have enough for the week." The sleeves of her black sweater fell to the middle of her thickly veined hands. She lifted a shaky hand and settled it atop Cash's hand. "How are you, Cash?"

She held his gaze, and in her silence he heard a million accusations. Vetta had never blamed Cash for Samuel's death, but that didn't mean that Cash didn't blame himself, or assume she secretly did as well. He drew his eyes from the picture on the wall to her heavily hooded eyes.

"I'm well. How are you, Vetta? Is there anything I can get you? Do you need the trash taken out? Your heat adjusted?" It was always too warm in her apartment. Cash didn't know what Samuel had taken care of before the fire, so he tried to do as much as he could to help her. Vetta didn't have any children, and he hated knowing she was alone. No matter what Cash did, it would never be enough to fill the void of losing her husband of sixty-seven years.

"Oh, you know, there is a box of pictures in the bedroom closet that I would love to see, but they're too heavy for me to take down. And the heater in there seems to be stuck on high."

Cash was on his feet and across the room in seconds. "I'll fix that right up." He stood at the edge of the bedroom, staring at the double bed, and felt his heart squeeze. Anger clawed at the back of his neck. He pushed himself to enter the bedroom and check the heater, which clicked down to low without hesitation. Then he opened the closet doors, where a handful of clothes hung from wire hangers, two pairs of orthopedic shoes neatly placed beneath them. He grabbed the cardboard shoe box from the top shelf and hurried back into the living room.

"You are such a doll. Just set it down here." He put the shoe box on the coffee table. The box was filled with envelopes of all sizes and colors. "Would you be a dear and hand me the envelope there? The blue one?"

He grabbed the blue envelope nearest the top. Handwritten in pencil on the front of the envelope was *1967*. He handed it to her.

"Ah, yes. Each of these envelopes represents a year we were together. Some of them have a few years, because you know, it's hard to catalog a year. Some years only have three or four pictures, and honestly, some years aren't even in there. Life goes by so fast. Sometimes twelve months would go by in the blink of an eye, and we'd realize we hadn't taken a single picture." Her arthritic fingers wrestled with the photos as she withdrew them. "In 1967 Samuel was still working as a doctor at the hospital. That was before his eyesight began to fail. He cared for a boy—Paul was his name." She handed Cash a photograph of Samuel with a little boy. Dressed in a lab coat, Samuel was wearing a wide smile, his arm draped over the little boy's shoulder.

"Paul's cute."

"Yes, he was." She caught Cash's gaze and held it. "Paul's

heart was bad, and there was a procedure that might or might not save him. Samuel and Paul's family had to make a very difficult decision." She paused and shifted her eyes away, as if she were watching a scene unfold before her eyes. "Funny how pictures can jog a memory."

Cash's muscles tensed.

"They proceeded with the surgery, and Paul made it through, for a day or two, and then his little heart gave out." She knitted her brows together and lowered her eyes to the photograph. "Samuel was eaten up over his passing."

Cash dropped his eyes to the floor. "I'm sorry."

"Oh, honey, there was nothing anyone could do. Samuel did the best he could." She covered Cash's hand with her own. "That's all anyone can ever ask."

I didn't do the best I could. I should have fought harder to get into the apartment and save him. Cash had a stellar record. Nobody died on his watch. *Until Samuel.* Cash's pulse sped up. He sensed that she was telling him the story to make him feel better, but guilt gripped his chest, heavy and dense, just like the beam that had kept him from making the rescue. *Inescapable.* Cash took a deep breath. *Samuel was trapped.* Anger and guilt coalesced, sending him to his feet.

She squeezed his hand as he rose.

"Vetta, I'm sorry…"

"You have nothing to be sorry for, dear. Samuel believed strongly that when it was time, it was time. Everyone has an expiration date, Cash. We just don't know when it is." She smiled, and Cash choked behind a cough. "Goodness, are you sure you're okay?"

"Yes." He coughed again, trying to dislodge the lump that had settled in his throat. "I…uh…" He eyed the box. "Would you like me to put these in an album for you? Something you can flip through, maybe?"

"You don't have to do that, Cash."

"I'd like to." She'd lost her husband because he'd been weak, unprepared. He should have anticipated the beam burning through and moved faster instead of taking the time to look up and assess the ceiling. The least he could do was make it easier to keep Samuel's memory alive. "I'll bring these back as soon as I can. Are you sure you don't want me to warm up that spaghetti?"

"No, thank you." She rose to her feet, pressed her thin lips together, and her gaze softened. "Cash, tell me about your work before you go. Did the storm bring many emergencies?"

He clenched his jaw. "I wasn't on duty."

"So you didn't have to rescue anyone?" Her gray eyes didn't stray from his.

"Yeah. I actually did. A woman ran off a back road just outside the city. I rescued her." *And she was a big pain in my ass.*

"With your unit?"

"No. I was on my way to see my brother. It was after my shift." *My shift.* Cash took pride in being a firefighter, and he knew that Tommy was right. The guys had been giving him shit for taking unnecessary risks and going too far during rescues. It was only a matter of time before the chief put him on desk duty to handle administrative paperwork, supplies, coordination of schedules. It just about killed him thinking about the very real possibility. He had to pull his shit together. The thought of the alarm sounding and the clamor of the men slamming their feet into their boots and shouting to one another and knowing he wouldn't be leaving with them made his gut burn. But he'd be damned if he could stop taking the risks that—ever since

Samuel's death—seemed vital. He had less to lose than the other guys. Almost every one of them had a girlfriend or a wife, and they risked their lives every day because it was the nature of their job. Lately, Cash had taken that to the extreme, leaving his partner behind and ignoring orders to evacuate when there was still a victim inside. And now, standing with Vetta, he felt the air being sucked from his lungs. He had to get out of there. He picked up the box and she touched his arm.

"Cash, I'm sure that woman was very thankful."

He thought of the venom in Siena's eyes when he'd told her to get back into the car, the way he could barely think when he was leaning over her in the truck, and the way she thanked him without even meeting his eyes. *She's anything but thankful.* "She's unharmed. That's all that matters."

Chapter Four

NIGHTCAPS WAS AS busy as ever when Siena arrived. She wasn't a big drinker, but after the day she'd had, she jumped at the chance to meet her brothers Dex and Sage and Sage's girlfriend, Kate, for a good, stiff drink. She weaved through the crowd and found them at a booth in the back of the bar. Dex waved and she felt instant relief. Her brothers had that effect on her. They'd always been there for her, and tonight she could think of no place she'd rather be. She hung her coat on the end of the booth and slid in beside Dex.

"You look determined." Dex scanned her face. "Bad day on the runway?"

"Ha-ha. Hey, Sage, Kate. Where's Ellie?" Dex had recently been reunited with a friend from their childhood, Ellie Parker, and Siena had been the only one in the family not to know they'd been madly in love with each other for years. Well, Siena and apparently Dex, but he figured it out pretty fast, while Siena was left dumfounded. She adored Ellie, but as Dex's twin, she was shocked that she didn't have some sort of twin intuition. A sixth sense or something.

"She's working with the other teachers on the software project." Ellie was a teacher who specialized in education for low-income kids. She'd won a grant to develop an educational software program specifically aimed toward low-income children. She and several other teachers were working with Dex and a few of his employees to develop the program.

"Wow. She's working late. She's really jumped in feet first."

"What're you drinking?" Sage asked. He'd cut his dark curls when he'd gone to Belize, where he met Kate, and now they were growing back, framing his handsome face. Siena had always been envious of his thick, curly hair. And now, watching him with his arm around Kate, she was envious of their relationship, too. Their love was a painful reminder of what Jewel was making her do.

"Something strong enough that you guys are going to have to walk me home." Siena picked up Dex's beer and took a sip.

"That bad?" Kate's long dark hair fell over her shoulder as she reached across the table and touched Siena's hand. The sleeve of her navy-blue sweater flared at the end and covered all but her fingertips. "Anything Sage and I can do?"

Kate had been living with Sage since they returned from Belize, where Kate had been running a nonprofit program for artists to aid newly developing nations. Sage had joined the project, and recently, they had founded their own nonprofit. Siena had never seen her brother look happier, and Kate had already become like a sister to her. She was warm, friendly, smart, and industrious, but what Siena loved most about her was that she was as genuinely caring as Sage was, and completely disinterested in his wealth. She longed to find someone who would love her for who she was and not what she had.

"Not unless you can erase the memory of a really handsome asshole from my mind, convince my agent that I shouldn't date an athlete, and explain to the rental car company…Oh, never mind." She sighed and rested her head on Dex's shoulder. "I'm glad you guys are here."

Sage returned with a shot of tequila and a glass of sangria. "To soothe my baby sister's soul." He leaned over and kissed her head.

"Thanks, Sage. I can't do a shot by myself." She eyed each of them, and they all held their hands up.

"I've got a meeting with Mitch and Regina in about an hour, and I'm three beers deep already." Dex's hair hung over his eyes. He wore a black T-shirt emblazoned with some PC game character on the front.

"Lightweight," Siena teased.

"I'm painting tonight, so one more beer and Kate and I are out of here." Sage shrugged.

She should have guessed. He had on one of his many paint-streaked long-sleeve shirts. "So I'm on my own?" Siena sighed. "Fine." She sprinkled salt on her hand, licked it, then sucked back the tequila and chased it with sangria. "Ah. That's a start."

"Wanna tell us about the handsome asshole?" Dex pulled her close. "Want me and Sage to take someone out?"

"Ugh. I ran off the road last night in a rental car, and—"

"Wait. Stop." Dex pulled back from her with an angry look in his eye. "You were out in that storm? What were you thinking?"

"Siena, really?" Sage took a swig of his drink.

"Sage, don't be so judgmental." Kate crossed her arms. "Siena, really?"

Siena laughed. "Okay, so it was stupid. Willow called me from her parents' house and invited me for dinner, and I'd just gotten home and had three messages from that jerk I went out with last week. The snow wasn't that bad when I left..." The snow wasn't that bad when she'd rented the car, but it was definitely bad within minutes of leaving the rental car parking lot.

Kate shook her head. "That's really dangerous."

"Thanks. I wish you would have told me that before I went over the edge of the road," Siena said with a sigh.

"But you were okay? Jesus, Siena." Dex pulled her close again.

"Yeah, fine, until this smart-ass fireman rescued me."

"You were rescued by a smart-ass fireman? Sounds good to me." Jack's fiancée, Savannah, pulled up two chairs to the end of the booth. She was tall and slim with thick, auburn hair that cascaded over her shoulders. Savannah was an entertainment attorney, and she must have come directly from the office, because she wore black slacks and a white silk blouse beneath a tailored jacket.

"Hey." Jack towered over Savannah and tugged on her hand with a teasing scowl. At six four, he always towered. *Like Cash.* "Hey, Siena." He leaned down and kissed her cheek, then held a hand out toward Kate, who was too far away to hug. "Kate, good to see you."

"Hi," Kate said.

"Hi, Jack." Siena had hoped to avoid Jack finding out about her accident. He was so protective of her that she knew she'd be in for a lecture.

They settled into their chairs. "Tell me about the sexy fireman." Savannah shot a glance at Jack. "I just want to get caught up. No one is sexier than my survivor man." She wrapped her hand around the back of Jack's neck and kissed him.

"*Smart-ass* fireman," Siena corrected. "He laid into me about not being prepared and…" *And then leaned over me and nearly drowned me with his virility.* She cleared her throat. "And he was really sweet when he was guiding me to safety, but then once I was safe, he was just an ass."

Savannah glanced at Jack.

"What?" Jack wrinkled his brow.

"Sounds like something you did when we first met." Savannah kissed the back of Jack's hand, which she held in her lap. "Jack was all over the place when we first met."

"I was a broken man, no doubt." He took a swig of his beer. "But you healed me." He wrapped his arms around her and kissed her temple. "Sometimes arrogant men make the best partners, or at least that's what I'm told."

"No, thank you," Siena said. She leaned against Dex's shoulder. "I want romance and sweetness. I want to be treated like you guys treat Ellie, Kate, and Savannah."

Kate and Savannah exchanged a glance.

"What?" Siena asked.

"I think that look was supposed to mean that we're not all romance and sweetness. Besides, do you really want a pushover? Siena, you're a strong woman." Sage leaned back and held Kate's hand. "You're not a wallflower. You need a guy who can stand up to you when you get…"

Siena narrowed her eyes.

"When you get the way you get." Sage lifted his beer bottle. "You know I love you."

"What the hell does that mean?" Siena looked around the table. "Come on. Am I a bitch?"

"Oh my God, no." Savannah narrowed her green eyes and smacked Jack's arm. "Tell her she's not a bitch. You guys are awful."

"You are not a bitch, Siena. In fact, you're hardly ever

bitchy. But if you hook up with a guy who's not a challenge, you'll be bored in a week."

"Why? Am I that…? What? What would that even make me? I love romance. I love that you guys would do anything for the women in your lives. I love that if Kate called Sage at three in the morning and he was painting, he'd drop everything and go home."

"I would." Sage pressed a kiss to Kate's lips.

"And that Dex lied to us about having a meeting because he's really going to take a cab down to get Ellie so she doesn't have to ride home alone." She smirked at Dex.

"How can you possibly know that?" Dex asked.

"Because Ellie told me last week when you did it, and she said you never let her go home alone at night." Siena looked at Jack. "And you, Jack. You have Savannah's coffee ready every morning before she's even awake, and then you walk her to the subway. Like it or not, you guys are total romantics, and I don't think there's any reason I shouldn't expect the same thing."

Siena had a pretty face and a body that men were drawn to—a lean figure, long legs, and full breasts that weren't made of silicone—and sometimes those were exactly the things she hated about herself. She attracted the attention of the wrong kind of men. Men who thought she was brainless and easy just because she was a model. Little did they know that her four-star-general father would have none of that beauty-trumps-all philosophy. He'd pushed her and her five brothers to be the best they could be, and though she'd been modeling since she was eight, she now boasted a degree in biology that she'd never do anything with professionally, but she was proud to have accomplished it just the same. Siena was smart, and she was pretty, and that was enough to make certain women hate her and to intimidate men who weren't part of the wealthier crowd. It had turned into the bane of Siena's existence for the past two years. There was a time she reveled in the attention and feeling as if she were somehow more special than others. But that got old—and lonely—fast. Now she just wanted to be loved and cherished. Romanced, not taken out to dinner with the expectation of sex. She didn't want over-the-top dates and diamonds on every finger. She wanted a man who would look at her like her brothers looked at their girlfriends and fiancées, like they were the oxygen they needed to breathe, for no reason other than who they were on the inside.

Jack took Siena's hand and looked at her with a soft gaze that said, *My little naive sister, let me teach you.* "Honey, you need a guy who's a challenge, like Sage said. And we are romantics, but we're also men. Real men. Men that Dad raised, which means that we get angry, and we get ornery, and we act like Neanderthals when we're challenged. Don't lose sight of that; otherwise you've completely emasculated every one of us." Jack squeezed her hand. "Now, tell me what the hell you were doing that he had to lecture you about."

Shoot. She thought she'd gotten off home free. She pulled her hand from his and scooted closer to Dex.

"She went out in the storm and drove off an embankment," Kate said.

"Hey!" Siena glared at her.

"It's like a Band-Aid. Rip it off fast and it'll sting less." Kate snuggled against Sage.

Siena watched Jack's jaw clench and his dark eyes narrow.

Savannah ran her hand down his arm. "Jack."

"You could have been killed in that storm." Jack's tone was unyielding. "Why didn't you call me? I would have driven you anywhere you needed to go."

"Jack, I'm twenty-six, not fifteen."

"Yeah, well, I don't care if you're twenty-six or thirty-six; you'll always be my little sister, and if you ever do something stupid like that again, I'll—"

"Jack." Savannah shook her head. "He just loves you, Siena."

"I know." *Jesus, that was way too reminiscent of Cash.* "Sorry, Jack. If it makes you feel better, I learned my lesson."

"Damn well better have." Jack shook his head, then blew out a breath and leaned forward again. "Siena, listen, the weather can turn in an instant. I'm sorry I got so mad, but people die in flash storms all the time. I don't want to find out that I lost you to something like that."

That's when it hit her. Jack had lost his wife in a flash storm a few years earlier. Guilt prickled her limbs. "I know. I'm sorry."

"Now, tell me if the guy said anything that I need to beat his ass for, or was he just an ass in general?"

Siena sighed. "He was…like you were just then."

"Good man." Jack smiled.

"*Ugh.*"

"I guess you probably don't want to tell us about the dating an athlete thing, huh?" Kate asked.

Siena rolled her eyes. She'd had enough frustration for one night. She didn't want any more lectures, and she didn't want to talk about the awful situation Jewel was thrusting upon her. One more glass of sangria to dim the memory of Cash Ryder, and then she'd have Dex walk her home, where she'd cuddle up under her blankets, call Willow, and commiserate with someone who would say nothing more than, *Aw, that sucks*, or, *What an ass*, whether she believed it or not. Because that's what friends—

instead of women who were like sisters—did.

"WHAT THE HELL is all that?" Tommy stood in the doorway of the firehouse bedroom.

Cash looked up from where he sat on one of the beds, surrounded by photos of Vetta and Samuel. "What does it look like?" He took a picture and slid it into a vinyl pocket of one of the photo albums he'd bought. When he left Vetta, he hadn't been able to stop thinking about Siena or Samuel, and after working out for an hour and a half and still feeling like a bundle of nerves, he'd gone out and bought three big photo albums.

"Yeah, I get that they're pictures, but who are they of and what are you doing with them?" Tommy came into the room and stood over him, arms crossed, shaking his head. "You've lost it, man."

Cash clenched his jaw.

"I have forty-eight off. C'mon. Let's go grab a brew."

Cash blew out a breath and held his hand out, as if he were displaying the pictures. "They're Vetta's. I figured if I give her something to remember him by, it'll ease the guilt."

"I get it," Tommy said. "Dude, you're a good man. She knows that. You said yourself that she doesn't blame you."

"Yeah, she doesn't, but that doesn't mean I don't."

"You've been doing this for a decade and he was your first loss," Tommy said with concern in his eyes.

Joe Arlen strolled into the bedroom and flopped on a bed. "Hey."

"Hey, Joe. We're taking off." Tommy nudged Cash's arm. "C'mon. Let's get outta here."

Cash knew the drill. He was off. Joe was on. The bedroom belonged to Joe and the other guys who were on duty now, and they didn't need him there keeping them awake. He gathered the photos into the shoe box and put them and the photo albums into his locker.

Tommy reached for the magazine on the top shelf. "You stole the Remington mag? I thought you were just taking it into the bathroom. Dude, that's so uncool."

Cash grabbed his hand before he could snag it and glared at him.

Tommy cocked his head to the side.

"Remember the woman I rescued last night?"

He shrugged. "Yeah."

Cash nodded at the magazine.

"No fucking way."

"Way." Cash slammed his locker shut and locked it.

"So…What? No way. Did you ask her out?"

They headed down the stairs and onto the street. "No. She's a pain in the ass. You know the type—entitled, belligerent."

"Hot."

"Like the world owes them something." Cash rounded his shoulders forward against the cold. "NightCaps?" The local brewery, and their preferred hangout, was right around the corner from the station.

"I was going to suggest Bart's for a change, but Kelly hates that waitress who hits on me all the time. NightCaps it is." Tommy shoved his hands in his pockets.

A few blocks later they opened the doors to NightCaps and headed inside. "Not too busy. Happy hour must be over. Grab us a couple of beers and I'll snag a table." Tommy scoped the place out and Cash headed to the bar.

"Four Killian's Reds." Cash leaned on the bar and turned to look for Tommy. He spotted him leaning over a table of women in the back of the bar. He laughed to himself. Leave it to Tommy to zero in on the chicks despite having avoided Bart's because of the waitress. *Selective avoidance.* He paid for the beers and snagged a table. Cash had no interest in making small talk with anyone tonight. He shrugged off his coat and settled into a seat to wait for Tommy.

"Cash!"

Goddamn it, Tommy. Tommy flagged him over to the table, where he was lowering himself to a chair between two women. *Shit.* He rubbed a knot tightening across the back of his neck and weighed his options. Ignore him. Sit with him and dodge questions all night about how big his hose is and if he was good at yielding his ax. *Same old shit, different babe.* He finished his beer and pushed the empty bottle aside. Ignoring Tommy was looking better by the second. His cell phone rang, and he pulled it from his jeans pocket. *Chief Weber. Great.*

"Hey, Chief." He rubbed his temples with his finger and thumb.

"Hey, Cash. How you doing?"

Cash had worked under Chief Jon Weber for the last eight years. He was a fair and honest man. Tough as nails and one of the most capable firefighters Cash had ever known.

"Good, Chief. What's up?"

"We need to talk, Cash. When are you on again?"

He knew his days were numbered. He had to get back in the game soon or he'd be out of a job. "Wednesday morning, nine to five; then I'm off till Friday at five."

"Great. My office. Eight?"

"You got it, Chief." Cash ended the call and ran his hand

through his hair, eyeing Tommy, and wishing he'd get the hell back to the table so he could talk this shit out. All he had to do was get his head back into a safe place. Taking unnecessary risks on the job was bullshit. If he could quell the goddamn guilt that had swallowed him ever since he'd been blocked by that damn beam and dragged out of there before he could save Samuel, then... *What the hell?* Cash squinted across the bar at the woman climbing from a booth, her hand linked to some dude with longish hair and a tattoo on his neck. *Siena.* She dragged her hand over the shoulder of the dark-haired guy sitting at the end of the table. *What the hell is she into?* She headed toward the stairs that led to the bathrooms.

Without thinking, he crossed the floor.

"Cash, come here, man."

Cash ignored Tommy and followed Siena down the stairs. The delicious curves that he'd known were beneath her jacket last night, the ones he—and every other man on earth—saw in that goddamn Johnnie Walker ad, swayed seductively in front of him. She pulled her cell phone from her pocket and pushed a button. Cash turned his back as she turned around.

"Hey, it's me."

Mmm. Her voice was sweet, friendly, nothing like she'd sounded when she'd been demanding to get to her car.

"Yeah, I'm at NightCaps. I'm gonna have Dexy walk me home, but I'll call you after I'm there. Will you be around? Yeah, I have some stuff I want to tell you before tomorrow."

Dexy? You're ditchin' the dude you're with and then calling another? Damn. You're worse than I thought. Cash had half a mind to turn around and call her on it.

"'Kay. Cool. Okay, call you soon."

He heard the bathroom door open and he spun around,

only to find himself eye to eye with Siena. A redhead, who had apparently been the one to open the bathroom door, pushed between them and headed up the stairs.

"You." She narrowed her eyes.

There's that angry voice again. Damn, she was hot, and he couldn't stop picturing her in those pink panties she had on in the magazine. "Siena."

"Are you going to lecture me for drinking now, too?" She clutched her phone in her fist.

If he didn't stop picturing her in those panties, he was going to lose it. He closed the gap between them, his voice a heated whisper. "I saw your Johnnie Walker ad in that magazine."

She was breathing hard, and she smelled too fucking sweet.

"Congratulations. So did about two million other people."

He couldn't think of a single thing to say. He shoved his hands in his pockets to keep from backing her up against the wall and shutting her up with a rough kiss on those gorgeous, pouty lips of hers. *I'd like to tangle my fingers in your long hair and—*

"Siena." Harsh. Clipped. The dark-haired guy who'd been sitting at the end of the table hustled down the stairs, his eyes locked on Siena.

Cash knew a warning when he heard one. He took a step back.

Siena rolled her eyes at the guy, whose jaw was clenched tight.

"Jack…"

Jack?

Jack's thighs were as thick as tree trunks. He crossed his arms, his eyes darting from Cash to Siena.

Fuck. There was only one thing Cash could do to defuse the situation. He held his hand out. "Cash Ryder."

Jack stared at his hand. "Siena?"

"Jesus, Jack. This is the guy who rescued me from the accident last night." She turned away.

Jack's clenched jaw eased. "The asshole fireman?"

Siena glared at him.

Asshole fireman? "That sounds like me," Cash said. *You were talking about me.* He drew his shoulders back and sucked in a breath, then nodded at Jack and pushed his hand forward again. "Cash."

Jack shook his hand, both men angling for the strongest grip. Jack looked down at their hands at the same time Cash did, and they released their grips in unison.

"I'm Jack. Thanks for getting her home safely," Jack said.

"It's what I do." *Home? Who the hell are you? Her husband?* He hoped Jack didn't realize he practically had wood just being near her.

"I appreciate it. I've had a talk with Siena. She'll be prepared from now on."

Siena groaned. "Why don't you two just finish your little date? I'm going to use the ladies' room." She pushed past Cash and stormed into the bathroom, mumbling under her breath.

Between her boyfriend, husband, lover, or whoever he was and being close to Siena, Cash's gut twisted and every nerve burned. He had to get the hell out of there. "Nice to meet you, Jack." Cash took a step toward the stairs.

Jack wrenched his arm. He narrowed his dark blue eyes and looked down his nose at Cash. "Thanks for all you do for the city. Your whole unit. We appreciate it." He shook out a curt nod, then released his arm.

Siena burst through the bathroom door. "*Ugh.* You're both

still here?" She pushed past them and stomped up the stairs.

Cash waited for Jack to ascend the stairs before following him up. He had no idea what was going on, but clearly Siena had a line of men at her disposal, and he had no interest in being one of them—even if his body seemed to want to push its way up to the front of the line. He grabbed Tommy's arm and dragged him to their table.

"Dude, what the hell? Those girls were hot."

"Kelly?"

"She's not here." Tommy picked up his beer and waved at the table of hungry women that were leering after him.

Cash couldn't tear his eyes from Siena even if he wanted to. The guy whose hand she'd been holding climbed from the booth and stood beside her. She hugged Jack, then the woman next to Jack, and then she hugged the other couple, whom he hadn't even noticed before. Jack was obviously with the auburn-haired woman who had her finger hooked in his belt and a whopping diamond on her left hand. The tall, dark-haired guy in the gamer shirt whose hand she'd been holding draped an arm around Siena's shoulder.

"Isn't that the model?" Tommy said as she approached.

"Shut up," Cash snapped. He eyed her as she passed, and he couldn't help but size up the guy she was with.

"That's her brother. The gamer guy. What's his name?" Tommy snapped his fingers. "Dex. Dex Remington. Crazy smart dude who sold a million PC games right out of college."

"Her brother? You're sure?" He shot a look at the table again, wondering if the similarities between the other two men that were beginning to take shape were all in his head. "How many brothers does she have?"

"Hell if I know." Tommy finished his beer.

Brother? If Tommy was right, then that answered one question, but she still had some guy on the line whom she was calling after she got home.

"You've got that I'm-gonna-fuck-someone-up look on your face." Tommy winced. "Oh, man, my stomach is killing me. I might need you to fill in for me tomorrow at that calendar shoot."

He was too tightly wound to think straight. *Calendar shoot? Not a chance in hell.* "No way."

Tommy winced. "Seriously, dude. I think we better get out of here. My gut is complaining big-time."

Cash downed his Killian's and followed Tommy out, wondering if Siena had felt the same jolt of electricity between them that he had before Jack had come down the stairs and he'd tried to convince himself he didn't care.

Chapter Five

"THIS IS MY favorite shoot of the year." Willow Preacher adjusted the strap of her red bikini, then elbowed Siena. "All these hot firemen. *Mmm-mm.* Look at them. And there's only you and me. No competition. Take your pick."

Top Models had been working with the local firehouses for the past two years for their holiday calendar shoots. Siena would bet they sold millions of the holiday calendars. Women loved hot, nearly naked firemen, and having female models in the shots with them always added a little lust, which translated steamily in the pictures. The firemen filed into the studio wearing nothing but their turnout pants, red suspenders hanging from their waists, their ripped, delicious bodies glistening under the heat of the studio lights. Siena would have to be blind for her heart not to beat a little harder at the sight of them. Her mind drifted to the sexy fireman who had rescued her. These weren't pampered male models who were paid to look rugged, who spent hours with personal trainers and were artificially tanned. These were *real* men. She thought of the way Cash had taken control the night of her accident. He wasn't the least bit frightened. He knew just what to do. Oh yeah, he was a real man. Rugged, hard, and devastatingly handsome.

Siena raked her eyes down their bodies as they tossed the hoses, boots, and hard hats to the side, their muscles twitching and jumping beneath their taut skin. These men were out every day saving lives and fighting forces of nature so strong that it scared her to even think about it. There were a dozen of them there for the holiday calendar photo shoot, each more rugged than the next, and not one of them aroused her in the way that Cash did.

"Oh my goodness, look at that guy who's coming in." Willow's thick Caribbean accent hadn't faded one bit since she came to the States and began modeling a year and a half ago, and with her dark skin and thick, wild ringlets, she looked like an exotic goddess.

Siena lifted her eyes just in time to see Cash walk through the door. *Holy crap. No way he's modeling.* His sexy dark eyes scanned the room, his jaw muscles working hard to keep the scowl on his handsome face.

"Shit. That's him." Siena sucked in a breath at the sight of his naked bare chest, his olive skin stretched tight over hard muscle.

"No way. That's the asshole?" Willow placed her hand on Siena's shoulder. "Honey, I don't care how much of an attitude he has, you oughta redirect that anger into something useful, like hot, animalistic sex."

Siena couldn't concentrate. How could she when his pants hung just low enough to reveal the curve of his abs where they sank below his hips and dipped toward the center in a sexy V as they traveled south? She felt her cheeks flush, and when he ran his hand through his dirty-blond hair and it fell, disheveled and sexy, over his brooding brown eyes, she was struck dumb. Every time she saw him, the attraction grew stronger. Last night had been like fighting her way back from a riptide when she'd walked away. *How on earth am I going to make it through this?*

"Stop staring." Willow laughed. "Siena! He's watching you stare at him. C'mon, girlfriend. Someone needs to protect you from yourself." Willow grabbed her arm and dragged her away.

"Oh my God. He saw me staring? What is wrong with me?" Siena wanted to look over her shoulder, but she couldn't do it. She wouldn't give him the satisfaction.

"He's watching every step you take, so I'd say, yeah, he saw you." Willow narrowed her eyes. "And he's not smiling, so…"

"What is wrong with me? I never ogle. Ogling is gross. And he's a jerk."

"He's definitely ogle worthy. And you could always kiss him until he can't speak, or a silk tie might do the trick."

Siena gasped.

"What? Just sayin'."

"Cash Ryder, Joe Arlen, Mike Shilling, I want you guys over here. Ladies, let's get this show on the road," the photographer, Trey Michaels, directed.

Siena had worked with Trey enough to know that he was a no-bullshit photographer. There were photographers that would allow improvisations, jokes, and even banter between the models and the photographer's assistants, but not Trey. Trey was a forty-something straight shooter. His ponytail and rail-thin, cotton-clad body gave the impression of a guy whose life was full of nothing but chilling out and maybe smoking a little weed. That couldn't have been further from who he was. Trey was known for his risqué photo shoots, and despite his laid-back appearance, he was a professional who demanded respect from not only his assistants, but the models as well. When he spoke, everyone listened and acted. Immediately. Siena stood up straight, pulled her shoulders back, and prayed she could get through the shoot without a scene. She avoided looking at Cash, whose dark glare was burning a hole right through her.

"Where would you like us?" Siena asked, hoping her elevated pulse wasn't noticeable in her too-fast speech.

"Siena, you here." He pointed to an area behind Cash. *Shit.* She moved into position and looked down at him with what she hoped was an equally harsh glare.

He shifted his eyes to her, his chiseled, clean-shaven jaw clenched tight.

"I can't believe you're here."

"Me either." His voice was deep, gravelly, sexy...and ice-cold.

Jesus. That goddamn voice. Every muscle in her body tensed. *Crap. Calm, calm. Ocean breeze. Babies. Flowers.* She had to be in the zone to model, and his being there was totally throwing her off her game. Trey would be pissed if she couldn't find her groove.

"Cash, on one knee, ax in your left hand, and I want Siena pulled in tight, her hip at your jawline and your right hand reaching around the back of her legs."

Great. Intimate positioning with the iceman. Siena maneuvered around him. *Pretend he's someone else.* She closed her eyes just long enough to envision the Ralph Lauren model she'd worked with two weeks ago. A smile lifted her lips, and in the next breath her eyes were open and she was following directions like the professional she was known to be.

"Closer, Siena."

She inched closer. His face was right next to her left hip, radiating heat like an oven.

"That's it. Now, Cash, get in there like you can't get close enough." Trey motioned with his hand as Cash moved closer. His hard, muscled shoulder brushed against Siena's thigh, knocking her just enough that she had to hang on to him to remain stable on her stilettos.

He looked up at her and grimaced, his dark eyes narrowing again.

She took her hand off of him as fast as she could. *Asshole.*

"Good. Good. Now, Willow, over here." Trey positioned the others while Siena and Cash held their positions.

Siena could hold a pose for hours if she had to. It was one of the reasons photographers requested her so often. She had approached modeling the same way her father had taught her to approach everything in life. *Be better than everyone else. Stronger. Smarter. More worthy of the next step in your career.* There was a method to her father's madness, and it had served her well. Between her determination, intelligence, and her confidence, she wasn't easily manipulated by peer pressure or questionable financial advice. She kept the reins tight on her spending, so even if her career ended tomorrow, she'd earned enough—and saved enough—to be financially secure living off of just the interest of what she'd already earned.

Cash bumped against her thigh, and she gasped a breath, reaching for his shoulder again, then thought twice about it and stumbled backward instead.

Trey shot her a dark stare. "Problem?" He raised his brows.

"No. Just…off-balance. I'm sorry."

Cash looked over his shoulder and smirked.

Two can play at this game.

Willow caught her eye and knitted her brows together in two quick repetitions. The rest of her body remained perfectly still. Model code for, *What the fuck are you doing? He'll make this miserable for us. Cut it out.*

Siena widened her eyes and shot a glare down at the edgy man in front of her.

Willow rolled her eyes.

After an hour of shooting as a group, Trey gave them a two-minute break. Siena steered clear of Cash, drinking ice water through a straw, while the makeup artist touched up her foundation.

Siena narrowed her eyes in Cash's direction and said to Willow, "If you don't keep that ass away from me, I'm going to say something I shouldn't." He and the other firemen patted one another's backs and flexed their biceps as if they were competing with one another. *Neanderthals.* She remembered Jack's comment and cringed. *We get angry, and we get ornery, and we act like Neanderthals when we're challenged.* He was *nothing* like her brothers.

Willow rested a hand on Siena's shoulder and leaned in close. "I swear when Trey positioned you near the black-haired guy, Mike, Cash was drinking you in like tequila." Willow wiggled her shoulders seductively. "I like that one. The one with the thick waist—a waist I can hang on to—and the brown hair. *Joe.* Baby, Joe could put my fire out any day of the week."

"Ugh." Siena couldn't wait to get out of the shoot and away from Cash. She was tense. Her muscles hurt from arching her back and craning her neck, and her feet were burning from the stilettos.

"Okay, now we're going one-on-one," Trey announced.

"Lucky you," Willow teased. "Cash looks like Bradley Cooper, so suck it up and pretend it's Bradley. Man, what I wouldn't do for a night with Bradley. You know, if you close your eyes and pretend…"

I thought the same thing when I met him.

"Hard to do when he acts like Mel Gibson."

Chapter Six

CASH WAS STILL reeling from seeing Siena in the bar last night and wiped out from staying up half the night wondering who the hell she called after *Dexy* walked her home. There was a reason Cash never volunteered for this promotional shit. He hated everything about it, from the stupid poses to the idea that women bought the damn calendar to stare at pictures of his buddies, like firefighters were slabs of meat instead of the toughest guys around, risking their lives to save others, with more important shit to worry about than how they looked. Hell, if those women took one look at them after a rescue, they'd see their faces black with soot and tense with stress. *Not so pretty then, are we?* And now they'd be looking at him on the stupid calendar, too. That made him no better than Siena in her pink fucking panties. *Goddamn Tommy.* Tommy was up feeling sick all night, and if Cash didn't pitch in, they'd have only eleven guys for the shoot. He'd do just about anything for Tommy. Now he was stuck modeling with Siena fucking Remington. One of the most sought-after—and from what he could see, stuck-up—models in the city. Within the first five seconds of seeing her, Cash had decided to ignore her, but there was no *ignoring* Siena Remington. Every goddamn pose was seductive as hell. From the first second they'd been positioned together, his nerves had knocked him off-kilter, and he'd knocked right into her. *Twice.* She looked at him like he should bow down to her. *Fuck that.* Cash Ryder didn't bow down for anyone who hadn't earned their position in life the hard way—through hard work and dedication. And he certainly wasn't about to cater to some spoiled model who had no idea what real life was all about.

"Siena, Cash." Trey pointed to the door to the stairwell. "Grab the hose, hat, and boots," Trey yelled to an assistant.

What the hell? He followed the photographer through the heavy door.

"Cash, pull those trousers down a bit. I want to be so close to the danger zone my lens is smokin'." Trey tugged on Cash's pants.

Cash fought the urge to smack the photographer's hand away from his pants, if only to keep from also snapping at Siena, whose eyes were locked on him. Holy hell, she was making him nervous, and that pissed him off.

"Siena. On the steps. Darling…" Trey pointed to the jeans-clad assistant who carried a hard hat and boots. "Hat, boots," he barked to an assistant, then he pointed to Siena. "Where's my hose?" he snapped at his staff.

The assistant helped Siena out of her stilettos and into the fireman boots; then she put the hard hat on her and it slid right down over her eyes. She looked crazy adorable, pulling a reluctant smile from Cash's lips, which he quickly tamped down to a sneer.

Siena stood with her arms a few inches from her body, allowing the assistants to adjust her bikini, shimmy the top of the boots around a bit, and then angle the hat so her eyes—*Holy shit.* She had gorgeous, sea-blue eyes. How had he missed those before?

Trey positioned her on a lower step, with Cash stretched out on his back along the concrete stairs. What the hell did a fireman need to lie across steps for? If he were knocked on his ass in a rescue, he sure as hell wouldn't want to have a photo taken. *This* was why he hated this shit.

Trey took Siena's hand and led her up to a higher step; then the assistant wrapped the hose between Siena's legs and she held it like a python above Cash's chest. From his angle on the stairs, he couldn't help but look right at the underside of her full breasts, which stretched the material of her tiny, red bikini top, pulling it away from her torso and revealing a sliver of the flawless, milky skin of her breasts.

Siena was totally focused on the directions of the photographer, as if Cash didn't exist at all. Her long brown hair wasn't terribly thick and hadn't been overly styled for the shoot. It cascaded naturally over her shoulders and down to the middle of her back. Cash was hyperaware of every inch of her long, lean legs beside him, her curvaceous hips, and her slim waist, which he suddenly longed to wrap his hands around and pull toward him. *Holy hell, what am I doing?* He felt a tightening in his groin and knew he was in deep shit. He shifted his eyes to the wall. *Ugly Betty. Ugly Betty. Ugly Betty.* Shit. It wasn't working.

"That's too stiff," Trey snapped.

Fuck.

Trey grabbed the hose and repositioned it over Siena's shoulder. "Better. Siena, lean over him and stick your butt out."

Siena did as she was told, bending at the waist. Her hair tumbled onto Cash's face, sending all sorts of erotic thoughts through his mind.

"Sorry," she said, making no move to clear her hair from his face.

"Arch," Trey commanded.

Cash watched her ass inch up, her back sink down.

"More," Trey coaxed. "Eh. Eh. Perfect!"

Cash heard him move by his feet and click off a few shots. "Darling, come sweep her hair. I need to see Cash's face."

The assistant carefully placed Siena's hair over both shoulders and down her back, giving Cash a clear shot of her cleavage. *Fuuuuck.*

Click. Click. Click.

"Cash, look at her like you want to bed her."

"What?" Crap. He knew that look, and he was damn good at it, but doing it on demand—and to her?

"We've got a rise. Hurry up. This is a great shot." Trey dropped his eyes to Cash's formidable erection.

"Shit." Cash narrowed his eyes and looked at Siena; embarrassment deflated his arousal.

"Siena," Trey said with a sigh. "Show him. Hot. Sexy. I want to fuck your brains out."

Without a word, she slid her eyes to Cash and locked them, half-mast, on his. Her lips stuck out just a little, as if she were going to pucker and stopped short, and then they parted just enough for her tongue to run slowly in between.

Holy fuck. Erection in full bloom—and totally forgotten— Cash couldn't pry his eyes from hers. Somewhere in the back of his mind, he heard the camera, noticed the adjustments to the lighting, heard Trey's voice, but none of it registered. And when Siena lowered her body along the steps and slid her leg over his, then her hand along his chest, the skin-to-skin contact had him reaching for her.

"What are you doing? He didn't tell you to do that," she snapped.

"What?" His eyes darted to Trey, standing on a step beside him, looking down through the camera. *Well, fuck me.* Now she'd completely thrown him off-kilter, stolen his ability to think clearly, and pissed him off to boot.

FIVE HOURS OF shooting wasn't that long in modeling terms, but five hours of shooting with full-body contact, with an experienced, arrogant firefighter who for some stupid reason had Siena's body craving his touch, was exhausting and titillating at the same time, rendering Siena beyond frustrated. She'd worked with the hottest male models around. She'd been on the arm of the *real* Bradley Cooper, and never had her body burned as white-hot as it had in the stairwell.

In the dressing room, she zipped her jeans and slipped into her tight V-neck T-shirt, forgoing her sweater. She was still too damn hot.

Willow wiggled into her dress. She always wore dresses, while Siena tended toward jeans. She watched Willow's ass as she fixed her hair in the mirror, and she cast a look over her shoulder at her own ass and wondered if Cash thought she had a nice one. *Oh my God. I have to stop thinking about him.* She needed a distraction. She eyed Willow.

"How do you get that curve at the top of your butt? Mine is so flat." Siena reached a hand out.

"Wanna feel it? It's like being pregnant; everyone wants to touch." Willow laughed. "You can't get this real estate at the gym. You gotta be born with it."

"Jeez, that's awesome."

"Turn around." She held up her index finger and moved it in a circle.

Siena did, looking in the mirror over her shoulder.

"Girl, you have a fine ass. What are you worried about?" Willow put on lipstick and smacked her lips. "Besides, Cash, Mike, and Joe were totally into you. Did you notice that some of those other guys barely said two words?" She didn't give Siena time to answer. "Mike, Joe, and I are heading over to NightCaps. Do you guys want to go relieve some tension?"

Siena washed her face and patted it dry. "Are you referring to me and Cash? We're not a *you guys*."

"Whatever. You know what I mean."

"I want to hang with you, but I'm not sure I can take sitting with Cash for ten minutes, much less all night. Besides, he doesn't seem like the kind of guy who would want to go hang out. He seemed like he was hating every second of the shoot." She thought of him reaching for her on the stairs. *Well, almost every second.*

"Come on." Willow grabbed their purses and pulled Siena out the door. "You never know how he'll be when he loosens up."

Siena didn't believe he knew how to loosen up, but she couldn't quite pull the words *No thanks* from her lungs.

Outside the studio, Willow and Joe piled into a cab. "We'll meet you there," Willow said as she closed the door with a wink.

Great.

Cash stood beside her with a scowl on his face. "Guess we're sharing a cab."

"Whatever." *This was a big mistake.* "I can't believe you're even going."

"What's that supposed to mean?"

"Just that you seemed like you couldn't wait to get out of there."

He clenched his jaw and flagged down a cab. As they climbed in, he said, "Perceptive, but only partially right."

Siena had no idea how to respond to that. Did that mean he didn't want to go? Then why was he? She let out a frustrated breath and set her purse between them. She needed some kind of barrier. As much as she wanted to stay away from him, she felt a stirring down low every time she looked at him. She turned and looked out the window. *Better. Safer.*

"Oh crap."

She shifted her eyes to him.

"I've got to stop somewhere before I go to the bar. Why don't you drop me off and I'll meet you guys there?" He rubbed his hand nervously down his face.

"That's the lamest thing I've ever heard. If you don't want to go, just say it. I don't care. It's not like you'll hurt my feelings." Her stomach clenched, and a twinge of hurt squeezed at her heart, causing her mouth to run a mile a minute. "It's not like I want to go with you anyway."

"What are you talking about?"

"This bullshit excuse. *Someplace to go.* That's as transparent as a girl saying she has a headache."

His nostrils flared, and he fisted his hands. "Who are you to decide if I'm telling the truth or not? I don't make up excuses. If I didn't want to go to the bar, I wouldn't go."

So you want to go. Heat shot through her. "Right. Like you want to spend any more time with me than you have to."

"You don't believe me?" He leaned forward and gave the

driver an address. "You're coming with me."

A command. Why the hell does it turn me on when you do that?

"I'll show you who's a liar and who's not."

"I'm not going with you on some fake errand that you made up to make yourself look better." She crossed her arms over her chest to calm her racing heart.

"Fake errand?"

He leaned in close. So damn close she could smell the mint he'd eaten ten minutes before.

SIENA REMINGTON WAS the most frustrating woman he'd ever met, and Cash was done playing. With his lips an inch from hers, he whispered, "Unlike women, I never fake a damn thing."

Her body visibly shuddered. Exactly the reaction he'd hoped for. That would shut her up.

"I've never faked a damn thing in my life," she shot back. Her eyes darkened, filled with challenge.

I bet you haven't.

"Can you stop at the florist on the corner first, please?"

He caught Siena's confused expression and chose to ignore it. Vetta hadn't been eating much lately, and he wanted to check on her. Flowers might just cheer her up if she was feeling sad or lonely.

The cab pulled over. "I'll only be a second." He looked from Siena to the cabbie. "Don't leave," he said to the cabbie. "I'm the one paying your fare."

He returned to the car five minutes later with a bouquet of

daisies. "Thanks," he said to the cabbie.

Siena stared at the flowers. He knew she wondered who they were for. *Good. Let her stew.* He wished he'd had time to go to the grocery store even though Vetta had said she didn't need anything.

When they pulled up in front of Vetta's apartment, Cash's eyes never left hers as he paid the driver. "Stay there," he said gruffly to Siena.

He stepped from the cab and then opened Siena's door for her. "You coming or what?"

"You just told me to stay here like a dog." She stared straight ahead.

"I meant I'd open the door."

She glared at him.

"You're so fucking crazy. You can call me a liar, but I'm not going to let you make me into something I'm not in that pretty little brain of yours. I open doors. It's who I am." They stared at each other so long he thought the cabbie was going to charge him extra. "Are you getting out of the car?"

She huffed as she climbed out, her arms crossed firmly over her chest. She looked up and down the block. He headed into the brick apartment building. When he opened the door and held it without going in, she rolled her eyes and passed through.

"Where are we?"

He had no idea why he'd told her to come with him. Siena had pissed him off too many times. Cash was a lot of things, but a goddamn liar wasn't one of them. He thought of his meeting with the chief and knew that telling the chief he'd get himself under control would be a lie. He had no control over what had become a *need* to take extra risks on the job—if only to prove that if he could help it, they'd never lose another life while he was on duty. He pushed away thoughts of the chief. The chief could wait until tomorrow. He needed all of his focus to make it through tonight.

He knocked on the door, keenly aware of Siena's angry breathing beside him. He heard the click of the dead bolt, the slide of the chain. Cash drew in a deep breath and pulled his shoulders back. His eyes slid to Siena. Tension lines gathered around her beautiful eyes, across her forehead, and framed her sweet, pouty lips. The click of the last dead bolt drew his eyes back to the door.

"Oh, Cash, you brought my favorite flowers." Vetta pulled the door open and was startled when she spotted Siena. "Goodness. You've brought a friend."

Siena's eyes shot to Cash; then her lips lifted to a practiced smile and her face softened. "Hi, I'm Siena Remington."

It was all he could do not to call her on her ability to morph from Modelzilla to sweet Cinderella in the blink of an eye.

"Siena Remington. I knew a Remington once. Please, come in." Vetta moved slowly toward the living room.

Cash held out a hand, guiding a path for Siena to enter before him.

"I'm Vetta Miller. Please, sit down." She settled into the chair, leaving the sofa for Siena and Cash.

"I'll put these in a vase." Cash headed into the kitchen. He pulled open the refrigerator, noticed the spaghetti hadn't been touched, and closed it again.

Vetta spoke quietly, but not quietly enough for Cash to miss what she said—and Siena's answers.

"Siena, how do you know Cash?"

"I...We..."

Cash stilled his hand from arranging the flowers, listening

intently.

"I ran my car off the road the other night and he rescu—helped me."

Rescued. I rescued you. Was she too stubborn to admit he'd rescued her, or did she dislike him too much to give him credit? His gut tightened at the latter.

"Ah. You're the one he told me about. He's a nice man."

He held his breath, waiting for Siena's response.

"Is he?"

Am I? What kind of response is that? He shoved the flowers in the vase and took a step toward the living room, then stopped at the sound of Vetta's voice.

"Oh yes. He visits me several times each week, brings me dinner, fixes things."

Cash closed his eyes, waiting for the bomb to fall. *He killed my husband.*

"He's a dear."

His eyes flew open. *A dear? A dear.*

He waited another beat, but when neither said anything further, he cleared his throat and came into the room, setting the vase on the coffee table.

"Now, those brighten this room right up, don't they?" Vetta gazed up at him with a kind smile. "Cash, won't you sit down?" She pointed to the vacant seat beside Siena on the small sofa.

He didn't trust himself next to Siena. His body reacted to her in ways he couldn't control and she tweaked his last nerve, causing him to be even gruffer than he normally was.

"I'm good. I'll stand."

"You should sit," Siena said, patting the seat beside her with a smirk on her lips.

You know just what you're doing to me.

"Yes, Cash. You're making me nervous." Vetta nodded toward the sofa, and he reluctantly sat beside Siena. The scent of her sweet perfume wrapped around him, and when she leaned toward Vetta, so close to his lap that she was practically on it, every muscle tensed.

"Vetta, you said you knew a Remington?"

"Yes. A Joanie Remington. She used to bring crayons and paper to the kids in the pediatric ward where my husband worked. It was ages ago."

"That's my mother."

"Oh, isn't that a coincidence. I wonder if she would remember my husband, Samuel." She looked up at the photo on the wall and sighed.

"Is he…?" Siena glanced at Cash.

Cash felt the air leave his lungs. *Here it comes.*

"Oh, he passed a few weeks ago. Heart attack." She reached for Cash's hand. "Cash has been checking on me ever since."

Why are you doing this? Just tell her. Get it over with. He could barely breathe.

Siena searched Cash's eyes, and he drew them away, sure she could see the guilt that haunted him every second of the day.

"Really?" Siena said quietly.

"Oh, yes. He's quite a gentleman."

"Okay, this is a little uncomfortable for me." Cash rose to his feet. "I just wanted to stop by to see if you needed anything before I headed out for the night. I noticed that you haven't touched the spaghetti I brought last night. Was something wrong with it? Do you want me to get you something else? I have time. I can go get something now."

"Oh, no, thank you. When you get up in age, hunger doesn't hold as much of a priority."

"Are you sure? I mean if you need to see a doctor, or need different foods…"

"No, no. You're such a doll, Cash. I'm fine, really. You kids run along. I'm fine." Vetta pushed to her feet, and Cash reached a hand out to her lower back and kissed her cheek.

"Lock this behind us, please."

"I always do," Vetta said with another smile.

He opened the door for Siena, and after she walked out of the apartment, Vetta touched his arm.

"Let her see you like I see you," Vetta whispered. Then she nodded and gave him a little shove out the door.

He joined Siena in the hallway. She tilted her head to the side and looked him over with an assessing gaze, as if she were seeing him for the first time. The energy rolling off of her had changed from sharp to soft, as if she were looking at a big stuffed teddy bear and thinking, *Aw, aren't you cute.*

Had everyone in the world lost their minds?

Chapter Seven

THE BRISK NIGHT air stung Siena's cheeks as they headed to NightCaps. She didn't know what to make of the angry and arrogant man Cash Ryder appeared to be as he walked beside her in silence, or how that part of him fit in with the empathetic, gentle giant she'd seen a few minutes earlier. She had so many questions, and she knew she shouldn't care about any of them. What did it matter how he treated an old woman who had lost her husband? Or that he'd brought her flowers or fixed her stuff? He wasn't that man around Siena, and that should be enough to send her hightailing it in the opposite direction. But she couldn't turn away. She was intrigued.

She stepped over the curb, and he grabbed her arm and held her still. She shot a look over her shoulder.

"You didn't even look for cars," he snapped. His eyes narrowed, and the muscle in his jaw bunched up.

The angry man is back. She'd been hoping to hang on to the softer side of him for a little while longer. Maybe only little old ladies got that pleasure. "I did, in my peripheral vision."

He lifted his chin to the illuminated red hand on the crosswalk sign. "See that?"

"Yes, but there are no cars coming."

He shook his head, still hanging on to her arm, his body pressed against her side. She couldn't pull away. She didn't want to. She liked the feel of him against her, the way he was looking at her like he wanted to devour her and yell at her all at once.

She yanked her arm out of his grasp. *What is wrong with me? He is so not the man for me. He's mean, testy, unpredictable.* She thought of the way he'd looked at Vetta when he'd kissed her cheek, the flowers he'd brought her, the concern in his voice when he'd asked about the spaghetti. He made her spaghetti?

"Fine. Walk out there. Kill yourself. Just don't expect me to rescu—help you."

"You're so…so…" She turned away and shoved her hands in her pockets before stomping across the street—after the crosswalk sign flashed the image of the person walking. She felt him behind her, felt his elbow touch her back when she slowed to walk around a couple.

"I didn't lie," he seethed.

She didn't outwardly acknowledge the truth of it, but inside she was still warm with the knowledge that he'd delayed their trip to the bar to check on Vetta. Most men wouldn't let anything steal a second of their time when they were with her, and most women would love that. Siena found herself even more attracted to him for having delayed their evening. She chanced a look at him, his eyes focused on the people walking toward them on the sidewalk. He was obviously aware of his surroundings at all times. She guessed that was part of his whole *being prepared* thing. He shoved his hands in his coat pockets. His cheeks had darkened since he first arrived at the photo shoot and were now peppered with evening stubble that she desperately wanted to touch. *Stop it.*

You're not a liar.

But you are an asshole.
Sort of.
Sometimes.

He held the door to the bar open, then pulled out a chair for Siena when they found the others at a table near the bar.

Okay, so sometimes you're a gentleman. The realization stilled her mind. She scrutinized him as he shrugged off his coat, looking way too hot in a tight fire department T-shirt and jeans that hugged his thick, powerful thighs. She swallowed against the attraction that coiled in her belly.

"What're you drinking?" he asked gruffly.

She pushed to her feet. Cash settled his hand on her shoulder and gently but firmly pushed her back down to her seat, sending a shiver down her spine. *A hot iron leaving its mark.* She sensed Willow's eyes tracking their every move.

Cash pinned her to the chair with the same heated stare he'd stilled her with in the truck. Damn, he could pin her anywhere he wanted with those eyes.

"It's who I am, remember?" he asked sternly.

Everything he'd done since they left the studio had thrown her equilibrium off. Siena wasn't used to not being in control, especially not with a man. She arched a brow and in her most seductive voice said, "I'll have a screaming orgasm."

His Adam's apple jumped in his throat. His fingers curled around her shoulder, gripping it tightly.

"Maybe two," she added before turning her attention to Willow.

SHE'S FUCKING WITH me. Cash tried to stifle the rush of

desire that burned through him as he ordered two rounds of screaming orgasms for everyone at the table. *Maybe two.* He scoffed. Hell, one night with him and she'd be screaming for more.

He set the drinks in front of her.

"Only two?" He shook his head. "I had you pegged all wrong."

He doled the rest out to the others, sensing her eyes on him.

"You're not really my type, but I'll take it." Mike's harmless flirting had never gotten him into trouble. He was married with a three-year old daughter. He fluttered his dark eyelashes and flashed a crooked smile. He ran his hand through his military-short black hair.

"Well, he's definitely my type," Willow said, lifting her shot glass. She winked at Siena.

"Damn, I was hoping I was your type," Joe said, pulling his lips into a frown.

Willow leaned over and kissed his stubbled cheek. "Baby, you're all my type."

Siena rolled her eyes.

Cash sat across from her and lifted his glass. "To screaming orgasms."

The others mirrored his toast and sucked down their drinks. Siena held his stare, then tossed her head back and swallowed the shot.

"Hm. Not quite as good as I remember." She arched a brow.

He felt his lips lift into a smile. *You wanna play?* He knocked back his second shot, slammed the glass on the table, and locked eyes with her again. "Sometimes it takes a few before it hits the spot. But if you can't keep up…" He shrugged.

Willow tossed back her second drink. "Oh, we can keep up, all right. Mike, get a few more rounds."

Siena's eyes never left his. She licked her lower lip, leaving it wet.

Damn.

"I usually get it right the first time. The rest is just for good measure." She tossed back her drink. "Ah. That was a little better."

Mike brought two more rounds to the table. "Yeah, baby. Now we're talking." He glanced around the table. "I figure I have another fifteen minutes or so before I need to head home."

Cash's pulse raced. The challenge in Siena's eyes was more than a drinking game. He knew lust when he saw it—and when he felt it.

Siena stood. Cash did the same.

"I'm going to the ladies' room."

"I'll walk you."

She kicked her hip out to the side and leaned across the table. "Suit yourself."

Cash felt as if he were walking in a path of fire as he followed her through the bar and down the steps. He tugged his collar away from his neck as his feet hit the floor. Siena cast a glance over her shoulder, ran her eyes slowly down his body, then sauntered into the ladies' room.

He followed her in.

"It wasn't an invitation," she said coldly.

He pushed open each of the stalls, confirming that they were empty. Two steps brought him to her, his nerves tight, his body hot. She looked up at him without a word. He took a step closer. Her back met the wall; his hips met hers. Christ, she felt good. Too damn good. She was breathing as hard as he was.

Her breasts lifted and fell against him. She had to feel his hard desire against her. He leaned forward, his lips a breath away from hers, and rested his forearm on the wall beside her head. Her lips parted, her eyelids hung heavily, seductively, as he drank them in; then he lowered his gaze to the pulse point on her neck, which was beating fast and hard. He dropped his eyes lower, lingering along the line of her collarbone, then the dip of her chest as it disappeared beneath her shirt.

He licked the sweet alcohol from his lips and lowered his cheek to hers.

"Careful," he whispered. "You're playing with fire, and I'm a master at controlling the flames."

Chapter Eight

SIENA LET OUT a breath and watched him stroll out of the bathroom as if he hadn't just made her damp with nothing but his voice—and his hard body pressed against her—leaving her aching for more. *Jesus.* She panted out several loud breaths and ran a shaky hand through her hair. *What the hell was that?*

She ran her hands under cold water, hoping to cool the heat that had taken over her brain. It didn't help. Nothing would help. He was in her brain. His masculine smell lingered around her. He was powerful, edgy, dangerous. A cheetah. And holy hell did she want to be his prey. *Pounce, baby, pounce.*

Siena took a deep breath and walked out of the bathroom. Cash was waiting for her by the stairs. She stopped cold. Swallowed hard.

He waved a hand toward the stairs, and she took a step, then stopped. He waved her forward again, and she walked tentatively up the steps.

"It's just who I am," he said quietly.

"A stalker?" Her ploy at levity failed. Even she wasn't laughing.

She sensed him behind her. He leaned forward, and his hot breath warmed her neck.

"No."

His stern answer made her shudder.

"A gentleman."

Her heart softened a little more.

Willow was putting on her coat when they arrived back at the table. "Hey, we're gonna go see if Cheri is working over at Studio Twenty-One. Want to come?"

Shit. Studio Twenty-One? She and Cash locked eyes. What was she doing? She had no idea what she was doing, but the idea of going to Studio Twenty-One didn't sound great. She couldn't look away from him. She wasn't done with Cash Ryder. *Not nearly.* One thing was for sure: She was *not* going home with him.

Siena took a deep breath and steeled herself to go home and spend an evening reading. Or watching television. Or…lying in bed thinking about Cash. *Goddamn it.* She glanced at the table and caught sight of four full shot glasses. She and Cash hadn't had their last two rounds. *Thank God. Just what I need to calm my engine.*

She hugged Willow. "I'll catch up with you tomorrow. I'm going to hang out and finish my drinks and then go home. Mike, Joe, take good care of her."

"I'm going home to my wife." Mike winked at Cash. "Thanks for a fun night."

"You know I'll take care of her," Joe said on the way out the door.

Cash pulled out Siena's chair for her, and as she sat down, she wondered if she'd made a huge mistake. She wanted the drinks, but when Cash sat down across from her, she saw him through entirely new eyes. She'd seen the softer side of him at Vetta's, and now…she'd seen a purely sexual side. Damn, how was she supposed to go back to seeing him as the ass she'd thought he was?

He picked up a glass and narrowed his eyes. "To screaming orgasms."

Big. Giant. Mistake. She downed one shot and then the other as fast as she possibly could, relishing in the sweetness as the liquid coated her throat. *Numb me, baby.*

"Whoa, I didn't peg you for a wham, bam, thank you, woman."

A nervous smile brought an even more nervous laugh. She had to get control. *Focus. Like at a shoot.* Her mind immediately recalled the image of Cash sprawled on the stairs with a massive erection. She felt her cheeks flush and dropped her eyes. *This is bad. So very bad.*

"Who…who was that woman you visited? Vetta?"

Cash looked at his watch. "It's late, and I've got an early meeting with my chief." He pushed his chair from the table and rose to his feet.

You're blowing me off? She couldn't wrap her arms around the idea. *You're blowing me off?*

"Come on. I'll walk you wherever you're going."

Reeling from being blown off, she was caught off guard by his kind tone. "No demand?" Siena leaned back in her chair, contemplating how she might piss him off next just for the hell of it.

He shoved his arms into his coat and shrugged in response.

"I'm fine. I'll get myself home."

Cash sighed heavily. He looked around the bar, then went to her side and leaned in close.

Siena's pulse ratcheted up a notch.

"What would Jack say if I let you walk home alone?"

"You're using my brother as a...a-against me?"

"I wondered if he was your brother. Not against you. He'd kick my ass if he thought I let you walk home alone after four screaming orgasms." He flashed a cocky-ass grin.

She rose to her feet and grabbed her jacket. "I guarantee that if you told Jack you gave me four screaming orgasms, you'd never speak another word, much less walk anyone home."

"Got you moving, didn't it?"

"WHERE TO?" CASH asked Siena as she zipped up her coat and rounded her shoulders forward to ward off the cold. He had an urge to wrap her in his arms and keep her warm, craving the close proximity after feeling her heat in the bathroom at the bar. How could a woman who looked that damn hot in a bikini look equally as hot in a quilted coat and jeans?

"I can get home myself." She walked into the road to flag down a cab.

"Are you always like this?"

"What?" She waved at a cab.

"So...autonomous." He lowered her hand. "It's a hell of a lot cheaper to take the subway."

Siena wrinkled her nose. "The subway? You're kidding, right? At night?"

"Let me get this straight. You're not afraid to walk around the city at night, or take a cab with a stranger driving you, but you won't take a subway with thousands of people around you at all times?" He shook his head. "No. I guess you wouldn't."

"What's that supposed to mean?"

"Forget it." *I should let her climb into a cab and move on.*

"Are you implying that I think I'm too good for the subway?" She stepped closer to him and poked her finger into his chest. "Because I sure as hell don't. I thought a cab was safer at night."

He looked down at her delicate finger poking him and almost laughed. She thought she was so tough. She was a definite pain in the ass, but tough? Not in as many ways as she thought, and after watching her all day in that sexy bikini and then seeing her defenses melt away in the bathroom, he didn't care how much of a pain in the ass she was. She'd fucked with his head enough that he couldn't think past her, and he'd be damned if he was going to let anything happen to her on the way home from the bar.

"Whatever. All I care is that you get home safely." He flagged a cab.

"Forget it. I'll take the subway." She spun around and walked away.

Goddamn, you're a pain. He hurried after her.

"I can take the subway by myself, thank you." She took fast and determined steps, her hands shoved deep into her coat pockets.

"Yeah, give up on that one. It's not happening." Why did he even care? He should go back to the station house to...*Damn it.* He'd just think about her all night.

The subway was standing-room only. Siena held on to a rail by the door and Cash squished in behind her. He reached around her to hold on to the railing and stifled a groan when the subway began to move and rocked her hips against his. He shifted to the side to alleviate the contact and the subway car shifted again. *Fuck it.* He stopped trying to control it and let the subway stir up all the heat it wanted to.

Siena turned her head sideways and said, "I could have done this by myself." She gripped the handrail so hard her knuckles were white. Her body shivered against him.

Cash settled his hand over hers and felt her flinch beneath his touch. He pressed his cheek to the back of her head. "Your hand is freezing."

"I…forgot my gloves."

He reached for her other hand. She resisted his touch, but he held tight. "I'm just warming your hands. Stop freaking out." That's what he told himself, too. Her hand was feminine and small, completely covered by his. He rubbed his fingers along the back of it, his thumb along her palm, until it warmed, and she stopped shivering. Remarkably, the tension in their hands eased, confusing him even further.

The subway stopped on Bleeker Street in the Village, and they followed a group of young kids onto the sidewalk. A breeze kicked up, and Siena curled her shoulders against it. Her hair blew across her face. She spun to the side, trying to escape the wind, and her hair blew in the other direction. She swatted to move it from her face.

Cash stepped in front of her and held her shoulders. "Stay still."

She looked up at him with her brows knitted together as she swiped a few strands away from her eyes.

He gathered her silky hair in his hands, suppressing the urge to run his fingers through it. "Better?"

She nodded.

"Do you have one of those things girls keep on their wrists?"

She laughed. "No. It's not the eighties."

"Then you'll have to make do with me." He draped his arm over her shoulder, holding her hair in his clenched fist.

"Between this, the accident, and the gloves, maybe I need to give you a little lesson in being prepared."

She didn't say a word.

She felt damn good pressed up against his side. This was the longest she'd been silent since he'd met her, and he wondered how he'd pissed her off now. *My arm. Presumptuous. I'm ruining her image.* He'd almost forgotten that she was Siena Remington. No wonder she was hesitant to take the subway.

"Don't yell at me when I touch your hair." *Why do I sound so angry?*

She narrowed her eyes as he moved behind her and gathered her hair, then tied it into a knot.

"That'll keep it from your face." He shoved his hands in his pockets and stepped away from her.

"What, did your arm get tired?" she snapped.

"Let's just say I'm good at reading nonverbal cues."

"Nonverbal cues? What are you talking about?"

He stared straight ahead. He wasn't going to argue with her. "Where's your apartment?"

"Three blocks up." She was shivering again.

"Come on." He pulled open a door to a café and waved her by.

She stood on the sidewalk staring straight ahead.

"Christ. What is it with you? It's not like I'm dragging you out on a date."

She drew her brows together.

"I was going to get you a cup of hot chocolate. You're like a little bird shivering in the cold. You need something warm in you." His mind immediately swapped *something warm* with *me.* He had to stop thinking about her in that way. "And I figured you didn't want me messing up your image. Hot chocolate was the next best thing."

"Messing up my image?" She folded her arms across her chest.

"Look, I forgot who you were when we were walking. I was trying to be nice by holding your hair out of your face. I lost my fucking mind, okay?" His voice escalated, and his heart raced again. Damn it. He couldn't even walk away. He had to see her home safely.

She took a step closer to him, her lower lip shivering. "Thank you. Okay?" she said with as much venom as he had. "I *liked* that you held my hair."

"Then why'd you stop talking? You never shut up. If you're not telling me off, you're sneering at me and making a smart-ass comment."

She stomped away.

He was right on her heels. "Oh, now you're mad again?"

"I'm freezing." She turned off the main road onto a dark side street.

"That's why I was going to get you hot chocolate." *Jesus, does it take a rocket scientist to put two and two together?*

"Yeah? Well, don't."

"What is with you?"

She focused on the ground, and he grabbed her arm again. Damn, he had to stop doing *that*, too. He lifted her chin, and she shrugged out of his grip, but not before he saw a softening in her eyes that didn't match her angry tone.

"You allergic to hot chocolate?"

"I fucking love hot chocolate." Her shoulders were shivering so hard her teeth chattered.

"I never claimed to know much about women, but you're seriously messing with my head." He tugged his coat off and put it around her shoulders.

"Don't," she snapped, wiggling against him.

"Stop it." Yes, it was a command, but damn it, she needed his coat, and he wasn't going to watch her freeze. She was so slender compared to his breadth that he was able to slide her arms into the coat and zip it up. Then he took a hat out of the pocket of the coat and pulled it low on her head, covering her ears.

"Really?"

"Don't worry. You look goddamn adorable and you're still beautiful, and as a bonus…" He knew he was growling and he couldn't stop himself. The entire day he'd been repressing his attraction to her, and the desire had grown from a dull ache into full-blown need. Every damn thing she did and said was frustratingly seductive in some crazy way that made no sense at all, and yet he was powerless to walk away. "No one will recognize you. So I can't mess up your image." The words tasted like acid coming off his tongue.

The sleeves of his coat hung down to her knees, the waist hung just about as long, and Cash was so fired up that he didn't even feel the icy air slicing his skin.

"What did you say?" She angled her head up and pushed at the hat with the floppy sleeves of his coat.

"Here," he snapped, and rolled up the sleeves. Then he shoved his hand deep into the far pocket of his coat and took out a pair of thick gloves. "Gimme your hand."

She lifted her arm, and he pushed the sleeve higher and slipped the glove over her hand. She lifted the other arm and he did the same.

She shoved the hat higher onto her forehead and met his angry stare with her softened gaze. "I'd like that hot chocolate now."

"You…Christ Almighty. Let me get you home so you're

warm; then I'll go get it for you." He took a step forward, and this time she grabbed his arm.

"No. I want to go with you."

Her lips had that pouty thing happening again, which tugged at his heart and made him want to kiss them until they were smiling again.

She turned around and headed for the café.

"Is it just me that you mess with, or are you this much of a pain to everyone?" he called from behind her.

"Just you," she said, as carefree as if she'd just said, *I love ice cream*.

There wasn't a single seat available in the café. Siena stepped up to the counter, and her pout transformed into a warm, friendly smile for the older, gray-haired gentleman behind the counter. The hat had slipped down low again, and Cash couldn't see her eyes, but when she spoke, her voice carried a happier inflection.

"Hey, Bogey. How are you?"

Bogey?

"Siena? I didn't recognize you in there. Warm enough?" He looked from Siena to Cash and wrinkled his brow.

"Yeah, now I am." She looked up at Cash. "He was kind enough to lend me his coat."

What the hell was she doing?

"Very chivalrous on a night like tonight," Bogey said with a wink.

"Yeah, well, someone has a hard time with the idea of preparedness." He nodded at Siena.

Without missing a beat, she threw her elbow back into his gut. He caught the damn thing right before it connected and held tight, forcing a smile for Bogey's sake.

She looked up at him and fluttered her lashes. "Oops. I slipped." She turned back to Bogey. "Can we get two hot chocolates, please, with whipped cream?"

"Anything for you," Bogey said and set to work making them.

Cash pressed his body against hers as he leaned in close. "Slipped, my ass." He reached for his wallet and realized he'd shoved it in his coat pocket. Without saying a word, he thrust his hand in the coat pocket, *accidentally on purpose* feeling around for the wallet as his hand grazed the curve of her hip and slid to her inner thigh.

Siena cleared her throat, shooting daggers through her narrowed eyes.

He pulled out the wallet and wiggled it between his finger and thumb. "Oops. I slipped." The solemn tone returned to his voice, as he tried to quell his raging desire. He had to bite the inside of his cheeks to keep from smiling at her fierce scowl.

Outside, Siena sipped her hot chocolate and looked at him over the top of the cup. She lowered it slowly and licked the chocolate from her lips.

Cash groaned. He wrapped his arm in hers and pressed his body against her as they walked. "You're going to be the death of me."

Siena slowed her pace. With both hands wrapped around her warm cup, she nearly came to a stop each time she blew at the steam.

"Maybe we could move a little quicker. It's about ten degrees out here and I have no coat."

"Nope."

"Excuse me?"

"No. I don't think we can walk any quicker." She eyed her

hot chocolate. "I don't want to spill my hot chocolate." She smiled up at him, her hair blowing behind her from beneath his hat.

"It's a damn good thing you're…" *Sexy as hell.* "Cute." They passed a bench in front of a market. "Hey, here's an idea." His voice grew louder with feigned excitement. "Why don't we sit down and just relax a little while?"

"Oh! Great idea." Siena wiggled her butt onto the bench and patted the seat beside her.

"I see sarcasm is over your head." He sat down beside her. "If we're going to sit here and freeze, then you're sharing your warmth." He pulled her against him, and Siena snuggled in beneath his arm, pressing against his chest. *Dangerous. Way too dangerous.* He gulped down half of his hot chocolate to warm his body. If Siena kept wiggling her ass against him, he wasn't going to need anything to keep him warm.

"See? This is nice." She leaned her head back and looked up at him. "Oh, I know how I can keep you warm." She set her cup on the ground, then took his from his hands and did the same before climbing onto his lap and settling her hands on his shoulders. "Warmer?"

He couldn't talk. Could barely breathe. He was too busy trying to keep himself from getting another hard-on.

SIENA KNEW SHE was torturing Cash, and it was bringing her way too much pleasure to stop. Who knew that inside that brash, cranky man was a romantic, chivalrous softy? She couldn't even pretend to figure out why he was smoldering hot one minute, sending her insides into a frenzy of need, then icy cold the next, but when he'd warmed her hands on the subway, he'd given her pause. And when he held her close, keeping her hair from the wind, she thought it was about the most thoughtful thing he could do. But she'd been wrong. Wrapping her in his coat after she was such a monster to him topped the list and softened her heart toward him even more.

In his eyes she saw that he was just as confused as she was. It was the tenderness she'd seen when they'd visited Vetta, the same tenderness she saw right now, that made her *want* to understand him—*and torture him.*

"Still cold?" she asked.

"Feels like summer." His lips curled into a mischievous grin.

She wiggled her hips against him, feeling his thick, hard need beneath her.

"You take wicked to a whole new level."

She wrapped her arms around his neck. His brows knitted together. With her heart hammering against her ribs, she brought her lips closer to his. His eyes searched hers as she grazed the corner of his mouth with hers, wanting oh so badly to take his luscious lips in a greedy kiss. She forced herself to push past those full, delicious lips and press her cheek to his before running her fingers through his thick hair and whispering, "Still an expert at controlling the flames?"

He buried his hand in her hair, drew her head back so they were eye to eye, and growled, "Do you want me to be?"

Oh God, no. She opened her mouth, but words didn't come. She licked her lips, knowing the effect it'd had on him before.

"Siena." Her name was one long, heated growl.

God, she loved that guttural growl.

He cupped the back of her head. "Do you want me to control the fl—"

She was breathing so hard she thought she might hyperventilate. "No. God, no."

He settled his lips over hers and took her in a greedy, passionate kiss. His tongue moved fast at first, hungrily taking what she had to give, exploring every crevice, the lines of her teeth, the roof of her mouth. *Oh God*, she never wanted the kiss to end. He tasted of hot chocolate and lust, and his embrace felt like heaven and earth combined—strong, protective, and loving all at once. She clutched his hair in her fists, kissing him harder and moaning for more. He captured her moan in his mouth, then pulled back fast, leaving them both panting.

"More," was all she could manage before he lowered his lips to hers again and sent heat searing through her center. He slowed his tongue, stroking her with a slow tease. Holy hell. She'd never been kissed with such virility one second and tenderness the next. His hands slid around the bulky coat and pressed against her back. The sheer power of his hands spurred her body into motion. She pressed her chest to his. Another moan escaped her lips before she remembered where they were. *Outside. A bench. Holy shit.* She dragged her tongue along his lips as she drew back, panting. Wanting more. Needing more.

Needing to pull herself together.

"Go out with me." He said it urgently.

"Now?"

He shook his head and cupped the back of her head again. God, she loved that.

"Tomorrow night. A date. A real date."

She nodded, unable to stop the smile from spreading across her lips. "Okay." Her voice was a ragged thread.

He kissed her again, and she nearly lost it right there on the bench. He was right. It did feel as hot as summer. *Only better.*

Chapter Nine

THE FIREHOUSE SMELLED like pancakes and sausage when Cash arrived the next morning, thoughts of Siena running through his mind. He hung his coat by the door as Tommy came down the hall.

"Heard you guys had a hell of a night." With a flick of his chin, Tommy's hair swung out of his eyes. He carried a plate stacked high with pancakes and sausages doused in syrup.

Cash eyed him, freshly showered, color in his cheeks, full of energy. "You better?"

"Oh, yeah. Totally cool. C'mon. Get some food."

He followed Tommy into the kitchen, smelling a rat. Joe, Mike, and three of the other guys were at the table scarfing down breakfast.

"Hey," Cash said as he filled his plate.

"Missed you at Studio Twenty-One last night. Dude, killer night. Willow's got dance moves hotter than a six-alarm fire." Joe waved his hand up and down his chest as if he were fanning flames.

Not as hot as Siena. "That right?" He sat beside Joe and focused on breakfast. The last thing he wanted to do was let those magazine masturbators know he had a date with Siena tonight. It pissed him off that they'd seen her wearing practically nothing. Hell, the world had seen her wearing practically nothing. Jealousy ran its nasty claws down his spine.

"Caribbean women. *Mm-mmm.*" Joe elbowed Cash. "How about you? Siena Remington. Dude. Can't do better than *that* piece of ass."

Cash gritted his teeth against the urge to grab him by the neck and slam him against a wall. These were his buddies, the guys he lived with more often than he lived at his dink-ass apartment. The guys who'd give their lives for him. He eyed Tommy, who'd been ready to do just that a few weeks earlier.

"So?" Mike leaned across the table, mouth full of pancakes. He often stayed at the firehouse overnight, but when he did go home, he was always back for breakfast before his shift. "Where'd you guys end up? You didn't come back here."

Cash lifted his eyes to Tommy, head still down as he spoke to Mike. "Thought you went home last night."

"I did, spent time with Lisa." Mike and Lisa had been married for five years. They were good together. Lisa understood his need to unwind with the guys, and he was a caring and attentive husband and father when he was home. "Katie was asleep, so I came back around two. I didn't want to wake Lisa when I left in the morning. Stop changing the subject and answer the question."

"Walked her home." He shoved a forkful of sausage into his mouth.

Mike didn't take the *shut the fuck up* hint. "Damn. You went home with the pink panties girl? And?"

Cash sprang to his feet, sending his chair skidding across the floor. He glared at Tommy, then dumped his food in the trash and stood in front of the sink, scrubbing his plate beneath scalding-hot water.

"Shit, man. I guess you didn't get any." Joe laughed.

Cash threw his plate in the sink with a loud *clank* and spun around, breathing fire, ready for a fight. He didn't want them talking about Siena that way, much less thinking about her that way. His biceps burned. He fisted his wet hands.

Tommy put a hand across Joe's chest. "Dude, back off."

"What's got your balls in a bundle?" Mike asked around a mouthful of pancakes.

Cash shot him a sneer before turning back to finish cleaning his dishes.

Tommy came to his side. "What the fuck?" he whispered.

Cash shoved his dishes in the dish drainer, wiped his hands on his jeans, and dragged Tommy by the arm into the next room.

"You tell me," Cash snapped.

"What?"

"Sick, Tom? Sick, my ass." He pulled him into the television room, out of earshot of the others.

"My tummy ache got better yesterday morning." Tommy rubbed his stomach. The right side of his mouth lifted in a sarcastic smile, and Cash knew damn well that he'd been had.

He shook his head. "You frigging set me up. You know I hate those damn calendars."

"And I also know you rescued Siena from the side of the road and shoved the magazine with her picture in it in your locker. What am I, blind?" He crossed his arms, a challenge in his blue eyes. "Shit, I did you a favor."

Yeah, he did, but Cash wasn't about to let him know that. He was still confused as hell by Siena's turnaround—and his own. "I need another."

"You give me shit, then ask for a favor? After I already gave you a handout?" Tommy shook his head and flopped onto the couch. "Sit down and tell Uncle Tommy all about it. What do you need this time? A date with Angelina Jolie?"

Cash kicked Tommy's boot. "Ass." He'd been thinking about where to take Siena for their date. He'd Googled her name last night to get a feel for her lifestyle, knowing full well that he was setting himself up for heartache. What he'd learned was that she'd been photographed with most of the hot, wealthy men in New York City, coming out of expensive restaurants and exclusive venues. But Cash had looked past the Armani suits and capped teeth of her suitors. He'd looked past her four-inch heels and even—after first memorizing every curve of her incredible body—looked past her slinky clothing and perfectly applied makeup. He'd spent most of the night staring into Siena's eyes in each of those pictures, and what he'd seen had shocked him. In the eyes of other women in similar pictures, he'd seen an almost magical look, as if they were living the dream. Siena's eyes had felt lonely to him. Maybe it was wishful thinking that she might be a different type of person than those other women, but damn if he didn't see eyes that were searching for something more. Maybe he could be that something more.

Chief Weber poked his thick neck and enormous head into the room. "Ryder, ten minutes. My office."

Reality slapped him back to the present. Why the hell Cash thought he could be that something more was beyond him.

"Got it, Chief."

"What's the favor?" Tommy leaned forward.

"Get Paul to cover for me tonight? He's sleeping, and I don't want to wake him."

Tommy laughed. "What's goin' on tonight?"

"Nunya." He glared at him.

"You're pulling a *nunya*? You can't pull a nunya. The last time you pulled a nunya, you asked out my sister."

Shit. He'd forgotten about that. He hadn't even wanted to date her. He'd just wanted to piss off Tommy for something, and now he couldn't even remember what it had been. "Can you ask him or not?"

Tommy stood and placed his hand on Cash's shoulder. "Sure, whatever. But I do for you, you do for me. Whatever's mine's yours kind of thing…" He winked, translated as, *I'll ask, but I get to ask out Siena.*

Cash knew Tommy was just trying to piss him off, the same way he'd been when he'd asked out Tommy's sister. "Did I already say you're an ass, 'cause if I didn't, let me clarify. You're a jackass. Don't forget, 'kay? I know he's free. He told me yesterday, but I wasn't sure I'd need him to cover." Cash headed for the chief's office, turning back before leaving the room. "Hey, Tom."

"Yeah?"

"I'll let you know tomorrow if I owe you a thank-you for yesterday or if I need to kick your ass."

Chief Weber was sitting behind his desk, his hands steepled together beneath his chin, when Cash walked in.

"Ready for me, Chief?"

Chief Weber nodded, his face unreadable.

Cash took a deep breath, steeling himself for Chief Weber's reaming. Cash had wondered how long it would be before the chief brought him in. He liked to let the guys hash out their own shit, but people who hashed things out with Cash typically lost. He'd been pulled from the third floor of the burning building kicking and fighting to get back up there to try to save

Samuel. He'd been visually unscathed. His emotional scars, however, were taking much longer to heal.

"How you doing, Cash?"

Cash nodded. "Pretty good."

The chief lifted his chin, his dark eyes filled with concern.

Cash let out a breath. He had too much respect for the chief to tell him an outright lie. "I'm getting over it, Chief. Much better."

"*Getting* over it?" He leaned back in his chair and crossed his arms.

Eight years was a long time to work with someone, and in the eight years he had worked with Chief Weber, he'd never had his integrity questioned. Cash knew that if ever there was a time that he deserved it, it was now. He tried to formulate an honest answer, and no matter how he strung the words together in his mind, he came out looking like a pathetic hotshot, a weak excuse for a firefighter, and Cash was anything but pathetic or weak.

"Cash, I know you're struggling. I got a call from Patti Forsythe."

Cash held his breath. He knew he shouldn't have spoken to the damned therapist, even if his chief required it.

"Don't worry. She didn't break any confidences. But she did say you'd stopped seeing her rather abruptly and she was concerned." He rose and closed the door. The room suddenly felt much too confined.

Cash adjusted himself on the chair and cleared his throat. Adrenaline rushed through him.

Chief Weber sat on the corner of his desk, arms crossed. "I know being blocked by that beam pissed you off, Cash, and better men than you have walked away from this work after the same type of situation."

I can't breathe.

"I've been right where you are, Cash. You hear the alarm go off and I see you sweat like never before. Your face turns beet-red. Guilt and anger are eating you alive."

Cash ran his hands down his thighs, just to feel something. To make sure he was still breathing.

"I remember when you used to panic after being trapped in the firehouse for too many days without a fire to fight." He smiled, nodded. "The way I see it, you've got two choices. You quit the bullshit risk taking—listen when you're told to evacuate, or not to enter a portion of a building. Stay with your partner when I tell you to—and get back on the horse like the commendable firefighter you are, or you walk alongside it."

"It's not about being blocked." His voice was so quiet, he wasn't sure he'd really said the words.

"Sure it is. The beam trapped that man in the apartment, and it kept you from doing your job."

"No. It was the guys who kept me from doing my job. If they hadn't dragged my ass out of there, I might have saved that old man." He forced himself to say the man's name. "Samuel. I might have saved Samuel."

"You knew if you went in there, you might not come out alive. You calculated the statistics in seconds, Ryder. In the blink of an eye, you knew what the chances were of you getting in there and making it out before you were both swallowed by flames. You knew that another beam would mean the end of it all."

Anger pushed breath from Cash's lungs hard and fast. "I was willing to take that risk. I could have saved him."

"Cash, it's nothing to be ashamed of. Every firefighter experiences a loss at one point or another. Frankly, I don't give a damn if you're walking the horse or riding it for the next six months, but I gotta know what's what. You're one of the best men we have, so if we can fix this shit, let's figure it out."

Cash stood and paced. He ran his hand through his hair and fisted and unfisted his hands. "It's *not* that I'm ashamed, Chief. He was Vetta's husband. I saved her. I should have tried harder to save him."

"My ass, Ryder. You tried everything you could. Those men saved your life. I can think of a hundred valid, shitty-ass reasons you'd have perished in that fire if you'd have gone in, and so can you."

"No." Cash stood before Chief Weber, eyes locked on his. He was panting, sweating, his muscles tight. "I don't give a damn if I could have died. That's my job. I put my own life on the line every time I walk into a fire—just like everyone else in this damn firehouse." He tried to tether his anger, but it had been gnawing at his gut for too damn long. "It was the guy I couldn't save." *Say his name. Fucking give him a face.* "Samuel Miller." He sucked in another breath and blew it out fast. "*He* wasn't doing his *job*. And he was my responsibility. Mine, and I didn't just let him down. I killed him." *Killed him. I killed him.* Cash paced again, unable to sit still.

Chief Weber sighed. "Cash, you know the risks of the job. You know the realities that go along with it. You've been doing this a long time. You know damn well that you didn't kill that man. You didn't start that fire. Your job is to come in, put out the monster, and save the victims that you're able to save. You were blocked. Hell, the truth of it is that you almost lost your life when the ceiling came down. If Tommy hadn't risked his own life, you very well could have died right along with Mr.

Miller."

Cash stopped pacing. "Those were *my* zones."

"He had a heart attack, Cash. We looked into it, as we always do. He didn't die of smoke inhalation. He didn't burn to death. His heart failed him, not you." Chief Weber's eyes softened.

"Would he have had the heart attack if I had gotten him out? He was ninety-two. Scared shitless, I'm sure. And every time that fucking alarm goes off now, all I can think of is that I went to school for that shit. Fire protection engineer. If any one of us should have known the dangers, it was me. I should have acted faster to beat the beam burning through."

"Cash, you know that's messed up, right? You were in the belly of a five-alarm beast. You got four people out of that fire alive." Chief Weber stared him down, meeting his angry gaze, his own filling with strength. "Sit down," he commanded.

Cash sat down and leaned his elbows on his knees, locking his eyes on the floor.

"Here's how this is gonna go. You can believe whatever you want about Mr. Miller. There's no way of knowing for sure if his heart would have given out if you'd saved him or not. You're a good man, Cash. You've stepped up to the plate. Mrs. Miller has called me several times to commend you for your chivalry."

"She called you?" *Goddamn it.* "So you've known I've been hung up on this the whole time?"

Chief Weber shook his head. "How the hell could I not? You're out there at every fire running in before your partner, disregarding evacuation orders long after the rest of the team has pulled out, and generally putting your life even more at risk than your job demands. And by doing that, you're risking the lives of your brothers. You know this shit. You used to drill it into guys' heads. The guys covered for you the first few times, but I finally noticed for myself the way anger and guilt are practically propelling you into the fires with a wild look in your eyes. And that is when the warning bells go off. I've seen it before, as I said. Now it's time to fix it."

"Don't you think I would if I could? Don't you think I want my life back?" Cash sat up straighter. "When I'm not one hundred percent prepared and doing the goddamn right thing, and when I know those guys are worried about me being a hotshot, I feel pathetic. But goddamn it, Chief. I got their backs, and they have to know that. I've got less to lose. They've got wives and girlfriends, and if someone needs rescuing and it's a little risky, who better than me to take it?"

"I know you feel that way."

"I'd give my life for any of them."

"Absolutely."

Cash lifted his brows.

"That's why I'm giving you a choice. They respect the hell out of you, but if you don't fix this shit, and you end up on the desk, they'll ride you like a girl."

"I thought I'd be over this shit in a week, maybe two, but it's killing me." Coming clean to the chief felt like a great weight lifted from Cash's shoulders. Coming head-to-head with a choice made him feel like he was sinking under a new weight. "Choice?"

"That's right. I've talked to Regan."

"Regan? What the hell for?" Ari Regan ran the New York City Fire Academy and was one of the fiercest, most ornery men Cash had ever run into.

"To figure this shit out. I figured that if Patti couldn't help you, then you needed tougher love." He circled his desk and pulled a folder from the top drawer, then slid it across the desk to Cash. "Here's your choice. Figure it out and fix this shit now. And when you're in the fire, you use your goddamn breathing pack, you hear me?"

"I hate that fucking thing."

"I don't give a shit. You're risking your life, which means you're risking the lives of the team. Whatever you need—another therapist, time off—you tell me. If you can't rein in your risk taking, I'll have no choice but to put you on desk duty. Formally. We change your position. Everyone's aware what's what and knows what to expect, who's going to be where. That's important for morale and for structure."

"Or?"

"Or you're back with Regan—three times each week until you've got this behavior under control." He lowered himself into the chair beside Cash and softened his tone. "Listen, what you're going through isn't new. It's not like no one else has gone through it. Remember when Mike found that four-year-old in the closet? Or when Tyrone thought he got to that twenty-seven-year-old guy, and he died in his arms? Death happens. It sucks. It's not easy to deal with, but, Cash, it's up to you to decide how much of your life you let this steal."

"And how is retraining with Regan supposed to help me? I can fight a fire blindfolded, and you know it."

"Damn right I know it, and so does Regan. But what's going on inside your mind has nothing to do with skill or reflexes." He pointed to his head. "It's all up there, and until you beat that very real beast, you put every man in our unit at risk. Regan's good. He's helped guys through this before, and he's succeeded."

"Tough love."

"The toughest damn love you'll ever know." Chief Weber shrugged. "Choice is yours."

There was no question in Cash's mind about what he wanted to do for the next thirty years. He just wasn't sure even a hard-ass like Regan could stop the strangling of guilt that had been his constant companion since the fire. But the idea of training with a bunch of rookies was causing his gut to twist into a knot.

"I don't suppose Regan would be planning on doing this solo?" Not his style. Regan would humiliate the shit out of him just for fun if he *wasn't* there for help. The fact that he was going to rely on Regan would only give the guy more reason to mess with his head.

Chief Weber rose to his feet again. "Not a chance in hell."

'Course not. He scrubbed his hand down his face, thinking of his date with Siena. She was tough as nails, and if he didn't know her, but knew she dated a firefighter who put his unit at risk, he'd almost feel sorry for her. She deserved a man who always did the right thing.

"There's nothing I can't beat, this goddamn gorilla on my back included."

Chief Weber smacked him on the back. "That's the Cash I know."

He narrowed his eyes at the chief.

Chief Weber grabbed his keys from the desk. "Don't look at me like that. I knew which way you'd go."

Cash left his office and headed for his locker, feeling the pressure of goddamn Regan breathing down his back. He grabbed the box of photos, intending to throw a few more into the photo album, but the magazine lured him in. He picked it up and flipped through to Siena's picture. He studied her eyes as he'd done the evening before, and this time, he didn't see a hint of loneliness in them. He saw a woman who was exactly where she wanted to be, and he had no idea what that could possibly mean.

SIENA HAD BEEN staring at the gift registry for what felt like hours, and she still had no idea what to get Savannah for her bridal shower. She clicked to the next set of gifts on the kiosk and felt her mother's hand on her shoulder.

"Want to try another store?" Joanie Remington ran her hand gently along Siena's shoulders. "You're so tense. Is everything all right?"

"Yeah." *No.*

"Uh-oh." She gently turned Siena to face her. They had the same electric-blue eyes and stood nearly eye to eye, but while Siena wore a pair of boot-leg jeans, heeled boots, and a designer waist-length, double-breasted jacket, her mother wore a pair of wide-legged wool pants and two layers of cotton shirts beneath a long cotton sweater. She wore her long gray hair loose, adding to the bohemian style she was known for. Joanie was an artist through and through. She had a tender but very direct way of approaching Siena and her siblings when they were having a hard time, and Siena knew from the sound of her voice that she'd read her like an open book.

Siena feigned a smile. "It's nothing. I'm fine."

"Fine..." She took Siena's hand and headed out of the store and onto the street. "Fine is not a way of life. Fine is something that we are when we wish we were something else." She opened the door of the next store and they headed for the women's section. "Do you have any idea what you want to get Savannah for her bridal shower? I'm at a total loss. I mean, what do you get a lawyer who isn't materialistic? The two don't seem as though they jive, do they?" She laughed.

Jewel had called Siena that morning and told her to expect Gunner Gibson, the quarterback of the New York Furies, to pick her up at seven on Friday. She'd tried again to get out of the date, but Jewel talked her into it. Again. *This is your career. Don't fight battles that will make you lose if you win.* After kissing Cash, going out with Gunner was even less appealing than it had been the first time Jewel had brought it up.

"I don't have any idea what to get her. She doesn't ever ask for a thing, except for time with Jack." Which Jack wanted as much as she did. "They're happy, right, Mom?"

"Jack and Savannah?" She laughed softly. "They're so perfectly suited for each other. I can't imagine either one ever being happier. Don't you think so, or am I missing something?"

"No. I know they are. We met for drinks the other night, and you can see it when they're together. They're always holding hands. He watches out for her like he watches out for me."

"Which you sometimes hate."

"Maybe. But I still love it."

"Maybe we're wasting our time shopping for Savannah in the city. Maybe we should focus on something she can't find here." Her mother tapped her lip, her brows drawn together.

"I have an idea of something she might like, but I don't know if it's appropriate for a bridal shower." Siena stopped to look at a sweater. "I feel like she can buy anything she wants, so whatever we buy, while it's nice, it's not really...I don't know. Special? What about putting together a photo album with pictures of Jack from when he was growing up, and we can get pictures of her from her dad, and we can make kind of a side-by-side album of where they were in each phase of their lives when they weren't together."

Her mother's eyes lit up. "I like that, but what about Linda?"

"Well, I thought about that, and I guess I was thinking that we could make a single page to cover those years and title it *The In-Between Years*, or something like that. And while I wouldn't put Linda in those pictures, I think we could put pictures of Jack in the Special Forces, and then maybe at the bottom of the page, you know that picture that you have of Jack sitting on the boulder in your backyard?"

"The one taken after Linda died, when he was so devastated?"

"Yeah, that's the one. That would be the only reminder of what happened, and then we put pictures from when they met and since. You've talked with Savannah about all that. You know she feels like they were brought together at the right time for *them*. That if they'd gotten together ten years earlier, they wouldn't have been the people they were now and all that." Siena expected her mother to say it was too morose of an idea, or too much of a painful reminder for Jack—or even Savannah. "It's okay if you think it's stupid, Mom. It was just an idea."

"I think it's brilliant. There's a shop around the corner that makes wooden photo albums that are worthy of mantels and coffee tables. Want to go take a look? If you want, we could even get one that's unfinished and I could paint it." They headed back outside.

"That sounds perfect. From the heart." *Like Cash giving me his coat.* Siena pulled her jacket closed against the frigid air.

Cash's voice sailed through her mind. *Maybe I need to give you a little lesson in being prepared.* She'd like him to give her something all right, but it had nothing to do with preparedness.

"Feel better now that you have that figured out?"

Siena hadn't been one of those teenagers who lied to her parents. She wasn't a saint, but her parents had brought her up to be honest above all else. And now, as she heard the concern in her mother's voice, she felt ashamed for agreeing to go out with Gunner. At the same time, it wasn't like she was crossing any moral lines. At least that's what she'd been telling herself since Jewel called. Being with her mother had her rethinking that stance.

"It wasn't that." Siena slowed by a coffee shop. "Can we grab a warm cup of coffee and talk a minute?"

"Sure, honey. Whatever you'd like."

After getting their drinks and settling in at a table, Siena readied herself to talk about the situation that had been nibbling away at her nerves.

"Mom, how do I know where to draw the line with my career? I mean, we've talked about the bigger stuff, and you know I'd never sleep with some guy to get ahead or anything like that, but what about the gray areas?"

Her mother reached across the table and touched her hand. "Gray areas? Siena, what exactly are you contemplating?"

Siena's phone vibrated. "Sorry, Mom. Just a sec." She read the text from Cash. *Hi. It's Cash. Still on 4 tonight?* She felt her cheeks lift into a smile as she texted back. *Duh. I have ur name and number in my phone. Yes, still on. Unless u want to blow me off.* She pushed her hair over her shoulder and met her mother's gaze as she arched a brow.

"What?" Siena felt her cheeks flush, knowing Cash would

fume when he saw, *duh*, in the text.

Her mother smiled. "Nothing." She glanced at the phone in Siena's hand. "Okay, gray areas, right?"

"Oh, right." *Focus on Mom, not Cash. Or the amazing kiss. Oh my God. I can't focus. Shit.* It was much more fun to think of teasing Cash than to tell her mother about what she'd agreed to do. She took a sip of her coffee, sensing her mother's patience growing thin. *Time to rip off the Band-Aid.* "Jewel wants me to date an athlete."

"Why on earth would she want you to do that? Does she have someone in mind?"

Siena glanced around the busy coffee shop, then leaned forward and spoke quietly. "Gunner Gibson. She thinks it will get me more modeling jobs and ensure longevity."

"I have no idea who that is, but, Siena, you work all the time. You seem to always have jobs lined up. Is there something I'm not seeing? Are you losing modeling opportunities for some reason?"

"No." Her phone vibrated. "Sorry, Mom. Last one. Promise." She read the text from Cash. *I forgot. I have to work. Sorry. Maybe another time.* Siena's jaw dropped open. She read the message again. And again. Then she put her phone down on the table with an audible groan.

"Problem?"

"No," she snapped. *He's blowing me off? Fine. I didn't want to go out with him anyway. The big pain in the butt.* Her phone vibrated and she glanced at her mother, who waved at the phone. Siena rolled her eyes and pressed her lips together, furious with herself for even thinking that there was more to that arrogant man. She read another text from Cash. *Just controlling the flames. Lol. Does 7 work?*

"Ugh!"

"What is it?" her mother asked.

"Nothing," she said sharply as she texted back. *Fine. Don't b late.* She pressed the send button, then decided to mess with him right back, and she texted again. *And don't come early, either. I hate when men do that.*

Let him stew over that for a while.

"Whatever you're texting about must be pretty steamy. You're blushing." Her mother sipped her coffee and raised her brows.

"What? No." *Yes.* Sometimes she forgot how observant her mother was. "Gray areas. Let's focus on those." *And not think of Cash and coming in the same sentence again.* She explained why Jewel wanted her to date Gunner.

"And what do you want to do? If you date this man, Gunner, what does that tell the world? And why do they care so much? That always baffles me."

"I don't want to do it, but you know how this industry works. It's all about who you're seen with. Remember when you met Josh Braden—Savannah's brother, the fashion designer? Remember how he said he was sick of the same thing before he met Riley?" Before reuniting with his childhood crush, Riley Banks, and subsequently hiring and then falling in love with her, Josh had dated the type of women a man of his social status was expected to date, and he'd hated it. He and Riley had the same small-town family values and the same interests.

Her mother nodded, and Siena continued. "It's part of the fashion world. It's part of acting, modeling, and probably the sports industry, too. In fact, Jewel might have some sort of deal with his agent because it'll probably do just as much for his visibility as for mine." Her phone vibrated, and she slid it from the table to her lap to read the text from Cash.

Would u blow me if I did?

Siena gasped. *What the hell?* Her phone vibrated again and again in rapid succession. She scrolled through the texts.

Off! Damn phone! Blow me off!!!

I hate phones. Seriously. I'd never say that.

4Get it. Mortified.

Siena laughed.

"Okay, now that's just rude. You either have to share those texts, which I'm assuming you have no inclination of doing since your cheeks are bright red, or you have to tell me what's going on. I didn't come out with you today to watch you text with someone else." Her mother's words were firm, but her eyes were smiling.

"Let me tell him I'm shutting off my phone." She texted quickly. *With my mom 4 lunch. Looking forward to 7!* She put her phone in her purse and sighed again, this time a happy, relieved sigh. "I met this guy, and that's who's texting. We're going on our first date tonight, but he walked me home last night, and he's the guy who…" She remembered that she hadn't told her mother about the car accident.

"Would this be the fireman?"

"Is nothing sacred in our family?" Siena knew the Remington grapevine would reach her parents about her accident and about Cash, but she hadn't thought it would happen that quickly.

"Jack came by to talk to your father, and he mentioned that he'd met you and your brothers for drinks. You know Jack."

"So why didn't you say something earlier? And what did Jack say, exactly?"

"I figured you'd tell me what you wanted me to know when

you were ready. Jack said he met him. Cash, right? And that he didn't find him to be an ass." Her mother reached out and touched her hand. "Is he why you're so upset about the whole dating an athlete thing?"

"No, Mom. He's not." She leaned back against the seat and rubbed her temples. "Maybe a little, but not really. I didn't even have this date scheduled when Jewel told me I needed to do it. And I can't tell anyone that the date's not real, so please don't, because then I'd get bad press." She leaned forward and spoke in a harsh whisper. "It's such a mess. If I go, everyone thinks we're dating, which shouldn't really matter, but I know it's not true, and that bothers me. Then there's Cash, who drives me insane half the time because he's arrogant and cocky…"

"Then why accept a date?"

"Because he's also so much more than I ever imagined, so I wonder *why* he's so arrogant and cocky. I keep going back to Jack and how he was when he met Savannah. I mean he was borderline mean. Not that Cash is mean." She groaned again. "I can't explain it. He challenges me, and I challenge him right back, and I have no idea why I do it, but it's fun."

"Uh-huh." Her mother leaned back and crossed her arms over her chest. "And how is he *so much more?*"

"Every way possible. Like when we were walking home, he actually took off his coat and put it on me. Hat and gloves too, and I didn't even ask for them. That sounds stupid now, but last night it was really romantic. Or it seemed that way." She furrowed her brow. "Oh God, am I wrong?"

Her mother laughed again. "Look at you all tied up over a man. I'm not sure I've seen this side of you before. At least not as an adult."

Siena rolled her eyes again, a common occurrence when she

was with her family. "Am I wrong about him being romantic? He saw my teeth chattering and bought me hot chocolate, and last night on the subway he—"

"He got you to take the subway at night?"

Siena fiddled with her napkin again. "Yeah. I know. I never realized a subway was safer than a cab."

"Depends who you ask," her mother said.

"I guess. Anyway, I don't know. He warmed my hands, but now I wonder if he was just trying to get close to me. But it didn't seem that way. Well, maybe a little, but at the bar…" Her voice escalated. "At the bar, that was romantic. He pulled out my chair, and held the door, and when we saw Vetta…" Her shoulders dropped as she sighed, as if deflated. "Oh, Mom, I almost forgot. She said she knew you. Her husband was a pediatric surgeon."

Her mother wrapped her hands around her coffee mug and stared into it, as if deep in thought. "Vetta Miller?"

Siena shrugged. "I'm not sure. But her name was definitely Vetta. Her husband died a few weeks ago. Samuel, I think."

"Oh, poor Vetta. Yes. I knew them years ago when he worked at the hospital and I volunteered. If you see her again, please give her my condolences. I'll have to send her something. So Cash visits her? Are they related somehow?"

"I don't really know how they know each other, but he visits. He brought her flowers, and I think he helps out, fixes things for her."

"Well, Siena, sounds like you are in quite a conundrum. I can't advise you about Cash except to say that if you feel he's more than meets the eye, then see if he is. But be careful. Jack's a special man, but most men who are arrogant and pushy aren't as kind underneath."

"Dad is," she said softly, catching her mother's eyes.

"Yes. Your father is. But you know your father and Jack, and you love them. As I said, not all men who are that arrogant are equally as kind or loving. Just go into this with your eyes open and until you're sure that he's not too aggressive, maybe stay public?"

"Mom, I would never date someone I think could be too aggressive. And aggressive is probably the wrong word for Cash. He's…very male."

"Well, that's a whole different thing altogether." She finished her coffee and set a stern stare on Siena. "So are you going on the date with this Gunner man?"

"I think so. I'm not sure I can get out of it."

"Siena, you always do the right thing, and I trust you. If you think you're doing the right thing for yourself, then you probably are. We have to get a move on anyway if we're going to buy that photo album."

On the way out the door, a fire truck's siren sounded and Siena's heart raced. *Cash.*

"By the way, don't think I'm not upset about your accident. We raised you to be more careful than that. Remind me to thank Cash if I ever meet him."

"Okay, Mom. We'll see if he passes the first date test."

"There are tests for dating now? That would have made it much easier to weed out the losers in my day," her mother teased.

"I have this mental checklist. I date so many guys who are with me just for the photos, or to say they dated me, which I don't usually find out until after. You know what? Dating sucks. They do need real tests."

"Tell me about this checklist."

"Okay, it's kinda silly. The first thing is when he picks me up. Does he look in my eyes first? I mean, all men check you out, but in that first second. That's what matters. And does he walk right into my apartment or wait to be invited? If he's in the apartment, is he focused on figuring out where the bed—Where everything is, or is the apartment secondary to his interest in me or whatever we're talking about. Then, when we're out, do his eyes wander? Is he looking to see if people are noticing that we're together? That one's weird when I date celebrities, because you have to be able to tell if he wants them to look or not. And he can't be on his phone. Total turnoff. And—"

Her mother shook her head as they walked around the corner to their destination. "You can stop right there. I can't even imagine having all that in my head on a first date. In my day, we were happy if our suitors opened the car door for us and treated us like ladies."

"Well, isn't that what I'm saying?"

"I have no idea. There are so many things on that list that I've already forgotten most of them. Do you have many second dates?" She laughed.

"I suck, right?"

"No, you don't suck. Only you know what type of person you want to accept into your life."

"All I'm asking for is someone who's as good to me as Sage is to Kate, Dex is to Ellie, and Jack is to Savannah. And even Dad, how he is to you." Siena draped her arm over her mother's shoulder. "What can I say? The man that ends up in my life has a lot to live up to." And, Siena realized, there was something else she wanted in a man. She wanted a man who would challenge her.

Chapter Ten

SIENA STOOD BEFORE the full-length mirror in her bedroom sizing herself up. She had no idea what a guy like Cash would wear on a date, and he'd given her no indication of where they were going. In her leather leggings and thick, white Gucci cowl-neck sweater, she was comfortable and she wouldn't be overdressed for a restaurant, a café, or whatever he had in mind. All men seemed to want to wine and dine her. *Ugh.* She hoped Cash wouldn't want to. She got the feeling he wasn't really a wine and dine kind of guy. She checked her makeup and put on a pair of small dangling earrings, slipped on her Melody wedge booties, which would bring her closer to his insanely delicious lips, and brushed her hair one last time.

The doorbell sounded and she froze. It was only six forty-five. He was early. Her pulse sped up as she crossed the expansive wood floor of her loft. *Calm down.* She drew in a deep breath and blew it out slowly, trying to center her mind before opening the door and finding an empty hall and an enormous box at her feet tied with a big red ribbon.

"Cash?" She poked her head out the door and looked around. No answer. Intrigued, she carried the box inside and kicked the door closed. Anticipation tore through her as she untied the giant bow, then tore the box open. Inside she found a pair of thick black gloves, a red scarf, and a cute black knitted hat with a card tucked inside the hat—and another box beneath it all.

"No way." She tried on the gloves, which fit perfectly and were so soft she wanted to cuddle with them, wrapped the scarf around her neck, and read the note.

Siena,

I couldn't stand the idea of you being cold for one more second. If you don't like my taste, don't tell me. Smile like you do in your pictures and tell me they're perfect.
—Cash

She pressed the note to her chest. When she lifted the box from the larger container, she saw there was yet another beneath it, and she went to work opening the next box. Her eyes widened and her jaw fell open.

"Oh my God." The box was empty, except for a note.

S,

It's the thought that counts, right? I thought about buying you a warm coat, but then you'd have no reason to want to get closer to me. Again. You know the drill. If you hate the idea, lie to me.
—C

There would be no lying tonight. She'd been *so* right about him. She felt her heart open just a little more. The third and last box had a smaller note taped to the top. Before reading the note, she picked up the box and shook it. *Clank, clank!* She read the note.

Lush,

Inside this box are the ingredients for a screaming orgasm (or two). Don't have them too early. I hate when women do that.

Your personal bartender,
Cash

"Ha!" She opened the box, and sure enough, she found a bottle of vodka, Baileys Irish Cream, and Kahlúa. "Oh, you are bad. Bad, bad, bad." The doorbell sounded, and she glanced at the clock. Seven o'clock on the dot. "And that makes you oh so good." With a grin she didn't have a chance in hell of quelling, she answered the door, and her breath caught in her throat. Cash's broad shoulders filled the doorframe.

"Hi." He placed a hand on her hip as he leaned down and kissed her cheek. "It's so great to see you."

Eyes. Check. His lips were soft, and his scent was intoxicating. In his black V-neck sweater and thick black parka, he was even more strikingly handsome than she remembered, and she'd thought about him so often that she was sure she'd had every bit of him memorized. She was wrong. God, was she wrong. *Forget the checklist.* She dropped her eyes for an instant, drinking him in. He looked hot in a pair of Levi's that hugged his hips perfectly, the fabric stretched tightly across his thick thighs.

"Hey, my eyes are up here." He used his index and second finger to point to his eyes.

Oh crap. I failed my own checklist!

"I see you got the package." He looked at the gloves, which were still on her hands; then he gently grasped the ends of the scarf, which was wrapped around her neck, and reeled her in close.

Siena's pulse kicked up a notch. "You didn't have to buy me anything." *Kiss me. Just kiss me.*

"I know, but if you're going to go out on a date with a fireman, you need to be prepared for anything."

Anything. She liked the sound of that. She could think of a million things she'd like to do with him. None of which required gloves.

"They were the most thoughtful gifts I've ever received." She flushed, remembering the third box. "Especially the second box…even the third box."

His grin reached his eyes, which looked seductive as hell—narrowed just a hint, darkening a little more with each passing second—and they hadn't shifted from Siena's face for a second, other than to look at the gloves and scarf.

"And I didn't come early, just as you requested."

Siena sucked in a breath.

He shifted his eyes over her shoulder to the box, sitting just beyond the door in the middle of the floor. "The question is, did you sneak in a screaming orgasm—or two—before I arrived?"

Shut up and kiss me. She couldn't breathe. Hearing the word *orgasm* come from the lips she'd thought about for the last twenty-four hours set a swarm of butterflies loose in her stomach, and feeling the heat radiating from his body sent lust-filled signals from her brain to her most private places. She swallowed past the desire to kiss him and forced herself to take a step away.

"Come—come on in." She prayed her weakened knees would carry her forward. She sensed him close behind her.

"Do you want to grab a coat and we'll go?"

He wasn't going to even try to delay? Every guy tried to get things moving sexually before—or in lieu of—the date. She was relieved and curious. Maybe he didn't feel the same rush of heat that she did. *Oh God, what is wrong with me? Stop thinking about kissing him!* She smiled up at him. *Easier said than done.*

"Sure, let me grab it. Where are we going?"

"It's a surprise."

Siena grabbed a coat from the closet, and as she slid her arm into the sleeve, Cash gathered her hair and held it, easing the shoulder of the coat over her sweater. Siena felt herself swooning over his tender touch and tried like hell to tether her impetuous thoughts. *I'm never like this. What is wrong with me?*

Cash checked the lock after she closed the door behind them.

"It locks automatically."

"Just want to be sure your screaming orgasms are safe."

Oh, you are bad. Very, very bad. Siena had a feeling he wasn't kidding about his ability to control the flames. He knew just how to stoke her fire.

Chapter Eleven

IT TOOK ALL of Cash's focus not to take Siena into his arms the moment she'd opened her apartment door. He'd thought about her sweet lips all afternoon, and when he was shopping for her gloves, he could practically feel her hands in his. Their size was ingrained in his palm from when they'd ridden the subway the evening before. But when she looked up at him with her big baby blues, he knew if he kissed her, he wouldn't be able to stop. And even though he hated the idea of not kissing her, whatever it was about her that had fed his edge the evening before had softened it the minute their eyes connected tonight. No one had ever had that effect on him before. And now, as they stood in front of the Rockefeller Center ice skating rink and her eyes lit up at the sight of the Christmas tree, the urge to kiss her gripped him again.

Siena leaned over the rail and sighed. "There's nothing as beautiful as a Christmas tree."

Cash leaned his back against the rail and shoved his hands deep in his coat pockets to keep from reaching for her. Damn, this was going to be harder than he'd imagined. He wanted to kiss her more than he wanted to take his next breath.

"I think Christmas trees are beautiful, but I'd be lying if I didn't say that you were far prettier than that tree. And I'd imagine that every guy around here would agree."

Siena turned her body so she was facing him. "That's so sweet."

"Christ. Don't say that too loud. No man wants to be known as sweet." *Sweet? Fuck that.* He needed his edge back. "Want to skate?"

"Oh, no. I think my older brothers got all of the athletic talent in the family."

"That makes it even better. Come on." He pushed away from the railing and headed toward the rental counter. Siena didn't move. "You coming?"

"I really can't skate. I suck at it."

"I highly doubt you suck at anything. Come on." He reached for her hand.

She shook her head.

From the look of her clenched jaw, he knew there was only one thing that would make her get on the ice. "Yeah, you're probably right. It's much harder than being pretty." He turned back to the rail.

He shot a glance at her and saw her eyes narrow, her shoulders stiffen.

"It's okay. We can just hang here and watch everyone else. I probably should have booked a nice restaurant or something. My bad."

"I'm telling you, I suck at it." She knitted her brows together, but he could see by the tension in her shoulders that she was getting irritated.

"Whatever. Look, no biggie." He turned away from the rink. "I knew it was a long shot when I brought you here, but I thought…" He shrugged. "Hell, I don't know what I thought.

Look, let's go sit in a nice restaurant and talk about celebrities."

"Oh my God. Is that what you think I do?"

He shrugged again, forcing himself not to smile.

"Ugh. Fine. I'll show you that I can't skate." She stalked off toward the rental area. "But if I break my ankle, you have to explain it to my agent."

Twenty minutes later, Siena clung to the edge of the railing, her ankles wobbling from side to side.

"I hate you for this," she snapped.

"I can live with that. Come on. I'll help you." He reached for her hand.

"I don't need help. If *you* can do this, *I* can do it. I haven't tried since I was a kid."

That's my girl. "Yeah?"

"Yeah. Go ahead. I'll catch up in a sec."

He pointed to the center of the rink, then to his chest. "You're trying to get rid of me?"

"No. I just want to see that you can skate and that you're not just going to make fun of me when you can't move off the railing either."

"Oh, I can move off the railing." He set his jaw to let her know he was serious.

"Prove it."

"I can't just leave you here to fall and get slaughtered by children as they skate over you."

"See? You really can't skate."

"Shit. Watch and learn." He sped around the edge of the rink and turned around, skating backward at a fast speed, locking eyes with Siena as he came back around. He cut to a stop beside her, spraying chips of ice up around them.

She lifted her chin and crossed her arms, immediately losing her balance. She reached for the railing and he reached for her, catching her just before her fingers hit the ice.

"You okay?" He slid his hands down to her waist. Jesus, she felt good.

"How do you know how to skate like that?"

"Too many lonely nights. C'mon, I'll show you." He held on to her waist and skated behind her. "You know the general premise, right?"

"Of course. I'm not an idiot."

"I never said…Never mind. I'm going to hold on to you from behind. I'll hold you up; all you have to do is move your legs."

She glanced over her shoulder with her lip trapped between her teeth. "Now I get it. You brought me here so you could feel me up." The mischievous look in her eyes made his head spin.

"I don't need an ice skating rink for that. But hell, now that you mention it." He pressed his hips against her and felt her body stiffen against him. He lowered his head and placed a soft kiss just beside her ear, then whispered, "Stop trying to cop a feel with your ass and skate."

NOT ONLY COULD Siena not skate, but every nerve in her body was on fire. How was she supposed to concentrate on anything with his hard body against her and his hands on her waist? She felt his hips press against her butt, his leg forcing her right leg forward, then her left. Shit, he was taking her out on the ice. She gripped his hands, adrenaline pushing her to concentrate on every slide of her foot, every press of his knee against hers to help her along.

"Look at that," he said in a gravelly, sexy voice. "Little Siena Remington is skating."

"Shut up. I am not. I'm being pushed."

"Want me to let go?"

"God, no. Don't you dare." She pressed her hands tightly against his, trapping them at her waist. She noticed a group of guys eyeing her from the other side of the rail, and she glanced at Cash, who was too focused on her to notice. *I love that.* She didn't care that she might be making a fool of herself. She didn't care what she looked like to anyone other than Cash.

As much as Siena hated feeling like there was anything she couldn't do, she was enjoying having Cash take care of her, and for just a second, she thought she understood why some of the most capable women she knew would act less so around the men they dated. In the next breath she remembered how much it turned her stomach when they did that, and the understanding was shot to hell.

She felt Cash's grip loosen and she sucked in a breath.

"What are you doing? Don't let go." Panic surged through her, and she grabbed the sleeve of his parka with both hands.

"Relax." His commanding voice was back. He slid his hands around to her front as he skated adeptly around her, then gripped her hips once again—from the front this time—and skated backward.

"Oh my God, you scared the daylights out of me. I'm fine if you're holding me, but the minute you let go, I'm going to fall, and it's not gonna be pretty." *Or feel good!*

"Don't give me that garbage. Focus on me, not your feet."

No hardship there. The earnest look in his eyes reminded her of the night they'd met, which brought to her mind the moment he'd leaned over her in the truck. She felt her knees go weak, and without a second's hesitation, his hands gripped her tighter.

"I've got you. Tell me about your brothers. How many do you have?"

"Five. You met Jack at the bar—the really tall, protective one. The other guys at the table were Sage and Dex. Sage is an artist, and he's wicked athletic, and Dex is the one who walked me out. We're twins. And then there are my other brothers, Kurt—he's a writer, but he almost never meets us for drinks—and Rush. He's a professional skier." Her feet were sliding along, one leg after the other, and her ankles were no longer keeling to the side.

"I never put two and two together. Rush Remington? The Olympic skier?"

"The one and only."

His eyes filled with mischief. "So who's the evil twin?"

She concentrated on the way his hips moved beneath her hands. Strong and sure. "Um…depends who you ask."

He raised his brows. "Maybe I'll have to come to that answer on my own after I know you better."

She studied his face, the way his glances behind him were swift and careful. When he spoke, he focused on her eyes, but when another skater neared, his eyes trailed them and his grip on her became firmer, more protective. When her ankles tilted, he reflexively held her up. How could he be so focused on her while moving backward on skates?

"So were you a spoiled princess growing up? Because I can't even imagine you as that."

"Ha! My family is *not* like that. Hardly. I mean, my brothers have always been good to me, but my dad is tough. Military tough, and being a girl didn't carry any weight. Tell me about your family."

"I will. My family's as big as yours, which is weird. But I want to know more about you. How did you end up modeling?"

She rolled her eyes. "I hate to admit this because it comes out all wrong."

Cash scratched his cheek, a smile stretching slowly across his handsome face. She loved how a little crease formed just to the left of his lips when he smiled, and—*Holy shit! He's scratching his cheek.* She looked down and his other hand hovered just to the side of her hips. She was skating on her own.

She grabbed his parka.

"Look at you. A model who can skate. Now I've seen everything," Cash teased.

"Oh my God. Hold me. Put your hand back. I'm going to fall."

"No, you're not." Another command.

"Cash."

"I'm here. You dip, I catch. It's what I do."

Is there anything you don't do? She sucked in a breath and concentrated on moving her feet. *Oh my God. Oh my God. Oh my God!*

"Siena, focus on me. Tell me about modeling."

"I'll fall."

"You're holding my arms so tightly that if I lifted them, you'd come with them. You're not going to fall. Modeling. You. The story."

He narrowed his eyes, and she nodded, drawing in a long breath again and blowing it out slowly.

"I was eight. In a mall with my mom." She tried to calm her racing heart. She was skating. *Skating!* Even though it never came up in her daily life, she'd always wished she could skate. Her mother had tried to show her how. Even Dex had when they were kids, and she couldn't do it. She fell on her ass a hundred times an hour and finally had just given up. And now...

"Okay. The mall. A guy approached my mom about taking pictures of me. He said he was a photographer, and he gave her a business card. She didn't pay him much attention, but after that, it was all I could think about. I went home and looked at magazines all afternoon, searching the models' faces, memorizing the poses."

His eyes traveled from hers, to her mouth, then back up again, and he smiled.

"I convinced her to take me for the pictures, and from that moment on, I was hooked."

He nodded. "That explains it." His hand slid around her waist again, and he skated beside her.

"Explains what?"

"Nothing. Just that how much you love your job shows in your pictures."

She reached for him. "Wait. I'm going to fall."

He laughed and pressed his arm to her back. "I've got you. I just wasn't holding tight. You've got this. You need me like you need makeup."

"What does that mean?"

"It means you don't need anything or anyone to help you be more than you are."

She didn't know what to make of that. She didn't need makeup? She didn't need a man? Was she too bullheaded? Too conceited? Why was he looking at her like that? She couldn't read the sort of smile on his lips, and when she tried to figure out his stare, he drew it away.

"Christ."

"What did I do now?"

He guided her over to the railing and placed her hands firmly on it. "Stay here."

"Cash!"

He skated off at racing speed, passing everyone, bent forward like a practiced skater, and he went around the rink once, twice, three times, before skidding in beside her, red-faced and breathing hard. She watched his eyes. He had to be showing off. Siena glanced around the rink, searching for a pretty girl, someone he was showing off for. She scrutinized him, bent over now at the waist, panting, his eyes locked on the ice.

"Sorry." He looked up at her and shook his head. "You get this look, and…"

A look? I had a look? She had many looks when she modeled, but with Cash, she hadn't needed to fake a single one.

He pulled himself up to his full height, and her stomach fluttered—*so broad, so masculine.*

"I just needed to go fast."

"What look?"

He shook his head. "It's a…thing you do. Your eyes get all serious, like your mind is going a hundred miles an hour, and then your lower lip sticks out a little in this crazy seductive pout, and…" He ran his hand through his hair and looked away again. "Jesus. I can't do this."

She sighed, frustrated at herself for opening up. "I knew it. I shouldn't have told you about the mall. I know I sound shallow when I say it."

He looked down at her, his nostrils flaring. He inched closer, their thighs brushing. *Oh God.* She wanted to reach up and touch his strong, clenching jaw, feel the muscles pulsating. She wanted to place her lips on his, to have him wrap her in his arms, and she'd ruined everything. Sometimes she hated who she was—a talker, too stubborn, too pretty—as much as she loved it.

In the next breath, he lowered his lips to hers and kissed her deeply, stroking the worry right out of her mind and stealing her breath. One strong arm caught her as her knees weakened, pulling her against him as he deepened the kiss. Safe in his arms, she let go of the railing and ran her hand along his jaw. *Oh God. Oh God, you feel so good.* When he drew back, he took her remaining breath with him, leaving her panting for more.

He released the pressure on her lower back, and as cool air filled the space between their bodies, she stifled a moan. His intense gaze didn't falter; his brows drew together.

"I'm sorry," he panted. "That look gets me every time."

"Then I'll have to do it more often." Without thinking, as skaters sped past and people looked on, she pulled him into a sweet, soft kiss, wishing she knew what look he meant.

CASH HAD NEVER before wanted to remember a moment so badly in all his life, but the look in Siena's eyes the second before she drew him in for another kiss sent chills right through him. And the way she kissed him, soft and tenderly, left him craving more. Now, as they shuffled through the crowds along Times Square, everything felt different. He felt different. Cash wasn't easily intimidated, but as he fought the urge to drape his arm around her neck, he realized that he was intimidated. She was Siena Remington, and to everyone else in the world, that meant something completely different than it meant to him. To others, she was a gorgeous body, a pretty face. A top model. Of course she was all those things, but when he looked into her eyes, he saw things that he didn't understand—and desperately wanted to. Vulnerability. Pent-up frustration. Intelligence. Hell, the list went on and on.

A man pushed past, wrenching Siena sideways. She sucked in a breath. "Ow!"

Cash locked eyes on the guy's back as he hurried away. *The hell with being intimidated.* She was who she was, but he would never hesitate if he liked any other woman the way he liked her. He wrapped his arm around her and pulled her close.

"You okay?"

"Yeah. Fine. People are always in such a rush near the holidays." She cuddled closer to him and he tightened his grasp.

That was where she should be, close enough that no one could hurt her. Safe. Protected.

"Hungry?"

She shrugged. "A little."

"What's your pleasure? A woman cannot live on screaming orgasms alone." He loved teasing her, seeing her strength rise in her shoulders and settle in her eyes as she contemplated a feisty retort.

She slowed her pace and looked up at him from the corner of her eyes. "I'm sick of having them alone." She trapped her lower lip in her teeth, her cheeks flushed.

Holy hell. He was struck dumb. It was all he could do to keep his legs moving. He was breathing too hard, his muscles tense. She pressed her body closer to him, giving rise beneath his zipper. How the hell was he supposed to navigate these flames? His body wanted to race back to her place and make love to her all night, his heart told him to pace himself, and his mind had no idea which way to go.

Food. He'd concentrate on food. He had no idea what she'd eat. Models had to be careful; that much he knew.

He cleared his throat. "Want to...um...salad? Does that work?"

She smiled up at him and narrowed her eyes. "Let's be bad."

Christ. She can't mean...

She took his hand and dragged him across the street and into a small pizzeria. At the counter, she moved in front of him and settled his hand on her waist; then she reached back, brought his other hand around her waist, and relaxed against his chest.

Life doesn't get any better than this. Without thinking, he kissed the top of her head. The scent of coconut shampoo filled his senses. In that one small positioning of him against her, she'd stolen any lingering intimidation, and as her head lolled back against him, fitting perfectly between his pectoral muscles, he let out a sigh he hadn't realized he'd been holding. Siena covered his hands with hers and he rotated his wrists, taking her fingers in his. At that moment, nothing else existed. His hunger was forgotten; his heart was full.

"Next." The large, dark-haired man behind the counter drew his attention.

Siena looked up at him. God, she was beautiful. "Veggie," she whispered.

He nodded. "Two slices of veggie pizza, please."

The man skillfully boxed two pieces faster than Cash could contemplate taking his hands from around Siena and digging out his wallet. Which he did reluctantly. He grabbed the box from the counter, and Siena wrapped her arm in his as they walked outside. He'd been so wrapped up in her that he'd almost forgotten the tickets he'd purchased for the other part of their date. He looked at his watch.

"Okay, don't hate me, but we have to hurry."

"Where?"

He held tight to her hand and walked fast, feeling Siena practically running to keep up. "I'm an idiot. I bought tickets to a carriage ride tour and almost forgot. We have to be at the center of Times Square in seven minutes." He glanced at her just long enough to see her eyes widen.

"You did?"

"Yeah, dumb, I know. I thought it would be romantic and maybe something you didn't do all the time."

They ran by festively decorated storefronts and reached the carriage just as it arrived at Times Square. Cash helped her into a seat and sat beside her, both of them breathing hard.

"Wow, sorry. It was supposed to be one of those magical moments you see in movies." He shook his head. *I'm such a fool.*

She stared at him without saying a word.

"Stop looking at me like that." He looked straight ahead, knowing he'd just messed up their evening. She'd been so close to him. He'd felt it. He'd seen how much she liked him in her eyes, and now…now she'd think he was a total idiot. Who took carriage rides through the city when they lived there year-round? Why did he even think it might be romantic?

The carriage moved slowly along the road, and Cash settled back into the seat for the longest ride of his life.

"You're a hopeless romantic."

He shifted his eyes to hers, his head still facing forward. "Cut it out."

"No," she said sharply. She placed her hands on his thighs

and leaned closer. So close he could see tiny flecks of white in the blue of her eyes.

"You are." Her lips curved into a smile. "Look at you. Mr. Macho Fireman planned a romantic carriage ride." She lifted his arm and snuggled in beneath it. "I like it."

"You're making fun of me, right?"

"Nope." She reached for the pizza box. "But now I'm hungry." She took off the gloves he'd bought her and set them in his lap.

He liked her ease of using him as a table, as strange as that seemed. It made him warm all over. The slice of pizza looked too big for her, and as she opened her mouth to take a bite, her eyes widened. He could stare at her all day and never get sick of her expressions.

After they were done eating, he set the box beside him and wiped a spot of pizza sauce from her cheek with his thumb.

"I forgot to tell you, I'm a pig when I eat. It's a really bad thing. My brothers tease me about it."

"A piglet maybe, but it's not a bad thing. It was a spot of sauce." *And your cheek was so soft that I want to touch it again.*

She shook her head. "You should see me with ice cream. It always ends up on my shirt."

"There's one way to fix that."

"A bib?" she teased.

He nuzzled his cheek to hers and whispered, "Don't wear a shirt when you eat it." He drew back slowly, his lips grazing her cheek, testing, weighing her reactions, looking for signs of whether they were in sync. She touched his cheek again, the way she had at the rink, and the intimate touch answered him. Oh yeah, they were in sync. Her lips parted as she turned to him, and he settled his mouth over hers for another deep, sensuous kiss. She slid her hand beneath his jacket and urged him closer, sending a surge of desire through him. There was no misconstruing the heat between them, and he had no interest in controlling the flames anymore.

Half an hour later, they were climbing out of a cab in front of his apartment building. Why he took her there instead of her apartment, he had no idea. His apartment was small, ridiculously so, but he wanted her to see the real him. And with Chief Weber's vote of confidence, he hoped the other part of the real him would one day return.

He took her hand and led her upstairs to the second floor, seeing the interior of the building through new eyes. He'd never noticed the chipping plaster or the worn carpet. He cringed as he unlocked the old door.

"It's not what you're used to, but…" He shrugged as the door swung open. "After you." He watched her scan the small living room, just large enough for a love seat, coffee table, and a bookshelf. The exterior wall was raw brick, with a window overlooking the street. She walked to the window and looked out, running her fingers along the windowsill; then she turned back to him and tilted her head to the side, as if she were putting together the image of him and the apartment in her mind. He shrugged out of his coat and hung it up on a hook beside the door.

"Come on. I'll give you the tour." He reached for her hand, and in a few short steps, she was beside him again. He unzipped her coat and drew it down her shoulders. The way she was looking up at him made him feel as if he were taking off something much more intimate. He lifted her hands and gently removed her gloves, then put them in the pocket of her coat and hung it next to his. He liked seeing it there. Cash had had women in his apartment before, but never anyone he wished would stay. He envisioned Siena in every room of the small apartment: looking up from a seat on the couch as he came from the kitchen to the living room, waking up beside him in his king-sized bed, cooking dinner at his side, with no elbow room, in the kitchen. He pushed the silly thoughts aside, and with her hand in his, brought her into the kitchen.

"This is so cozy," she said sweetly.

"That's code for small, and yeah, it is, but I like it." He'd bought the apartment a few years earlier, and he and Tommy had refinished the hardwood floors, painted, replaced the cabinets, and remodeled the bathroom. It was far from high-end, but as Siena ran a hand over the dark marble counters, he filled with pride.

"Cozy is homey to me. Small is nice. But I've seen small apartments that feel cramped and, I don't know…not homey. This is lovely."

He nodded, unsure how to react to his apartment being called *lovely*. He pointed to an alcove between the kitchen and the living room with two doors. "Bathroom. Bedroom."

She dropped his hand and opened the door to the bathroom. "Oh my God, I love all this stone."

"Really?" He looked over her shoulder at the tiny bathroom. Cash had a thing for texture, and Tommy had given him hell about the bathroom sink, because each stone had to be hand placed. He'd taken a dark bathroom vanity and removed the top, then inset stones of various sizes and shapes and set the bowl of the sink inside them. A thick glass top covered the stones, and Cash had been proud of the outcome. The bathroom floor was dark granite, and the walls were painted cream. He'd trimmed the bathroom with mahogany wood, having negotiated a killer deal in exchange for visiting the salesman's daughter's school to talk about being a fireman.

"The whole thing is so masculine." She squeezed between him and the doorframe and poked him in the stomach. "Suits you perfectly."

In the alcove, Siena glanced at his bedroom door. Cash reached around her and pushed the door open.

"Don't even think about making a move on me. I'm just giving you the tour."

"I think I can control myself."

Cash waited outside the room when she walked in, positive he could *not* control himself. Seeing her beside his bed was difficult enough, and when she flopped down on it and flashed a smile as she fell back, her arms out to her sides, he nearly lost it.

"Ah. This is so comfy." She turned and faced him, her legs dangling off the end of the bed, her body completely open to him.

He clung to the top of the doorframe, his muscles twitching. "You're too damn trusting." He didn't mean to sound so gruff.

She narrowed her eyes. "You spend a lot of time telling me what I do wrong."

Shit. I do?

She rolled onto her side and propped her chin up on her elbow. "But I don't think you do it because you think I'm stupid. I think you do it to protect me. To point out what I should be careful of."

He raked his eyes along the arch of her back, following the curve of her hips—hugged by her black leather pants as if they were her second skin. His chest tightened as he dug his fingers into the edge of the doorframe above his head.

"Is that what you think?" he managed in a hungry growl.

She crawled across the mattress on her knees, like a sex kitten on the prowl, then slid from the bed and closed the gap between them. She ran her finger slowly from his waist to his chest and looked up through her thick lashes. Her lips parted, and when she spoke, her voice was thick with desire.

"It's exactly what I think."

She slid between him and the doorframe again and disappeared into the living room, leaving him rock-hard and confused as hell. After several deep breaths, he joined her in the living room, where she sat on the couch, her booties on the floor beside her, her feet tucked beneath her. She held a picture frame in her lap and looked up from it as if she hadn't just teased him to the edge and left him hanging.

"These are your siblings? Our families are so similar." She ran her finger over the images of his brothers and sister. "Handsome family."

He loved the sweet look in her eyes as she gazed at the photo of his family and hated himself for the jealousy that clutched his heart.

She sat up a little straighter and lowered the picture so he could see who she was pointing to. "Who's this? Look at those eyes. Wow." She ran a finger seductively down her neck, lingering at the edge of her sweater.

"Duke."

"*Mm*. Duke. I like that name." She tilted her head to the other side, flipping her hair over her shoulder. "And this cutie, with the crooked smile? Who's that?"

"Blue." He gritted his teeth as she nodded and assessed his photo.

"Now, that's a sexy name. Blue Ryder. I bet he has no trouble reeling in the women."

He took a step closer, intending to snag that picture right out of her hands, but her look stopped him cold.

"Then again, it doesn't get much sexier than Cash, does it?"

You're going to drive me fucking insane.

He narrowed his gaze, locking eyes with her. "Not in my world it doesn't," he growled.

She turned back to the picture. "Now, this one, he looks my age, and this other one, oh, he's wicked cute. He's kinda got a surfer dude thing going on." She pressed her lips together and furrowed her brow. "What are their names?"

"Jake and Gage." He sat beside her and leaned his elbows on his knees, one hand clenched into a tight fist, the other wrapped around it.

"*Ooh*, Gage. That's intriguing. And you have a sister. She's gorgeous."

He snagged the photo from her hand. "Trish," he said angrily as he leaned over her, pushing her back against the arm of the couch with his chest as he set the frame back on the end table.

She didn't say a word, and he couldn't think past the feel of her delicious curves beneath him and his thundering, jealous heart beating in time to hers.

"It took you long enough. I thought I was going to have to act attracted to your sister, too."

His hand slid to her hip, inciting a groan. "You have to be certain you want me, because if I kiss you, I'm not going to stop."

"Good." She grabbed his sweater and pulled him against her. "I'd be disappointed if you did." She slid her legs down the couch beneath him.

"Siena, I'm not your typical date. I'm not made of money. I don't have fancy clothes. I live in a box."

"I love your cozy little box," she said in a heated whisper.

"Don't toy with me. If I make love to you, my heart's in it, not just my body."

"Don't make promises you can't keep."

The challenge in her eyes spurred him on.

He lowered his mouth a breath away from hers. "Don't fuck with my heart. I can't afford any more scars." He searched her eyes, seeing the want there, the need, for him.

"I don't scar," she whispered. "I soothe."

She ran her hand along the back of his neck. Their mouths met in a frenzy of need, a rough, animalistic kiss that sent shivers through his body and an ache between his legs. God, she tasted good. He had to have more of her, and as his lips found her jaw, she clung to him. A sexy little noise escaped her lips and drew his mouth back to hers. His hands traveled up her sides, then back down along the sleek leather as he rode the curves of her hip, her thigh. Then his hand found the edge of her sweater and slipped beneath. He captured her moan in his mouth, needing more of her, wanting to taste every inch of her. She buried her hands in his hair and pulled his head back, staring hungrily into his eyes.

"Cash." She breathed heavily.

He tried to read her thoughts. Should he stop? Kiss her? Somewhere in his searching, he became aware of her hand on his jeans, tugging them, fumbling for the button, and heat seared through him. He grabbed her wrist and shook his head, breathing too hard to speak. She fought against him, reaching for him again, and when he released her hand and drew her sweater up, he thought he'd never seen anything so beautiful. He'd seen her body before, in the photo shoot in the magazine, but nothing came close to knowing that her heart was pounding for him, the desire in her eyes was for him—and him only—not a damn camera.

TOUCH ME. KISS me. Taste me. Lying beneath Cash wasn't enough. She was beginning to see that nothing with Cash was enough. She'd had more fun on their date than she'd ever had on a date before, and the minute they walked into his apartment, she'd wanted to back him up against the brick wall and kiss him until he thought of nothing but her. But he was so damn careful. She thought the bedroom might lure him in, but no. She'd worried for a second that he'd think she was too easy, but when she'd brushed by him, his body exuding the same need as hers, she didn't care. He'd find out she wasn't easy, that what she felt for him was different, magnified, new.

He lifted her sweater, and she held her breath and closed her eyes, anticipating his luscious lips on her skin. His hands found her ribs again. They were so big, so strong, and making her so damn crazy as his thumbs brushed against the bottom of her breasts. He kissed his way up her stomach, then between her breasts.

"Yes," she said in one long breath. She reached for his hand and brought it to her breast. God, she craved his touch. And, oh, did he feel good, caressing her through her lacy bra. She needed to feel his skin against hers, and she reached for the clasp between her breasts.

He looked up at her, breathing hard, his eyes mirroring the

aching need in her body. "You sure?"

She nodded, and then his fingers replaced hers on the clasp.

With one swift twist, the clasp released, and he moved the cups to the side.

"Christ. You're gorgeous."

He lowered his mouth to her breast, his tongue stroking her sensitive nipple, then sucking, kissing, and slowing to slow, hot strokes again. She arched into him as he moved to her other breast. A shock of cold air swept across her wet breast, and she sucked in a breath. His hand found her then, and his finger and thumb worked her nipple until it was hot, sending a shudder right through her. She urged his hand lower, needing more of him, and held her breath as he slid his hand beneath the waist of her pants, along the swatch of her thong.

"Cash," she panted.

He moved down her body then and hooked his hands in the waistband of her pants.

"You sure?"

She nodded frantically. *Hurry. Hurry.*

He stopped and raked his eyes down her body again, her sweater pushed up to her chin, breasts bared before him, her chest heaving with every heavy breath. He lowered his lips to her belly and pressed a soft kiss there. She moaned again, waiting, wanting to pull her own damn pants off. And then it hit her. Media. *Fuck.* She closed her eyes and tried to quell the panic blooming in her chest. She hated herself for even worrying about this, but she'd once been with a guy who sold the story of their intimacy to the press. She had to be careful.

"Wait."

He released her pants, and his eyes shot to her.

"You wouldn't. I mean, I know you wouldn't." *Shit, shit,*

shit. She hadn't been intimate with a guy in so long that she didn't even know how to say what she had to.

He slithered up her body. "What, baby? Tell me."

His voice was so tender, his eyes so trusting. She had to close hers just to get the words out. "You wouldn't somehow leak this to the press or something, would you?"

His eyes narrowed and filled with unmistakable anger. "Are you shitting me?"

"I'm sorry. I'm sorry. It's just…I don't think you would. I just have to say something because…because it's happened before. That's why I never sleep with anyone. It was years ago, but it really hurt and I can't go through that again."

His jaw clenched again; his nostrils flared. "After what I said to you, do you think I'd hurt you?" He pulled back, and she grabbed him and held him still.

"No, I don't. But I have a hard time with this stuff."

He let out a breath and ran his hand through his hair. Then he took her in his arms and held her close. His cheek felt so good against hers, and in his arms she felt safe. Safer than she'd ever felt. Her heart swelled, embracing him and aching for the pain she'd caused him at the same time.

"Whatever we do, it's between us," he whispered. "Sex isn't a game to me, Siena. You're not a game to me."

She didn't need anything more to know the truth. She drew back and touched his cheek. God, she loved his face. How could every fiber of her being feel like it belonged to him when they'd known each other for only a few days? "I'm sorry. I didn't mean to break the mood."

He shook his head. "I want you just as badly, but knowing you've been hurt makes my heart hurt, too. And I want to pamper you instead of ravage you."

"Ravage me now. Pamper me later."

In the next breath, she was in his arms, being carried into the bedroom. Her lips met his and kissed him like she wanted him to kiss her—greedy, demanding, needful. When he lowered her to the edge of the bed, she reached for his pants, wanting more of him. Her fingers hesitated, and she pushed up his sweater, then brought her lips to his hard stomach, wanting him to feel the same luxurious love that he'd given her. She wrapped her arms around his waist and rose slowly to her feet, kissing her way up his ripped, muscled torso. He reached behind with one arm and drew his sweater over his head, taking the T-shirt beneath with it. She gasped a breath. When they'd been in the photo shoot, she'd been totally focused on *not* focusing on Cash. Instead she'd focused on the photographer's directions, the lighting, making love to the camera. Now. Here. Everything was different. Heat radiated from him as she ran her hands up his body, then brought her lips to his chest, grazing his nipple with them and leaving a light trail of wetness from her tongue. He drew in a breath. His hands found her hips, and then he drew her sweater over her head and gently, delicately, slid her bra strap from each shoulder. She closed her eyes, having never felt so much tenderness and emotion from anyone. The few men she'd been with had moved fast; their lovemaking had been urgent. A minute of kissing, five minutes of foreplay, then three minutes of intercourse. Ungratifying at the worst. Lonely at best.

His tongue slid along the curve of her shoulder, sending chills down her spine and heat to her center. Her body trembled with need, and she steadied herself with both palms pressed flat against his beautiful chest. She brought her tongue to his nipple and teased him, loving the way his breathing hitched with each stroke of her tongue. She slid down his body, her tongue leading the way, and settled herself on the bed before him as she adeptly unbuttoned his jeans and worked the zipper. With one finger, Cash drew her chin up. Her eyes met his as he shook his head. Then he lifted her to her feet again and wrapped her in his arms, chest to chest, skin to skin, and looked deeply into her eyes.

"You're not going to go tell the press you slept with me, are you?" he teased.

"What'll you give me not to?"

With their chests pressed together, hearts beating in tune to each other, in the safety of his bedroom, he kissed her again. She never wanted to leave his arms, and when he hooked his fingers in the waistband of her pants again, she didn't stop him. He drew them down, then crouched before her, running his hands along her thighs before lifting each foot, freeing her from her pants. She shivered with anticipation and need as his hands slid sensually up her inner and outer thigh, kissing the space in between. One leg was numb, the other aching with jealousy, and her center was yearning for contact.

He laid her on the bed and brushed her hair from her cheek. "I saw pictures of you with other men," he said softly, without accusation.

She swallowed, not knowing how to respond.

"I don't care about them, but when I looked into your eyes, something was missing." He kissed her cheek, her forehead, ran his finger down her cheek. "You looked…lonely."

How could he possibly have seen that? No one saw the truth of her heart. She couldn't move.

He ran his hand gently down her arm and smiled lovingly. "What's missing, Siena? I want to fill that spot."

Oh God. She was drowning in need, trying to breathe past a lump that was forming in her throat. How could someone so virile be so observant? Honesty slipped from her lips without thought.

"I don't know what it is, exactly," she whispered. "I just feel this hole inside me." She'd never told a soul how she felt, but it had always been there. A sliver of emptiness that kept her from fully embracing all that she had. Except when she modeled. When she was in front of the camera, that sliver disappeared.

"Then I wasn't imagining things."

He pressed his lips to hers and wrapped her in his arms again. She loved being there, in the cocoon of his strength.

"When I touch you, I feel so much," he whispered between kisses as he moved slowly down her body. "It's more than your beauty. It's your heart." His hands caressed her hips as he drew his mouth lower. "The woman behind the snarky comments and tough, gorgeous exterior."

He kissed along the edge of her silky, black thong. She arched her hips, wanting more of him. His fingers traced the thin line of fabric across her hip, then followed it down to her center, where he slipped beneath the damp fabric with a groan. She sucked in a breath, clenched the sheets in her hand as he teased her softly, her inner muscles pulling for more contact. Then his mouth was on her inner thigh, sucking the sensitive skin, running up to the edge of her panties, lingering, licking, as his fingers slid in deep. She moaned with need, arching, urging, wanting more. Cash read her perfectly, and when he slid the fabric over and licked her lightly, it was all she could do not to thank him. She lifted her hips as he drew the thong off and tossed it aside, then grasped her inner thigh, massaging it as he brought his mouth back to her again. Every stroke of his tongue brought her closer to the edge. His hands found her bottom and lifted her up, just a hair, just enough that her knees fell open, and then his hand found her again. Harder, deeper, his thumb stimulating the sensitive nub that sent her heels pressing into the mattress.

She gasped a breath. Then another. "Cash." She'd never felt like this before. *Oh God. Oh God. Oh God.* He didn't stop, and every lick, every swipe of his thumb sent a million needles through her limbs. And then—*Oh God*—he slid his fingers inside her again and a million lights exploded behind her clenched eyes; her inner muscles pulsated against him. And she cried out in an indiscernible cry of pleasure, panting, unable to concentrate on a single thought.

She felt his body meet hers, his lips on hers, his hand still pressed against her center, as tiny pulses sent aftershocks through her body. She couldn't open her eyes, could only revel in the blissful feelings. His mouth found her neck, kissing, then sucking lightly, drawing her need out again as she wrapped a leg around him, feeling the rough scratch of his jeans. She opened her eyes and tugged at them.

"Not yet."

She whimpered. "Torture. You're torturing me."

"I seem to remember..." He kissed his way back down her body. "That you liked *maybe two* screaming orgasms."

She laughed. "Okay, okay. Come up here and let's see how good of a bartender you are."

He narrowed his eyes, and with the sexiest growl she'd ever heard, he said, "I'm an overachiever," and slid his hand between her legs again.

Less than three minutes later, she was in the midst of another climax. "Cash. Cash. Cash!"

He was relentless in his pursuit of her pleasure, teasing her at the peak and drawing it out for so long she could barely remember her name when his mouth finally found hers again. She tugged at his jeans, pulling back from the kiss with urgency.

"Off. Please. Off," she said between heavy breaths.

He was quick to comply, and was beside her again, naked, his hard length against her thigh. She reached for him, and he rolled over to the side. He grabbed a condom from the nightstand, ripped it open with his teeth, and rolled it on quickly.

"Hurry," she pleaded.

He used his knees to draw her legs apart and settled himself above her. She clutched at his hips, pulling him forward, breathing so hard she thought her heart might explode. His eyes were nearly black as he looked down at her, every muscle taut. His chest heaved forward with each breath. She felt the tip of his desire against her center, and she pressed his hips, urging him forward. In the next breath, he slid inside. Deep. Hard. They both drew in a deep breath as they came together. He moved slowly at first, every thrust bringing them closer together, their eyes locked, their bodies as one.

"Kiss me," she whispered.

She melted into the kiss, as he lavished her mouth with soft strokes, moving in time to his hips, and she arched up, meeting his efforts with her own. Her body tingled with the tease of another orgasm as he quickened his pace, and she couldn't help but wrap her legs around his waist, allowing him to drive in deeper, thrust harder, fill her completely.

"Oh God. Cash." She clenched her teeth against the mounting pleasure.

"Tell me what you like," he said.

"You."

One simple, honest word, and she was rewarded by his moving at the perfect rhythm to bring her up and over the edge again to the most powerful, mind-blowing climax she'd ever experienced. She cried out again and again, and he followed her over the edge in his own intense release, holding her tightly and groaning her name against her ear—the most glorious sound she'd ever heard—and she couldn't wait to hear it again.

Chapter Twelve

CASH COULDN'T REMEMBER a time that he didn't think of his apartment as *that dink-ass place* he lived. Sure, he was proud of the work he and Tommy had done, but he spent most of his free time at the firehouse. When he thought of a home, he thought of his close-knit family and the home they'd shared when he and his siblings were growing up. When he'd moved to New York, he'd hoped to one day have the same feeling in his own home. But it hadn't felt like a home for a very long time. Now, lying in bed with Siena's scent surrounding him, her head on his chest and her lean, silky leg draped over his—as crazy as it was—it felt like someplace he'd like to spend more time. *With Siena.*

"Stay over." He kissed the top of her hair, inhaling her coconut scent again.

"*Mmm.*" It wasn't an answer, but it sure felt good as she touched his stomach lightly with her fingers.

"I want to wake up next to you."

"So…we're going to sleep? *Hm.*" She turned her head and smiled up at him; then she shimmied up his body so they were eye to eye. "What will you think of me in the light of day? We've gone on one date and I ended up in your bed, letting you do all sorts of dirty things to me." She lowered her voice to a whisper. "I've seen you naked."

"Well, there is that. I've ruined you for all men, haven't I? How can you ever go back to typical when you've had...Cash Ryder?"

"True." She wrinkled her brow. "If you look at it that way, then I've ruined you for womankind as well."

He laughed; then he rolled her over onto her back, pinned her to the bed, and kissed her softly, contrasting his forceful hold. He was as attracted to her sense of humor as he was her sensuality.

"You might just be able to convince me." She drew him into another kiss. "Can I borrow a T-shirt to sleep in?"

"Sure, but you might not wake up in it."

She sighed. "Promises, promises."

BY THE TIME the sun rose, Cash had been awake for an hour. Siena was draped over his body like a blanket, stealing his warmth, he guessed. Her arm rested on his stomach, her left leg was over his thigh, and her cheek was pressed against his chest. He listened to her soft, even breaths and couldn't remember ever feeling so happy. He'd like nothing more than to lie with Siena all day, and as he thought about the day ahead, his mind drifted to his conversation with Chief Weber.

He wondered if meeting with Regan might do some good. As far as an instructor went, Regan was a prick. There were no two ways about it. But as a colleague, a man Cash held in high regard, Regan was right up there near the top. If anyone could get his head back in the game, it was Regan, which was as much of a relief as it was a worry. What if he was too damn scarred to ever find his way back?

"Morning," Siena said groggily, smiling up at him. Her eyes were at half-mast, but the contented, trusting look in them was far from the fiery stares he'd received the first time they'd met—and on too many occasions to count since. "Are you going to dress in those sexy turnout pants and fight fires today?"

If they were going to try to make a go of this thing, she deserved to know that he was going through a rough time. *A rough time. Way to minimize it, asshole.* Before he could answer, she leaned up on one elbow, her tousled hair tumbling over her shoulders and bare breasts.

"I bet women fake emergencies all the time just to see you show up in your sexy uniform, with your big axes and rippling muscles and—"

Shit. How could he tell her that he'd turned into the guy who pissed off the other fighters? "No, they don't." His voice was gruff, though when he tucked her hair behind her ear, he was tender, careful. He grabbed the T-shirt she'd had on for all of ten minutes the night before and handed it to her.

She pulled it over her head and he helped her pull it down to her waist. The sleeves hung down to her elbows, the 2XL shirt billowing around her. She looked too damn cute for words.

"I don't go in until later. I thought we could spend some time together—unless you have other commitments."

OTHER COMMITMENTS. SHIT, *shit, shit.* Friday night. Her date with Gunner. *Ugh.* She sat up and ran her fingers along the ends of her hair, training her eyes on them to avoid looking at Cash. The idea of going out with Gunner made her sick to her stomach now that she and Cash had been together.

"I need to go home and change," she said softly. *I should tell you. You'd understand. Wouldn't you?* Of course he'd understand. She ran her eyes up the muscular planes of his abs to his wonderfully broad chest: tight, hard, and corded with muscles beneath deliciously taut skin. He was larger than most men she'd dated. Actors tended to be smaller, leaner. She thought about their interactions. He was definitely more dominating, more masculine. Male, he was all male. He'd never understand. How could he? Pride alone would keep him from understanding.

"Why don't we shower here? Then we'll go to your place so you can change and we'll hang out for a while. I need to do a few things for Vetta, but other than that, I don't need to be back at the station until around five."

Siena's stomach clenched. He'd find out about Gunner; he'd see the photographs. That was the whole point of the date, wasn't it? She contemplated telling him the truth. *It's a date I have to go on. My agent set it up. It's good for my career.* She sounded like one of those guys who had an excuse for everything. They'd gone on only one real date. What if he wasn't all she thought he was? What if the romance, the tender side of him, the fun possessiveness wasn't real? *That would make me a very bad judge of character.* She thought of the last few guys she'd dated. *Yeah, okay. Point taken. Maybe I'm not a great judge of character.* She fiddled with her hair again, wanting to spend the day with him more than she'd wanted to do anything else for as long as she could remember.

"That sounds perfect." He continued to surprise her with

how sweetly he spoke to her and the gentleness of his touch.

When they stepped into the shower together, his massive body took up almost the whole thing. She crossed her arms over her chest to ward off the cold air.

"I can wait until you're done," she said as she stepped from the shower. She felt his large hand on her shoulder.

"Oh no, you don't."

His commanding voice sent a thrill right through her. She turned back to him. Good Lord, he was too sexy to deny. Water dripped down his thick shoulders and perfectly sculpted body. She couldn't help but follow the stream south to his—

He pulled her back into the shower, against his chest. "Hey. My eyes are up here."

"Maybe so, but something else is trying to burrow a hole into my hips."

He lowered his mouth to hers and ran a slow slick of his tongue over her lower lip before taking her in a greedy, hard kiss. His rough hands grabbed her ass and pulled her against him again. His urgency drove her desire, and she grabbed his ass right back. He drew back and looked hungrily into her eyes. His eyes darkened, narrowed. His chest heaved against hers. He lifted her up and pressed her back against the cold tiles.

"Fuck." He drew his brows together, pressing his hips against her to keep her up.

"That's a little harsh, but okay." She laughed.

"Jesus, Siena. I don't have a condom." He looked down at his erection, standing sentinel between them. "I thought I could make it through the shower without…*Good Christ.*"

"I'm on the pill," she said halfheartedly.

He searched her eyes. "That's not the only reason to use a condom."

"No shit, Sherlock." She narrowed her eyes. "What kind of girl do you think I am?"

He set her back down. "That's not what I was implying."

"No?" She turned her back to him, anger mixing with the fire he'd sent soaring through her. *How did we end up here?*

He spun her around and held her arms, breathing hard, searching her eyes. "You have no idea who I've been with."

"Is that a brag? Because it's not very attractive." *Jesus.* Tears pressed at her eyes. She ripped her arms from his grasp.

"I can't even talk when I'm around you. You fuck with my head too much." Anger rolled off of him like flames. "That's not what I meant at all. I meant how can you trust that I don't have an STD? You're too trusting."

"I am not." Now her damn lower lip was trembling. *Ugh!* Her whole body was shaking.

He dragged his eyes down her body, and his gaze softened. He gently wrapped her in his arms and pressed her to his chest, his hands running up and down her back.

"You're cold."

"Am not. I'm fine, and I'm getting out anyway." Damn it, why did he have to feel so good? She tried to turn away, to walk out of the shower, but his grip was too tight.

He looked down at her with a grave stare. "Siena, I wasn't bragging. I was just saying that we need to talk about those things if we're going to date."

She fisted her hands and pressed them to his chest. "I know we do." Anger pressed her lips into a tight line, then pushed her words out with way too much force. "I've never had anything."

"Neither have I," he snapped. "We have to make a decision. If we're exclusive, no condom is okay, but if we're not, neither of us can afford that risk." The anger left his voice as he moved a wet strand of hair from her forehead. "That's all I wanted to get out in the open. Being prepared is everything in life. One wrong move and..."

He kissed her forehead, and she saw a shadow of sadness in his eyes. Just as quickly as it appeared, it was gone.

She tried to wrench out of his arms again, and this time he let her. She wished he hadn't. He was right. She knew he was, but her body was still riled, and aroused, and the goddamn tears that had pressed at her eyes were now streaming down her cheeks. *Exclusive.* That's exactly what she wanted, but then how should she deal with the date with Gunner? Was it fair to be exclusive if she'd already accepted the date? The thoughts pulled more tears from her eyes.

Water sprayed her back, and tiny splashes landed on his shoulders and chest. She could walk right out of the shower, get dressed, and walk away. Just go home and forget the date ever happened. But that's not what she wanted. She wanted to be close to him. She leaned her side against him, unwilling to give up all her defenses, but wanting to desperately.

"I'm sorry." He kissed the top of her head. "All I wanted to do was the right thing."

She looked into his brown eyes, and she didn't even have to think as she reached up and touched his cheek. "I love that about you. But I also hate it."

"Then our relationship will never get boring." He lowered his lips to hers, and it took only a few strokes of their tongues before they were clawing at each other again. "Exclusive or not? We should decide."

"Exclusive from my end." *Except the date. Oh God. The damn date with Gunner.* She wasn't going to sleep with him, so it didn't count. That was wrong on so many levels, she nearly kicked herself for thinking it. *I have to tell him. I can't keep it from him.* Another pang of guilt struck her. She'd promised Jewel she wouldn't tell anyone.

"Mine too."

He lifted her in his arms again, and with the cold tiles at her back and the shower beating on their adrenaline-filled bodies, she wrapped her legs around his waist and took in every blessed inch of him.

"Good Lord," she whispered as she clutched his wet hair in her fists. Sex had never felt so good. He loved her so adeptly, his hands gripping her ribs, pressing her against the tiles as if she weighed nothing at all. Each thrust was expertly timed as his lips found the curve of her neck and his tongue caressed her sensitive skin until her eyes fluttered closed, her entire body in the clutch of a brain-numbing climax. He was right there with her, her name spoken through clenched teeth as he followed her over the edge.

Chapter Thirteen

CASH HADN'T TAKEN the time to really look at Siena's loft when he'd picked her up the evening before, and when they walked in, he did a quick visual sweep of the open space. Sunlight burst through the enormous windows that lined the exposed brick walls and glared off of the light oak floors. The expansive space was sparse, save for a large wooden dining room table off to the right and a sofa, two leather chairs, a coffee table, and end tables at the far side of the room. At the far right of the room was the kitchen, separated only by a bar with four leather-topped stools, and beside that was the bedroom, which he could see through the open door. His entire apartment could probably fit in that bedroom. The boxes he'd left at her door were still sitting atop the coffee table.

Siena hung up their coats by the door and began picking up the empty boxes. "Gosh, I forgot I left these out. Last night seems like it was ages ago, doesn't it? Or is it just me?"

He took the boxes from her hands. "Everything feels like it was ages ago with you. I feel like we've known each other for years, but that's probably because we bicker like we have."

She turned to him and gripped his cotton shirt in her fingers. "We don't bicker."

"What do you call it?"

She wrinkled her brow. "Banter?"

"Ha. Yeah, we can go with that. You'll tire of it soon enough." He carried the boxes to the door, trying to pretend that those words didn't just send a spear of longing through him. "Want me to run these down to the dumpster real quick?"

"I won't get sick of it, but you might. My brothers tell me I'm a stubborn pain sometimes." She spun around and fluttered her lashes. "But I think I'm just spunky."

"Oh, you're spunky, all right." He raised his brows and laughed a little.

She tossed him her keys. "Here. If you take those down, I'll change really quickly. Then we can go do something before the whole day gets away from us."

Cash carried the boxes down the stairs and realized he liked doing that type of little chore for her. *Weird.* On the way downstairs, he thought of telling Siena about what was going on with him and his work. He needed advice he could count on, and he knew just where to get it. After placing the boxes in the dumpster, he pulled out his cell phone and called his eldest brother, Duke.

"What's up, little brother?" Duke's voice was deep, upbeat.

"Not much. I need to ask your advice on something." Cash and Duke had always been close. Duke had been the one to steer him toward his degree and toward his profession. He'd told Cash that no matter what job he did, he'd get sick of it at some point, so he might as well do what he loved for as long as he could while he enjoyed it. After that? When it was no longer fun or interesting? Then, he'd said, it was time to move on. Cash wasn't ready to move on, but he sure as hell wasn't having any fun, either.

"Yeah? Go ahead. I've got about fifteen minutes before I need to hightail it outta here for a meeting."

Cash took a deep breath. Admitting what was going on to Duke wasn't easy, but it'd be a hell of a lot easier than admitting it to a woman who saw him as they all did—an in-control, virile firefighter who put his life on the line every day. When he was in the belly of the beast recently, he wasn't in control.

"Here's the deal. You know that fire a few weeks ago when I told you it was my worst one ever?"

"Yeah, 'course." Duke's voice filled with a sympathetic tone.

"Then you remember that a guy died because I couldn't get to him. An old man. He was ninety-two." Cash's body went hot. He wiped a bead of sweat from his brow.

"I remember. That sucks, man. At least he had a long life."

"Yeah. Right, that's what everyone says. But here's the thing. I can't get it out of my head. Just the idea that he died because of me. If I hadn't been blocked, I could have gotten to him, and I—"

"Dude, you were blocked by burning beams. What the hell are you talking about?"

"Thanks for the sympathy." Cash took the stairs two at a time up to Siena's apartment. "Listen, here's the thing. It fucked with me, okay? I don't like it and I don't even understand it, but ever since, I'm taking risks, Duke. It totally fucked with my head. I'm doing shit I'd never do before, like leaving my partner behind and staying in after the evac call. Tommy and the guys covered for me at first, but they're giving me shit, and the chief is, too."

"That sucks, Cash. What do you think's going on? PTSD?" Duke asked.

"Who the fuck knows? I talked to a therapist, but it didn't

help."

"You could ask Boyd. If anyone knows about PTSD, he does."

Duke was right about that. Boyd had lost his parents in a fire, and had the scars to show it. Cash's parents were like second parents to Boyd and his siblings. But Boyd wasn't around right now, so he said, "Here's the deal. I'm seeing this woman, and I'm not sure if I should tell her or not." He sat on the top step outside Siena's apartment and lowered his voice.

"Do you like her?"

"Yeah. A lot."

"Then what's the question? Honesty, man. You know that. Without that, you don't have shit."

Cash nodded and ran his hand through his hair. "Right. I know that. I just needed to hear it from someone else."

"Anytime, bro. I need to run, but listen, if you want to talk about this, call me or come see me and we'll try to figure it out. Part of me says just force yourself to stop taking risks—or pull out. You can't put Tom and the other guys' lives at risk. You know, face your fears and all that, but I don't know if that's the right thing to do or not. I'm just throwing it out there."

He pictured Duke in his business suit and tie, his dirty-blond hair just mussed enough to add an edge to his otherwise pristine image. As a real estate investor, he spent his days negotiating and traveling and his nights in the arms of some of the most beautiful women in the world.

"Thanks, Duke. I appreciate it. Good luck at your meeting."

"Luck? Skill, baby. Love ya, Cash. We'll have to meet for a beer at some point, preferably when there's not a snowstorm. Hey, that woman you rescued was okay, right?"

He thought of Siena, naked in his bed beneath him, his name on her lips as she came.

"Perfect."

"You just gave away your hand, my friend."

"Whatever. Go to your meeting. I have to get inside. Thanks, Duke." He ended the call and stared at the door to Siena's loft. He had to tell her, especially after the discussion they'd had in the shower. Just thinking about the shower aroused him. *Christ.* He had to get his emotions under control.

SIENA ANSWERED HER cell phone as she pulled a sweater over her head.

"Hi, Mom. What's up?" She pulled on a pair of jeans and went to the bathroom to put on makeup.

"Hi, honey, I just wanted to see if you'd called Hal Braden yet about the pictures."

Shit. She'd forgotten. "I had that date last night, and it slipped my mind. I'll call after we hang up." She leaned over the sink and applied a thin line of eyeliner.

"A date? Oh, I almost forgot."

Sure you did.

"Did he pass your checklist?"

Siena heard the smile in her mother's tone, and she pictured her lifting her eyebrows. "With flying colors."

"Oh. Goodness." Her mother paused. "So, you'll see him again, then?"

"Yeah. We're spending the day together today. Actually, I'm about to head out with him." She heard the door to her apartment open, then close.

"I won't keep you. Are you going to tell him about the date with that athlete?"

Siena's stomach clenched again. "No." She looked at herself in the mirror and watched her smile fade.

Her mother didn't respond.

Damn it. She knew how her mother felt about honesty. She didn't have the time—or the desire—to argue with her mother about her dating life. She wasn't exactly thrilled about going out with Gunner, and talking about the situation only made her angrier.

"Mom?"

"Yeah. I'm here, honey. Okay, well, you know how to handle your affairs, so…"

Siena sighed. "Mom, it's not like I enjoy keeping it from him. I want to tell him, and I know it's the right thing to do, but I told Jewel I wouldn't, and this isn't a game. It's my career." She pulled her shoulders back and looked in the mirror. "I need to go. I'll call Hal." She ended the call and tried to separate herself from the guilt that gripped her. If her mother were there, she'd see the conflicting emotions in Siena's eyes. She only hoped Cash couldn't.

She found him standing by one of the windows.

"You don't like curtains, huh?"

"You noticed." She joined him and looked out over the streets below. The snow had nearly all melted, leaving the sidewalks and streets clear but wet. "I've always hated them, and no one can see in up here, so why block the light? I noticed that you had bedroom curtains, but I don't remember seeing curtains in the rest of your apartment."

"I hadn't thought about it, but I guess you're right. But I'm a guy. I always thought women liked their privacy."

"I do, but I also like the light. No one can see in. My loft is too high."

"Makes sense to me." He put his hand on her lower back and kissed her cheek. "You look beautiful, and you smell delicious."

His lips on her cheek and his low, sexy voice sent a shiver through her. "Thank you." She hooked her finger in his jeans. "Before I forget, I have to make a call real quick. Do you mind? I can make it while we go."

"No need. Go ahead and call and we'll leave after you're done."

She walked to the kitchen as she scrolled through the numbers in her phone. She didn't have Hal's number, but she had Treat's. He answered on the second ring.

"Siena Remington. How is my soon to be sister-in-law?" Treat was Savannah's eldest brother. At six foot six with dark hair and darker eyes and a body that rivaled even Cash's, he was quite a catch for his pregnant wife, Max. Max was beautiful in her own right, petite and dark haired, smart and strong willed. Siena was excited to become an official part of their family once Jack and Savannah married.

"I'm well, Treat. How are you? How's Max feeling?" She sank into the couch.

"She's feeling well, a little tired, but you know Max. She never stops moving."

"Wonderful. Three more months until the baby's due, right?" She watched Cash as he moved through her kitchen as if he lived there. He looked comfortable as he reached into the cabinet for a glass, then filled it with orange juice from the fridge.

He held up the glass and mouthed, *Want some?*

She shook her head and mouthed, *No, thanks.*

"Yes, three months. She's really looking forward to Savannah's bridal shower, and we're all looking forward to seeing everyone."

"That's kind of why I'm calling. My mom and I want to put together a photo album of Jack and Savannah. Something that shows them through the years, sort of side by side. You know, like when Jack was in the army, it'll have pics of Savannah doing whatever she was doing during those years, all the way up to now. I was going to call your dad, but I didn't have his number."

"That's such a thoughtful gift. I can get you pictures. That's what you need, right? Just tell me how many and I'll send them out tomorrow."

Treat was always generous and accommodating. It dawned on her that all of the Bradens were, Savannah and each of her five brothers. And of course their father, who had raised them alone after their mother passed away from cancer when Treat was only eleven.

"We don't need too many. Maybe a few from each year? Do you think your dad will mind? I don't want to take them if he'll miss them."

Cash finished his juice and washed his glass in the sink, then dried it and put it back in the cabinet. Siena watched him with interest. How many men would be so thoughtful?

"He won't mind one bit. You know my father. He lives and breathes for romance. Anything else you need?" Treat asked.

"Nope, that'll do it. Thanks, Treat. Let me give you my address." She gave him her address, and he said he would FedEx the pictures the next day. She ended the call and apologized to Cash.

"No need to apologize for a phone call. I was trying not to eavesdrop, but I heard something about a photo album. I'm making albums for Vetta." He reached for her hand and helped her up from the couch.

"Really?"

"Yeah. She had this big box of photographs and they were all in envelopes. So I figured it was the least I could do."

She noticed his jaw clench, his eyes narrow.

"I mean, putting them into albums would make it easier for her to look at them. I figured she would want to see her husband now that he was gone."

She felt herself open up to him even more. "That's the sweetest thing I think I've ever heard. How do you know her?"

He grabbed her coat from where it hung by the door and held it open for her, then helped her into it. "Her apartment was in a fire we handled." He pulled on his coat and opened the door. "Have your purse? Keys? Gloves?"

She grabbed her purse from the coffee table, her gloves from her coat pocket, and she looked at him with her hand out for the keys. He placed them in her palm, and she pulled him down by the collar and kissed his lips. "Yes. Yes. Yes. See? I do listen."

They walked down to the café where they'd had hot chocolate and ordered croissants and coffee, then ate them as they walked through the Village.

"At least it's not freezing out today," Siena said as they slowed to look into a store window.

Cash draped his arm around her neck and pulled her close. "I liked it when it was colder. Then you cuddled up to me."

"I'm an expert at pretending." She nuzzled against his side. Each time he pulled her close, she felt guiltier for not telling him about the date she was supposed to go on.

"So, tell me what I don't know about Siena Remington," Cash said as they walked down Fifth Avenue toward Washington Square Park.

"What you don't know? Let's see. You already know I can be a little stubborn, and you know I like hot chocolate, and about my family."

"That's all the first date stuff. I want to know about you. What do you love to do? What do you despise? What are you afraid of? What's your favorite color?" He held her hand as they entered the park.

"That's pretty easy. I love to dance, and I love to eat ice cream, even if it ends up all over my clothes. I like to shop, but I don't really love it unless I'm doing it for someone else." She breathed in deeply. "And I love this. Being here with you, without a plan."

His eyes grew serious and he asked, "How do you know I didn't plan this?"

"Did you?"

"No, but…"

"Ha! See, I knew. Oh, maybe you didn't know that about me. I'm really intuitive." She tossed her hair over her shoulder.

"Yeah, right. If you were intuitive, then you would have known I wasn't bragging in the shower." He pulled her close and wrapped his hands around her waist and gazed into her eyes.

"So I lied. I'm not that intuitive, but I knew you didn't plan this."

"You do know I wouldn't brag about stuff like that, don't you?"

The way he looked at her sucked her right in and sent desire rushing through her. His eyes locked on hers, filled with sincerity; his brows furrowed just a little.

"I do now," she managed.

His lips met hers, and everything else faded away. The sound of the birds, the din of the other people in the park, the noises from the cars on the road. It was just the two of them, his tongue caressing every part of her mouth as if he were memorizing it. His lips pressed firmly against hers, the peppering of stubble scratching lightly against her upper lip.

When they drew apart, it took a minute for Siena to catch her breath. She didn't have long to figure out how to breathe again before Cash was dragging her over to the area where people played chess in the park. They walked hand in hand behind the tables. Cash scrutinized each one. Siena loved watching the competitions. She always had. There was such rich diversity among the players. She loved watching an older African American man playing with a twenty-something guy who dressed like Eminem, and a middle-aged Rastafarian playing against a gray-haired older man with a beard that touched his protruding stomach. Later in the afternoon, the older crowd would be joined by higher-thinking school children trying to show their skills.

Cash stopped beside a table. "What's it cost to play?"

"Play?" Siena watched the bald African American gentleman scrutinize the board. His eyes darted from one spot to the next. The man he played against looked homeless. He wore three old, wrinkled coats, one atop the other. His brown beard and hair were a scraggly mess, and his hands looked like they were stained with dirt.

The bald man eyed Cash, then Siena. The edges of his lips curled up. "Two bucks."

Cash pulled out his wallet and set two dollars on the side of the board.

"You're going to play?" she asked.

He draped an arm over her shoulder and held her close. "Nope. You are." He didn't look at her. He watched the game unfolding before them, studying every move.

She stepped out from under his arm. "What? No way. I hardly know how to play." She'd played chess with her brothers when they were younger and she'd lost every time. Strategy games were not her forte. "Scrabble or Boggle—those I can play, but chess? I'll lose your money faster than you can say...*oops*."

His eyes shot to her, another firm look. "It's worth it."

She tugged his hand and stepped away from the table, sensing the eyes of the players on them. "I can't play. I seriously suck," she whispered.

"Don't give me that pouty look. You know it kills me."

Good to know. She honed it a tad, sticking out her lower lip a little farther and drawing her eyebrows together.

He kissed her forehead and shook his head. "You also said you couldn't skate, but you could. One game. That's it. Just one."

"But—"

"For me?" He took both of her hands in his and stuck out his lower lip.

She laughed. "You need to work on that pout. Maybe if you're lucky I'll show you how to do it someday." God, she loved how he pushed her. Even though she knew she'd lose, she felt the competition he'd sparked, and he gave her just enough of a doubt in her own belief that she sucked that she accepted the challenge. "Fine. One game. For you."

He pulled her close again.

"But don't think I'm going to enjoy it." She turned back to the game, suppressing a smile, and studied the board. It had been so long since she'd played that she hardly remembered how each piece was allowed to move. As she watched the two men near the end of their game, it came back to her. And she also remembered how it felt to lose. This was not going to be fun, but at least it would be over quickly. *Another Band-Aid.* She looked up at the smile on Cash's lips and wondered why he liked to challenge her. Her next thought was that she hated that their afternoon was passing by so quickly.

The man with the layered coats lost the game and relinquished his bench to Siena. Her leg bounced a mile a minute beneath the table. She was suddenly chilled, and she put her hands in her pockets and rounded her shoulders forward.

"I'm Siena."

The bald man nodded and moved a pawn. "Frank."

She smiled. "Hi, Frank. Oh, my turn. Sorry." She had no idea where to move. She moved the same piece of hers that Frank had.

Cash stood behind Siena and settled his hand on her shoulder. The intimate, strong touch helped to ease her nerves.

They took their turns in silence, though it was killing Siena not to talk. She knew better than to talk through a game of chess in the park. Everyone knew better than to do that. These players were competitive, which was precisely why she had no business playing with them.

Cash leaned down and whispered against her ear, "You're doing great," before kissing her just below her earlobe, which Siena found terribly, excitingly, distracting.

When their game was almost over, Cash set down two more dollar bills on the side of the table.

Siena looked up at him. "I'm not playing again. I've lost this game in less than five minutes."

He was looking so intently at the chess table that she wasn't sure he'd heard her until he squeezed her shoulder again.

"Are you going to play?" she asked.

"Yeah. I'll give it a shot."

Frank lifted his eyes to Cash, and Cash smiled. "If you don't mind. I mean, I'm not much better than her, but I can't really ask her to put herself out there without being willing to put myself in the same position." He shrugged.

Frank nodded.

Three moves later, Siena lost the game. She let out a breath, relieved to be out from under the pressure of it, even if it had lasted only a few minutes.

"Okay, you're in the hot seat, Cash." She stood beside the bench where Cash sat and watched as the two men leaned over the board and began playing. Cash took less than three seconds to decide on his moves, while Frank studied the board a little longer, lifting his eyes every few seconds to glance at Cash.

Siena ran her hand along the back of Cash's neck, then rubbed the tension she felt there. Not a word passed between the men. Cash sat with one hand on his thigh, elbow out, the other on the edge of the table. He was taking Frank's pieces, so he must be doing well, though Siena thought Frank was taking a lot of Cash's pieces, too.

Cash wrapped his arm around Siena's legs and ran his hand down her hip while his eyes remained trained on the board. She hadn't seen Cash so intent on anything other than her body, and the memory made her shudder. She loved seeing this side of him, knowing his mind was strategizing, calculating, and also knowing that somewhere in that mind of his he was thinking about her at the same time. His intensity made him even sexier. *Everything makes you sexy.*

Frank's eyes narrowed, his hand hovering over his pieces. He shot a look at Cash, then eyed the table again.

"Check," he said, his shoulders easing just a hair.

Cash clenched his jaw repeatedly as he looked over the board. A few seconds later, he moved a piece, sat back, wrapped his arm around Siena's waist, and pulled her down on the bench beside him.

"Checkmate." He kissed her cheek.

Frank lifted narrow, angry eyes at Cash. He nodded as Cash slid the money off the table and Frank grabbed his hand. He held his stare, and Siena's heartbeat sped up.

"Well played," Frank said.

Cash's lips lifted into a crooked smile. He nodded curtly, then guided Siena away from the table.

"WHAT WAS THAT?" Siena asked in a hurried whisper. "Did you just use me as a setup? You're some kind of chess whiz, too?"

Cash waited until they were beneath the arched entrance of the park before answering. He gazed down at the pinched look on her face.

"I'm not a chess whiz. We play at the firehouse," he answered as they left the park.

"Come on. You swindled that guy, and I was the bait, or whatever you call it." She stopped walking and poked him in the side. "You could have let me in on that."

He caught her finger midpoke. "You're always poking me."

He laced their fingers together. "I didn't plan on playing, and I didn't win much. I saw the chess games and thought it would be fun to see you play, and when you said you couldn't, well, I had to do it then."

"Why?" She pulled her hand from his and crossed her arms.

He smiled, trying hard not to laugh at her angry stance. He closed the distance between them and put his hands on her cheeks. "Because there is nothing that you can't do, and I would be a horrible boyfriend if I let you walk away from things because you thought you couldn't do them."

"But I couldn't. I lost." She pressed her lips into an angry line again.

"Sure, you lost, but you made some good moves. If chess were something you were interested in, you would spend time playing it and I have no doubt you'd master it. I watched you figuring out the game when we first stood by the table. You were doing more than just watching."

She rolled her eyes. "Yeah, like remembering how to play."

"Maybe, but I saw more than that. Like the gears in your mind were turning. And your moves were good."

"Why do you think I can do things? First skating, now this." She tilted her head in his hands, and he felt the tension easing from her jaw and neck.

"Because you're smart and you're stubborn as hell." He pressed a kiss to her lips and shrugged.

She reached for his hand as they walked down the sidewalk. "Boyfriend, huh? It's been a long time since I've had a boyfriend."

"Yeah, I can tell." He leaned away like he was escaping a poke.

She swatted him and he pulled her close again.

They walked and talked all afternoon, and telling Siena about his work weighed heavily on Cash's mind. They'd had the most wonderful afternoon together. They laughed, they kissed, they talked. He now knew her favorite color was indigo, her favorite food was a brownie fresh from the oven with vanilla ice cream on the side, and the thing she hated most was seeing other people suffer—emotionally or physically. They stopped to have lunch and he made up his mind. He was going to tell her after lunch, before he walked her back home.

The restaurant was cozy and quiet. Cash and Siena were taken to a booth near the back. Siena slid across the red vinyl seat, and Cash couldn't stand the thought of not being right beside her when he told her about what he'd been going through. He slid in beside her instead of sitting across from her. He wanted to feel everything she felt.

"What?"

"Nothing. I've never been with a guy who sat on the same side of a booth with me." She snuggled against him again. "I like it. You're like this swindling bad boy who keeps surprising me with romance."

"That's as bad as calling me sweet." Cash shook his head while secretly tucking away the compliment. "How hungry are you?"

She shrugged. "Salad hungry. What about you?"

"Full cow hungry."

"Great. Let's see if they offer full cow with a salad on the side."

Siena poked at her salad while Cash downed a thick roast beef sandwich. It would be easier to tell her on a full stomach. Because if she dumped him, he knew it would take a while before he'd feel like eating again.

"It's three o'clock. I'm afraid I have to go after I walk you back to your place. I want to stop by Vetta's before work." Cash put his arm around Siena and noticed she hadn't eaten much of her salad. "Wasn't it good?"

"Yeah. It's really good. I'm just not that hungry." She stared at the plate with hooded, sad eyes.

"What's wrong?" Maybe she was as bummed as he was that their day together was ending. Or maybe he'd totally misread her and she just realized she'd had the most boring day of her life.

Siena turned in the booth and faced him with a scowl.

"Uh-oh." He wiped his face and set his napkin down on the table. "What'd I do?"

She touched his thigh and shook her head. "Nothing. You're great. I loved our day together and our night together."

"Then why do you look like I just killed your kitten?" He pulled his shoulders back, bracing himself for the Dear Cash conversation. A million thoughts ran through his mind at once—none of them good. *You realized I'm not model boyfriend material. I'm boring. I'm too aggressive. God, I am gruff. That could be it.*

She dropped her eyes and licked her lips. When she looked up again, it was guilt he saw in her eyes. Plain as day. He'd recognize that look anywhere, because it was the same one he saw every morning when he looked in the mirror.

"Jesus, tell me what it is, Siena. It can't be that bad. Even if you don't want to see me anymore, it can't be as bad as what I see in your eyes." He took her hand in his, his heart pounding against his ribs.

"Not see you anymore? Cash, I want to see you *more*. I haven't enjoyed a date this much in forever." Her lips were pouty, but her forehead was creased, worried.

"Then what is it?"

She blew out a fast breath. "Okay. Please don't hate me."

Great. Anything that starts with *Don't hate me* never ends well. "No promises."

She looked down at their hands. "I'm not supposed to tell this to anyone. Not even you." She met his gaze again. "Especially you," she corrected herself.

"Why *especially* not me?"

"Because if anyone was going to rat on me, it'd be you. I need you to promise me that what I tell you will never go further than you and me. No matter what. Even if we break up." She clung tightly to his hand and pressed her lips together as she searched his eyes.

"Come here." He pulled her into a hug with absolutely no idea what could possibly have gotten her this worried. "Whatever it is, if you ask me not to tell anyone, I promise you, I won't tell anyone."

She drew back and looked at him again. Her big baby blues opened wide, full of hope. "Even if I…" She leaned in close and whispered, "Killed someone."

"Come on. You're going to make me lose my mind." He shook his head. His gut was tied in such a knot that he wished he hadn't eaten that sandwich.

"Okay. But you really can't tell anyone, and I mean it." She scooted closer to him. "I trust you, Cash."

"Good. You should."

"Okay. God, this is hard. I've never done anything like this before, and the timing is really bad. I mean, I've *really* never done anything like this, and I don't like that I have to do it now."

Cash's muscles tensed. His chest tightened. "Spit it out. Please. You're killing me."

"My agent is making me go on a date with an athlete tonight. I don't want to, and I tried to get out of it, but it's for exposure, and nothing more. I don't like the guy. I've actually never met him. And I—" She shook her head and spoke fast, her eyes trained on his chest.

"Hold on. Slow down. Let me get this straight. Your agent is making you date someone." He looked away and ran his hand through his hair. What the hell? Was she making this shit up?

"Yes. Gunner Gibson."

"Gunner...the quarterback? The guy who gets thrown out of strip clubs every week? Seriously?" He pulled away and scooted over on the bench. "Siena, if you want to date other guys, and what you said this morning was just said in a moment of passion, that's cool. Just tell me." *I'll fucking hate it, but at least I'll know.*

She reached for his hand and he pulled it out of her reach. Her eyes filled with sadness. She opened her mouth, but no words came out.

Christ. He had to man up and let her off the hook, no matter how much it hurt. He made a mental note that women sucked ass. "Listen, we had a good time." He started to move out of the booth, and she grabbed his hand. He looked down at her grip on his wrist. Her knuckles went white.

"Don't. Please." Her eyes pleaded with him. "Listen to me, Cash. I don't lie. Please. Talk to me."

He settled back into the seat, jaws clenched, biceps twitching.

"Cash." She spoke in a harsh whisper. "I know how it sounds, but I'm not lying." She ran her hand down his arm, then held his hand in hers. "I'm not that kind of girl, Cash."

One look in her eyes was all it took to see that she was telling the truth. He felt it in her touch—she couldn't be faking that, the way she clung to him like he was life itself.

"Why are you telling me? Why didn't you just let me go to work? You could have gone out with him and I'd never have known."

She dropped her eyes and his muscles clenched.

"Why?"

"Because I don't want to keep anything from you. I really like you."

She sighed, and he knew there was something more. Every second he waited felt interminable.

"The reason she's making me do it is for exposure, which means that pictures will be all over the Internet and the papers. They alert the press for these things." She gripped his hand tighter. "It's one date."

"Right now. Right now it's one, but what if that goes well? Then it's two, or…" *I sound like a jealous ass.* He rubbed the back of his neck where an ache was needling his nerves. "Fuck it."

"What does that mean?" Her angry tone drew his eyes to hers.

"It means that I'm not interested in competing, Siena, but I'm also not a child. If you have to do this for your career, fine. I trust you. You know, you always hear about this shit, but I never thought it was real." Jealousy clutched his heart, and he rolled his shoulder back to try to disengage from it. She didn't have to tell him. Sure, he'd see the papers eventually, but if she didn't care about him, she wouldn't have said a word.

"Oh, it's real, all right. I've just never been told I had to do it before. And, Cash, believe me, I tried to get out of it. I tried everything, but Jewel, my agent, thinks if I don't up my exposure, I'll start losing jobs." She touched his cheek. "It's dinner. One dinner at a fancy restaurant. Nothing more."

He nodded, gritting his teeth through the anger and jealousy that was eating him alive. "So I should prepare myself for what? To see pictures of you and him walking arm in arm?"

She shrugged and nodded. "I guess."

He envisioned so many other things. Gunner Gibson was a burly, handsome millionaire, with dark hair, blue eyes, and rock-hard muscles that women crooned over. He thought of her being one of those women, and it sickened him. He breathed harder, thinking of seeing pictures of her kissing him, holding his hand, like they'd held hands all afternoon. *Shit. Goddamn it.* What choice did he have? End things here and now based on jealousy, or trust her and be man enough to weather the storm of photographs? He thought of the pictures he'd seen online of her with various handsome men and the loneliness he'd seen in her eyes. The loneliness that wasn't there when they were together. That gave him a modicum of comfort.

"You told me not to tell anyone, but it'll be in the papers? I don't get that at all."

"The date's not real. I'm not going out with him because I like him. So if you tell the wrong person that I'm doing it for press, I'll get bad publicity, and that would be a nightmare." Her eyes still pleaded with him.

"And what about us? We pretend we aren't going out?" He felt his nostrils flaring. This was a nightmare.

"I've never done this before, so I don't really know how to navigate it all, but I think we can still go out. I mean…I guess I need to talk to Jewel, because the press is sure to be all over me."

She turned and faced the table. "Oh God. Cash, I have no idea." Her voice shook, and when she met his gaze again, her eyes were damp. "I'm so sorry."

"Shit. Come here, baby." He cupped the back of her head and drew her to his chest. He had no idea what to do. He sure as hell wasn't going to have a secret relationship. That was bullshit. But with Siena clinging to his shirt, her cheek pressed against his chest, his vehemence fell away.

"We weren't going out when Jewel told me I had to do it. I'll call her now. Let me call her." She pulled out of his hands and dug her phone out of her purse.

"Wait." He lowered her hand that held the phone. "This is your career. Before you call, whatever you have to do, it's fine. We'll figure it out." *Fuck.* Where the hell did that come from?

"Oh, Cash." She wrapped her arms around his neck. "I'm so sorry. Thank you."

They left the restaurant, and Siena called Jewel as they walked back to her place. Cash purposely walked a few feet behind her, to give her space as much as to give himself time to think. He was a simple guy with a simple life. The last thing he needed was to be part of some high-profile love triangle, but when she ended the call and looped her hand in his arm and looked up at him with eyes full of hope, he was no longer sure of anything at all. Except that he wanted to be with Siena.

"That's a relief. I'm so glad I called." They entered her building and rode the elevator upstairs. "She doesn't know that I told you. I just said I was dating someone and needed to know the game plan."

"Yeah? And?" He needed her to cut to the chase. The whole afternoon had thrown him off-kilter. First their closeness had sent his heart reeling and filled him with hope for more, and now this conversation had knocked the wind right out of him.

"She said that since the press hasn't been following me around, that they probably wouldn't start now, so I can just live my life as normal, and if that means we go out together, then we do. She's going to tip off the press when I meet up with Gunner, so it's not like they're actively seeking me out. Jewel said she just needs enough to get us into the rag mags. You know, *Are these two the hot new couple* kind of thing."

"Oh, is that all?" He was sure she could see steam coming out of his ears. He clenched and unclenched his hands as she opened the door to her loft.

She pressed her hand lightly to his chest. "Is that anger or jealousy? Because you sound like you're ready to kill someone."

Her seductive tone wrapped around his thoughts. Gunner would be hearing that voice tonight. "Both."

"Then you'll be glad to know that I told her to change the date. If all they need is us to be spotted together, why go to dinner? I hate going to fancy restaurants with people I don't know." She hung up her coat, eyeing him as he stood rigid, feet planted hip distance apart, muscles tense, his hands shoved deep in his coat pockets. "We're meeting at a bookstore instead."

"Better." *Bookstore. Christ.* At least a bookstore didn't require a sexy dress and six-inch heels.

"Were you telling me the truth about him and strip clubs?" She drew her brows together and went to her bedroom. "I'm going to get my iPad." She came back a minute later, and he hadn't moved. He couldn't move. He was too angry.

She searched Gunner's name and her eyes widened. "Holy crap. Why would she do this to me? I'm Googling the other guys she wanted me to go out with." She searched, and a few seconds later she said, "Oh my God. Cash, all three of the guys she wanted me to go out with have really bad reps. My reputation is totally clean. I've never been caught doing anything bad. Goddamn it." She paced, her arms crossed.

"Maybe that's it. You're too squeaky clean." He pulled her into his arms, his muscles still tied in knots. "Hell, I could have helped you dirty up your reputation." He rested his cheek on her head and closed his eyes, feeling his heart swell. How the hell had she become so important to him so quickly? There was no way he'd tell her what he was going through now, not knowing she had all this shit going on in her life.

"So we're cleaning up his act and I'm making mine more controversial?"

"Sounds like it."

"Thanks for not bailing on me," she said.

"I said I'd try. No promises." He might not be making verbal promises, but he was tossing out silent prayers to the powers that be and hoping he could keep from falling into jealousy hell and ruining what was quickly becoming the most important relationship he'd ever had.

Chapter Fourteen

WHEN THE ALARM sounded that night, Cash suited up with the rest of the men. He climbed onto the truck, muscles burning, adrenaline searing through his veins.

"Dude, don't pull any shit today," Tommy yelled into his ear.

Cash could barely hear past the sirens and the rumbling of the engine as it sped out of the firehouse. He'd stewed all evening over Siena's date with Gunner, and as much as he wanted to be understanding, he was having a hell of a time letting go of the fact that she was spending time with a cretin like Gunner. If that jackass laid one finger on her, he'd kill him.

He narrowed his eyes and gave Tommy his darkest, meanest stare, hoping he'd leave him the hell alone. He wanted nothing more than to get into the belly of the monster and tame the jealousy that was clawing at his insides, and he knew that wrestling a fire was about the only thing that would do the trick.

Thankfully, Tommy got the message.

They arrived at a home on a residential street with flames billowing against the windows and the two upper floors engulfed in flames.

"We're looking for three children. Three, five, and seven years of age. They were asleep on the second floor. You know the drill," Chief Weber yelled as they sprang into action. "Cash…" He narrowed his eyes and pointed angrily at him. "Don't pull any shit. You and Mike stick together; you hear me?"

All Cash heard were the voices in his head. *Three children. Three, five, seven. Second floor. Get 'em the hell out of there.* Joe did a quick 360 sweep of the exterior of the building while the roof crew ventilated the fire, containing it to the rooms it had already swallowed.

Cash grabbed Mike's arm and headed into the building.

"Stay with me, Cash. I'm not fucking around," Mike said.

Adrenaline pushed him forward, and he ignored Mike's warning. Fear pulled at the edges of his mind. *Get in. Make the save. Get out.* In one breath, Cash sized up the surroundings. *No fire on entry. Smoke coming from stairwell.* He crossed the floor to the stairwell in three determined steps. *Solid, walkable.* He took them two at a time to the top. Thick, pitch-black smoke illuminated by flames to the left. No line of sight. Cash hit the floor with Mike on his heels, feeling with his hands, listening to the roar of the fire as he felt his way along the floor.

"Get the right. I got the left," Cash hollered. He heard Mike crawl to the right. "Anyone in here?"

No response.

He crawled along the floor in the dense smoke as if he were blind. "Stay low. If you can hear me, make a sound."

No response. *Fuck.*

He felt a bedpost, swung his long, powerful arms under the bed, striking something solid. He dragged it out. A duffle bag. Unzipped. Full of balls. *Seven-year-old.* He heard the roar of the flames, saw the flash of light as they engulfed the doorway behind him. His heart thundering against the hardwood floor, he used the toe of his boot to push himself forward as fast as he was able. He used his finger to feel the edge of the floor where it met the wall, and when the wall ended, he found the closet. *Always the fucking closet.*

Mike's voice cut through the smoke. He couldn't make out what he said. No time to waste, Cash pulled open the closet door and felt around. No kids. *Shit.* Flames licked the floor, heading for the bed. *The bed.* Cash stood in the thick smoke, eighty pounds of equipment weighing him down, the heat of the fire strangling him. He hit the floor, crawling to the other side of the bed and feeling around again. No kid. *Goddamn it.* With his heart in his throat, he made his way through the flames to the hall, still unable to see. With no idea where Mike was, he crawled along the floor, feeling for the next doorway. Instinct told him to move toward the fire, not away. He turned back, felt for doorways again, and that's when he felt it. A child's foot sticking out of a hole in the wall, limp. *What the fuck?* He reached into the wall and grabbed the child as flames chased his efforts. With the child against his chest, he threw caution to the wind and stood, blinded by smoke, one hand on the child's back, the other on the wall, feeling for the stairwell, coughing, breathing heavily and wishing he'd put the goddamn air pack on. *Damn it.* He hated the fucking air pack. He hit the stairs and got the child outside. Met by the EMTs, he handed over the child.

Outside the building, red lights blinked, spectators watched, hollering to the firemen. It was all a blur to Cash. He had one focus. The children.

"More?" he asked the EMT through heavy breaths.

"Three-year-old."

Cash headed back into the building with Joe on his heels. "Mike?" he yelled.

"Not out yet," Joe called. "You gotta use your breathing pack if you're in there!"

The hell I do. It was a visceral reaction born of habit. He was too focused to remember that he'd wished he'd had it on only a few minutes earlier.

"Tommy?" he asked one of the other guys.

"Out. Safe."

Cash hit the stairs running. Flames engulfed the hallway. *Goddamn kids.* With no idea where Joe was and thinking of Mike, he found his way on his stomach through the flames to the hole in the wall where he believed the other child might be hiding. *Fucking Mike. Where are you?* He ripped the drywall out of the wall, grabbed his air mask, and shoved it on the little boy's face, pressing him against his chest. He had no idea if the child was alive or dead, but he knew he had seconds to get him out as flames tore at his sleeves and his back, making even thinking beyond getting out impossible. *Out. Out. Out.* He crawled to the stairs. Hands tore the child from his chest; heavy boots thundered down the steps.

"Out, Ryder!" Chief Weber yelled.

"Mike out?" Cash hollered, pressing the mask to his face and breathing deeply. His lungs burned, ached.

"They'll get him," Weber said.

"He's got a kid." Cash had to get him out of there. He was back inside the smoke-filled house when he felt Weber grab his arm.

"Out! Now!"

Like hell. Vetta flashed into his mind, then Lisa and Katie.

He had less to lose than Mike did, and he'd be damned if he'd have to look into Katie's eyes and tell her what a great guy Mike had been. Cash wrenched his arm from his grasp and hit the stairs two at a time, ignoring Chief Weber's command that followed him through the front door—*Use your goddamn breathing mask!* He crawled in the direction Mike had gone, ignoring the angry commands coming from the stairs. A window shattered. *Venting the room.* He followed the sound of coughing.

"Mike!"

"Ryder, get outta there!" one of the guys from the ventilation team hollered through the window. "We got him!"

Cash pushed to his feet and stumbled forward toward the coughing sound he'd heard. He found Mike, tossed him over his shoulder, and brought him to the window to the ventilation team.

"Get Mike out," Cash hollered. He turned back, but the flames were too thick, the smoke too dense to pass. He could barely breathe, though he didn't notice. Adrenaline sent him onto the sill, and he rode down with the ventilation team, bitched out the entire way.

"What the fuck was that, Ryder?" Chief Weber stood over him as he sat on the running board of the ambulance, mask on his face, sucking in air. "You're dangerous. Fucking more out of control than ever."

"I got 'em out, didn't I? How's the kid?"

"Shit shape, but he'll make it, they think." Chief Weber paced, his fisted hands shooting right and left as he hollered at Cash. "Damn it, Ryder. We talked about this. You didn't just risk your life. You risked the lives of your team. If you got stuck in there, we'd have men risking their lives trying to save your ass."

Cash pulled the mask from his face. "But I didn't."

"That doesn't fucking...Forget it. This is your last warning. It's time to get over what fucked you up or get out. This loose cannon shit isn't you, Ryder, and you know it. You're forcing me to make a decision, so take this warning seriously, because your ass won't like desk duty."

He watched Weber stalk off. Yeah, he was right, but hell, if Cash knew how to rein it back in, he would do it. If he'd taken a chance that night, Samuel might still be alive, and how the hell was he supposed to get past that? His mind drifted to Siena, and he knew he had to figure this crap out fast. *Regan?* The idea pissed him off even more.

SIENA THOUGHT SHE might lose her mind if she had to spend one more minute with Gunner Gibson. She sat at a table in Corner Reads, the bookstore where they had planned to meet at seven—and he'd shown up at seven forty. Jewel had told her to just look interested in him, gaze at him, engage him in conversation. She said they didn't have to look like they were in love; they just needed to look interested to pique the public's interest. Siena still didn't get the point of the whole situation. She was a model, not an actress, and practically no one outside the industry knew who she was beyond being a pretty girl they'd seen in a magazine. But Jewel had assured her that this was what her career needed for her to remain as one of the top models, so she sucked it up and put on her best *interested* face as he scrolled through his text messages.

"Gunner, what do you like to read?" *Jesus, what am I going to talk to this guy about?*

His eyes remained trained on his phone. "Eh, you know, sports stuff mostly."

No wonder you have to rely on strip clubs. Siena didn't see anyone taking pictures, and she wondered how long she'd have to sit there pretending that she was okay with a guy focused on his phone and wasting her time. But she knew how to get guys like that to talk.

She fluttered her lashes—of course he wouldn't see her doing it, but it put her in the right frame of mind—and in her best fan girl voice, she asked, "Tell me what it's like being out there on the field with all those big men rushing after you. Aren't you scared?"

Bingo! His eyes found hers. The hand holding his phone dropped to his lap, and a smile graced his full lips and pushed at his high cheekbones. Maybe she'd think he was handsome if he weren't such a nimrod.

"Scared? Hell no. I'm as big and strong as they are. But a normal guy, yeah, they'd be worried. My guys have my back, and if one of the other team break through…" He patted his chest three times. Hard.

Siena envisioned Tarzan banging his chest, and she stifled a laugh.

"I can handle myself. You know, I've got the second-best record in the league." He leaned forward, elbows on the table, biceps flexing beneath his black T-shirt. "Best record in the bedroom, too. We could blow this bookstore and go have some real fun."

Siena narrowed her eyes at him and held his stare. She leaned forward with a smile on her lips, and in the most seductive voice she could muster, she said, "How about we get through this impossibly boring situation, get the pictures taken so the press thinks there's a chance in hell I wouldn't despise everything you just said, and then we move on with our lives?" She fluttered her lashes again. She was damn sure he saw it this time. His hands fisted, and he tilted his head.

"Your loss." He shrugged and turned his attention back to his phone.

Siena glanced out the front window of the bookstore and finally noticed two guys with cameras. *Damn, they're good.* No wonder they caught so many celebrities off guard. She'd had no idea they were even there. She focused on Gunner, smile in place, and said under her breath, "Cameraman. Front window. Act interested."

On cue, Gunner lifted his eyes and reached across the table, grabbing her hand and gazing into her eyes with an almost-as-believable look in his blue eyes as Siena knew she had in hers.

Several flashes later, cameras still clicking away, she rose to her feet. "I think they have enough." She picked up her purse, and when she turned back to him, his lips were on hers. She pressed at his chest. *What the fuck?* With camera flashes in the window, she was all too aware of the situation at hand. She pushed him away with the smile still in place. "That wasn't part of the deal."

"Like you minded." He put his hand on her lower back and walked with her out the door.

She stood rigidly beside him, her insides churning with anger, but when her feet hit the pavement, she still flashed a smile while flagging a cab. She couldn't get inside the cab fast enough, and when he started to slide in beside her, she pushed him out the door. "We're done." She slammed it behind him.

She rested her head against the seat and let out a breath.

God, that was awful. She told the cabbie to take her to the firehouse. She needed to be with Cash. On the way over, she called Jewel. Her call went straight to voicemail.

"Jewel, the guy's an ass. How can you do this to me? This can't be a necessary part of being a model, and if it is, then we need to discuss my future." She ended the call after leaving the message.

When the cab reached the firehouse, Siena was still shaking with anger. She debated not going in and texting Cash instead, but she wanted to see him, needed to feel his arms around her. She walked into the empty bay, the heels of her boots clacking across the concrete floor.

"Hello?" she called out. When no one answered, she walked through a door to her right that led her into the station house. A burly man with a mustache and thick brown hair sat behind a desk in the front of the station, a phone pressed to his ear. Her nerves tingled, making her want to turn around and walk out. *Why did I come here?* She knew absolutely nothing about firehouses. What if there was some sort of guy code where the firemen weren't supposed to bring their girlfriends around?

"Yes. Thank you." He hung up the phone and turned his attention to her. "Can I help you?"

She debated saying she was lost and making up something that would allow her to leave gracefully when the sound of the fire truck returning pulled the man's attention toward the garage.

"Um..."

"Sounds like the guys are back. Are you looking for someone?"

Shouts and laughter, cursing, and heavy booted footsteps filled the hallway she had just come through. Siena's stomach twisted. She found herself eye to eye with several soot-covered, bare-chested firemen, who were standing in the hallway staring at her. It took her only a second to find the tall, handsome blond man she'd come to see and to recognize the anger in his eyes as they narrowed. He parted the bodies between them, pushing them to the side as he barreled his way through.

"Siena." His eyes darted to the men beside him.

She watched his shoulders draw up, the ridges of his muscles tighten around his neck and arms.

"Siena? Isn't that the girl from the magazine?" one of the guys asked as he pushed past Cash.

"Yeah. You're the Johnnie Walker girl." He ran his eyes down Siena as if he were imagining her in the pink panties. His eyebrows rose, and his pectoral muscles jumped. He nodded. "Oh, yeah, you are."

Cash's hand gripped his shoulder.

The guy glanced back as Cash moved him aside and grabbed Siena's hand, then dragged her down another hallway and into a room with a television. He looked her up and down, surveying her. He was taking stock, not sexually drinking her in.

"You okay?"

"Yeah," she managed, her voice weakened by the weird night and the scene with his friends.

He leaned down and kissed her, a quick, welcoming kiss. "Why are you here?"

"I..." *Shit. I needed to be held? I'm such an idiot. What am I? A weak girl? Oh my God, what am I turning into?*

He searched her eyes and pulled her against his bare, sooty chest. His hand cupped the back of her head. "You're trembling."

He kissed the top of her head, and she cursed herself for

loving every second—and needing every moment—of his warm embrace. She'd had a shitty evening. Why on earth would that bring her here? How could she need him so badly, so fast?

Because she hadn't wanted to meet Gunner in the first place.

Because she'd rather have been with Cash.

Because she'd allowed Jewel to talk her into something she didn't believe in.

Cash smelled like smoke. *Oh God.* He was out saving lives and risking his own, and there she was whining about an uncomfortable meeting with some guy. She stepped back.

"I'm sorry. I shouldn't have come. Are you okay?" Jesus, he was sexier than any man she'd ever seen, and the way he was looking at her—his dark eyes caressing every inch of her in a protective, caring way—drew her to him again.

"Sorry," she said against his smoky chest. "Just one more second. I just need one more hug." She drew in a deep breath and then stepped back again. "Okay. Sorry. You were at a fire?"

He took her hand and drew her down to the couch. Siena recognized the brown-haired guy who poked his head into the room from the photo shoot. Joe.

Cash glared at him.

"Sorry, man." Joe went away, leaving them alone again.

"Residential fire. What's going on? Did something happen with Gibson?" He tightened his grip on her hand.

"Not really." She wanted to tell him about the kiss, but suddenly she felt silly. Like a tattletale. So what? The guy stole a kiss, and he was an asshole. *And it will be in the papers.*

"Siena." In his eyes, she saw it. He was calling her on the bullshit.

She sighed. "When I stood to leave, he kissed me, and they

took pictures. I didn't kiss him back, and it's not a big deal, but—"

His eyes darkened and his chest expanded as his anger rose to the surface. The oblong muscles along his jaw flexed. Siena felt the couch buckle as his massive thighs tightened and he pushed himself to his feet.

"Not a big deal."

"Cash…" She'd known he'd be upset, but she also knew he'd see it in the papers. That was the point of the whole damn evening, but he'd be hurt and angry if she didn't tell him about the kiss before the papers came out. She went to his side.

"So every guy here is going to see you sucking face in the newspaper with some guy. And I can't tell them it's not real?" he said in a harsh, heated tone, his eyes burning a path to hers.

"Do they even know about us? Because it didn't look that way." She turned toward the door. "I'm not even sure why I came here. I don't know why I said what I said. I don't care if your friends know we're dating or not." She heard anger in her voice, but it wasn't anger she felt. It was frustration at herself for putting them in this position in the first place. She wasn't upset about his friends not knowing about them. Hell, she hadn't even had time to tell Willow yet.

He stepped in front of the doorway, blocking her from leaving. "No, they don't know yet. But it's not for whatever reasons you might think."

"I don't care, Cash." Her words lost their oomph. She was tired and confused. "That doesn't matter to me. I came here because I was so mad after he kissed me that the only place I wanted to be was in your arms; then I saw all those guys looking at me, and…" She brushed her hair out of her face. "And I got nervous. I mean, here I waltz into the place you work and expect you to just take me in your arms. Which you did." *You really did.* "And maybe in a firehouse that's totally the wrong thing to do. I don't know. I don't want to mess up whatever relationships you have here by being the needy girlfriend—"

"Christ, Siena. You can be the needy girlfriend. It doesn't make you any less of a strong person. You think I don't know how tough you are? And you aren't going to mess up my friendships with the guys." He cupped her cheek with his sooty hand and his eyes softened. "I haven't told the guys about you because they're gonna ride me about it. And..."

"And?" What else could there possibly be? Wouldn't he be proud that he was dating her? Shouldn't he be as proud as she was about dating him? She was proud, she realized. Even with his gruff exterior, she liked who Cash was. A lot. And she wouldn't be embarrassed to be seen with him anywhere.

"Look, I'm a private guy, okay? And that magazine you were in, it made the rounds before we started dating. Every one of those guys has seen you in your...*pink panties.*"

"In my..." Oh shit. To Siena, modeling was a job. Something she loved doing. It was her career. She'd thought about guys leering at her, or doing God knew what while looking at pictures of her, and sure, it had bothered her, but she'd gotten used to it. It was part of her job, and she wasn't exposing her private bits to the media and the masses. The men she'd dated hadn't given a hoot about it, other than to be proud. Cash's jealousy was new to her, though not new to their relationship. She'd caught glimpses of it earlier in the day, when she told him about the date with Gunner. But she hadn't thought about that jealousy infiltrating other parts of his life. And now that she realized what was going on in his mind, it made sense that he'd drag her away from them without an introduction and send Joe away until he figured out how to deal with things.

Things.

Pink panties.

"Cash, I only came here to be with you. I'm sorry if your buddies saw the ads I was in, but it's my job. It's not like I'm posing for them. And to be honest, I don't really care if they know about us or not, but I would care if I couldn't come see you when I needed or wanted to." She ran her finger through the soot on his chest and then looked down at her jacket, now covered with soot.

"Sorry." He wrinkled his forehead. "You came here because you wanted to be in my arms?" He reached for her hand. "I like that."

"Yeah. Me too. We have a weird relationship." The words came out before she could think about them.

He clenched his jaw again, and she was sure he agreed with her.

"I don't mean that in a bad way, Cash, but it's true. We have this connection that feels so deep, and so real, and then we have this thing between us that makes us bang heads." She dragged her finger across his chest again and wrote her name in the soot.

Cash looked down and laughed softly. "Marking your territory? Or leaving a memory behind?"

She drew her brows together, as if she were thinking it over. "Definitely marking my territory. I ran to you, remember?"

"Well, with that soot on your face and all over your clothes, I'd say I marked my territory, too." He pulled her close again. "Yeah, we have a weird relationship. But what really matters is that we have an honest relationship. The rest will settle down at some point."

She pulled back to see the look in his eyes, and she saw just what she thought she would—uncertainty. It tugged at her heart.

"Or it won't," he said with a shrug. "More important, do I need to have a talk with Gunner Gibson?"

"A talk?" She imagined him stalking Gunner—angry fireman against oblivious quarterback. The thought made her smile. "No. I can handle him as long as you can handle me afterward."

He slipped his hands around her waist and pressed his cheek to hers. "Babe, you're not someone I need to handle."

He paused just long enough for his warm breath to circle her neck and send a chill down her back.

"You're like a fire. I want to study you, understand you, and learn what makes you lose control."

He kissed her neck, and between the heat of his bare chest pressed against her, his heartbeat hammering in time with her own, and his sensual whispered words, Siena could barely breathe. *Yes. Oh God, yes!*

Chapter Fifteen

THE NEXT MORNING, Cash headed into the kitchen hoping none of the guys had gotten industrious and gone to the convenience store. If Siena's picture was on the cover of the gossip magazines at the newsstand, he at least wanted coffee before facing it. He'd hidden out in a back room last night to avoid the litany of questions he was sure they'd bombard him with after Siena left, and he'd worked on Vetta's photo album until long after the other guys were asleep, and he'd heard from Siena, indicating that she'd arrived home safely.

"Shit, man, what happened to you in that fire last night?" Joe asked Mike. "Find a *Playboy* and take a break?"

They were sitting around the kitchen table eating breakfast. Cash patted Mike on the back. "Glad you were all right, man. Could happen to any of us." Cash glared at Joe, though he enjoyed razzing the guys just as much as Joey did. That was part of the firehouse brotherhood.

"Cash, you still okay to help me move my brother's desk today?" Tommy asked when he came into the kitchen.

"Desk? What are you talking about?"

"I told you about two weeks ago. I need help moving my brother's desk. You got plans?" Tommy sat down with a plate of eggs and stared at Cash.

"Uh, no, man, that's fine. I don't remember talking about it, but whatever. Sure. I'm on until tonight anyway." He pulled out his cell phone to send a text to Siena.

"What happened to that magazine that was in the TV room?" Joe slid a look at Mike.

Mike cleared his throat. "I don't know. Tom? Where'd that thing go?"

Tommy eyed the two of them and shook his head.

"I'm heading over to the medical supply store this afternoon to see if they have a walker. Anyone wanna go?" Joe asked.

Cash fisted his hands.

"Johnnie Walker?" Mike asked.

"Yeah. I heard he's got a sweet pair of pink—"

"All right. Enough." Cash pushed himself up from the table so quickly his chair crashed to the floor. He stared them down.

Mike and Joe laughed.

Tommy eyed the men again and shook his head. "Why're you always pokin' the bear?"

"Oh, man, because nothing else is quite as much fun." Joe set his breakfast on the table and speared a hunk of eggs.

"Her name is Siena, and I'm dating her, so keep your traps shut. Got it?" Cash threw his plate in the sink and crossed his arms, looming over Joe.

"Dude, she's in a magazine. It's not like you can stop anyone from seeing her." Joey shoved a forkful of eggs into his mouth.

Cash leaned down and said in an angry, even tone, "Think I don't know that? But I can sure as hell stop you two from disrespecting her."

"All right. Fine. So what's the deal? You're dating now?"

Mike looked at Tommy, who shrugged. "Dude, we were all there for the photo shoot. You could have said something."

Cash trusted these guys with his life. Why on earth was he having such trouble telling them about Siena? Why did he feel like he needed to protect her?

"I wasn't dating her then. But yeah, we're dating now." Cash locked eyes with Tommy, who sat back, crossed his arms, and arched a brow. Cash knew that smirk on his face well. He was enjoying every second of Cash's discomfort. "Look, I know you've seen the ads. Hell, everyone has. Just…Goddamn it." He turned around and began scrubbing his dishes. He didn't know what the hell he wanted. They'd seen her. Big fucking deal. The picture didn't show any more than a bikini would.

"Man, it's not like we'd make a play for her now that we know you're dating her." Mike took a bite out of his toast. "Especially after you saved my ass."

Cash blew out a breath and faced them again. He slapped Joey's shoulder. "Ease up on the Johnnie Walker talk. That's still a little raw."

"That's what she said," Mike joked.

Cash shot him a dark stare.

Mike held his hands up in surrender. "Sorry. Kidding. Kidding. Seriously, though, you're not exactly a sensitive guy. How'd you hook up with her?"

Cash rubbed the back of his neck as he headed for the stairs. "She likes my dark side." He pulled his cell phone out again and texted Siena. *Told the guys about us. U free later?*

"Come on, man. We gotta go." Tommy held up his keys and rattled them.

"Oh, right. Almost forgot." He grabbed his coat and they headed out to the car. "How long's this going to take?"

"Not long." Tommy drove through town in silence.

He glanced at Cash a few times, and when he turned in the opposite direction of his brother's house and headed toward Randall's Island, Cash fisted his hands in his coat pockets.

"What the hell, Tom?"

"Chief Weber said I had to do it, so don't give me shit." He stared straight ahead, his dark hair poking out from beneath his knit hat. He gripped the steering wheel tightly with his gloved hands and shot a glance at Cash.

"Regan? Really, Tom? You didn't think that maybe you should clue me in on this?" He didn't know if he would have taken the step to see Regan on his own or not, but he hated the idea of the chief forcing it on him, and he hated Tommy agreeing to it behind his back even more.

Cash's phone vibrated. He pulled it out and read a text from Siena.

I'm never free. I cost ice cream or hot chocolate. Xox.

Cash texted back. *Cheap date. I'll call after my shift.* He thought about adding an *X* or an *O* or both, but it felt girlie. He hit send and shoved his phone back in his pocket.

"Chief Weber was pissed yesterday, Cash. You gotta get this shit under control or you're going to be on the desk." Tommy pulled onto the Fire Academy grounds and parked by the office.

"This is the last thing I want to do today. You know that, right?" Cash shook his head. "Why are we even here?"

Tommy shrugged. "Chief said to make sure you're here. That's it. That's all the direction I got. You're here. I did my part. Come on. Let's get this shit over with."

They found Ari Regan in the office, sitting with his feet up on the desk, blue baseball cap covering his bald head. He smiled when they walked through the door, flashing bright white, crooked front teeth, which looked even brighter against his olive complexion. He lifted his square chin.

"Tommy and Cash." He didn't move to greet them, didn't offer them a seat. His smile remained, and to anyone who didn't know him, they'd think he was happy to see them by that dashing smile.

Cash knew better. He saw the gears of Ari Regan's brain working in his dark stare. Regan—always Regan, never Ari—had obscenely large biceps, especially for a guy who was only about five ten. He looked like he'd swallowed two small watermelons that planted themselves in his arms, second only to his thickly muscled shoulders and broad chest. Tattoos slid out from beneath his tight sleeves. He wore a watch on his left hand and a silver chain around his neck. Aviator sunglasses perched above the rim of his hat.

"Regan," Cash said with a narrow gaze.

Regan glanced at his watch, his smile fading. "Sit." He rose to his feet as Cash and Tommy sat across the desk from him, a tactic Cash should have expected and had almost forgotten. Regan came around to where they sat and leaned against the desk, spreading his legs out, one enormous foot in front of each of them. His black cargo pants stretched tight around his powerful thighs. He lifted the brim of his hat, then settled it above his eyes again.

"Tell me why you're here." He locked dark eyes on Cash and crossed his arms.

Cash shook his head. He was in no mood for games, and the crappy part was that he knew Ari Regan didn't play games. He was dead serious, and the answer, *You know damn well why I'm here*, wouldn't get Cash anything more than a scowl and harsher treatment than whatever Regan had in mind.

"Because Tommy dragged my ass here without my consent." Cash slid a deadpan stare at Tommy.

"Hey, man. I just do what the chief tells me to."

Regan's eyes never wavered from Cash's.

"Cut the shit. You're wasting my time, and I don't have a lot of it."

Cash leaned his elbows on his thighs, fisting his hands. He cocked his head to the side and forced his clenched jaw to unhinge enough to speak. "Apparently, I'm taking risks and I guess I'm here for you to beat that need out of me."

Regan smiled and leaned back, arms still locked across his chest. "Risky business. This is going to be some fun shit, but first, Ryder, as I recall, you're Mr. Prepared. You call people on risky stuff. Want to give me the dirt, or do we have to play games to get there?"

In his peripheral vision, Cash saw Tommy rubbing his hands on his thighs, then crossing his arms and uncrossing them.

"Can you let Tommy go? This isn't his issue."

Regan looked at Tommy, then back at Cash.

"He stays."

Fuck. The last time Cash was at the training center was when he was tasked with bringing a rookie down to be broken of his fear by Regan, and Cash had to remain there for each of the poor guy's humiliating sessions. Two weeks later, the rookie quit. Cash wasn't a quitter, and he sure as hell wasn't a rookie. He could take whatever Regan wanted to throw at him. He just didn't want to be responsible for Tommy going through the same shit.

"A few weeks ago I lost a guy. Beams blocked my way. I wanted to make the rescue, and the guys dragged me out. End of story." Tommy was one of those guys. Tommy probably saved his life that day, but Cash didn't care. Someone else lost his.

"If that was the end of the story, then you wouldn't be sitting in my office right now, would you?" Regan uncrossed his arms and leaned his palms on the edge of the desk. "Seems to me like you do want to play games, and, Ryder, I love games."

"Regan, let's get your torture over with." Cash sat up straight, holding Regan's stare.

"My torture? Let me ask you something, Ryder. Do you remember what happened seven years ago with Chuck Tooler? Let's talk torture." Regan rose to his feet.

Cash's chest tightened. He remembered what happened to Chuck. In gruesome detail.

"Chuck Tooler had been with his unit for what? Six years?" He slid along the desk until he was right in front of Cash. "Remember why he ran back into the building after it was evacuated?" Regan paused. "I asked you a question, Ryder. Remember what happened to hotshot Tooler?"

"Yeah, I remember." The words felt heavy leaving his lungs. He did not want to relive Tooler's demise. Hell, if he never thought about it again, it would be soon enough.

"Tell me why he ran back in."

The room was silent save for the sound of Cash's blood rushing in his ears. He clenched his jaw and shot a glance at Tommy, who looked down, refusing to meet his eyes. Cash pulled his shoulders back and sat up straight, out of respect for Tooler; that's what he told himself. The truth was, he was warding off the idea that he was anything like Tooler.

He rubbed the tattoo on his left arm, remembering when he and Tommy had gone to get it shortly after Chuck had been swallowed by the fire—he'd added another piece after Samuel died. Cash had no idea what the meaning behind the tattoo was, but the minute he'd seen the image, he'd felt the pain of Tooler's burns, the reminder that the beast—the fire—was stronger than any one of them but not stronger than the team of them. The top of the image reminded him of the thick eye of the beast—and the screams that came from Tooler's lungs. The markings at the bottom of the tattoo that looked like long, pointed, spidery legs, were reminders of how fast the beast had turned on Tooler and swallowed him whole. He only now realized that after Samuel died and he'd added another layer to the tattoo, he'd also blocked its meaning out completely. He'd stopped looking at it because it was so painful a reminder. *How the hell could I have blocked that out?*

"Spit it out, Ryder," Regan urged.

"He said there was another guy in there and it was his job to get him out." Cash's mind flashed back to the day before, when he disregarded his buddy's warning and then the warning of the ventilation team. He wiped a bead of sweat from his brow, then rubbed the thighs of his jeans, pressing hard just to feel that he was grounded, safe. *Not Tooler.*

"Tell me what you felt when he ran in. Tell me how your body reacted," Regan pressed, making his fucking point loud and clear.

Cash could smell the smoke. He could feel the heat of the flames, could feel the fear, the twist of his gut. *It's out of control. We gotta get him.* "Chief…" His goddamn voice was shaking. Aw, shit, so were his hands. He cleared his throat and sat up straighter. "Weber wouldn't let us go after him."

"Not what I asked. I want to hear what you felt, Ryder."

Cash narrowed his eyes, breathing hard. There was no slowing down his heartbeat. *Fucking Regan.*

"You see your buddy run into the fire." Regan leaned forward, lowering his voice to just above a venom-filled whisper. "You know the upper floors are about to crash down on your buddy, on the guy who took you and Tom under his wing, and that beast is going to burn every inch of his body." An inch from Cash's face, Regan's eyes went almost black, his voice filled with anger. "What the hell is going on in your gut, Ryder?"

"I fucking wanted to go in after him," Cash yelled. "We all did, but the guys from the second engine held us back. No one got in. No one." He pushed to his feet and paced the concrete floor, anger seething through his body like poison.

"In your gut?" Regan uncrossed his massive arms and shoved a finger into Cash's stomach. "What's going on in there?"

Cash stared at him, breathing hard, wanting to push him out of his face—one hard shove—but that wouldn't get the images to disappear. It had taken years to bury those images, and now…now they were back, and Cash saw himself in them.

"I fucking hated him for putting us in that position. I wanted to beat the shit out of him and rescue him at the same time. I wanted to puke my guts up, and I wanted to kill someone. Hell, I wanted to kill everyone."

"And?" Regan yelled.

"And he should have fucking known what he was doing to us. He knew the risks. He knew we couldn't go in." Cash panted, pacing again. He walked behind Tommy, who was leaning forward, elbows on his knees, hands buried in the sides of his thick hair, and he remembered the weeks that followed. The promise he'd made Tommy swear to. *Man, if I ever turn into the guy who does that, drag my ass out of this unit.*

Regan closed the distance between them, stopping Cash from pacing any farther. Cash had six inches on Regan, and still Regan's presence was that of a brick fucking building. Impossibly wide shoulders, massive arms, and a stare that would knock the wind out of many men.

"And now you tell me how what you're doing is any different." His command came with a calm voice, though his eyes were cold and harsh. Without turning, he pointed at Tommy, holding Cash's stare. "Tell me, Ryder." He stepped closer. So close, Cash could see his pupils dilate, could smell coffee on his breath, and could feel his anger filling the slither of space between them, thick and inescapable.

Cash shifted his eyes to Tommy, then back at Regan. The truth sent a piercing pain through his body. He opened his mouth to respond: *There's no fucking difference. Point made. I'm an ass. I'll fix it.* No words came.

"You have three seconds to tell me how it's different, Ryder. I'm not a patient man."

"It's not fucking different. Okay? I get it." He pushed past Regan, knocking into his shoulder on the way.

Regan grabbed his arm and spun him around. "I didn't dismiss you." He moved in on him again, a breath away. "Now, you tell me what you saw when Tooler came out."

Christ. Cash's muscles tensed. His legs were rooted to the floor. He forced himself to answer through gritted teeth. "He crawled out…dragging the guy alongside him."

"More."

Fuck you.

"Two seconds," Regan pushed.

"You want to know what I remember? I'll fucking tell you. The smell of burned flesh—I can still smell it." He rounded his shoulders forward, fisted his hands. "The guy was dead. He saved a dead man and lost his life."

"How?" Regan took a step closer, backing Cash up toward the concrete wall.

Cash's body told him to knock Regan out of his way and outrun the memory. His mind knew it was impossible.

"Details."

Cash looked away.

"Ryder!"

He snapped his attention back to Regan's flaring nostrils and angry stare. "In the hospital. Burns over ninety percent of his body, his family by his side, drugged to escape the pain."

"Did you see his wife? His kids?"

He'd never forget the devastation in their eyes or the pain that was still present every holiday when Cathy Tooler brought gift baskets to the station. He couldn't forget his little girls' tears that couldn't have been stopped by anything other than their daddy being healed, and the way the two of them, five and seven at the time, clung to each other, as if they couldn't remain erect if not for the other's legs.

"Yes," was all he could manage.

"You tell me, Ryder. Do you want your unit going through that? Your brothers? Do you want them to make a choice between saving your ass and saving their own?" Rhetorical questions, spoken as if they were each beaten into him with a hammer. Regan walked around to the other side of the desk and pulled out a photograph from the drawer. He threw it across the desk to Cash. "What do you see?"

Cash shifted his eyes and remained where he stood, a few inches beside where Tommy sat.

"My unit." *The guys I love. My brothers. Aw, hell.*

"What else?" He repeatedly tapped his index finger on to the picture.

"Brothers. Trust. Loyalty. Courage. Bravery," Cash shot back. He ran his hand through his hair to break the streak of anger between them. It didn't work.

"Your risk taking puts every one of those guys in the same damn place, Ryder." His stare softened just enough for Cash to become aware of the man he was beneath the fury. The man he respected. The man who taught him to respect the beast and the men whose lives depended on him.

Cash set a hand on Tommy's shoulder and felt the knotted muscles beneath his palm. No matter how he tried to formulate a response, the words felt wrong. *I know* indicated that he knew what he was doing when he did it. The truth was, at those moments, his mind went blank. It shot back to the guys pulling him away from saving Samuel Miller. *I'm sorry* would be worthless spoken to Regan, and maybe even to Tommy. Words felt too weak for the shame and sorrow that he felt. Regan was one hundred percent correct, and it slayed Cash to know that he'd risked putting his friends in such an awful position.

"Sit down." Regan nodded to the chair beside Tommy.

Relieved for the direction, Cash did as he was told.

"You got a girlfriend, Ryder?"

Cash rubbed his tattoo as he answered, silently swearing he'd never let Tooler's images get away from him again. He needed that reminder. "Yeah."

"New relationship? Old?"

"New."

Regan leaned across the desk. "The next time you go into a fire, I want you to ask yourself if you want to see that woman's face standing over you in the hospital—or worse—standing beside you when you're visiting a fellow firefighter in the hospital because of some stunt you pulled. We clear?"

When Cash first began as a firefighter, it was his family's images that he kept in his mind as he prepared for each rescue. He told himself it was them in the fire. That's what kept him focused and allowed him to push the fear away—because fear existed no matter how often he and the guys pretended it didn't. Now it would be Siena's face he'd picture, and she wouldn't be in need of rescue. He'd picture her waiting for him safely away from the fire. Waiting for him to come back to her. Holy hell, how hadn't he realized how much he wanted that until just then?

Chapter Sixteen

SIENA SAT ON her couch with her feet propped up on the coffee table staring at the front page of *Us Daily* with her cell phone pressed to her ear, listening to Jewel rave about the exposure. The headlines read, *Is It Love?*

"Jewel, this is such garbage. I read all about Gunner. He's fixing his rep with me, and…I can't believe this will do anything other than ruin mine."

She'd gotten up early to scour the gossip magazines down at the café. She'd ignored Bogey's disapproving headshake while she'd paid for a handful of them. She wasn't front-page news on the other magazines, but she was a few pages in and mentioned on the cover. *Hot new couple! Gunner Gibson scores Siena Remington.* Her stomach had been off ever since she brought them home and memorized every word of the articles. She felt dirty and ashamed to have faked the date. She kept flashing to Cash's face, the way he'd looked so stricken when she'd first told him what she had to do and the way he'd spun it in his head to try to get past it. Getting past an idea was one thing. Getting past seeing your girlfriend on the front page of a magazine kissing another man was another.

"Look, we all know you're a top model this week, but it's a

fickle business." Jewel sighed. "You know all this, Siena."

"You know what? I don't think it is. I have solid contracts with Chanel, H&M, and Revlon. I've been one of your top models forever and this…" She tossed the magazine onto the coffee table with a sigh. "It just makes me feel cheap."

"Funny. It'll have the opposite effect on your contracts."

She pictured Jewel touching her hair, sitting with her legs crossed, looking out the window of her penthouse apartment with a satisfied grin on her thin lips.

"Well, it's done. At least that's good. Now I can go back to my normal life." *And forget about the stupid picture.* Another call interrupted theirs, and Siena glanced at the screen. *Savannah. Great.*

"Well, not exactly. You need to meet Gunner again. His agent called this morning, and Gunner's popularity rank soared after the picture came out. You're trending on Twitter. Did you know that?"

Oh God. "No, I didn't, and if we're gaining that much attention, why do I have to meet him again? Have you met him? He's a pig." Siena had a Twitter account, but she rarely used it, and it was the last thing she wanted to check as she thought of the headlines all over the Internet. How could she even ask Cash to deal with something like that? She wasn't sure she would be able to do the same for him.

"A handsome pig. It's not like it's a hardship for you. Spend an hour pretending you're having a good time. Dinner. Later this week."

Siena lowered her feet to the floor and pulled her hair over one shoulder, then ran her fingers through the ends. "Jewel."

"One more date. That's it. One dinner to feed the media."

One dinner. One night. She wanted to refuse so badly she

could hear the word coming from her lips, but she was in this deep. The damage was already done.

"Fine. But this is the last time."

"I'll text you the details. Remember, Siena, keep your eye on the prize."

Unfortunately, Siena was beginning to think that she and Jewel had different ideas of what that prize was. The prize she was thinking of came in an attitude-laden, six-foot-four handsome package of sheer masculinity on the outside and mushy romantic on the inside.

After she ended the call with Jewel, she read the texts that had come in while she'd been talking. Willow's was the first to appear. *You didn't tell me?* Then she read a text from Savannah. *Call me!* And she had a voicemail from her mother. She texted Willow first. *Spur of moment. Will catch up w/u l8r. K?*

Her phone vibrated before she could make a decision about who to call first, Savannah or her mother.

Fine. Just 1 question. Did u spend the night alone? Siena loved Willow, but she wasn't the type of friend she could spill her guts to. Willow loved drama too much, and she had loose lips, and while Siena liked drama, she hated being the center of *this* type of drama. She texted back. *YES! More l8r. Gotta run. Xox.*

She answered a knock at the door, and when she saw the FedEx man through the peephole, it took her a minute to remember that she'd asked Treat for the photos of Savannah. She opened the door, accepted the package, and when she closed the door behind her, she leaned against it, wondering why Cash hadn't texted her. He could be busy. She had no idea what firemen did all day. Surely they couldn't be out rescuing people every minute. She remembered his sooty body, hyped up with adrenaline, pressed against her the evening before, and a shudder ran through her.

Her phone rang, pulling her out of her thoughts. *Savannah.*

"Oh my God. You went out with Gunner Gibson and didn't tell me?"

"I was just about to return your call." Siena sat on the couch and opened the package, smiling as she leafed through the pictures of Savannah.

"How did you even connect with him? He's my friend Aida's client and he's a handful, Siena. You'd be better off with the smart-ass fireman than Gunner."

Siena felt like she and Cash had been together longer than a few days, and it felt weird that Savannah didn't know about them yet. She reminded herself that no one knew about him yet—except her mother. And the guys at the station, according to Cash.

"Yeah, about him…" She bit her lower lip, contemplating what to say about Cash. "I'm actually dating him now."

Savannah laughed. "No way! Jack told me there was something in the way you talked about him that made him think you liked him."

"Really? How could there have been? I didn't even know I liked him in that way." She remembered how Cash had met her at the bottom of the stairs and how her heart had leaped into her throat and the way her body had reacted to being so close to him.

"If you'd seen me when I first met Jack…Oh my God, Siena. He was so abrasive, but there was this underlying current that was too strong to turn away from. You didn't feel any of that with Cash? Because Jack bet me twenty bucks that you'd end up dating him."

"My brother bet on me?" She couldn't imagine Jack doing

that. Building a brick wall between her and any man, she could see, but betting on her? No way.

"He liked him. He said you guys reminded him of me and him. But if you're dating him—"

"Cash."

"Sorry. If you're dating Cash, why were you out with Gunner?"

"It's a long story." *And I can't tell you anyway.* She set the pictures down on the couch. "Are you excited about your bridal shower?"

"Yeah. More about seeing everyone than the actual shower. I'm excited about seeing my dad. I haven't seen him in a few months." The shower was going to be at her father's ranch in Weston, Colorado.

"Well, I can't wait. I'm excited to see everyone, too."

They talked for a few more minutes about the shower, and after ending the call, Siena debated texting Cash. She was torn between calling him and talking about the pictures and texting him and acting as though the meeting with Gunner, and the pictures, never happened. Of course, he might be avoiding her *because* he'd seen the pictures. They were supposed to see each other in a few hours, and she had no idea where they were meeting. The perfect excuse to text. *Only a few hrs until I get 2 see u. Where do u want 2 meet?*

Her stomach fluttered nervously as she waited for him to respond. Ten minutes later she worried he'd seen the pictures and was having second thoughts. She sank down on the couch, let her head fall back, and closed her eyes. When her phone vibrated five minutes later with a text from Cash, she was afraid to read it. She stared at the message indicator, then set the phone in her lap and twisted the ends of her hair. *It's fine. It's fine. It's fine. Just read it.*

She picked the phone back up and held her breath as she read the text. *Ur place? Around 6?*

She should be relieved that it didn't say he couldn't make it. Or to bug off completely because of the pictures, but she wasn't relieved. She had hoped for something more. *Miss you? Can't wait?* Anything to indicate he was glad to be meeting her. *Oh my God, I'm overthinking again. He's a guy. Guys don't do that.* Having eased her mind enough to respond, she texted back. *Perfect. Can't wait.*

Siena called her mother to let her know that she had the pictures from Treat. She'd kept the interior pages of the photo album and her mother had taken the wooden binder home to decorate.

"Hi, Mom. I got the pictures of Savannah."

"Oh, good, honey. I have Jack's right here. I'll have to bring them to you. Oh, dear, I'm not sure when I can get into the city."

"Just FedEx them. That's what Treat did. I'll have them by Tuesday or Wednesday. I can't get out to your house before that anyway."

"Okay, that's smart. I'll do that. How are you otherwise?"

Siena walked to the window and looked outside, wishing she could take back the time she'd spent with Gunner. To the rest of the family it would just look like she'd gone on a date with him, but her mother knew the truth. And so did she, and the truth of it made her stomach feel sick again.

Might as well get it over with. "I guess you saw the pictures?"

"I haven't seen them in print, but I saw them online. It looked like you had a nice time."

That was her mother's way. She wouldn't make Siena feel

bad, and she wouldn't assume anything negative. She'd allow Siena to reveal what she wanted to reveal. The problem was, with her mother she rarely needed to *reveal* anything. Her mother could read her voice better than anyone ever could.

"Not really." Siena turned her back to the window. "He's a dumb, jocky jerk."

Her mother laughed. "The kiss didn't look like you felt that way."

"*Ugh*. I hate this. The whole thing is so ridiculous. It's a ruse, nothing more."

"I suppose, but do you think Cash will see it that way?"

She sighed. "I don't know. I ended up telling him it was a fake date, so you should be glad that I listened to you."

"I'm glad you listened to your heart, or your conscience, whatever drove you to be honest with him instead of leaving him in the dark. You can't build a relationship on legs made of lies."

Siena sighed. She just hoped she had a relationship left to worry about.

Chapter Seventeen

CASH FINISHED PUTTING away the groceries he'd brought for Vetta, then sat on her sofa thinking about his meeting with Regan. He couldn't believe he'd blocked out the very thoughts he'd gotten the tattoo to remember. He looked down at the tattoo and traced the sharp lines, and his mind moved to Samuel and the instant he'd realized that he wasn't going to be able to save him.

He looked at Vetta's bedroom door. She'd excused herself to take care of something, and he could hear her moving around in there. While he waited, his mind drifted back to that awful day. He could almost feel the heat of the flames licking at his back a foot from the entrance to their burning apartment. He'd heard a crack and looked up as a beam, engulfed in flames, came crashing through the ceiling, bringing flaming debris with it, blocking the entrance to the apartment and missing Cash by inches. Someone tugged at his arm, pulling him away from the apartment. He pushed forward, and someone grabbed his other arm. He spun around. *There's a guy in there! I can get him!* Tommy shook his head, shouted something Cash couldn't make out. He pointed to the ceiling. Cash knew the risks. One beam down, flames covering what was left of the ceiling—they had a minute, maybe, before it came tumbling down. He could do it. He could get in there, grab the guy, and get out—but he was being dragged down the stairs. *No! Let me go!* He fought against them. He'd saved the man's wife and she'd pleaded, *My husband. Please, get my husband. He has a weak heart.*

He ran his fingers through his hair with a shaky hand as she made her way across the small apartment. His mind fell back to the fire again.

He'd had to tell Vetta he wasn't able to save her husband, and she had grabbed his arm and held on tight. *I know you did the best you could.* That was the moment things changed in Cash's mind. He could have done more, and he promised himself he would from then on, no matter what the risks were to himself. He had so little to lose compared to some of the other guys.

The pull to continue pushing himself past what was acceptable was so strong it was like another person inhabiting his body. *Keep doing more. For Vetta. For Samuel. For all they lost.* Then his mind returned to Siena, and the guys in his unit, and he fought against that pull with the realization of the risks he was taking—and the danger he posed to the other guys in the unit by his hotshot behavior.

Pride and guilt tangled together.

"Why are you making fists?"

Vetta's worried voice brought his attention back to the present. He hadn't even realized what he was doing, but his fists were clenched so tightly that his knuckles were white.

He sat back, opened and closed his hands, then placed his palms flat on his thighs. "I'm sorry, Vetta. I was thinking about...work." He lifted his eyes to Samuel's picture.

Vetta's eyes remained trained on him. "Yes, I suppose you

were. You always are, aren't you?"

The concern in her voice brought the truth to his lips. "Yes."

Vetta reached for his hand. "Well, then, let's talk about something to unfurl those fists. Tell me about Siena. She seemed like a nice girl. Are you sweet on her?"

Cash almost laughed. *Sweet on her* was an understatement. "You might say that."

"And is she sweet on you?"

Cash felt heat rush up his neck.

"Oh, goodness, I've embarrassed you. I'm sorry. It's none of my business." She set her hands back in her lap and fidgeted with a tissue that she held in one hand.

"No, it's okay. I'm just not used to talking about…" What? Dating? Women? He talked about women all the time with the guys at the station, but usually they were quips, jokes. Siena wasn't a joke, and he'd be damned if he'd let anyone make any more quips about her.

"It's okay. You're a private man, and I respect that. If you'd ever like to bring her by, it's okay with me. I enjoyed seeing you two together. She softens you."

Softens me? "Is that supposed to be a good thing?" *Softens. Sweet. What are these women doing to me?*

"Why don't you ask her that?" she said with a warm smile that left him completely confused.

AN HOUR LATER, Cash was on his way to Siena's apartment. He'd purposely stayed away from magazine stands and avoided looking at the newspaper or Internet, given what she'd said about the possibility of seeing a picture of Gunner kissing her. He'd received a text from Tommy about twenty minutes earlier, which he'd ignored. *Better look at Us Daily before ur date.* Two minutes later, the text was burning a hole in his pocket, so he deleted it. He told Siena he could deal with the situation, but the truth was, he worried that once he saw another man's lips on hers—in a picture that the world would believe meant something more than it did—he wasn't sure how he'd react. Better to ignore the situation until he was forced not to.

She opened the door, and a rush of longing whipped through him. It had been only a day since he'd seen her, but it felt like so much longer as he reached for her.

"How could I have missed you so much?"

Her eyes widened, and her lips curled into a smile as she grabbed the collar of his parka and settled in against him.

"I might have missed you a little, too."

He nuzzled against her cheek. "You smell amazing."

He kissed her cheek, and she turned in to the kiss, sliding her hands up his neck and burying them in his hair. He felt himself getting hard, and with his hands wrapped around her waist, he walked them inside, his lips never leaving hers. He kicked the door closed and told himself to pull away, but that was the last thing he wanted to do. Her sweet curves felt so good against him, and kissing her was like falling into heaven. He never wanted to stop. When she ran her hands beneath his coat and over his shoulders, dropping his coat to his elbows, then pressed her hips against his, he knew they were completely in sync.

"Siena," he whispered between kisses, shrugging out of his coat and catching it in one hand. He drew back, long enough to glance at his coat and remember he should hang it up. He reached behind him and hung it on a hook, then ran his hands through her hair and searched her eyes, just to be sure her desire wasn't all in his mind. She was breathing hard, clinging to his shirt, her heart slamming against his.

"I'm not usually like this," she said.

"I'm not complaining." He pressed a soft kiss to her lips, lingering in the soft pillows of them for a beat before drawing back again and running his hands up along her ribs. God, she drove him crazy.

"I…"

He pressed soft kisses along her collarbone, then licked the indentation in the center.

"Oh God." She closed her eyes as he brought his hands up her body and cupped her breasts, trailing kisses along the curve of her neck. "I…I thought about us all day."

"Me too." Jesus, he had to have more of her. She felt so damn good. He slid his hands down her back and cupped her ass, pulling her against him.

"I was afraid you'd break up with me when you saw the pictures," she said in a heated whisper.

"I didn't look at them."

He took her in a deep, greedy kiss, burying the thoughts of the pictures in their heat as they stumbled toward the bedroom. She moaned into his mouth, a feminine, urgent sound that made his entire body hot. She cupped his balls through his pants, and when his hands pressed against her bare stomach and slid down the front of her jeans, she arched in to him with another wanton moan. Jesus, she was so hot. He buried his fingers inside her and settled his teeth along the silky flesh of her neck, sucking and stroking her with his tongue as she writhed against him.

"Cash," she whispered.

He pulled back and searched her eyes again, making sure he wasn't taking them too far too fast. She locked her eyes on his and reached for the button on his jeans, adeptly releasing him from the tension as they fell open and she drew the zipper down. He brought his mouth to hers and ran his tongue along the swell of her lower lip.

"The bedroom seems very far away," he whispered against her lips.

She slid her hand inside his boxers and wrapped her fingers around his hard length. "Bedrooms are overrated."

She playfully backed him up against the bar that separated the kitchen from the living room and trapped her lower lip between her teeth, looking at him with a mischievous glint in her eyes. He reached for her, and she pushed his hands away and shook her head; then she hooked her fingers into the waistband of his pants and yanked them down, taking his boxers with them. She raised her eyebrows and dragged her hands sensually up his bare thighs.

"Siena..." Her name came out as one long breath as he watched her take him in her hands and lower her mouth around his throbbing erection. "Holy hell, Siena." He buried his hands in her hair. She looked up at him as she licked the length of him, then took him in her mouth again. She clutched his hips and swallowed him deeper, then drew him out slowly. He groaned, trying to keep from coming apart. She was like his every fantasy come true. She took one last lick of the tip as she shimmied her way back up his body, and in one quick move, she took off her shirt and tossed it on the floor, revealing the sexiest lacy bra he'd ever seen. It barely covered her nipples, and pressed her perfect breasts together, creating cleavage so deep he wanted to bury himself in it. Cash reached one hand behind him and ripped his shirt from his body, then pressed her against him.

"You've still got too many clothes on." He grabbed her ass, then sank his teeth into her neck.

She gasped a breath, and he released her and kissed the tender spot. Siena hooked her thumbs into the waist of her jeans and wiggled out of them. *Christ.* She stood before him in a black thong and that damn lacy bra, and he could barely breathe. He stepped from his pants and wrapped his arm around her waist, then backed her up against the counter while running his hands over her hips. He licked along the crest of her breasts, to the deep cleavage in between.

"You can't be this beautiful," he whispered.

She guided his head to her breast, and he licked her through the lacy material, feeling her hard nipple against his tongue. She grabbed his face in her hands and brought his mouth to hers, then kissed him forcefully, sucking his tongue as if she were between his legs again. This time the moan came from his lungs, and when she reached for his hand and pressed it to the damp fabric between her legs, he thought he was going to lose it. She released his tongue, breathing heavily.

"Touch me," she commanded.

Jesus, she was going to drive him right over the edge. "You little sex kitten, you."

"Make me purr."

He unhooked her bra and ripped it off, then took her breast in his mouth, roughly sucking one, then the other as she pressed the back of his head, urging him to take her harder, more aggressively. His hands found her hips, and he lifted her to the counter, searching her eyes, making sure they were still in sync. The smile that curved her lips told him everything he needed to know. He slid his fingers beneath the swatch of fabric that separated them and entered her, then massaged the sensitive nub that had her clawing at his shoulders.

"Lick me." She pushed his head down.

He pulled her panties to the side and licked her slowly at first, then hungrily as she moaned and writhed, burying her fingers in his hair and guiding him to the pace she wanted. He felt her thighs tighten around him and he lifted his head and pulled her mouth to his, kissing her as she rode the wave of her climax, shuddering against him again and again, her insides pulsating around his fingers, her tongue licking her own juices from his. He had to make love to her. He drew back as the tiny pulses against his fingers slowed, and she panted against his chest.

With her palms against his chest, she pushed her head back enough to look him in the eyes. She licked her lips and whispered, "Make love to me."

She gripped his biceps as he lifted her from the edge of the counter and wrapped her legs around his waist, then buried himself inside of her. *Good Christ*, she was so wet and so hot, and the way she moved, clutching his arms for support, drawing herself up along his entire length, then burying him again, drove him closer to the edge. Then she was coming apart again, clawing at his shoulders and whimpering against his cheek. As much as he wanted to let himself go, he wanted to love her properly—in a bed, feeling her luscious curves beneath him. Still buried deep, he carried her into the bedroom, lowered her onto the bed, and made sweet love to her, slowly and lovingly.

Caressing, tasting, touching every inch of Siena's flesh and bringing her over the edge two more times before finally allowing himself to find his own earth-shattering release.

Chapter Eighteen

SIENA ZIPPED HER jeans and pulled a long-sleeve shirt over her head, listening to Cash in the bathroom, drying off from the bath they'd just shared.

"I'm not usually the type of guy who'll let you take advantage of him without at least taking me on a date, so don't think I'm just here for the taking whenever you want," he called into the bedroom.

Siena peeked her head in the bathroom. "That's what they all say."

He tied the towel around his waist and grabbed another one, then chased her around the bedroom, flicking her with it. "Oh yeah? So this is how you treat all your dates?" He paused. "Wait. Don't answer that."

"I'll never tell."

She laughed as she dodged the flick of the towel and jumped onto the bed. He threw the towel and tackled her, pinning her to the mattress as she giggled and wiggled beneath him.

"Careful wiggling like that. You might get me all hot and bothered again."

She whipped the towel from around his waist with a burst of laughter, and he trapped her laughter in a sensuous kiss.

"Now look what you've done." He shifted his eyes to his erection.

"Yeah, well, you'll have to wait. I'm hungry." She pushed him onto his side and wiggled her eyebrows. When she saw his eyes narrow, then widen with understanding, she whispered, "Whoa, dirty boy. I meant for real food." She flipped her hair over her shoulder as she rose to her feet. She felt his hands encircle her waist as he tugged her back down to the bed.

"You think you're so funny." He pressed a kiss to her lips and smiled down at her.

"Well, not *so* funny, but clever," she teased.

"Okay, I'll give you that."

The way he was looking at her, like he felt the same rush of emotions she'd felt from the moment she opened the door, stole her next breath. She ran her finger along the line of his jaw, unable to find the right words for what she was feeling. *I love being with you. I wish you were always right here. Don't move. Let's just stay here forever.*

"What?" He searched her eyes.

She shook her head, still unable to voice what she felt.

He kissed her, a soft, tender press of his lips that asked for nothing more. "I'm going to get dressed so you don't get any other dirty ideas."

She watched him move around the bed and leave the room to retrieve his clothes. Her heart squeezed in her chest. She'd never been so forward with a man before, and with Cash she had no hesitation. She had been ready for a nice night out, maybe to catch a movie or take a walk, but the minute she'd seen his smile and locked eyes with him, her need to be close to him was greater than any other need she'd ever felt.

He came back into the bedroom fully dressed, running his

hand through his hair; then he picked up the two towels and took them into the bathroom. When he returned to the bedroom, she noticed how comfortable he appeared, like he lived there, and she liked it. His cell phone vibrated, and he didn't reach for it.

"Aren't you going to check it?" Siena rose to her feet, and he took her hand as they walked out of the bedroom.

"You're right here. Who else is important enough to interrupt our date?"

"I don't mind. What if it's Vetta? Or work?"

"I have a special ringtone for work. I guess it could be Vetta, but I visited her before I came here. She asked me if I was sweet on you."

Siena laughed and put her hands on his hips. "Are you?"

"Maybe a little." He kissed the tip of her nose. "She also said you soften me, whatever that means."

"Did she?" Siena pulled on a pair of leather boots, proud that Vetta had attributed a change in Cash to her being in his life. "I think I just bring out the softy that's always buried deep inside you."

"No man wants the word *softy* linked to his name." He shook his head.

"Okay," she whispered. "I won't say it too loudly. What did you have planned for our date?"

"It's a surprise." He crossed his arms.

"I love surprises."

"I never realized I did until tonight." He took her in his arms and narrowed his eyes. "Everything you do surprises me."

"I'm going to hope that's a good thing."

"It is." He glanced around her loft.

Siena followed his gaze from the large windows to the substantial wooden dining room table pushed off to the side, across the floor to the kitchen, the bedroom, then back down the other wall.

"What?" she asked.

He shook his head. "Nothing. I hadn't really taken in your place before. It's very open, clean. The exposed brick walls are cool, and the wide-planked floors are great. I don't think I've been in an apartment without walls before."

"It has walls." She pointed to the bedroom. "There's a wall between the kitchen and the bedroom, and the bathroom of course."

"I meant other walls. Most apartments have the rooms separated. You know, a kitchen, a living room, a dining room." He grabbed her coat from a hook on the wall and helped Siena into it.

"Yeah. I hate that. I like to see everything. When my family is over, we're always moving between the kitchen and the table, and someone's always sitting on the couch being lazy, and I like knowing I can see all of them at once."

"I would have figured you for a wall girl."

"Why?" She watched him put on his coat, which made him look even more muscular than he was. She felt her belly flutter when he reached for her hand.

"Because you were pretty protective of yourself when we first met. You had a pretty thick wall around you."

"I did? Gosh, I think of myself as a pretty open person." *Did I have a wall around me?* "You weren't exactly Mr. Open yourself."

"Yeah. I know." He pressed her hand to his lips. "But you make all my walls crumble."

"I'm not sure I ever knew I had walls around me until you

said that. Do you still feel like I have walls around me?" She made a mental note to ask Willow about that.

He pulled her close and smiled down at her. "Your walls didn't stand a chance against my charm."

She saw the tease in his smile, but the shiver that ran through her told her he was absolutely right. He might be too gruff for some women, but for Siena, he was just perfect.

"Now I have the very important job of making sure I'm worthy of your openness."

"The first part, that was cute. Let's not lay it on too thick." She grabbed her purse, catching a glimpse of the magazines on the coffee table. "Speaking of walls and worthy, you really didn't see the pictures from the bookstore?"

The tease in his eyes disappeared as quickly as the question left her lips. "No."

"I think you should see them. I don't want there to be anything weird between us, and seeing the pictures of me and Gunner for the first time when we're out together would definitely be weird."

He shoved his hands in his coat pockets. "I didn't look at them because I don't really know how I'll feel when I see them."

"At least you're honest." She laced her fingers with his and looked into his eyes, recognizing the worried shadow in them. "We just made incredible love, and you're the first man I've ever shared a bath with." She stood on her tiptoes and kissed his chin. "Whatever you feel when you see the pictures, at least you'll know those things." She pulled him toward the couch and pushed him down to a sitting position, then sat on his lap and leaned her forehead against his. "I hate that I had to meet him at all, and I hate that you have to see these. But it's better that we face them together than try to pretend they're not out there." *And I hate even more that I have to see him again.*

NO PART OF Cash wanted to see those pictures. He didn't have underlying curiosity about Siena and Gunner's meeting or feel the need to know what the world had seen that he hadn't. If he could ignore the fact that they were photographed together forever, it would make his life much easier. But he knew what he was in for. The guys at the firehouse had all seen the photos. After receiving Tommy's text, he was certain of that—and knew they'd razz the hell out of him. Cash rubbed the tattoo on his arm and felt a stab of pain that came with the memory of Chuck. He closed his eyes for a beat to center his mind and move past the ache of it. *Better to be prepared than blindsided.*

"All right, but no promises." He tucked a lock of hair behind Siena's ear, feeling so many contrasting emotions. His pulse was ratcheting up by the second. He felt closer to her than he ever had another woman, and somewhere inside his head, even though he knew it wasn't fair, he was hurt that she'd gone out with Gunner. They hadn't been dating when she'd agreed to the meeting, and hell if he didn't know that, but still…The hurt lay in wait, and he hoped to hell it wouldn't claw its way out.

"Here's the deal, babe. I could get pissed, and I might not want to go out after seeing them."

Her brows knitted together, and her beautiful lips pressed together as she nodded, as if she understood. "Okay," she whispered. "I understand. I still think it's better that we do this together."

She placed her palms on his cheeks and kissed him gently;

then she drew in a deep breath and reached for the magazines. "Ready?"

He shrugged. "No, but…"

"Okay. Here you go. This is the worst, because it's on the front page."

She held the magazine against her chest and searched his eyes. A shadow of fear washed through her eyes as she lowered the magazine.

With one large palm, Cash pushed it back against her chest. "Are you sure you want to do this? I'm fine with pretending they don't exist. More than fine with it." *Sort of. Shit, I have no idea if I'm fine with it or not.*

She nodded. "I would rather you've seen them. I'm sure someone will say something to you at some point, and it's better that you've seen them with me." She lowered the stack of magazines again, quickly flipped them around, and clenched her eyes shut.

The first glance sent a shudder of anger through him. One sweep of the cover. Gunner's hands were embracing each of her arms, their heads tilted, people behind them looking on. It was enough to make him want to stand up and walk out the door. He gritted his teeth so tightly that his gums ached. After the three-second sweep, he lifted his gaze to Siena, whose eyes were still clenched shut, and his anger softened just a little. She was right there with him, making them face the pictures together, and if the way she'd loved his body didn't already tell, that courage spoke volumes about what she felt for him.

He kept his eyes trained on her as he took the magazine from her hands. She opened her eyes and they found his, searching them for a response. He reached up and cupped her cheek.

"You know, if you were a stripper, I wouldn't have to deal with these types of things. I'd just have to stay out of strip joints and pretend you were a waitress." His attempt at levity didn't lessen the impact of the picture or the worry in her eyes.

"If I were a stripper, I wouldn't last a day. My father would drag me to a military academy. Then he and Jack would go kill anyone who had seen me, just for good measure."

She smiled, but it was forced, and Cash knew he had to take a better look and deal with what was right before them—and between them.

He dropped his eyes to the picture, and this time, he forced himself to study it, the way he had studied the pictures on the Internet, from a detached view. There wasn't a chance in hell that he was going to be able to separate himself from the pictures. He had no choice but to look at the pictures through *boyfriend* eyes. He trained his eyes on Gunner and avoided looking directly at Siena's image. Gunner was handsome, and in the picture—photoshopped or not, Cash didn't know or care— he looked bigger than life and like he was enjoying the kiss far too much. His grip on her arms was tight, his lips slightly open, his eyes closed. Cash narrowed his eyes, searing the image into his mind, feeding his hatred of the man. He felt Siena's hand on his forearm, but he couldn't meet her eyes. Not yet. He shifted his gaze to the image of her and quickly scanned it from head to toe, then tore his eyes away, closed them for a beat, and drew them back. Her fingers were splayed, not touching his body, but an inch from his side. There were inches between their torsos, as if she were pulling back as he was pushing forward. Cash glanced up at Siena, saw that the worry in her eyes had spread, bringing tension to her jaw and forehead. He dropped his gaze again, and he forced himself to look at her face. Really look. He saw the same tension in the line of her jaw. He was avoiding looking at the one thing that would tell him her true feelings. Her eyes. He'd been able to sweep past them, and now, as he allowed himself to focus on them, he realized they were open, her brows knitted together, much like they were now. He breathed a sigh of relief and closed his eyes for a second again, envisioning Siena's face when they kissed. Her eyes always fluttered closed; her sensuous lips were soft and tender, and her cheeks—he loved touching her beautiful cheeks—held no tension. They were relaxed, drinking in the kiss as much as he was.

When he opened his eyes, Siena still had a pinched look on her face. He felt a smile form on his lips, and as he reached for her with two hands, the magazines tumbled to the couch.

"Okay," was all he could manage to say. He took her face in his hands and brought her lips to his, and in that moment, as he felt the tension release not just from her mouth and jaw, but from the rest of her body as she melted into him, it was better than okay. The surety of them was perfect.

"Okay? So, you're not upset?"

"Jealous, maybe." He picked up the magazine again and pointed to her face. "See your face? I read all sorts of discomfort there. And when we kiss, unless I'm totally reading you wrong—and I could be; I'm no expert on women. When we kiss, you're fifty shades of comfortable."

She threw her arms around his neck. "Oh, thank goodness! I hated kissing him. I can't believe you can see that. I kinda hope the world can."

"No, you don't. That would defeat the purpose of the pictures." He patted her hip. "Come on. Let's go do something fun." They stood, and he handed Siena her purse.

"Don't you want to see the others?"

"Nope. You said that was the worst of them. I survived it. That's enough torture for one night." *For a lifetime.* "I'm glad it's done. There aren't going to be more surprises like that, are there?"

"What do you mean?"

"Dates with Gunner? Or anyone else? I mean, I know you agreed to meet him before we started dating, and you've fulfilled that commitment. So now you're all mine?" He pulled her close and felt her pull back. *Aw, shit.*

"Cash…"

"You're kidding, right?"

"Jewel said I had to meet him one more time, just to solidify it in the press. Then that's it. I told her I wouldn't do it again after that. We've come this far. It's one more time. That's it. No more. I promise."

Cash ran his hand through his hair and turned his back to her, trying to weed through his tangled thoughts. *Once more. It's her career. Shit, this sucks.* Anger brewed in his gut, but as he turned back to her and she reached for him, looking up with those trusting baby blues, full of worry, he wrapped his arms around her and tethered his anger.

"We can handle one more media splash." He rested his forehead on hers. "I wasn't ever a jealous guy until you came along. You're killing me in all sorts of ways."

"No. I'm making parts of you that you never knew existed come alive."

Chapter Nineteen

THE POET HOUSE was dimly lit with at least three dozen small tables squeezed so close together there was barely enough room to walk between them. Cash had always wondered what it would be like to listen to poets read their work, but since it wasn't the manliest thing to do, he'd never admitted it or taken the time to check it out. The women he'd dated in the past were all about the fast lane—loud bars and quick lays—which had suited him just fine because he knew they weren't right for him in the long run. Siena was more grounded than them. He could tell how important her family was to her, and her career. She wasn't a kid playing at the dating world. She was an adult living her life and doing all she could to make her mark in the world. He respected her. Hell, who was he kidding? He was falling for everything about her.

Siena leaned forward, completely focused on the poet and what he was reading. Her eyes widened; then her brows drew together with each passage, and when he finished, she placed her hand over her heart and sighed with a dreamy look in her eyes.

"That was so moving."

Cash had been so focused on her, he'd missed the last of the poetry reading. But watching Siena's facial expressions and the way even her breathing became lighter, as if she didn't want to breathe too hard or too loud for fear of missing a word, moved Cash.

"Yes, it was." He reached for her hand as her phone vibrated.

"Oh, gosh. I thought I turned that off. I'm sorry."

"It's okay. You can check it."

She pulled out her phone, mumbling as she scrolled to the text. "It's rude. I'm sorry." After reading the text, she shot a look at Cash.

"Everything okay?"

She texted back, then turned her phone off and shoved it in her purse. "Yeah. It was Jewel."

His stomach clenched.

"I have to meet him for dinner this week." She fiddled with the ends of her hair. "I'm sorry, Cash."

He forced himself to unclench his jaw and be civil, even though his gut was on fire. He shrugged. "It's one dinner. I can deal with it."

"You know I'd rather not go."

"True, but that doesn't change the fact that it sucks." He held her stare, trying to convince himself to ignore the anger, but as soon as that crossed his mind, he knew it wasn't anger at all. It was the green-eyed monster twisting his gut and pushing anger into his tone. "It's not the pictures that bother me. It's knowing there's some other guy who's going to touch you, kiss you, and…"

"But you knew that kiss wasn't real. You saw it on my face."

"Yeah. I did." He leaned back in his chair and looked around at the other couples, wondering how many of them had to deal with this type of shit. *None of them, of course.*

"I'm sorry. Last time. I promise."

It was all he could do to nod in acceptance.

THEY WALKED BACK to Siena's loft hand in hand. She could feel tension in his hand and she could see it in the lines that snaked their way across his forehead.

"Should we talk about it?" she asked.

He smiled down at her, a tense smile that didn't reach his eyes. "No. I'll get over it in a few minutes."

"You sure?"

"Yeah." They passed the bench near the café where they bought hot chocolate when he brought her home after the photo shoot. "Let's sit down for a few minutes."

She watched him draw in a deep breath of the crisp night air. She wore the gloves and scarf he'd given her, and she fidgeted with the edges of the scarf beside him.

"I'm not mad, you know."

"What are you?"

He lifted her chin so their eyes met. "Babe, how would you feel if I told you that Tommy set me up with his cousin and I had to go because she was family?"

She stopped fidgeting and put her hand on his thigh. "Did he? I thought we decided to be exclusive."

He laughed softly. "Yeah, so did I."

His brows lifted and his meaning became clear. "I'd hate it. But Gunner is work for me, not a date."

He shrugged again. "And mine's a familial commitment, not a date."

"Cash, are you telling me you're going on a date with someone else?" She sat back against the bench, her heart aching with the thought.

"I'm asking how you'd feel." He turned his body toward her and draped his arm across the back of the bench.

"I would be hurt. I wouldn't like it."

He lifted her chin again, and without anger, without accusation, he said, "Me too."

Shit, shit, shit. "But this is work. You know he's not someone I even *want* to spend time with."

"Babe, I know all of that. I'm just being honest with you." His eyes held steady. "Can I deal with it? For you? Yeah, I can deal with another date with Gunner. Do I want to? Hell no. But I will. I just want you to understand how it feels from my side."

She couldn't pull her eyes from his. She loved his honesty, and with every word, she hated herself a little more for what she'd agreed to do, and she owed him the same honesty.

"You're stronger than me, Cash. I don't think I could take you going out with someone else. It would hurt too much, even though we've only just begun seeing each other. It would be too painful."

"Then it's a good thing I'm as loyal as a retriever." He leaned forward, pressed his cheek to hers, and whispered, "And I'm falling hard for you, so if you're going to toss me aside, please drop the leash fast."

Her hands stilled. "Who are you kidding? I'm holding on to the leash with both hands."

Chapter Twenty

WAKING UP IN Cash's arms was the best feeling in the world. When they'd returned to her loft last night, they'd watched *P.S. I Love You*, and Siena swore Cash's eyes were damp, though he vehemently denied it. Neither one had wanted to be apart, and having Cash spend the night felt natural. Now, as sunlight brought in the promise of a glorious day, and he wrapped his arm around her and pulled her close, she wished they could stay in bed all day.

"Did you sleep okay?" Cash kissed the top of her head, which was all he could reach because Siena's arm and leg had him trapped.

"Better than okay."

"You didn't mind me taking up your entire bed?"

She moved up his chest so they were eye to eye. "I was just trying to figure out how I could skip my photo shoot and keep you here all day."

"As much as I would love that…And trust me, I would…" He grabbed a handful of her ass. "If you start canceling photo shoots, Jewel will have you dating the whole football team. Besides, I've got to finish Vetta's album, and I'm on duty for the next forty-eight hours after tonight, so I want to get a few things done."

"Forty-eight hours? That's a long shift, but the timing is perfect. Why don't we get together after my shoot, if you're free, of course?"

"I'll check my very busy calendar."

She ran her finger down his chest and felt his muscles jump. "Bring your stuff and spend the night."

"Careful. You'll get sick of having me at your beck and call."

He sat up, and she tossed the covers aside, loving the desire that filled his eyes as he raked them down her naked body and the way his body became instantly aroused. A rush of heat coursed through her, driving her to straddle him. His hands found her hips and expertly guided her over his erection, then buried it deep inside her.

"I love having you at my beck and call," she whispered as she kissed the sensitive skin beneath his earlobe.

Cash groaned with need. His hands tightened on her hips, moving her in pace to his efforts before lowering his mouth to her breast. She loved the way he touched her, with just the right mix of lust and something more. When he shifted positions and rolled her beneath him, then drove into her hard and fast, a thrill ran through her entire body. He kept up the quick, hard pace, causing every sense to heighten and every nerve to burn with desire. Moments later, her eyes slammed shut as an orgasm ripped through her, so strong she could barely breathe, couldn't hear past her own passionate cries. She felt Cash's muscles harden beneath her hands as he followed her up and over the peak of his own intense release, panting, gripped every few seconds with powerful aftershocks that rocked his entire body.

It took a minute for them to realize that his phone was ringing in the other room. His eyes flew open.

"Shit. That's the station."

He flew from the bed and ran into the other room buck-naked. She pulled the sheet over her chest and listened.

"Got it. Okay. Yes, sir."

Cash came back into the bedroom and went directly into the bathroom, where she heard him washing up. "Sorry, Siena. I gotta fly. There's a two-alarm, and everyone's been called in." His eyes were intense, calculating, as he hopped on one foot, tugging his jeans on, then pulled his shirt over his head. "Text me. I'll come over tonight."

"Be careful." She'd never seen him move so fast, and his intensity frightened her. He was literally going to walk into a fire. *Oh God, he could die.* His job hadn't felt real until that moment. Even when she saw him with soot all over his body, he hadn't been flushed with adrenaline, preparing to go into a fire. She wanted to cling to him and plead with him to be careful, maybe even not go. No. She would never ask that. She wasn't that selfish. But she couldn't keep her thoughts completely trapped inside her.

"Cash," she said a little breathlessly, "I'm counting on you to come back."

He leaned over the bed and kissed her—a quick peck. "Love you, babe. You can always count on me."

She didn't think he realized what he said. His eyes darted frantically around the room as he shoved his feet into his socks, then hurried into the living room. She threw on a T-shirt and followed him out.

He opened the door and pulled her into another quick kiss. "Don't look so shocked. I told you I was falling for you. Gotta go." He pulled the door shut behind him, leaving her stunned, frightened…and happy.

TWO ENGINES WERE on the scene when Cash arrived at the fire. He'd seen the billowing black smoke from several blocks away, and his mind instantly flashed to Chuck and Samuel—and then to the look in Siena's eyes when she'd said she was counting on him to come back.

Chief Weber brought him up to speed. "You're with Mike and, Cash, I'm not fucking around. This is a big one. Another engine is on its way. We need you focused. Don't pull any shit and risk our men's lives."

Cash thought of Siena waiting for him that evening and his talk with Regan. "Got it, Chief."

Chief Weber grabbed his arm. "Cash, don't fuck this up."

It wasn't a threat. It was an ultimatum, and Cash read it loud and clear. "I got this, Chief." He pulled his arm from his grasp and slapped Mike on the back. "Let's go." As they headed toward the entrance, Cash had a million things going through his mind. *Thank God it's a warehouse and not an apartment building. Don't fuck this up. Siena's waiting for me. I have something to lose.*

It was a fast-moving two-alarm fire, and it ripped through the two-story warehouse at record speed, burning everything in its path. The warehouse was filled with building materials, making their jobs even more dangerous. Dozens of firefighters fought the blaze from every angle with crews inside, crews on ladders outside putting out the flames from above, and entering the second floor through the windows. Cash heard a loud crack before he realized where it had come from. The ceiling crashed, sending three firefighters down to the first floor, flames coming at them fast. In the blink of an eye, he and Mike were there, carrying the guys to safety. They were blinded by the dense smoke and made their way out by following the path they'd memorized on the way in and the shouts of the team at the entrance. Cash ran back toward the building, coughing, having trouble breathing. He fought the idea of putting on the goddamn breathing apparatus with all he was worth. The chief's voice ran through his mind: *Don't fuck this up.* It was followed by Siena's: *I'm counting on you to come back.* With that thought, he pulled on his goddamn breathing pack and headed back into the fire.

It took more than two hours for them to extinguish the blaze. Cash stood beside Tommy, looking at the burned warehouse, their bodies black with soot and covered with sweat. He was still riding the adrenaline rush.

"Mike said you used your breather." Tommy wiped his forehead with his forearm.

Cash looked down and realized he was rubbing the tattoo on his arm. "Yup."

Tommy nodded. "That's good, Cash. I'm proud of you."

Cash slid him a look that said, *Proud of me? Shut the hell up.*

Tommy draped his arm around his shoulder and said, "You shut the hell up. I was sure this would be your last fire."

Cash elbowed him in the ribs, and Tommy dodged it with a laugh.

"What? You can be a stubborn ass when you want to."

"And that's a bad thing?" Cash climbed onto the truck and sighed when he sat down.

"Only when it can cost you your job." Tommy stared at him so long Cash felt a path burning between them.

"What?"

"I just want to know. Was it Regan, the chief, or Siena who finally got to you?"

"Why do you care?" Cash pulled out his phone.

"Well, the way I see it, if it was Regan or the chief, then it may not be a permanent change. You know, make little changes to keep your job, but in a week you might be back to barely breathing and hotdogging it. But if it's Siena, that's a whole different ball game."

He looked at his phone and was surprised to see a text from his brother Duke. *U at that fire?* He should have figured that after telling Duke what he was going through, he'd be on his case. He'd always looked after Cash, and Cash knew he always would. He texted back. *Yeah, and I used the fucking mask, so u can go back 2 work now.*

He texted Siena before responding to Tommy. *Just wanted 2 let u know I'm fine.*

Tommy's blue eyes were locked on him, and he knew he wouldn't get away without answering. He shrugged. "Some of each, I guess."

Tommy shook his head and grinned. "You're an ass, you know that?"

He laughed and read Siena's response. *Whew. I was worried. My place? 5?*

He wondered what was going through her mind right then. He hadn't planned on saying what he had before he'd left, but once the words were said, he knew they were true. Siena had been shocked, and he figured that shock would do one of two things as it simmered through the afternoon. It'd boil to full-blown fear and she'd put space between them, or it would make them even closer. Either way, he wasn't upset with himself for saying that he loved her. He did, and *that* was what drove him to put on the fucking mask.

Chapter Twenty-One

THE WIND BLEW Siena's hair across her face, and she fought the urge to cringe as it sliced into her bare legs. Photographers loved making contradictory statements with their pictures. Featuring girls in bikinis while lying on ice or women wearing summer outfits in the middle of a snowstorm. She'd been standing in the middle of some rich guy's yard for two hours already, wearing lingerie with high heels, the wind whipping against her flesh, wishing her body would go numb, but it refused. It didn't help that all she had been able to think about all day was Cash telling her he loved her and then running into a fire.

"Lovely, Siena. That's perfect." Henri Carpa was a heavyset man with a full beard, and one of the leading photographers in the industry. "Now, we're going to take a few more shots with the bushes in the background."

It was an honor to be chosen for the shoot, but that didn't stop Siena from hating Henri just a little each time the wind blew. They finally brought out the male model, Rodelpho Morenz. He moved with powerful grace across the lawn in his thick white robe. Siena had worked with him before, and with his high cheekbones and deep-set, piercing blue eyes that were every bit as electric as hers, he was devastatingly handsome. His dark hair was slicked back from his face, which made him look like a Greek god, and if that wasn't enough, when he dropped the robe from his shoulders, into the hands of an assistant, every muscle on his body looked as though it had been painted on. She watched him come closer, knowing she'd be pressed against his body in all sorts of compromising positions, which would thankfully bring warmth to her freezing limbs. She also knew that all those delicious looks fell to pieces the minute he opened his mouth, because Rodelpho had been blessed with a higher-pitched voice than most women Siena knew. The first time they'd worked together she couldn't get past the distraction of it. Now his voice was just part of the total package that was Rodelpho. He was a nice man, and at the moment, a welcome means for heat.

"Nice to see you again, Siena." He air-kissed her cheeks.

While on shoots, Siena and the other models were hypervigilant about makeup and hair, as messing with either could add significant time to the shoot.

"Hi, Rod." She tried to keep her teeth from chattering. "I'm glad you're here."

"Really? I figured it was just the tundra-like weather." He glanced at her breasts and winked.

Same old Rod. Their playful banter had begun during their first shoot, and now, three years later, it was still one of the things she enjoyed most about working with him. Though he was attractive, Siena had never been sexually attracted to him. In fact, she hadn't been sexually attracted to any of the models she worked with. As she analyzed that thought and her mind drifted to Cash, she realized that maybe it wasn't just male models she wasn't attracted to. It was all men who cared too much about what they looked like, or lived as if they did. It struck her as an odd thought for a model to have about other models. Even so, it was the truth of the matter. She eyed Rod as the makeup artist touched up his brows. Sure, he was well built, handsome, nearly perfect, if judged by looks alone. Cash was rugged, heavily built, virile, and red-blooded brave. He was handsome, but he was so much more. He was caring, tender, romantic, and without a doubt, strong willed. Cash was perfect inside and out, and she couldn't wait to be back in his arms again.

The photo shoot ran late, and she texted Cash from the cab on the way to her loft.

Shoot ran late. I'll be there by 5:20. Sorry! Xox.

She thought about those three little letters. *Xox.* Kisses and hugs, and it brought back the chill that ran though her when Cash had said he loved her. She wondered if things would be weird between them now. She hadn't said it back, and she definitely felt her heart wrapping itself around him, but she didn't want to be one of those girls who claimed their love because their boyfriend did. She wanted to say it when it felt right, and she made a promise to herself that that was exactly what she'd do.

Her phone vibrated with a text from Cash. *No worries. I'm here.* She loved knowing he was going to be there when she got home. Oh God, she loved so much about him. But it was all so fast—and that scared her as much as it excited her. Her phone vibrated again, this time with a text from Willow.

Girl, u r all over the press.

Her stomach tightened as she texted back, wishing she could tell Willow the truth.

I saw.

She hoped that short answer would nip the conversation in the bud.

Her phone vibrated again a second later with Willow's response. *Gotta get me a newsworthy date!*

Siena laughed, wishing she could text, *You can have Gunner!* Instead she texted, *You won't have 2 look long. Guys kill 2 go out w/you. Ur gorgeous!*

Willow's response brought another laugh. *I know.* Siena didn't respond. She had forgotten her gloves. She was freezing, her muscles ached, and she was dying to see Cash. She didn't want to be distracted by her cell phone. As she paid the cabbie, Cash met her in front of her apartment building with a black backpack over his left shoulder, his arms open wide, and a to-go cup in each hand.

Perfect. Inside and out.

Chapter Twenty-Two

CASH FOLDED SIENA into his arms. "How'd you make out?"

She looked up at him and laughed. "Man, I knew I forgot to do something. I didn't realize I was supposed to make out. I was saving all my kisses for you." She pulled out of his arms. "Let me just grab a cab and I'll go back to Rod."

"Get over here." He hooked an arm around her shoulder and pulled her back to him, then trapped her laugh with his lips and kissed her hard. He deepened the kiss as she pressed her body to his. When their lips parted, she was breathing heavily.

"Wow." She blinked up at him.

"Just a little reminder of what's waiting at home for you." He handed her a cup, and she could smell warm cocoa in the steam. "I figured you'd be cold." He touched her bare fingers. "Seeing how you're not the best at being prepared."

"Do you mind?" she asked as they walked inside and took the elevator upstairs. "I'm still riding the high of that kiss. Don't shoot me down so quickly."

"It's not your fault. I should have reminded you before I ran out." He held her cup while she opened the door to her loft.

"I'm a big girl. I should remember."

"Yeah, I'm thinking that's a long shot. Even I need reminders about stuff sometimes." *Like not to take risks that endanger my fellow firefighters. Or myself.*

After hanging up their coats and finishing their hot chocolate, Siena motioned toward the bedroom and said, "Do you mind if I put on something comfier?"

"Okay, but I'm not really in the mood. I like a little foreplay first," Cash teased as she walked into her closet. She came out in a pair of sweatpants, thick, fuzzy slippers, and a sweatshirt, looking all kinds of adorable. "Now, that is *hot*."

"You dirty boy. I was freezing," she said with her pouty lower lip sticking out.

She cuddled against him and he had to kiss her again.

"We'd better get out of this particular room, or my mind isn't going to think you're just adorable. It's going to wander to what you have on under there." They walked hand in hand past the kitchen counter, and Cash said, "Keep on moving, because that counter holds dangerous memories."

She laughed. "The couch is pretty safe."

"For now."

Siena sat on the couch, her back against the armrest, her knees pulled up to her chest.

"Let me grab you a blanket. Where do you keep throw blankets?" He looked around the sparse living room.

"Do guys even know about *throw* blankets?" She pointed to the closet by the door. "Up top, in there."

"Throw blankets? My mom has one draped over every couch and chair in the house, and she had them in each of our bedrooms when we were growing up. We were like the throw blanket family." He covered her with a chenille blanket and lifted her feet onto his lap.

"Want some wine? My brother Kurt gave me a nice bottle a few months ago, and I almost forgot about it until just now." She moved to stand, and Cash put his hand on her leg.

"I'll get it. Relax. Just tell me where it is." He found the bottle on a wine rack he had somehow overlooked near the kitchen, and he poured them each a glass, then carried the bottle and the glasses to the coffee table. "I'm taking mental notes. Screaming orgasms when you're flirty, wine when you're cold."

She smiled as she took the glass. "How do you know it's not screaming orgasms when I'm flirty and wine when I'm a sure thing?"

"I didn't, but I'm making another note." He lifted her feet onto his lap again and rubbed her foot as they talked. "Tell me about your shoot."

She rolled her eyes. "It was so cold. We were shooting lingerie outside, and I swear, I've never been so cold in my life."

"Were there pink panties involved?" He arched a brow.

She pushed his stomach with her foot. "I don't get to choose my shoots. No pink panties. Black and cream lingerie. I'll model it for you later if you want." She wiggled her eyebrows.

"Now I understand the perks of dating a model." He leaned in for another kiss. "I might just take you up on that."

"You'll love this. The guy I modeled with is really hot, but he—"

He held his palm up. "Stop. Please. Don't overestimate my ability to deal with this stuff."

She smacked his arm. "Really? If you're going to date me, you have to be able to deal with all of my career, not just the parts you want to know about. The same way that I have to deal with knowing you could die in a fire, or that you probably get hit on by a zillion women because you're a fireman. And when that calendar comes out, there'll be women all over New York doing God knows what to your picture."

He moved closer to her. "Is that jealousy I hear? Does the green-eyed monster live somewhere in that beautiful body of yours? I don't believe it."

Siena crossed her arms. "I am only human. Just like you. And don't change the subject. This is about you accepting my job."

"You're right. But do I have to hear about the hot guys? Couldn't you lie to me and say they're ugly?"

"You're such a pain. I was going to say his voice was higher than mine, and no, I won't lie. If you love me…" She narrowed her eyes and held his stare. "Then you have to trust me. I should be able to say anything to you without fear of you being jealous."

"Oh, I do love you. More with each frustrating second." He rose from the couch and paced.

"Wait. You love me, but you're leaving?"

He returned to her side and crouched beside her. "I'm not leaving. I was pacing. Baby, I have no doubt that what I feel for you is love." He could see her holding her breath, waiting for the *but*. "Breathe, baby."

She let out a breath. "Sorry. You love me?"

"I do. It's fast, and I don't expect you to miraculously say it back. But you know, life goes by quickly, and when I felt it, I said it. When I walked out that door, I was glad I did. I wanted you to know—just in case."

"Just in case…you didn't come back?"

"Fires are dangerous. But what we were just talking about, love, jealousy, that's really important."

"More important than you getting killed in a fire? Cash, that's pretty important."

"It is, and we can fret over it some other time, but right now we need to talk about that other stuff. Baby, if you think any man can handle hearing about the woman they love being in a half-naked man's arms—a man she describes as *hot*—and not be jealous, you're way off base. Part of loving someone is caring enough about them to not want them to be with someone else. It's not rational. Hell, it might not even be fair, but just as I have to accept hearing about hot guys, you'll have to accept hearing that I'm jealous. It doesn't have to break us up. I won't tell you not to model or not to be in pink panty shoots, but when you tell me the guys are hot, give me the space to cringe and take my ego slap. Hell, you'd be wise to throw in a compliment here or there about how I'm handsome too. That would buy you big bonus points."

"So, what kind of jealous are we talking about? Are you going to get angry every time I have a shoot?"

"Did I get angry tonight?"

"No."

"Of course not. I'm not a kid. I might even think awful things in my head about how the hot guys are really assholes. But I'll never try to control your modeling career." He went to sit down on the couch and stopped himself. "Wait. That's not exactly true. If you continue to date guys for press, that would probably piss me off enough to reconsider if we're really right for each other."

"I told you I'm only going out this last time with Gunner."

"I know. I'm cool with that. I meant, like, if three months from now you said you had to do it again. In my book, if we're an exclusive couple, that crosses a line. Job or no job."

She moved her feet so he could sit down and he pulled them back onto his lap. Her legs were tense, rigid.

"Siena, all you have to do is turn these situations around. Suppose I came home and said, *Hey, we rescued this hot woman today. I had to give her mouth-to-mouth and—*"

"Okay, okay. I get it." She shook her head. "I would like it better if you left off the *hot* part."

"Exactly." He took her hand in his. "Babe, your career will bring you into contact with some of the most beautiful, wealthiest guys around. I'm secure in who I am, and I know what I do and what I don't have to offer. But let's not pretend that it won't be hard sometimes. I don't wear my emotions on my sleeve for many people, but you see right through me. If I'm jealous, I have to be able to say, *Hey, babe. This is a tough one. Give me a sec.*"

"Okay, that's fair."

"And don't pretend that there won't be times you feel the same way. No matter how beautiful you are, I think if you saw pictures of me half naked with Willow, you'd feel a twinge of jealousy."

"God, I hate it when you make sense."

"I've just seen a lot of relationships go bad because people try to pretend to be something they're not. I can't do that with you. And if I ever act like a jerk, call me on it. Tell me to back off. I can't imagine I'd ever be that jerky. I trust you, and you don't act like you're Siena Remington, the model. You act like you're Siena Remington, my fun, interesting, sexy girlfriend."

"So, I don't act snobby?"

A smile crept across his lips. "Entitled, snobby…" He moved in closer. "Like you love and need everyone looking at you every second of the day."

She rolled her eyes again. "You're going to hate this, but when I first started really modeling, once I was old enough to see how differently I was treated, I was kinda that girl. It lasted about a few weeks, and I couldn't stand to be around myself." She laughed. "So...the next time you see a lingerie ad and the guys at your station all stare at it, what can I expect?"

Cash ran his hand down his face. "Those guys? You'll probably see me give them a look whenever you're around, and I may look angry, but it's not really anger. It's more..."

She nodded. "You don't have to name it. I saw that look at the bar with Mike and Joey. It was the *back off, she's with me* look."

"Sounds about right."

"I'm glad we're talking about this stuff, and I can hear exactly what you're saying." She smiled up at him. "I have to tell you, though, this whole sensitive thing you've got going on..." She drew a circle in the air in front of him. "Like the romantic side of you, it blows me away."

"Oh God. Please don't go sharing that I'm a sensitive guy. You'll ruin my rep."

She laughed. "Your secret's safe with me. Jeez, Cash, you keep doing things that totally throw me for a loop. I couldn't stop thinking about you all day."

"Even while you were in the arms of the hunky model?"

"Stop teasing. I could barely concentrate after what you said. I feel so much for you, and I was worried it was too much too fast." She licked her lips and ran her hand down his arm. "It's a little scary. I definitely feel myself falling for you, too. When you're not here, I wish you were, and when you are, I don't want you to leave."

Falling for. She's not there yet. Laying his emotions out on the table for Siena was risky, but that was one risk he couldn't afford not to take. "I didn't say it so you would. I said it because I felt it too strongly not to, and I don't want to hear it from you until you feel it so strongly that you can't hold it back."

She opened her mouth, but no words came out.

He ran his finger down her cheek. "Don't feel pressure. Even if it takes years, or it doesn't ever happen, it won't change what I feel for you."

Cash handed her a glass of wine and picked up his. "To us." He tipped his glass so it *clinked* against hers.

"I love us," she said.

"Careful. You're getting awfully close to the three words of the promised land."

They set their glasses on the table and she touched his arm again. "I do love us. Tell me about your tattoo."

He glanced at his arm and contemplated how much to tell her. She reached over and brushed his hair from his eyes. "You don't have to if it's too personal."

That was Siena. She didn't ask for more than he could give. And until he met her, he never realized how much he was capable of giving. Honesty wasn't hard to find when he was with her. He didn't feel the need to hide anything from her.

"I got it after a fellow firefighter died."

"I'm sorry. I didn't know."

He looked down at the tattoo. "After Vetta's husband died, I added another layer to it, and I sort of blocked the meaning of it out completely."

"Vetta's husband? Why? Were you close?" She scooted nearer to him on the couch and buried her toes beneath his leg.

"No." He looked into her eyes and saw how much she trusted him. "I was part of the rescue at the fire where he died. He was in a room that I was told to clear." His pulse took off with the memory. "The fire was really bad. There were dozens of us there, and I cleared the other rooms and got Vetta out. When I got back upstairs, a beam fell from the ceiling." He heard himself breathing harder, louder, and paused to swallow the panic that came rushing back to him. Siena took his hand in hers, but he couldn't look away from the scene as it unfolded before him.

"The beam was burning. It split on the way down, blocking the entrance completely. The smoke was so thick, and the flames were so high. I was right in front of the entrance. I had an ax, and as I swung back to break a hole through the wall, I heard the evacuation call." He shook his head, remembering his thoughts at the time, *No. Not yet! I'm going in!* "As I swung the ax, it stopped on my backswing, grabbed by someone. My buddy Tommy and another guy got ahold of me. I fought them, hollering for them to let me go. I wanted to save him. I needed to save him. They dragged me out, cursing a blue streak. I could barely breathe from the smoke, and they had to restrain me from running back into the building." He met her gaze and saw compassion and fear. "They saved my life. Before we hit the bottom floor, the ceiling in the hall collapsed. A ladder team got Samuel out through a window, but he'd had a heart attack."

"You blamed yourself?" she whispered tentatively.

"Kinda. I figured that if they'd let me go, I could have gotten in there and rescued him. Maybe he wouldn't have had the heart attack. Maybe…"

"Oh, Cash."

She wrapped her arms around him, and he buried his hand in her hair and held her close, soaking in her comfort without embarrassment.

He pulled back, unable to stop there. He had to tell her everything. If she was ever going to love him, she had to love him inclusive of his faults, and this was a big one.

"I was always the guy who was prepared, who didn't take unnecessary risks. I was the guy everyone else could count on. But after… After I lost Samuel, something in me snapped. There was no risk I wouldn't take to save a life. It was like I could make amends for losing him." He shrugged, locking his eyes on the tattoo. "I figured, I have less to lose than some of the other guys, with their wives and their children." He looked at her again. "And in some ways that's true. But my risks put everyone at risk, and it took someone pounding that into my brain for me to begin to see it."

"Pounding?"

"Not literally. There's this guy, he trains rookies, and he's a real hard-ass, but he's one of the best firefighters I know. I really respect him. He drilled it into me, and my chief laid it on the line. Stop taking risks, or he'd pull me from active firefighting duty and make me run the administrative desk instead." Cash shook his head. "And then I fell for you, and it all came together. Suddenly, I remembered—or realized again—or whatever—that I wasn't just risking my life. If I took a risk and failed, then someone else has to save me. And, Siena, my job is everything to me, and those guys, they're my brothers, my family. And you…Suddenly, I had someone who counted on me. Someone whom I loved."

He ran his hand over his face to steady his voice. "Today, in that two-alarm fire, I used my breathing mask. That sounds like nothing, right? Firefighters use them all the time, but ever since Samuel died, I haven't touched mine. I would wheeze and cough and barely breathe rather than breathe through the damn thing."

"You were punishing yourself."

"Yeah, I guess I was. But today I used it. I heard your voice in my head, and all that bullshit fell away. All that mattered was putting out that fire in the most skillful way I knew how, rescuing anyone who needed it, and making it back to you."

"What if I hadn't said that I was counting on you to come back to me?" She searched his eyes.

It was a question he'd asked himself a hundred times during the afternoon. "My love for you doesn't rely on your love for me. It's there, and if you were to break up with me tomorrow, what I feel for you would still be what pulled me back to safety." He smiled. "I should be thanking you."

"And Vetta? You didn't know her before the fire?" She scooted closer, nearly on his lap.

"No."

"Does she blame you?"

He shook his head. "Doesn't seem to. She lost the man she was married to for longer than I've been alive, and I have no idea what little things he'd done for her, like taking out the trash or bringing groceries. But I wanted to make sure she wasn't alone. After the first few visits, I looked forward to seeing her, even if it was a painful reminder of what had happened."

"Cash, that's so thoughtful of you." She traced his tattoo with her finger.

"The tattoo." He sighed. "I have no idea about its real meaning. Tommy and I went together to get it after we lost a buddy to a fire, but I added a layer after Samuel died." He ran his finger along a line that looked like a thick V and encircled the top of the tattoo. "I added that as a symbol of a life lost, I guess. I don't ever want to forget the fallen, you know?"

She nodded, and he could see how heavily this was hitting her. Wrinkles traveled across her forehead, her brows knitted together, and the edges of her lips turned down. As much as it pained him to see her sadness, he wanted her to know all of it. All of him.

"As a whole, what I see is a constant reminder of the power of the fire and the importance of teamwork. I lost sight of it for a while, but it's back, and it's here to stay. It's a reminder that the beast—that's what we call fires, beasts—possess more strength than each of us as individuals, but not more power than all of us together. See the top? That part that looks like an eye? I see that as the power, or the heart of the beast. Like the eye of a hurricane. And the markings at the bottom." He ran his finger along the spiky lines coming out the bottom like sharp, spidery legs. "They're reminders of how fast a fire can turn."

"You were going through all of this when we met? Carrying around all that guilt and taking risks at work and everything?"

"I guess. Yeah."

"No wonder you had a chip on your shoulder."

"I had a chip on my shoulder because a beautiful young woman was out in a snowstorm, completely unprepared, and she could have died." He pulled her onto his lap. "And you were so stubborn that I couldn't decide if I wanted to kiss you or shake you."

"Funny. That's the same way I felt about you."

"No wonder I fell in love with you. We were made for each other."

Chapter Twenty-Three

SIENA SPENT MONDAY morning working on the album for Savannah. She created scrapbook-style pages with pictures of Savannah and cute embellishments and captions, while leaving room for Jack's pictures to be placed on the same pages. She hoped to have Jack's pictures by Tuesday and the photo album complete by Friday. The bridal shower was on Saturday at Savannah's father's house in Colorado, and Siena was looking forward to seeing everyone again. She pasted the last picture of Savannah from her elementary school years on the page. She looked cute with long auburn ponytails, wearing cowgirl boots, a Western vest, and a broad smile.

Siena leaned back on the couch wondering what Cash was like as a boy. She pictured him as a cocky teenager, grumbling at everyone, maybe causing trouble with his brothers or friends. She wondered if they'd have ended up together if they'd known each other then. The thought brought her mind to all that Cash had revealed to her the evening before. She hadn't realized he was going through so much when she'd met him. Then again, there was a lot about Cash she hadn't seen when they'd first met. She picked up her cell and texted him.

Miss me yet?

Her phone vibrated a few seconds later.

I missed u the second I walked out the door.

She wiggled with happiness and texted back. *Me 2 u. Wish u were here. Do I really have 2 spend 2 nights alone? Want me 2 come by the station?*

Her phone vibrated a minute later. *You and coming at the station should never be used in the same sentence.*

Siena laughed as she texted back. *Naughty boy! Is there some kind of fireman club like the mile-high club?* She sent it with a smiley face and waited anxiously for his response.

Yeah, but we're not joining it.

Siena's smile faded to a frown. "Aw, come on," she texted back. *Why not?*

Seconds later she had her response. *You. Naked. My buddies. Not a good mix.*

She tried to come up with a playful response, and a minute later her phone vibrated again with another text. *But I'll bring home my fireman boots for u 2 wear & I can show u my fireman pole.*

Siena laughed. *God, I love you.* As she texted back she realized how true the thought was. *Oh my God. I love everything about you.* She tucked the thought behind her racing heart and texted back. *I'll wear my red lingerie w/the boots if u wear ur turnout pants.*

Her phone vibrated again and she picked it up, her heartbeat amped up at the thought of Cash in his turnout pants—and her love for him. The text was from Jewel advising her of her date with Gunner for dinner the following evening. Siena groaned.

Cash's text came through a second later. *What r ur plans tonight?*

She texted back. *Pole dancing, stripping, maybe turning a trick.* She set the phone down, thinking about how to tell Cash about her date with Gunner. He already knew they were going out again, but she hated to ruin their playful mood with that nonsense. By the time her phone vibrated again, she'd decided to wait and tell him when they were actually talking on the phone, maybe later that evening.

Cool. Save me a lap dance. Gotta go work out. Thinking about u in only my fireman boots. Love u.

The first thought that flashed through her mind was *love you too*. The second thought was a vision of Cash, bare chested, lifting weights. She wanted to tell him she loved him but not by text, and now that she had to fill him in on Gunner, she didn't think it was fair to say it and then spill the Gunner specifics. She'd deal with Gunner first. She texted back. *Call me l8r?*

Her phone rang a second later with a call from Cash.

Oh no, no, no. Not so soon! "Hi." She bit her lower lip.

"Hey, babe. What's up?"

"You didn't have to call right away." *Shit. Shit. Shit.*

"I'm your beck-and-call boy, remember?"

"How could I forget? I just wanted to…" *Tell you the date with Gunner is tomorrow night.* Only she didn't want to. Not then. "Say that I liked our flirty texts, so be sure to bring home your boots. And your turnout pants." She clenched her eyes shut, hoping he bought it. Another call rang through.

"Hold on a sec, Cash." She looked at the screen. "It's Dex. I'll call him back."

"You sure? I can hold on."

"Okay, one sec." She switched over to Dex. "Hey, Dexy. I'm on a call. What's up?"

"I'll make it quick. Wanna meet me and Ellie at around six

thirty at NightCaps?"

"Sure."

"Great. I'm not sure who else will be there."

"That's okay. Sounds great. I can't wait to see you and Ellie. I have to run. I'm on the other line. Love you." She switched back to Cash. "Sorry, Cash. Dex and Ellie want me to meet them tonight at NightCaps. I wish you could be there."

"So do I. I'd like to get to know your family."

Me too! The thought of Cash meeting her brothers as her boyfriend instead of the way Jack met him made her warm all over. "I'd like it if you met them. Jack's fiancée is having her bridal shower on Saturday in Weston, Colorado. I have to fly out on Friday."

"Weston? My brother Gage lives a few minutes from there. Would you be opposed to me flying out with you? I haven't seen him in ages, and I owe him a visit."

"I have to stay with Savannah and the girls, but yeah. That would be awesome. Do you think you can get flight arrangements this late? Wait. I can get them. I can probably pull some strings. Let me see what I can do. Are you sure you want to go? It's a fast trip. Out Friday and back Sunday night."

"A few hours with you in a plane and a day with my brother—what could be better? I can get someone to cover my shift at the station."

Siena was so excited to travel with him she could hardly see straight. "Super. I'll make arrangements. I need your birthdate, because they'll ask for it, and the name on your driver's license."

"I see. This was just a sneaky way to get my middle name. Nice," he teased. "Cash Martin Ryder." He gave her his birthdate and his home address, too, which she'd forgotten she might need. "I have to run in a sec, but I'm seeing Vetta later if we don't get called out. She'd love to see you if you want to come along."

Siena didn't have any plans for the afternoon. "Sure. When?"

"Whatever works for you, assuming I'm not out on a call."

"I'm meeting Dex at six thirty, so how about five?" She'd rather tell him about the dinner with Gunner in person anyway.

"Perfect. I have to run. I want to fit in a workout so I look good in my turnout pants."

Siena laughed. "I'll meet you at the firehouse at five." *And think about you in your turnout pants until then.*

AT FOUR THIRTY Cash came downstairs to the first floor of the station house with Vetta's photo albums in hand. He'd had only one call that afternoon, which left him plenty of time to put in the remaining pictures. He found Siena standing at the entrance of the TV room talking with someone. Her back was to Cash. Her long dark hair hung nearly to the waist of her tight-fitting jeans. She wore a white winter coat, and when her hand dropped to her side, he noticed she was wearing the gloves he'd gotten her. He came up behind her and settled an arm around her waist while glaring over her shoulder at Tommy, Joey, and Mike, who were sitting on the couch in the TV room with cocky grins on their faces.

"Hey, babe. Tommy didn't tell me you were here." He narrowed his eyes at Tommy.

"I'm early." She smiled, her eyes shifting from him to Tommy.

She touched his clenching jaw—a good reminder that his

emotions weren't invisible. He ran his hand through his hair to give himself some breathing space.

Tommy brushed past Cash on his way out of the room and whispered, "I'd stop taking risks for *her*, too."

I bet you would. "Hey, Tom, we're going to see Vetta. Call if you need me." He flashed a hot stare at Joey and Mike, then grabbed his coat and headed toward Vetta's apartment.

"You had that look in there," Siena said as she wrapped her arm in his.

"I'm sure I did."

"Why? They were just being nice."

"Yup." *And picturing you in your pink panties.*

"Is this one of those times you were talking about?" She looked up at him with her big blue eyes and he saw a little tease in them, but her steady tone washed it away.

"This is one of those times when I just needed to take a breath." *Shit.* He tried to figure out how to be honest with her without making her uncomfortable. "They were being nice, babe. But they're guys, so they were also just…"

"Checking me out?"

He pulled her close as they neared Vetta's apartment. "Yeah."

"Well, boys will be boys. Lucky for you I'm as faithful as a retriever."

Cash stopped walking, and with one powerful arm, he drew her to him. "That's my line."

She licked her lower lip, which just about killed him. "Well, now it's your turn to hold the leash."

He lowered his lips to hers and kissed her, reveling in the sweet, fresh smell of her, the feel of her body against his. *God, I missed you.* When he finally pulled back, she clung to the collar of his coat, looking at him with urgency in her eyes.

"What?"

She breathed hard, her eyes dark and serious. "Nothing. I'm just really glad you rescued me that night."

He held the door to Vetta's building open for her. "Because you hate to be cold?"

"No. Because I didn't realize how much was missing in my life."

Cash stopped cold. The current between them changed. It had been warm before, but now it drew him to her with magnetic force. "What does that mean?"

"Everything."

Her voice carried a thread of love that Cash could practically feel. And when she placed her hand on his chest and looked into his eyes, the love in hers nearly made him drop the photo albums.

"Siena." The whisper was all he could manage.

"Remember when you said that if you made love to me your heart would be in it?" She spoke softly, barely louder than he had.

Cash nodded.

"Your heart is in everything you do, and now it's part of my heart, too. I love you, Cash."

Cash opened his mouth to respond, but no words came out. His heart raced, and it was all he could do to focus on breathing. Siena drew her brows together, and when she continued, Cash still couldn't respond.

"I didn't expect it, and God knows you're as stubborn as I am. We'll probably always have this weird push-pull between us, but in some strange way, I think that's also what makes us work."

He lowered his forehead to hers. "Don't say it if you aren't sure."

"I would never do that to you. You might be a big, strong firefighter that everyone thinks is unbreakable, but you're also a…" She looked up and down the hall, then whispered, "A big old softy."

"Your big old softy, and if you ever say it aloud again, I'll—"

"Shut up and kiss me." Siena wrapped her hand around his neck and lowered his lips to hers.

"How am I supposed to focus on anything else now?" Cash took her hand in his, and Siena dragged him to the door to Vetta's apartment.

"Hopefully, we'll be together for a very long time, so you might as well figure it out now. And now that you've committed to traveling with me this weekend, you're kinda stuck with me at least until then."

As she knocked on the door, Cash knew he was, without a doubt, the luckiest guy on earth.

"Siena, Cash, how lovely to see you." Vetta opened the door, and Cash kissed her cheek as he passed.

"I brought you something," he said.

"Yes, you did. And she's lovely." Vetta winked at Siena. "Sit, please."

Cash set the photo albums on the table, and Vetta ran her shaky hand over the top of them.

"This was so nice of you, Cash." She smiled up at him, and her eyes moved between him and Siena. "You two look different."

Cash sat beside Siena and put his arm around her. "Well, the last time you saw us together we weren't exactly at our best. It had been a long, hard day."

"We'd spent the day doing a photo shoot together for Cash's annual firehouse calendar. It was a little stressful, and we were really tired." Siena patted his thigh.

"*Mm-hmm.*" Vetta nodded and picked up a photo album. She leafed through it, lingering over pictures and sighing. "This is…" She tugged a tissue from a box on the end table and dabbed at the corners of her eyes.

Oh, damn. Cash could handle a lot of things, but women's tears when not caused by a fire was not one of them.

Siena covered Vetta's hand with her own. "He did a nice job, didn't he?"

She folded her hands in her lap and her lips curved into a smile. "Yes. Cash always does his best. That's how I knew I could trust him with these pictures. Since I've known him, he's never let me down."

A sinking feeling settled into his gut. He lifted his eyes to hers, wondering how she could possibly say such a thing. He brought her out of the fire and came back empty-handed when he went to get her husband.

"He hasn't let me down, either," Siena agreed.

Christ.

Vetta set her other hand on top of Siena's. "You know, Siena. I think everything in life happens for a reason."

Siena smiled at Cash. "I think so, too."

Vetta locked eyes with him with a seriousness that he'd never before seen in her eyes. "Even death."

Holy hell. Are we really doing this? Here? Now?

"I'm not sure I follow." Cash shook his head, fighting the urge to flee her apartment.

"Me either." Vetta laughed softly under her breath. "But I'm sure we will understand it eventually. At least that's what

Samuel always believed."

Samuel. Shit. Here it comes. He drew in a deep breath. It was time for him to face the truth of what happened. He sat up tall and pulled his shoulders back.

"Vetta, I'm sorry about Samuel, but how can you just accept his death with such…grace?" *And not hate me?*

"What choice do I have?" Her eyes filled with compassion, and she glanced down at her lap for a second, blinking repeatedly, as if gathering her composure. She met Cash's gaze and sat up a little straighter. "I could let it eat me up inside, but Samuel wouldn't have wanted that. He was a pediatric surgeon. Did I tell you that?" She looked at Siena, then Cash, who nodded. "He helped save lives—like you, Cash, and also like you, he was a good man. He healed many, many children, but as with your job, sometimes the fate of those who relied on him was out of his hands."

Questions flew through Cash's mind at record speed. *Did Samuel ever feel that if he'd only done something more he could have saved someone he'd lost? If he did, then how did he handle it without going crazy? As a doctor, what could he have done? Donated his own organs? Given his own blood?* Would that have been the equivalent to Cash risking his life as a firefighter?

"Vetta." His voice cracked when he said her name, and he cleared his throat to gain control. "I…I take responsibility for not getting into the apartment fast enough, and I know words are never going to be enough, but I am truly sorry."

"I know you are, Cash. And you shouldn't feel responsible. I spoke to Chief Weber after the fire. I know that you fought tooth and nail to get into the apartment. Siena, do you know what a gem this man is?"

"I think I do," she answered.

She released Siena's hand and pushed herself up from her chair; then she took Samuel's picture off the wall and sat down beside Cash.

Cash reached for Siena's hand, clenching his jaw and fighting against the goddamn tears in his eyes.

"As I said, everything happens for a reason. Samuel's death brought you to me. He had a weak heart. We didn't know how long he'd live, and if I hadn't met you, I'd have been alone. *Really* alone." She paused, as if letting the words sink in. "Look at me, Cash."

He lifted his eyes and didn't see an ounce of blame on her face, the absence of which caused a thick lump to form in his throat.

"Chief Weber told me that you fought to save Samuel even though you probably knew in your heart that you would never make it out alive. For that, I will forever be indebted to you."

"Vetta, I didn't save him."

"No, you didn't. But you cared enough to try, and then, from what Chief Weber said, you sort of lost your mind a little." She smiled and set Samuel's picture in his lap.

He stared at it, his chest tight, muscles clenched. "Chief Weber told you I lost my mind?"

"No. Chief Weber said that you hadn't forgiven yourself. I made up the rest."

What the hell?

"Samuel would have done the same thing. He didn't lose many children, but when he did, he beat himself up for weeks. And it took a lot of love, and a lot of reminding, and a mountain of faith, to bring him back to who he was. Eventually, he understood that some things were stronger than his will to heal, just like some things are stronger than your will to save."

Cash looked at Siena, whose eyes were also damp. "That's why you said Siena softened me." *And you were goddamn right.*

"I've been around a very long time, and from where I sit, I see a couple willing to fight for each other. I could be way off base, an old woman rambling about nonsense, I suppose. But fate is a powerful thing, and I do believe Samuel was right. Everything happens for a reason."

Chapter Twenty-Four

CASH AND SIENA walked down the busy street hand in hand. Cash had been pretty quiet since leaving Vetta's, but when Siena asked him if he had time to just stop in at Night-Caps to say hello to her brothers, he seemed eager to join her.

"So, you love me?" Cash looked down at her and arched a brow.

"Well, how could I not? I mean, just look at you." She ran her eyes down his body. "*Mm-mm-mm.* You're easy on the eyes, and you're a fairly good lover…"

He spun her toward him. "Fairly good?"

Siena broke out in a fit of laughter in his arms. "And you're the…" She raised her voice. "Sweetest, softest man I know."

He backed her up against the front wall of NightCaps. "Hey. You're going to ruin my rep."

She tugged at his collar until his lips were so close she could feel his breath on hers. "Good. That'll keep the other women away." She kissed him, then pushed him playfully away. "Besides, I know it gets your back up, so the next time we're alone you'll show me the man you really are." She pulled open the door to the bar. Cash reached above her and held it open as she scanned the room for Dex and Ellie, finally catching sight of them, along with her other brothers, at a big table off to the side. She grabbed Cash's hand. "Come on. I can't wait for you to meet them. I can't believe Rush is here." As they approached the table, she realized her brothers weren't their usual smiling selves, and it occurred to her that she couldn't remember the last time Kurt or Rush had joined them for a drink.

"Hi, guys." She hugged Rush. "I didn't even know you were in town! Wow, look at you all tan in winter. I never get used to that."

"Yeah, well, spend enough time on the slopes." Rush hugged her and ran his eyes down Cash.

"Kurt, I'm so glad you're here, but you all look like something's wrong. Did I miss a memo?" Her phone vibrated and she read a text from Jewel. *My office, noon tomorrow?* She sent a quick confirmation and tucked her phone into her purse.

Jack rose to hug her, then extended a hand to Cash. "Nice to see you again, Cash."

Cash shook his hand. "Jack." He nodded.

"This is my boyfriend, Cash." She knew her smile was too wide, like a little girl showing off her first dress, but she couldn't help it. She loved Cash, and she hoped her brothers would, too. "Cash, these are my brothers." She pointed to each as she introduced them. "This is Kurt, who rarely comes out of his writer's cave. Dex and his girlfriend, Ellie; Sage and his girlfriend, Kate, and this is Rush, who is in the middle of his ski competition season, so I still can't believe he made it. And you know Jack. And this is Jack's fiancée, Savannah."

Each of her brothers stood to shake Cash's hand. Ellie, Kate, and Savannah said hello from their seats.

"So you're the fireman," Sage said with a nod. "Thanks for rescuing her from the snowstorm."

Cash smiled at Siena. "It must have been my lucky night."

He placed his hand on Siena's lower back, and even though he hadn't left yet, she knew she'd miss him when he did.

"How did you know he's a fireman?" Siena asked.

Sage cocked his head.

Rush laughed. "There isn't much we don't know about you, buddy."

"Mom?" She should have known. *The Remington grapevine at work.*

Sage shook his head and nodded toward Savannah.

"I might have let the news slip." Savannah lifted her shoulders with an apologetic smile.

"It's not like I wanted to keep him a secret, but…"

Cash helped her take off her coat, and she touched his chest, wishing he could stay and knowing he had to get back to the station.

"I wish you could stay. Thanks for coming with me to meet everyone."

"We'll plan a get-together when I'm not working. It was really nice to meet you all. Siena talks about your family a lot, so I hope we can spend some time together at some point."

Siena watched him walk out as she sat down beside Kurt. "I can't believe you're here. What's the occasion?"

Jack slapped *Us Daily* on the table, and suddenly all her brothers' faces had that *What in the hell are you doing?* look on them. The look they'd given her throughout her teenage and college years. She blew out a breath and rolled her eyes.

"So, what is this? Some kind of intervention?" She looked at Ellie, who shrugged. "Kate?"

Sage reached for Kate's hand. "Don't get mad at them, or Savannah. We threatened them with death if they said anything to you before we saw you."

"What's the issue?" *Other than the guy's a total prick that I know none of you approve of.*

"Well, I for one am totally confused." Kurt was the most reserved of all of her brothers. While the others wore their hair a little long and always appeared windblown, Kurt wore his dark hair short, and it was always perfectly combed. He preferred collared shirts to her other brothers' tees, and though he worked out daily and was equally as muscular as the others, his personality wasn't one of outward brawn. As a writer, he came across more academic than sporty.

"About what?" Siena asked, wishing she didn't feel like she was being scrutinized, even though she knew she deserved it.

"If Cash is your boyfriend—and from the look on your face when you introduced him, you're quite taken with him—then why go out with a troglodyte like Gunner Gibson?"

Kurt was the last person she'd expected to confront her, but then again, he was her older brother. There had been plenty of times he'd made comments that were just striking enough to have an impact on her decisions.

"It's not what it looks like." *And I can't tell you the truth, so let's just drop it.* "I'm with Cash, not Gunner."

Rush pointed to the picture. "That kiss looks pretty real to me, Siena."

Why can't they see what Cash saw when he looked at it?

"Is Cash a nice guy?" Dex asked.

"Of course."

"So he's not the smart-ass you portrayed him as last time we met for drinks?" Sage asked.

She rolled her eyes. "Yes, he's a smart-ass, but I like his smart-assness." She shot a look at Kurt. "I know that's not a word, so don't correct me." She leaned her elbows on the table and tried to figure out how to explain what she didn't even understand herself. "Cash is a smart-ass, and he's tough, but he's also kind and generous and funny..." *And an amazing lover.* "I *really* like him. I just judged him too quickly before."

"And is he romantic? That seemed to top your list when we were last together," Jack said.

"More romantic than any man I know. Including you." Siena smiled just thinking about how romantic Cash was.

"Okay." Savannah leaned across the table. "So why mess with his head?"

Siena flung herself back against her chair. "I'm not trying to mess with his head." Her brothers exchanged a knowing glance. "Gunner's just...He's nothing. Okay? And Cash knows that."

"I call bullshit," Rush said.

"Agreed," Sage added.

"And he's okay with you kissing the quarterback best known for bedding women and getting kicked out of strip clubs?" Jack asked. "Because, before you answer that, you need to know that I'm definitely not okay with you going out with this Gunner guy."

"Neither am I," Dex said. "And I gotta tell you, you have Ellie to thank for saving you from hearing from me the minute I saw the picture."

Ellie tucked her dark hair behind her ear.

"Thanks, Ellie," Siena said quietly. "It's not like you guys can tell me what to do."

They all turned dark stares on her. "Okay, fine. Maybe you can, or at least give me your two cents and I usually respect it, but this time..." She shook her head. "I have one more date with him tomorrow, and that's it. Then no more."

"Siena." Jack's deep, serious voice drew her attention to him. He crossed his arms; his biceps twitched against his broad chest. "This Gunner guy, he's not your type of guy. You've never been one of those girls who are all over these trashy magazines. Aren't you worried about your own reputation?"

Unfortunately. That's why I'm doing it.

"This Gunner guy is the kind of guy I hate. He uses his social status for all the wrong things, and you're our little sister, so the idea that he's adding you as a notch on his belt really pisses me off, Siena." Rush leaned forward with angry blue eyes.

She was frustrated that she couldn't tell them the truth, but now that the ball was rolling, she couldn't chance one of them saying the wrong thing at the wrong time. Savannah was an entertainment attorney. If she slipped up, it could bring Siena bad press.

She stared him down. "I'm not a goddamn notch on anyone's belt. Jesus, Rush. I met him at a bookstore. I didn't sleep with him." She heard the venom in her voice but was unable to quell her anger. "And yeah, Jack, I worry about my rep." *Too damn much, apparently.* She picked up the magazine and then threw it back down, pissed off at herself for agreeing to the damn date in the first place. Siena covered her eyes with her hands and sighed. She ran her fingers along the ends of her hair and dropped her eyes, feeling ashamed of what she'd done. If she'd gone out with Gunner on her own, without being forced to do so, she'd feel a whole lot different facing her brothers, but knowing she'd stooped lower than any of them ever would and had compromised her own beliefs, brought a heated flush to her cheeks.

Dex touched her hand. "Siena, we care about you. That's why we're here. Are you going through something that we're not aware of? I mean, you always seem confident, but did your ego take a hit or something? What would make you date this guy?"

She looked at the concern in Dex's eyes and knew that even if she wanted to, she couldn't tell him the truth. He'd think even less of her. But she wasn't going to lie, either. She pled the fifth and shrugged instead.

"Why don't we order some food and drinks and let this be for a little bit? Obviously this is a difficult situation for Siena, and if I were in her place, I think I'd feel a little attacked."

Siena raised her eyes, and Kate smiled at her.

"I know you guys care about me, and I appreciate that." Siena looked at each of her brothers. "All you need to know is that it's Cash I'm with, and he's the guy I hope to be with forever, so…"

The girls all leaned forward.

"Forever?" Savannah asked.

"As in always?" Kate added.

"You love him?" Ellie asked.

Siena bit her lower lip to keep from smiling too wide and proclaiming her love for Cash too loudly. She fiddled with her hair while she contemplated her answer.

"Siena?" Dex asked.

"I do. I really think I do," she finally said.

Sage, Kurt, Rush, and Jack exchanged a confused look.

"You've got a funny way of showing it," Jack said. "And if he's any kind of a man, then I doubt you'll keep him long if you're going on another date with that asshole."

Sage shook his head. "Sis, why go on another date with Gunner if you love Cash? Does he know you love him?"

"Mm-hmm. I told him tonight." She couldn't look them in

the eye. What they were saying made perfect sense, and it all made her chest hurt. Siena wasn't someone who cried often, but right then she desperately wished she could. She was sure it would make her feel a whole hell of a lot better than wallowing in shame.

Jack blew out a breath and ran his hand through his thick dark hair.

"Okay, now you even have me confused." Savannah picked up the magazine again. "I totally don't get any of this, but I know you said Cash reminded you of Jack, and if I'd gone out with another man, Jack would have killed him and ended things with me in a heartbeat."

"Okay, you know what?" Siena rose to her feet. "I know you guys love me, and I know this makes no sense, but I have to go. I just..." A tear tumbled down her cheek. "I have to go." She grabbed her coat and headed out into the night.

She hadn't taken five steps out of NightCaps before Rush caught up to her.

"Hey, sis, wait up."

"Go away, Rush." *I want to be alone. No. I want to go see Cash. Goddamn it. I don't know what I want.*

"Fuck no. We drew straws and I won."

"Don't you mean *lost?*" She pulled her shoulders in tight against her and walked out into the street to hail a cab.

"No. I mean won. We all wanted to talk to you." Rush flagged down a cab and climbed in after Siena. "Where are we going?"

"I'm going home."

Rush had a concerned and somber look in his eyes, one that Siena wasn't used to. He was an Olympic skier who spent his days training or competing and his nights gallivanting around whatever town he was in with whatever woman struck his fancy. Rush was thirty-two, and Siena doubted he'd ever settle down.

"Then that's where I'm going. You have alcohol?"

She thought of the ingredients for screaming orgasms that Cash had given her. "Oh, yes. I sure do."

"Good. We're gonna need it."

She gave the cabdriver the address of the firehouse.

"I want to see Cash first."

"That's cool. Whatever." Rush shoved his hands in his coat pockets and leaned his head back, then closed his eyes.

They arrived at the station a few minutes later, and Siena asked the driver to wait. Rush followed her out of the car.

"Don't think I'm not coming with you," Rush said. "I can't let my little sister go alone into a firehouse full of men. God knows what they're like."

"Really, Rush? What am I? A child? Cash is in there. Do you really think he'd let anyone bother me?" she fired back.

"Whatever, sis. I've got your back even if you don't want me to."

She groaned. "Fine, whatever."

Inside the firehouse, she paced as she waited for Cash to come downstairs. The minute she saw him, the tears she didn't realize had returned broke free and she ran into his arms.

"Babe, what's wrong?"

With one of his arms around her back and the other on the back of her head, she felt like she could finally breathe. He pressed her to his strong chest and whispered, "What is it? What happened?" He lifted his head. "Rush?"

"Hey, man. You have to ask her. Sorry," Rush said. "I'm only here to make sure she gets home okay."

"Thank you," Cash said.

He pulled back and looked into her eyes, which only made her cry harder, and thankfully, he held her close again.

"Whatever it is, I'm sure it's going to be okay," Cash said.

She pulled back again and took his face in her hands. "Do you know I love you?" she whispered.

"Of course."

"No. I mean, really know it? In your heart? Or do you think I'm messing with you?" She had to know, and she wanted to say so much more and wasn't sure she could.

"Of course not. What's going on?" He eyed Rush. "Excuse us a minute." He brought her around the corner and brushed her tears from her cheeks with the pad of his thumb. "Babe, tell me what's going on."

Siena took a few deep breaths and finally stopped crying. "I'm sorry. I never cry."

"Don't be sorry. I'm here for whatever you need."

"You know that I don't want to go out with Gunner, right? That none of that is real? That going out with him again tomorrow night is just to finish the whole publicity thing?"

"I didn't know it was tomorrow, but yeah. I know. You told me all of that." Cash pulled her close again. "Am I missing something?"

She shook her head and pushed away again. "No. My brothers are just giving me all sorts of crap, and I felt horrible. I needed to know that you trust me and that you know how much you mean to me."

"Of course. Did you tell them the date wasn't real?"

"No. I can't. I shouldn't have even told you, remember? But I couldn't hurt you like that and let you think it was real."

"Babe, they're your brothers. Don't you think you can trust them?"

"I know I can trust them, but one slip and going out with Gunner would have been for nothing. They would never mean to say the wrong thing, but if someone makes a comment to them, you know they'd slip and say it wasn't even a real date." She realized that Cash might do the same thing. "Oh God, Cash, how are you handling it with the guys around here?"

"I tell them to fuck off."

She rolled her eyes. "Really, come on."

"I do, but I also told them that it was a picture from months ago and that you had no idea how or why they printed it now." He kissed her. "See? I can handle anything."

"They bought that? What will you say after the next pictures show up?" *Shit, now you're lying because of me.*

"I already said that they'd probably see more of the same and that Gunner was probably trying to fix his rep or something. These are my buddies. The only reason they care is that they don't want you to screw me over. They couldn't care less who Gunner Gibson is dating, and they know you're not going to screw me over." He kissed her again. "Look, babe, your brothers are just looking out for you. I love that, and I have to tell you, I love that Rush is making sure you get home okay. But you don't have to worry about me. We only have to make it through one more Gunner date; then it's just you and me. Right?"

"Yes. Of course. I'm sorry I made a scene, and I'm sorry I overreacted." She wiped her eyes, feeling like a weepy, weak girl. She hated feeling that way.

Cash hugged her again. "You're only human, just like we talked about the other night. Honesty is what makes us strong as a couple. Jealousy, sadness, what's the difference? I'm here when you need me, and I know you'll be there when I need you."

That weak girl feeling slipped away, and Siena realized it wasn't weakness at all that she felt. It was the fear of losing Cash. With the certainty of his love for her, she headed home with Rush.

RUSH HUNG UP his coat and made them each a drink. Siena changed into sweats just to escape his silent, worried gaze. She eyed Cash's bag, which he'd forgotten when he ran out for the call, and shame clutched her again. *This is the last time I compromise myself for my work. Ever.*

She found Rush on the couch, drink in hand, reading the magazines with the pictures of her and Gunner.

"So, sis. What's the real deal?" His brown hair was tousled; his Rossignol shirt barely contained his brawny chest and arms. He kicked his long legs up on the coffee table and looked at her expectantly.

She slumped onto the couch beside him, and he handed her a glass from the coffee table. "This might make it easier."

He draped his arm over her shoulder and she sank against him. Siena was close with all of her brothers in different ways. Rush could always be counted on where controversy was concerned. He'd seen enough of it himself from his carousing in his younger years—although he'd been out of that part of the press scene for quite some time.

Siena sighed and took a drink. "I don't know, Rush."

"Well, I've never seen you run crying into a man's arms before, so it's something."

"Yeah, with Cash it's definitely something." She'd felt safer the second she was in his arms.

"And with Gunner?"

"It's definitely not…anything."

She felt him nod, then take a drink as she curled her legs up beside her.

"You know we weren't judging you, right?" Rush's voice was sincere, brotherly.

"I know." *I'm judging myself.*

"Look, Siena. You don't have to tell me anything. I just didn't want you to be alone tonight. I've sat in your seat many times. I've done lots of things I'm not proud of, for reasons I didn't even understand."

There it was, the honesty Cash was talking about.

"But that's how we learn," he said.

Rush still did things he couldn't possibly be proud of. Or maybe he was? How could she possibly know? He was a man, and men were so different. Still, she turned and arched a brow.

He knocked his shoulder gently against her. "Okay, well, that's how we're supposed to learn. I'm trying to be the good big brother here. All you really need to do is be able to sleep at night with your own thoughts churning through your mind. If you can do that, you're good."

"Can you?" she asked.

He set the magazines down beside him, closed his eyes, and let his head loll back. "Your goal shouldn't be to do as I do. But my advice is solid, so try to learn from it. I love you, sis."

She cuddled against him and pulled the throw blanket over her legs, glad he was with her. "I love you, too, Rush."

All you really need to do is be able to sleep at night with your own thoughts churning through your mind. There wasn't a chance in hell she was going to get a wink of sleep.

Chapter Twenty-Five

RUSH LEFT EARLY the next morning with the promise to see her soon, and by ten she'd already had texts from Dex, Sage, and Jack, each making sure she was okay. If she had ever wondered if her brothers cared about her—which she had never doubted—their sympathetic texts would have eased her mind. Now they just made her feel guilty about the date and about leaving NightCaps so abruptly.

The text from Kurt came while she was in the cab on the way to see Jewel. *I don't write romance, so I'm no good at this really. But if you want to talk about the troglodyte or Cash, you know how to reach me.* She loved that about him. Kurt never went all alpha male on her, and he didn't pretend to have all the answers, but he was there if she needed him. She texted back, *Thanks. Loved seeing u. Sorry I left early. I'm good. Xox.*

At noon Siena was sitting across from Jewel in her office, stewing over the date with Gunner later that evening. In the cab on the way over she'd decided that she was going to get out of it one way or another. Now her stomach knotted and her neck muscles felt bunched together into one big ache. The lack of sleep didn't help.

"You doubted the intelligence of my request, and I wanted

to see your face when I gave you this news." Jewel's navy pencil skirt and fitted jacket looked as if it had been made just for her, the perfect complement to her blond hair and fair complexion. She moved gracefully across the office to the bank of windows and touched the string of pearls that hung just below her collarbone.

"News?" Siena folded her hands in her lap in an effort to keep from fiddling with her hair.

"Track Sports is flirting with us." Jewel's coral lips spread into a self-satisfied smile.

"Flirting with? I thought they were married to Nicole Blessinger." Track Sports was one of the largest contracts in the sports industry, and Nicole had sealed that contract for the last five years.

"Nic's contract is up later this year. They were all over Chloe, but I was able to work a few miracles..."

"After one bookstore meeting with Gunner? That makes no sense. How can that possibly be?"

"That was just the tip of the iceberg. I've been in talks with them for months, but they didn't budge until they saw that you would take the steps that were necessary to help promote the brand *and* the industry." Jewel sauntered over to where Siena sat and put her fingertips on the desk. "I was greasing the wheels; now it's your job to make them spin."

Siena opened her mouth to ask how she was supposed to do that, but something told her that she already knew what it meant. More time with Gunner, or whoever else they decided she needed to be seen with.

"In case you're wondering, we're talking eight to ten million for a five-year deal, and let me just remind you..." She touched Siena's shoulder and her smile faded. "You're twenty-six. That'll carry you until you're thirty-one, which is considered older than middle age in model years."

Eight to ten million. "That's way more than Nic is making. Are you sure?"

"Am I ever not sure when it comes to dollars and cents?" She sat beside Siena, knees together, legs bent at a glamorous angle. "You were right. You don't really *need* this contract, and they know that. But you do need security, and this would be a nice little boost to your already ridiculous income."

"It's not that I'm not appreciative, but I have so much more than I could ever spend now."

"Yes, but what about when you find the man who makes your toes curl, and you decide to have a family? You come from a big family, don't you? Security for those children is worth a few dates, is it not?"

She knew Jewel was pushing her not just for her security, but also because she would earn a hefty fee for solidifying the contract. But she did have a point about children and family. What if she and Cash were married and eventually had children? What if he was injured on the job? Her stomach sank just thinking about it, but it was certainly a valid concern. And she loved children. How much money was enough money to secure a future for a child? She had no idea. And what if she didn't want to model after she had children? She knew she was reaching, but what if she didn't want to model and Cash was injured? They'd have to live on her savings. Would that be enough for her children's futures as well? She felt herself breathing a little harder. When did her life become so complicated?

"Yes, probably." *It's a hell of a lot of money.* She thought of Cash and her brothers. *Oh God. What am I doing?*

Jewel patted her arm. "That's the way I see it. Be sure to dress to the nines tonight. We want to keep them wowed." She stood and opened her door. A silent dismissal.

Siena thanked her as she walked nervously toward the door, her mind swimming in a sea of right and wrong.

"Oh, and, Siena. Tonight? Let's kiss with our eyes closed."

SIENA SNAPPED A selfie in her black Vera Wang dress that came to midthigh. The silk dress was simple, elegant, and sexy, arching over each breast where it met sheer material that clung to her chest, ending in a high neckline. The same sheer material covered Siena's arms, ending in wide silk cuffs. She texted the picture to Cash with the message, *Thinking of you.*

She'd been thinking about her meeting with Jewel all afternoon, and she decided that she needed to nail down what *a few dates* really meant. She needed to be frank with Jewel and tell her exactly where she stood with her relationship with Cash. As she waited for Cash's response, she assessed herself in the mirror again. She saw the shame that Jewel had missed. She felt it to her core. She looked down at her perfectly manicured hands, thanks to an afternoon of pampering at the spa around the corner. Happiness was at her fingertips, and she knew she was playing with fire.

Her phone vibrated with a text from Cash. *How am I supposed to think at all now? You are too hot for words. Can't you wear a paper bag on your dinner date?*

She laughed and knew exactly how to respond. She wished the whole thing with Jewel could be handled as simply as Cash's ego. *Lucky for u only u will ever see what's under this dress…or what's not. Love u. Xox.*

His response only made her feel guiltier. *Love u. Trust u. Have fun. C u 2moro after my shift?*

She responded as her doorbell rang. *Def. Let's stay at ur place. I'll bring my stuff. Ok?* She hated the idea of Gunner picking her up at her apartment, and she made a quick decision to stop him at the threshold.

"Coming," she called out on the way out of her bedroom. Her heart was beating so fast she had to remind herself to calm down—not for her date with Gunner, but with hopes that Cash responded before she answered the door. A second later his text came through. *Bring enough to stay forever.*

Oh God. Oh God. She did a little wiggly dance and texted back, *Forever and a day. Can you see my smile from there? I'm sorry but I gotta run. Love u. Xox.* She turned off her phone and answered the door. Gunner looked like a movie star rather than a quarterback in his dark suit, perfectly pressed white shirt, and a dozen roses in his hand. *Maybe he'll be easier to stomach tonight.* He slid his eyes down Siena's body; then, as slow as molasses, he worked his way back up. *Asshole.* Siena bit back the urge to slam the door in his face. She'd dressed up for *him*? She'd hoped his annoying behavior had been a one-time thing. Now she knew exactly why her brothers were so concerned. Well, she wasn't allowing even one toe of his into her loft.

"You look incredible."

His eyes finally met hers, and she was sure he could read the displeasure in her eyes. How could he not? The muscles beneath her eyes were practically pulsating. She didn't even try to force her normal smile.

"Thank you." *Asshole.*

He took a step toward the door and she pulled it closed a

little. "My brother is visiting and he's sick, so let me grab my coat and we'll be off." She left the door open as she tossed the flowers on the table—purposely forgoing putting them in a vase and giving him reason to come inside—grabbed her purse, phone, and coat, and headed out the door.

On the way to the restaurant, Siena sat with her hands in her lap, clutching her purse tightly, and thinking of ways to expedite the date.

"Look, I wanted to tell you that I'm sorry I was on my phone the whole time at the bookstore."

She looked up at him and, surprisingly, she saw sincerity in his eyes. "It's okay."

"No, it's not, really. I mean, maybe with other women, but not with all that's riding on these dates." He ran his hand over his freshly shaven cheeks. "Look, I have to clean up my act to keep my contract, and you need to be seen with the best on the field to land whatever contracts you're after. It probably doesn't hurt that I help you look less like a goody-goody."

He almost had her with his sincerity, but the goody-goody comment threw her off.

"Goody-goody?"

"Well, yeah. That's what my agent said, that you needed to get in the mix a bit, show you can hang with the dirtier crowd. The sports audience is completely different from all other audiences. They're anything but goody-goody."

The way he was studying her face unnerved her.

"Come on. You didn't know this? How do you think you ended up with me? They pick a woman who's never done a damn questionable thing in the press and throw her into the tiger's den. She's going to be eaten alive or learn to play."

"What does that even mean? Learn to play?"

"It means they're seeing how tough you are. Just like they're seeing if I can pull my shit together enough to convince the public I've changed my stripes." He leaned back and pulled out his phone, scrolling through his texts.

Really? The phone again?

"The way I see it, if we both play our cards right, we'll fool everyone." He glanced at her out of the corner of his eye.

She had a bone to pick with Jewel. She hated that he had a goddamn point, and she hated that he was blatantly honest, which she couldn't help but appreciate. But she hated herself a little more for playing the stupid game in the first place.

When the driver pulled up in front of the restaurant, paparazzi hovered around the car.

"Looks like our agents did their job and dropped the tip. Now it's time to play the game." He got out of the car and reached for Siena's hand with a perfect smile that reached his eyes. He was almost as good at modeling as she was, which was freaking scary as hell, because Siena knew how easily they could pull this off—and doing so with both of them fully apprised of what was behind the ruse made it feel a little less skeevy.

An hour and a half later, as he paid the bill, she realized that she'd had an okay time with Gunner, if she could look past his wandering eye. It was rude of him to check out other women while at dinner with her, but he wasn't really her date. She was just relieved that he wasn't looking at her like he was envisioning her naked, or scrolling through texts and ignoring her altogether. Stomaching dinner with him tonight was no different from going to dinner with a guy she was acquainted with who wasn't a friend and whom she had no romantic interest in. Like a business associate, which was exactly what he was.

He leaned across the table. She was fully aware of the photographers lingering outside, waiting for them to leave.

"Ready to hit the red carpet again?"

"Sure."

He didn't pull out her chair for her, which made her think of Cash, who always did the gentlemanly thing, and he didn't even angle his arm for her to take. He stood beside her, fixed his jacket, and handed her coat to her. Boy, did she ever miss Cash. They walked out side by side, and just as they hit the pavement, he slid his hand to her lower back and leaned in close.

"Try to look like I'm all you can think about," he whispered.

She thought of Cash and knew her eyes would translate the look he was going for. She closed her eyes when he kissed her cheek just before they got into the waiting sedan.

Inside the car he sighed. "Glad that's over."

"Thanks. Real nice." She rolled her eyes.

"No, not the night with you. I actually had a good time. Just the stress of the cameras. You know, making sure I'm not doing all the wrong things." He rubbed his hands on his slacks. "Tell me it's not a relief."

"It is." She looked down at her lap. The night hadn't been painful. It might not have been particularly enjoyable, but for the Track Sports contract, it was worth it.

"So, you're a straitlaced girl. Did I do anything wrong in there?" He turned to face her and again she saw sincerity in his eyes.

"You really want to know, or are you going to get angry if I tell you the truth?"

"Now you have to tell me the truth. What did I do? I looked you up online, and I tried to talk about things you were interested in and to stay away from sports."

"You did all that, and that was nice." She watched the lights of the city out the window, thinking of how Cash paid full attention to her all the time, whether they were out on a date or sitting at home. Maybe Gunner was trying to change. Maybe he would one day be a good boyfriend for some woman. She couldn't imagine it, but who was she to judge? Look at what she'd agreed to. "Okay, here's the thing. When you're on a dinner date, it's rude to have a wandering eye. It makes your date feel…I don't know. Insecure? Unattractive? Bad. It just makes them feel bad."

"Did I…In there?" He pulled his head and shoulders back, like he was shocked at the accusation. "Jesus, I didn't even realize I was doing that."

"You were."

"That is rude. I'm sorry. I guess I have a long way to go." He pulled out his phone.

"That's rude, too. Even if we're not on a real date, it's still rude."

He put it slowly back in his pocket. "Point taken. Do all women have such stringent rules?"

"I have no idea, but I would think that those who care about themselves do. And those who don't care about themselves? Well, that stuff will only make them feel even worse."

He scrubbed his face with his hand. "I think I need dating lessons."

Siena laughed.

"So, do you have a real boyfriend?"

She felt herself smile as she lifted her eyes to meet his. "Yeah. I do. A really great boyfriend whom I adore."

"Adore? Who says that?" He laughed under his breath.

She shrugged. "Maybe one day someone will say it about you and you'll find out."

The driver stopped in front of her apartment building.

"Your brother isn't sick, is he?"

She hesitated.

He shook his head. "It's okay. I kinda figured as much."

"Well, you checked me out so long I felt naked." She opened her door and stepped from the car. "I'm glad I got to know you a little better. Have a nice night, Gunner."

He nodded and flashed a broad smile. Siena thought he was going to make a smart-ass comment about hooking up and she moved to close the door.

He reached a hand out and stopped it from closing. "Thanks for being excruciatingly honest. We don't get that very often, do we?"

I do with Cash. "You asked me to."

"That I did. I'll watch my eyes, my phone usage, and…"

"Open doors for your dates. It helps. Good night, Gunner."

Chapter Twenty-Six

THE NEXT MORNING, Siena packed a bag with clothes for the next few days. As she packed her shampoo, hair dryer, makeup, body lotions, and other personal items, she wondered if she and Cash would eventually just keep one of everything at each other's apartments. She looked down at the toothbrush in her hand and wondered what it would feel like to see his hanging next to hers. To see his cologne on the dresser or smell his aftershave in the bathroom every morning. The idea sent a thrill through her, chased by a rush of heat. Her mind drifted to Cash's body and the feel of his hands as he gripped her hips when they were making love. *Oh my God, I'm turning into a nympho.*

She pushed her lustful thoughts away as she left her apartment and picked up the FedEx package that must have been left while she was in the shower. She'd almost forgotten about the pictures from her mother. She went back inside and packed the photo album pages, then headed downstairs to catch a cab. On the way to Cash's, she revisited the meeting she'd had with Jewel. She still had no idea what she should do, but after her enlightening date with Gunner, she was less apprehensive about spending an occasional hour or two with him—and a little concerned about Jewel's omission of the rest of the story. *So what if I'm squeaky clean?* She worked hard to be someone she could be proud of. Someone her father would be proud of.

And I ruined it pretty quickly.

No, I didn't ruin it.

The memory of her brothers' faces had her doubting her own ability to read the situation. The only thing she knew for sure as she stepped from the cab and headed inside Cash's building was that it was something she and Cash had to talk about. This wasn't a decision she could make alone if he was going to be part of her life.

CASH HAD THOUGHT about Siena in that sexy black dress all night and could barely think past wondering what she had on—or didn't—underneath it. She struck every nerve in his body with her feisty comments and sexual innuendos. God, he loved her. When he got home after his shift, he showered. Then he cleared out a drawer in the bedroom, made room in his closet for anything she might want to hang, and emptied a drawer in the bathroom vanity. And each area he freed brought a new and different level of excitement. He was getting way ahead of himself, but with his heart thundering in his chest, he didn't care. He couldn't help but think about waking up to her every morning and coming home to her at night. Walking into the living room and finding her snuggled under a blanket on the couch, wearing her baggy sweatpants or one of his gigantic T-shirts. It was almost too much to hope for.

He pulled the blinds closed in the living room and bedroom and lit a few candles. Then he turned on the stereo and paced.

He was being presumptuous, wearing nothing but his turnout pants. Maybe she had other ideas for the morning, but he wanted to be close to her. They were finally free of the Gunner noose, and it was cause for an intimate celebration.

A knock at the door made every muscle pull tight. What if he'd totally misjudged her playfulness? *Shit.* He looked around the apartment and debated blowing out the candles. She knocked again.

Aw, hell.

He pulled the door open, and Siena's eyes widened. In the next breath, she dropped her bag, shrugged off her coat, and jumped into his arms, running her hands through his hair and kissing his lips, his cheeks, his chin.

"Oh my God. We are so in sync." She kissed him again. "It's crazy."

With Siena in his arms, he kicked her bag inside and then threw the door closed, kissing her with the heat of passion that had been building for the last few hours.

"I missed you." He kissed her again. "You were so hot in that damn dress." He nuzzled against her neck and sucked the spot beneath her ear that brought a moan of want to her lips.

"Did you bring my boots?" She looked into his eyes, and he saw the flirtatious little vixen in her looking right through him.

"Oh, baby. I brought your boots, but once you get those clothes off, I'm not making any promises about waiting for you to put them on." He took her in another greedy kiss.

"Thought you were a master at controlling the flames." She licked her lower lip and he stifled a groan.

She wiggled out of his arms and began unbuttoning her shirt. "Where are they?"

"You're serious?"

"Hell yes." She tossed her shirt on the floor. "But if you don't hurry, I might be the one who's unable to wait." She wiggled out of her jeans.

Christ Almighty. She was standing before him wearing nothing but a tiny blue thong and one of those damn bras that barely covered her nipples, much less the rest of her delicious breasts. He moved toward her, hard and ready. She crossed her arms over her chest and turned from side to side.

"Boots?"

"You're killing me."

She looked around him. "You lit candles."

"You noticed." He was breathing so hard, she had to see the effect she was having on him. He took a step closer and she swallowed hard, then licked her lips.

"The boots," she whispered as he grabbed first one hip, then the other. "B-boots."

He lowered his mouth to her shoulder and dragged his teeth along the length of it to her neck. His hand slid up her side, his thumb grazing the underside of her breast.

"Boots," she whispered in one long breath.

"By the bedroom door," he whispered as he moved the cup of her bra and exposed one hard nipple. He took it between his finger and thumb, squeezing just a little before taking it in his mouth and loving her breast with soft strokes of his tongue and gentle sucks that brought her up onto her toes. He dropped his other hand from her hip to between her thighs and rubbed her through the silky fabric.

"Cash," she whispered.

"That's a lot better than *boots*," he said as he moved to love her other breast. He slid his finger beneath the fabric and couldn't stifle the groan this time. She was so wet, he had to taste her. He looked her in the eyes as he backed her up against the door.

"Don't move." It was a command, but damn it, he meant it. He retrieved the boots and set her feet into them. He ran his eyes down her body, and in his boots she was sexier than hell, and he felt himself get harder.

She grinned.

"I didn't think it was possible, but you just got ten times sexier." He pressed her to the door with his body as he kissed her hard, hungrily taking her every breath as his hands found her hips again. He loved her hips. Hell, he loved every part of her body down to her fucking toes. He fought the urge to drive into her right there. Instead he looked into her eyes as he used his feet to spread her legs. She sucked in a breath as he gave her another heated command. "Don't move." He pressed his hands to her chest just above her breasts, feeling her heart beating just as fast as his. Then he dragged his hands down her body, pressing her to the door and keeping his eyes locked on hers. His fingers splayed as they dragged along the lace of her bra, feeling her hard nipples beneath and amping up the urge to fill her with his heat. He felt her heartbeat through her breasts, and then his hands were on her ribs, which rose and fell with each heavy, intoxicating breath. She sucked in another breath, and he trapped her mouth with his again, loving, licking, tasting her tongue, the sides of her teeth, the roof of her mouth. He couldn't get enough of her. When his hands found her hips, he clenched them tight, as he'd learned she loved. She tried to arch against him, and he held her to the door, her legs spread, held apart by his bare feet. He licked her lower lip, and she whimpered against his tongue.

"Don't move," he said again. Hearing the gruffness in his

own voice only spurred him on as he kissed his way down the center of her body, then licked around her beautiful belly button before plunging his tongue into it. She cried out, an indiscernible stream of pleasure. He lowered his mouth to her inner thigh and ran his tongue up the length of it, stopping short of her thong; then he moved to the other side, feeling her legs contract and her hips tremble in his grasp.

"Cash, please."

He ran his tongue along the edge of her thong, just beside her sex, then sucked the sensitive skin, bringing her up on her toes again, her hands fisting on his shoulders.

"Oh God...not...fair."

He used his teeth to drag her panties to the side, revealing her swollen, moist sex. He stroked her with his tongue.

"Jesus," she cried.

She buried her hands in his hair and whimpered as he licked her again.

"You're so sweet," he said as he brought his hands to the front of her thong and fisted them around the fabric. "How much do you like these panties?"

She looked down at him, panting, confusion written all over her flushed face. In the next breath, he ripped them apart, right down the middle, and they fell to the floor. Siena breathed heavily as he licked her again, harder, and used his tongue to tease the sensitive nub, which brought her up on her toes again. He released one hip, holding her firmly against the door with the other, while he slipped his fingers inside her and drove her up and over the crest of a climax that shuddered through her entire body. With his fingers still inside her, he rose to his full height, his feet still holding her legs apart. He grabbed one wrist and held it over her head.

"Other hand," he panted. "Up."

She lifted her hand to his and he wrapped his hand around both of hers. Then he pressed his chest to her and took her in another urgent kiss as he teased her down below. She arched into his hand, moaning into his mouth. He drew back.

"Too much?" He searched her eyes, and she shook her head, her lips slightly parted, her breasts heaving.

"More," she whispered.

"Holy hell, I love you." He kissed her again, moving his fingers in and out of her faster, pressing his hard cock against her hips. Within seconds he felt her body tighten around his fingers, and she gasped another breath, stealing air from his lungs. She pressed her hips into his as she went up, up, up, then came down from the peak, her body still pulsing with tiny aftershocks, her heart hammering against his.

"More." She narrowed her eyes. A challenge.

He arched a brow as he stepped from his turnout pants. He threw her over his shoulder in a fireman hold, and in a handful of determined steps, they were in the bedroom, where he set her on the bed. She laughed and got up on her hand and knees, her hair cascading over her shoulder and down her back. Her eyes were at half-mast, filled with lust and sinful seduction. Cash hesitated, unsure of what she really wanted. The position was so open to him.

"Come on, big boy," she said.

He let his heart lead him to the bed behind her, her beautiful ass spread wide for him, her sex ready, waiting. He moved to flip her over, and she looked over her shoulder and shook her head. *Holy fuck.* He brought his hand to her center and could barely breathe with her looking back at him so seductively. Dirty thoughts ran though his mind, but he loved her too much to do anything that might hurt her. He brought the tip of his hard length to her center and she moved back, taking him in, then moved slowly and purposefully forward and back.

"Touch me," she whispered.

He brought one hand to her breast, the other to her center as she leaned back in his lap and he stroked her, groped her, and thrust into her moist heat, driving harder as the sensations grew. Flames gripped his thighs as his muscles tightened with each thrust. He lowered his teeth to her shoulder and grazed her skin as he sucked a moan right from her lungs.

"Oh, Cash, more. I want more of you."

A rush of carnal heat sent him up on his knees and her back down to her hands and knees as he thrust harder. She clenched the sheets in her hands as her inner muscles tightened. Cash's muscles corded as he gripped her hips and pulled her back against each of his thrusts.

She cried out and he stopped.

"Am I hurting you?"

"No, no. No. Don't stop."

Jesus Christ. Just as her sex tightened around him and she cried out his name, he felt his balls tighten. He drove into her again, and with the next pump of his hips, he filled her with his love, thrust after powerful thrust drawing the come right out of him. Breathing hard as she rode the crest of her release and then came down from the peak, he lowered his cheek to her back, feeling her heartbeat through her ribs. He placed soft kisses along her shoulders. He shuddered as he lowered them to the mattress, their bodies still joined together as one.

He wrapped his arms around her and kissed her cheek. "You okay?"

"Mmm. Better than."

"Was I too rough?" It would kill him if he'd hurt her.

"No. You were perfect." She turned to face him. "Was I too slutty?"

She bit her lower lip in the way that stole his heart. He kissed her forehead. "No, babe. When you're driven by love, nothing's slutty."

Chapter Twenty-Seven

LATER THAT AFTERNOON, Cash and Siena were cuddling on the couch watching the end of *Million Dollar Baby* when Siena's phone rang. She stood from the couch and looked around the room. "Do you know where my purse ended up?"

"Babe, I barely remember closing the door behind you." Cash got up and followed the sounds to Siena's bag on the floor by the door and found her purse beneath it. He handed her the phone and carried her bag into the bedroom.

"Hi, Mom."

"Hi, honey. How are you doing?"

"Fine, why?"

"I saw more pictures of you and Gunner…"

"Yeah, that should be the last of them." Jewel had said *a few dates*. She had no idea why she said that to her mother except that it was wishful thinking.

"Oh, good. Are you still seeing Cash? Has he seen these?"

She walked into the bedroom and found Cash putting her clothes into a drawer. She mouthed, *Thank you.* "Yes, I'm still seeing Cash, but I haven't even seen them yet."

Cash wrinkled his brow.

She held up a finger and walked back toward the living

room. She knew she was just delaying the inevitable.

"Well, you look like you are having a very romantic dinner in one, and in another you look like you're the perfect couple leaving the restaurant. There are others, but nothing too remarkable."

"Great, Mom. I'll take a look." She sighed as she lowered herself to the couch. They'd had such a nice day together, making love, eating lunch, and cuddling while they watched a movie. She hated to ruin the evening, but there was no putting off Jewel's mention of *a few dates*.

"Siena, are you sure you're all right?"

"Yes, and I'm sure you know about Jack and the others ganging up on me last night." She blew out a breath and collapsed back on the couch.

"I'm sure it felt that way. They just worry about you."

"Well, I worry about me, too, so I guess we all have that in common."

"Oh. Um. Well…"

"Don't worry, Mom. I'm fine." She leaned forward and asked quietly into the phone, "Has Dad seen the pictures?"

"Your father doesn't read those magazines."

"Good. Okay. Thanks, Mom. I'm at Cash's, so I have to run. Love you, Mom. Thanks for calling."

"Love you, too, Siena. And, honey?"

"Yeah?"

"I would never tell you how to live your life, but just be true to yourself, okay?"

Siena's chest tightened. "Yeah. Okay, Mom."

After she ended the call, she pulled up her big girl panties and went to talk to Cash. He was in the bathroom putting her toiletries under the sink.

"I hope you don't mind. I thought we might as well get organized."

She leaned against the doorframe thinking about how lucky she was. "You cleared space for me in here and in your bedroom?"

"I cleared space for you in my life." He patted her hip as he walked out to the living room. "There are things I need to know about you."

She followed him. "And things we need to talk about."

Siena sat back down on the couch, and Cash sat on the coffee table in front of her, his hands on her knees.

"Me first. I realized that I don't know a few important things about you. Like, your favorite flavor of coffee and your go-to snacks. Your favorite body lotion, which I think I just found out. Any special soaps you like to use? Breakfast foods?" He ran his hands up her legs, leaned forward and kissed her lips.

She touched his cheek. "French vanilla. Carrots and blueberries. Um…soaps? Gosh, Dove cucumber is my secret favorite, but the makeup artists like me to use this other expensive stuff. Breakfast foods? Fruits, I guess. A croissant when I feel like being bad and maybe egg whites when I'm starved. What's yours?"

"Black coffee and granola. I'm a guy, so lotions and soaps? Not really my thing."

"I love that you thought to ask these things."

"I have lots more questions, but I already know that you prefer salad to meat, silk to cotton." He moved in closer, and she felt a tug down low. "Cuddling after making love. And if I kiss you right here…" He lightly touched the spot just below her earlobe with his rough hand, and Siena held her breath. "It makes your whole body shiver."

"Every…thing you do makes my whole body shiver." She had the urge to pull him to her and make out like teenagers. It would be so easy to get lost in him instead of facing the Gunner situation, but she wasn't a coward, and she loved Cash too much to keep him in the dark.

He tucked a lock of hair behind her ear and rubbed the back of her neck. "Well, sweet Siena, I could say the same about you."

"Cash."

"That sounded too serious. Why do I have a feeling this has nothing to do with our favorite anything?"

"Because it doesn't. I met with Jewel again, and—"

He sat back and held up his hands. "Wait. Before we go down this road, if this has to do with Gunner, let me just say this one thing." He reached under the newspaper on the end table beside the couch and threw three daily gossip newspapers on Siena's lap. "Today's pics."

Shit. "You've seen them? I haven't even seen them."

He shrugged. "I picked them up on the way home. Better to be prepared." He placed his hand on hers. "It's okay, babe. I saw them, and they didn't change a thing. But I have to tell you, I'm glad we're done with this shit. I'm a pretty secure guy, but these…" He tapped the magazines. "These were tough. The one when you're leaving the restaurant especially." He whistled. "The look on your face…That's an ego slap for sure. But after I got home and stewed over it for fifteen minutes or so and I started to clear out the place and make room for your stuff, I got over it."

She looked down at the magazines.

"Page two." Cash flipped the page, revealing the photo of Gunner and Siena leaving the restaurant. She looked like a woman in love, with dreamy eyes as Gunner whispered in her ear.

"He said, *Try to look like I'm all you can think about*, so I thought of you." She ran her finger over the image of her face. "It worked, don't you think?"

"That explains it." He moved to the couch and draped his arm around her shoulder. "So, tell me what Jewel had to say."

She leaned against him, feeling his strength, and as he pulled her to him, she felt his love. "She said Track Sports is flirting with me. Thinking of giving me a five-year contract."

"That's good, right? Wasn't that the whole idea?"

"Yes, it's like a dream come true, but she also implied that I would need to continue seeing Gunner." She reached for his hand, and Cash slid his hand from beneath hers and rubbed his forearm. "Cash?"

He leaned his elbows on his thighs and rubbed his hands together. He didn't answer her, and he kept his eyes trained on his hands. Siena placed her hand on his back and felt him flinch beneath her touch.

"Cash? Talk to me."

He turned his head and met her gaze. An icy chill ran down her spine.

"Are you considering this?"

"No. Yes. I don't know." She pulled at the ends of her hair. "It's confusing. They're talking about a five-year contract and a boatload of money."

He leaned back and crossed his arms over his chest. She watched his biceps twitch and the pulse point in his neck throb. "And?"

"And? I'm trying to figure out what to do. I mean, you know I love you. Gunner knows I love you."

Cash closed his eyes for a second, then he planted his elbows on his thighs again and sighed. "I thought we talked about this."

"We did, but it's sort of changed. I mean, I told Gunner about you, and he's not just an asshole. He was better this time. Nicer."

"Better this time? Siena, I'm not following."

"Jewel said they're talking about a really lucrative contract."

"So this is about money?"

She heard anger creeping into his voice, saw his jaw clench, and then felt the pit of her stomach sink as she realized that, yes, part of this was about the money. "We're talking about me being the face of Track Sports. That's huge."

"Do you need the money?" He was dead serious.

"No, but—"

"Is this the contract you always dreamed of? The one that will bring your career to another level?"

"Not really, but it offers security."

"It offers the demeaning of our relationship. I don't know what you earn, and I don't want to know, but what's our relationship worth to you?"

Siena could barely breathe, much less think.

"What are they offering? Half a mil?"

She shook her head. "There's no offer yet, but they're talking twenty times that."

Cash lowered his forehead to his hands with a groan. "Shit. That's more money than I'd see in ten lifetimes."

He faced Siena and placed his hand on her cheek. She covered his hand with hers and watched as his eyes filled with sadness.

"Baby, I love you."

She felt his hand shaking. "I love you, too."

He lowered his eyes. "But I can't stand between you and an opportunity like this."

"Thank you, but I haven't even decided what to do. I just wanted to talk to you about it."

He dropped his eyes. "Siena, I love you too much to be the guy in the background."

"What are you saying?" She grabbed his arm and clung to it.

He shook his head.

"Cash?" Tears welled in her eyes, and her breath came in hindered spurts. "Cash…you're not…" Silence hung between them, sliced only by the sound of their heavy breathing.

"I said I would never get involved in your career, and I won't ask you to make a choice. Christ, how could you make a choice?" He put his hand on her thigh. "You have the opportunity of a lifetime in the palm of your hands. And for what? A few dates with some guy? Hell, it sounds insanely innocuous."

Siena laughed through her tears. "Yeah. It does."

"Except I'm a jealous bastard. I've kept it pretty well under wraps, but when we promised exclusivity, it meant something to me."

"It meant something to me, too. It means something to me." Siena grabbed his hand and brought it to her chest. "Cash, please. I love you. I didn't agree, really…" *Except I sort of did. Oh no, no, no!*

"The fact that you even considered it means the opportunity is pretty important to you. And hell, Siena, it should be."

"Cash, I don't want to lose you. I don't want to lose us."

"Yeah? Well, neither do I." Cash pushed himself from the couch and paced the living room.

Siena was on his heels. "Then why are we torturing each other? It's not like I've even been offered a contract. I just wanted to talk to you about it in case Jewel got an offer."

Cash stopped pacing. "Come on, Siena. You wanted to talk to me to see if I'd agree to your continuing to see Gunner."

"Jewel was talking about all that money and security for if I ever had children." She didn't mean to raise her voice, but she couldn't control it. "And I started thinking, you know? What if we got married and you got injured in a fire? And what if we had kids, and I wanted to be with them? What then?" She began pacing. "I thought…I thought…It might mean more security." She plopped down on the couch and covered her face with her hands. "Damn it, Cash. I don't know what I thought, but it has nothing to do with me wanting to be with goddamn Gunner."

He closed the distance between them. "I know that. Goddamn it, Siena. I don't think you like Gunner in that way. And I know you fucking love me."

She rose and stared him down. "Then what the hell is all this?"

"How should I know? I thought the whole Gunner thing was over." Anger rolled off his broad chest, forming a wall between them.

"It was."

"*Was* being the operative word." He narrowed his eyes and took a step closer. "This isn't even about Gunner. It's about what you are willing to give up or compromise for your career."

"Damn it, Cash. How did we get from there"—she pointed to the bedroom—"to here?"

He put his arms around her, and Siena felt his heart hammering against her chest. She didn't want to argue and was too confused to try to figure out any of this. Cash's hand slid up her back and cupped her head.

"I think this is one of those times when we need to call a truce and take a step back. We don't need to figure this out right now, do we?"

His whisper was in such sharp contrast to his tight muscles and racing pulse that she had to lift her eyes to his.

"No."

He kissed her forehead. "Okay, then we take a deep breath and try to enjoy some time together." His voice was gravelly, with an undercurrent of hurt and something more. Anger? Disappointment? She wasn't sure. He wiped her tears with his hand. "Everything happens for a reason, right?"

"According to Vetta."

He nodded. "Well, I say we live in Vetta's world for a little while."

"Do you still want me here? Do you still want to go with me to Colorado this weekend? I won't hate you if you ask me to leave." *Please don't ask me to.*

"Babe, I want you with me every minute of every day. That's the problem."

Chapter Twenty-Eight

WEDNESDAY AND THURSDAY passed with quiet contentment. Siena and Cash managed to take the issue with Jewel off of the table and focus on enjoying their time together. They went to the market and shopped for foods they both enjoyed, took walks, and skipped dinners in lieu of making love. They got up afterward and nibbled on snacks until they fell back into each other's arms. By the time Friday arrived, it would appear to a stranger that the discussion about Gunner had never taken place, but Cash's insides had been churning ever since.

As the plane descended, Cash felt Siena squeeze his hand. "Are you okay?"

"Yeah. I hate that we have to spend two nights apart."

She rested her head on his shoulder, and Cash's body reacted with a rush of love for her. He draped his arm around her, pulling her closer, wishing he could rip out the armrest and feel her entire body against him. He'd been stewing over their discussion, and not bringing it up was killing him. On the one hand, he didn't want to keep her from such an incredible opportunity, one that meant more income than he'd ever dream of seeing, for sure. And on the other hand, he loved her completely, and the idea of being the guy in the background would never work for him. He was a lot of things, and yes, maybe he was a softy when it came to Siena. He sure as hell had never been before her. But when it came to respecting their relationship, he wasn't going to back down. He also knew what that meant. Nobody—male or female, in his world—would willingly walk away from ten million dollars for someone they had just fallen in love with. Even if that love was so consuming that they could barely breathe without each other. He closed his eyes for a beat as the plane landed and felt in his heart that Vetta was probably right. Maybe he and Siena had fallen in love for a reason. To pull the reins in on his riskiness so he didn't kill himself or someone else and to bring her career to the next level. *Fuck, that sucks.*

"Are you afraid of landings?" Siena asked.

His eyes shot open. "No. Why?"

"Your entire body is like one big, tense muscle. And your jaw is clenching." She touched his thigh. "Feel that."

She knew him so well now that it hurt even more to think about losing her, and that brought walls up around his heart.

"I'm fine." *Damn it. Don't be a dick.*

"Okay, relax. So, what's the plan? You'll drop me at Savannah's dad's house and then go to Gage's, right? Then you'll pick me up Sunday morning?"

"That's the plan."

"Where exactly does Gage live?"

He knew she was trying to bring him down from his frustration. It was just another thing about her that he loved. Most people would go mute around his tougher side, but not Siena. She coaxed him out of it every time. But this time he wasn't so sure she could. Knowing that Jewel would eventually make her decide about Track Sports—and Gunner. The flames were lit.

The burn was raw. It was just the scar that hadn't set in yet.

"Mount Grail Road. Top of the mountain."

The plane touched down, and Siena picked up her purse and set it in her lap.

"Which means nothing to me. I know exactly one driveway in Weston. Hal Braden's. Lucky for me I'll have you to chauffer me around."

He almost said, *Always*, but he had to get used to the idea that he might not always be there with her. He kissed the side of her head. "Lucky for me. At least this time I know you're prepared for the weather."

"Yeah, well, I have a handy-dandy fireman who makes sure I am."

They came down the ramp hand in hand and went to gather their luggage. Cash slung his black duffel bag over his shoulder and carried the rest of their luggage to the rental car desk.

"Why do you insist on bringing that duffel bag? It's not like they're calling for a snowstorm."

It was his go-bag. The bag he'd had with him when he'd rescued Siena from the storm the first night they'd met, and he took it with him anytime he was in a car or on a trip.

"Wait. Don't tell me." She bumped her hip against his and put her hand flat on his stomach.

God, I love your touch.

"Because being prepared is everything." She kissed his stubbly cheek.

Which is exactly why my walls are going back up.

SOME TRIPS BROUGHT couples closer together and some

tore them apart. Siena and Cash had become so close since they'd met that she could feel changes in his mood like changes in the wind. The air around him would shift, his facial features tensed or became softer, more relaxed, his breathing became fast or shallow, and his eyes were like windows to his heart. Since their talk on Wednesday, she'd seen him go through every emotion under the sun, and she'd known he was fighting against himself to keep whatever was going on in that handsome head of his under wraps. But now, riding in the car with him, the shift in energy felt like a fissure between them, and it scared her.

"Cash, since we're going to be spending two nights apart, do you want to talk about stuff?" She slid her hands beneath her thighs to keep from fidgeting. She'd noticed that he reacted to her moods, and if he knew she was nervous, he'd probably clam up to avoid stressing her out before arriving at the Bradens' ranch.

"Not really."

Ouch. "But this whole thing with Jewel is a little like the elephant in the car, right? Or is that my imagination?"

He gripped the steering wheel tighter and narrowed his eyes, which never left the road. "Do you really want to do this now?"

"Well, no. I don't really want to do it ever, but..."

"Look, Siena. We've practically moved in together, and you're about to see your family and celebrate one of the biggest days in Savannah and Jack's lives. Let's not spoil it. We're fine. All this shit with your career will figure itself out, and we'll see where we end up." He glanced at her, then back at the road. "None of it will change my feelings for you."

Despite his reassurance, the fissure was beginning to feel like a ravine—and she had no idea how to cross it. "But you said you couldn't be the guy in the background."

He didn't respond, and she could practically feel his muscles flexing beneath his parka. She knew damn well that he'd never put her in the position she was putting them in. Even if she might be jumping the gun. She knew she wasn't. She knew Jewel too well. She wouldn't have pushed Siena if she didn't see a contract on the horizon. *Track Sports.* That would be huge, equivalent to her Revlon contract, only she'd be paid much more. Any model would jump at the chance, and she wondered if most guys would be as adamant as Cash about the whole Gunner thing. She didn't think so. Then again, she wasn't in love with *most guys*. And if she were honest with herself, she'd admit that she didn't even want to make the concession and date Gunner. But it was a lot to give up—if she were even offered the opportunity.

By the time they reached Hal Braden's ranch Siena decided she'd call Jewel later. She needed to know exactly what she was facing. Maybe she didn't really mean she had to keep seeing Gunner. Maybe she'd misread the whole thing. The thought made her breathe a little easier.

Snow flurries blew through the chilly air, landing on the six inches of snow that covered the ground. Cash, being the prepared boyfriend that he was, had checked and rechecked the weather before they'd left New York, and Weston was expected to have a few flurries, but nothing major. Cash opened the back of the Land Rover they'd rented, and Siena reached for her bag. He placed his hand gently on her hip and pressed his cheek to hers. She nearly melted, thankful for the intimate embrace after the chilly ride over.

"I love you, Siena," he whispered against her neck before pulling her close.

"I love you, too."

"I want you to focus on your family and friends. Have a great time. Don't worry about us, okay?" He searched her eyes, and she felt her heart swell. "Remember, we're living in Vetta's world. The right thing will happen, whatever it is. But don't let it ruin your visit. I'm sorry I was grumpy on the way over."

She kissed him softly. "I know. We're both confused, but I'm glad you came with me. Knowing you're so close is much better than thinking you're all the way back in New York. I know that seems silly, but..." She shrugged. She felt her phone vibrate in her pocket and ignored it. She wanted every second she could possibly have with Cash, and if it was Jewel, she'd just as soon not know what she had to say. At least not right then.

"It's not silly. It's why I came." He hoisted her bags from the car. "It's love, babe. Come on. Let's get you inside before your lips turn blue."

Hal answered the door wearing a thick flannel shirt with a white T-shirt underneath, a pair of Levi's, and a welcoming smile. "Siena. We're so glad you made it." He opened his arms and she fell into them. She'd loved Hal the minute she'd met him the day Savannah and Jack celebrated their engagement. At six foot six with thick hair that was more gray than black, kind, dark eyes that were mirrored in each of his handsome sons' faces, and shoulders almost as wide as the doorframe, he was like a big, comfortable bear.

"It's good to see you, Hal."

"Now, y'all come on in out of the cold and introduce me to your handsome beau." Hal held a hand out to Cash. "Hal Braden."

"Cash Ryder, sir." Cash shook his hand as Hal's eyes ran between the two of them.

"Nice to meet you, Cash. Are you staying with us this weekend?"

They left their shoes with the others near the door and walked into the spacious two-story ranch-style house. Hardwood floors paved the way from the spacious foyer to the open living room and the entrance to the kitchen. Siena looked around the room, remembering the last time she was there, when Savannah announced her engagement and Savannah's brother Hugh got married in their backyard. It was so romantic, she'd actually cried.

"No, sir. My brother lives up the mountain. I'll be staying there." Cash settled his hand on the small of Siena's back, and she filled with pride. She loved who Cash was. She knew he'd treat everyone with equal respect, from waitresses to businessmen, which was more than she could say for some of the wealthy men she'd been set up with in the past.

"Well, probably a good thing. Too many women in one house can drive a man to drinking." Hal winked at him as Savannah came out of the kitchen and squealed.

"You're here!" She hugged Siena. "And you brought the handsome fireman!" She hugged Cash and laughed. "I'm kidding, Cash. I'm so happy you came."

"Nice to see you again, Savannah. I'm not staying. I'm going to stay with my brother Gage. I'm just saying hello; then I'll leave you ladies alone to celebrate."

"He lives here? What a coincidence." Savannah looked toward the kitchen. "Do you have time to meet a few people before you go?"

"Sure."

She guided them into the kitchen, and Siena saw Hal hold Cash back for a second and whisper something to Cash that she couldn't decipher. Whatever it was, it brought another shift in the air around him. An unusual shift she couldn't read.

Treat and Rex, two of Savannah's older brothers, pushed away from the counters where they'd been leaning to greet them. Treat was the same height as Hal, and he had three inches on Rex. They shared the same black hair, though Rex's was tucked beneath a Stetson and hung to his collar while Treat's was cut short, more businesslike. Treat owned resorts all over the world, but when he'd fallen in love with Max, his now pregnant wife, he'd settled down on a neighboring property and helped his father part-time with the ranch while running his business from Weston.

"Siena." He embraced her, then kissed each cheek. "You look beautiful." He held a hand out to Cash. "Treat Braden, and this is Rex. We're Savannah's brothers. Well, two of them, anyway."

"Cash Ryder." He shook their hands. "Nice to meet you."

Rex tipped his hat after shaking Cash's hand and hugging Siena. He made a career of helping his father run the family thoroughbred business, and his body bore the fruits of his labor. While Treat standing by himself would have been a formidable presence with his broad shoulders and hard body, Rex's strength rippled beneath his tight gray T-shirt and snaked down his forearms in mountains and valleys. Six-pack abs were only a piece of his cowboy allure. And when his dark-haired girlfriend, Jade, came up behind Siena and hugged her with another squeal, then went to Rex's side, she thought they were the perfect couple. Just like her and Cash.

She reached for Cash's hand.

"Who's this handsome stranger?" Jade asked. She raised her eyebrows at Siena.

"This is my boyfriend, Cash."

"Cash? Great name. You know what they say: You can never have too much money or—"

"Hey." Rex pulled her into his arms. "You got enough of the *or*."

"See why I do that? Look what it gets me." She was a petite woman, and when she rose up onto her tiptoes, Rex lowered his lips to hers. "You know I only have eyes for one sexy cowboy."

Siena squeezed Cash's hand. That's how she felt about him. She only had eyes for Cash.

"Where's Max?" Siena looked around for Treat's wife.

"Right here." Max came through the door and embraced Siena. "Great to see you again." Her belly came between them, and Siena reached for it, then hesitated. "Oh, go ahead. Everyone does." She smiled at Cash. "Hi. Cash, right?"

He nodded. "Congratulations on your pregnancy."

Max brushed her dark hair from her shoulders and smiled at Cash, then looked at Treat. "Thanks. We're really excited."

"Okay, babe, I'm going to let you visit and head up the mountain."

Siena held tightly to his hand. She wanted him to stay, but this was Savannah's party, not hers.

"Cash, the men are all getting together tomorrow night while the girls celebrate. Why don't you and your brother join us?" Treat turned to Rex. "Have we decided where we're going?"

"What's wrong with here?" Rex looked at their father.

"Here? Aw, hell, Rex. You guys'll be up all night, and I'm an old man." Hal leaned against the wall and kicked one ankle over the other. "How about your place?"

"No can do, Hal," Jade said. "We're in the midst of painting, so the furniture is all misplaced. What about Treat's? I can't believe you guys didn't figure all this out earlier."

"I tried, but Treat said Rex was taking care of it," Max said with a smirk.

Rex eyed Treat. "He did, did he?"

"Um, I don't know what you guys had planned, but if you can make it up the mountain, I know Gage has his buddies over every week for poker night, so he's used to having his house overtaken by a bunch of guys. I'm sure he won't mind if you meet there. There's not much around except woods, beer, poker, and..." He shrugged. "I mean, unless this is a stripper party..."

"Um, that would be a hell no, thank you very much," Savannah said.

Treat and Rex exchanged a glance.

"Is he married?" Treat asked.

"Treat." Max settled her hand on her burgeoning belly.

"I'm only asking because if he is, it's not his brother he has to ask." Treat placed his hand on her shoulder. "We could have it at our house."

"What a bore," Rex said. "No offense, but I vote for poker on the mountain."

"See, you should have let me plan it," Max said, patting Treat's hand. "Poor Jack is going to be disappointed that you guys didn't go all out for him."

"You're kidding, right?" Savannah asked. "Jack hates this kind of thing. Besides, his brothers aren't here, so it's not like it's his bachelor party. His idea of a fun evening is sitting around with a beer, talking about surviving something. Anything."

"I didn't have a bachelor party," Treat added. "I think for

guys it's different than for women. Maybe if we were twenty-three and felt like our lives were over with the old ball and chain." He stepped away from Max as she swatted a hand toward him. "But we're old. To us, or at least for me, our wedding was the day I never realized I'd been waiting for, and the celebration was hearing Max say *I do*."

Siena sighed. "I love that." Cash squeezed her hand, and she knew she had that.

"That's Jack, too. You should go up the mountain and get lost in the woods or something. He'll love that. It's more than enough." Savannah looked at Cash. "Thanks for saving the day. I thought that after the way Treat helped save our cousin Blake's wedding, he would have had this one planned to a T."

"Excuse me. Blame Rex, not me."

Rex glared at him. "Kiss my—"

Cash cut him off. "Okay, then. Give me one of your numbers and I'll text you after I get there and run it by Gage, but I'm sure it's fine." Cash kissed Siena's cheek. "I better run. Oh, that mountain can be a bear at night. You have four-wheel drive?"

"No mountain's ever gotten the better of me." Rex crossed his arms, and Jade rolled her eyes.

Treat and Cash exchanged phone numbers, and Siena walked him to the door after he said goodbye to everyone else.

"That was really nice of you, but don't feel pressured to join them. If you want time alone with your brother, they'd totally understand."

He gazed into her eyes with an unfamiliar expression. "To be honest, I could use the distraction. I love my brother, but a night of just the two of us is not nearly as fun as a bunch of guys playing poker."

He pressed a sweet, loving kiss to her lips that wouldn't come close to holding her over for the next two nights. After watching him leave, she turned and practically ran into Savannah, Max, and Jade, who had formed a wall of concerned faces behind her.

Savannah took Siena by the arm. Jade took her other arm, and as they led her into the living room, the narrow look in Savannah's green eyes had her wishing she'd walked right out the door with Cash.

Chapter Twenty-Nine

CASH DROVE UP the mountain to Gage's house with the radio blaring, hoping his brother would have a cold beer ready for him. Maneuvering around deep ruts and potholes, he made a mental note to tell Treat and Rex about the sorry shape of the steep mountain road. He knew his brother wouldn't care if he invited them up, and he wasn't lying when he said he needed the distraction. He and Siena were a great couple, but he knew why she hadn't checked the text that came in when they were in Hal's driveway. She'd been hesitant to check her messages the last few days, and with each one, he'd watched her hold her breath. Cash had made up his mind. He wouldn't make her choose between him and the contract if it came through and held the stipulation that she continue to see Gunner or some other athlete. The only problem was, as right as he knew it was to let her take the opportunity when it came up—and he was pretty certain it was going to—he loved her too much to just walk away, and he knew himself too well to think he'd be okay with it.

Siena was the hottest model out there, and Track Sports would be lucky to have her. He even understood their goddamn desire to have her dating someone in the industry, even if he didn't agree with it. But he knew himself too well, and there wasn't a chance in hell he'd be okay with his girlfriend's lips on some other man for all the world to see. Just the thought of it made him want to kill someone. But the issue went deeper than that. Even though he knew it wasn't a fair thing to expect—and he never realized he believed so strongly in love until he met Siena—in his heart he believed that if she really loved him, she wouldn't consider the opportunity beyond a passing wonder. But then again, he'd never held the opportunity of a lifetime in the palm of his hand. Oh wait. Yes, he had, only his opportunity had to do with love, not money. *Siena.*

Gage lived on five wooded acres in a rustic, four-bedroom stone-and-wood home, which looked like it emerged out of the landscape instead of being built on top of it. The front of the house boasted deep-set windows, thick stone walls with chocolate brown trim, and an arched wooden door with heavy, black hardware that looked like it came straight out of a fairy tale.

He knocked twice before walking in.

"Gage?" Cash called into the large open great room.

The wide-planked floors were scuffed and worn and covered with a few strategically placed rugs with Aztec designs. The kitchen, off to his left with no real separation from the great room besides a massive wooden table, was lined with green cabinets with earth-tone marble tops. To his right was his favorite part of the house, a stone fireplace that took up about three-quarters of the far wall. There was a fire going, and Cash kicked off his boots, grabbed a cold beer from the fridge—he could always count on Gage—and sank into one of the leather recliners in front of the fire.

Just beyond the wall with the fireplace were two bedrooms

and a narrow stairwell that led upstairs to two more bedrooms and a loft. Cash listened for Gage, but the house was silent, save for the crackling fire. He looked up through the open-beamed ceiling at the loft and saw no sign of him there, either. Just as well. Cash needed a moment to decompress. He sucked down his beer and let out a long, needed sigh. As he leaned his head back, he caught sight of a photo tucked into a nook on the side of the fireplace. Cash smiled as he dragged himself from the chair and retrieved it. He and his brothers Gage and Duke were in the middle of a basketball game, shirtless. Gage was dribbling, Duke had his arms up in front of him, and Cash was below the basket. Blue and Jake stood off to the side, hands on their hips, while their sister, Trish, whom he hadn't seen in what felt like forever, sat on the grass beside the court in her bathing suit with oversized sunglasses on her face and a large glass of something beside her. He missed the days when they'd all hang out and annoy one another.

He heard the door open and set the frame back on the mantel, inhaling the woodsy smell of the fire, which made him wish Siena were with him. She'd love cuddling in front of the fire. He pushed the thought away. He might have to get used to trying not to think about her soon enough.

"Cash. Sorry, man. I was just out back getting wood."

Cash opened his arms and embraced his older brother. All the Ryder men were six three or six four, athletically built, and competitive as hell. "You need to go outside to get wood? I usually do that best in the bedroom."

"Yeah, well, I'm not as limited as you are." He flashed a boyish grin. His dirty-blond hair fell over his blue eyes as it had for as long as Cash could remember. "Besides, I can't seem to take things to the next level with Sally." Gage knocked the snow from his boots and coat and left them by the door. Then he grabbed a bundle of wood from the porch and crossed the room, setting it beside the fireplace.

"You still haven't made your move?" Cash asked.

"Well, I wouldn't say that. We're great friends."

"Christ. What is it with you and Tommy? I feel like you've both been playing this friendship game for years."

"It's not a game, and I have." He took a long pull of his beer and drew his thick, cable-knit sweater over his head, tossing it on the couch. "I don't want to talk about Sally. Tell me about you. Duke said you were risking your life or some shit like that."

Cash shifted his eyes away from Gage. *Goddamn Duke and his big mouth.*

Gage shook his head. "Cash, you gotta pull yourself together. Life or death, man."

Cash ran his hand through his hair. "I'm done with that shit, so don't worry. I pulled it together. It just took a little time, and believe me, I know just how stupid it was. I'm not proud of the shit I pulled." He rubbed the tattoo on his forearm, thinking of Tooler and Samuel.

"Yeah, well, if you ever need help again with something like that, you know Danica Carter, the woman who owns No Limitz, where I work, right?"

"Sure, you've mentioned her. What about her?" *Please don't try to set me up. I've got Siena and she's more than I could ever want.*

"She used to be a therapist. I can't tell you how many people she's helped at the youth center, and she's not even a therapist anymore. She can help if you ever get in that situation again."

Cash stood and paced. "Can we stop the self-help lesson now? Jesus, I came here to visit for a few days, not to be told how to fix the errors of my ways."

"Hey, whatever, man. I just want to help." Gage tossed a log onto the fire. "What's wrong with you? You're all pissy, like you haven't been laid in months. I thought you were here with your girlfriend. Siena, right? She holding out on you?"

Cash slid him a look, and Gage raised his hands in surrender. "Just asking."

"No, she's not *holding out* on me. I've just got a lot of shit on my mind that I haven't wanted to think about, and now that she's not with me, it's all I can think about."

"Grab another beer and we'll see if we can weed through whatever it is."

Cash headed to the fridge and brought back two beers. "Hey, before I forget, do you mind if a few guys come up for a guys' night out tomorrow? Siena's brother Jack is getting married to Savannah Braden. Her father lives in Weston, and the girls are having their bridal shower at her father's house, so the guys need a place to hang out for the night."

Gage shrugged. "It's cool with me if they can handle getting here."

"Great." Cash handed him a beer and relaxed into the recliner again. He texted Treat the address and directions; then he shoved his phone in his pocket and blew out a breath.

"So spill your guts, little brother. Let's see if we can get some of that piss and vinegar out of you."

Cash wasn't in the mood to talk. He was in the mood to fight. "You still chop your own wood?"

"If you're not talking sexually, yeah."

Cash set down the beer and headed for the door. "Get your

coat. I need to borrow your ax."

Cash tossed his parka to the ground after a few strong swings of the ax. "Nothing like splitting wood." His breath met the frigid air and bloomed into white puffs of smoke.

Gage leaned against the side of the house, arms crossed, eyeing Cash in the big-brother way he had. "Want to spill the beans now?"

Cash stopped in mid-backswing. He kept his eyes trained on the wood. "I love her, man."

Gage nodded, face still serious. "And?"

The ax came down on the wood and split it down the center with a loud *crack*. Cash tossed the wood to the ground and stood another slab on the wide tree stump. He dug his boots into the snow and brought the ax back again. Through gritted teeth, he said, "And her job has some weird shit that goes along with it." The ax came down hard, driven by his frustration, and split the sucker in two. The wood toppled off the stump, and he set another piece up to be split. He breathed hard. His lungs burned from the cold, but his body was hot with anger as he laid it all out for Gage—from the way he and Siena had met, to the dates with Gunner and the photos that followed, and the possibility of her dating Gunner, or some other athlete, while they were supposedly in an exclusive relationship.

He watched Gage closely, his eyes narrowing, his arms tightening across his chest. "So why date her?"

Cash set the ax down and leaned on the end of it. "Did I not just tell you that I love her?" He shook his head. *Dumbass.*

"Sure, but, dude. Look at yourself. And how much can she love you if she's gonna go out with some other guy? For work or not, that alone tells me a great deal about her."

Cash gritted his teeth. "Careful."

"I'm just sayin'. Sure, the first two dates. Whatever. You knew about that when you went out with her. But now? You're all but living together and she's talking about maybe going out with another guy?"

"Not out on a date like that. It's for work."

"Right. And how would she feel if you did the same thing?"

Gage came to his side and locked a serious stare on him. The stare he'd used when Cash was a teenager, about to do something stupid, like jump off the edge of a rock to a lake twenty feet below without first checking the depth of the water. Cash drew in a deep breath.

"I never would." *Fuck.* He needed to be told what he already knew like he needed a fucking hole in his head.

"Exactly my point. Wake the fuck up."

"Ten million, Gage." He watched Gage's eyes narrow. "That's probably what they'll offer her, and who am I to stand in her way?"

"Fuck."

"My thoughts exactly."

Gage took the ax from him and set it inside the shed. Then he grabbed Cash's coat from the ground and put his arm over his shoulder. "You don't need this ax. You need to get completely blitzed so you can't think about it."

"Now you're seeing my side of things."

"You know you can't influence her decision, right?"

"No shit." It was all he could think about.

"No wonder you're acting like your dick hasn't been drained in months."

Inside the house, Gage poured them each a glass of whiskey. "All you can do is wait this shit out." He handed Cash a glass of whiskey and held his up in a toast. "To being fucked by love."

"She could still make the decision that we're worth walking away from the deal."

Gage nodded. "As I said, to being fucked by love."

Chapter Thirty

SIENA WAS THANKFUL Saturday had flown by in a flurry of guests arriving and preparation for the shower. She hadn't slept a wink after Savannah, Max, and Jade drilled her about everything and anything Cash related. She didn't have sisters, and she loved the way they shared so openly, but talking about Cash all day and into the night had made the text from Jewel—*Track Sports proposed! Call me!*—and the ensuing phone call—*Nine point five million. Five years. There are a few stipulations, and I know your first question is about Gunner. The answer is yes. You need to continue a high-profile athletic association for the first two months of the contract and maintain a public alliance, which could be a friendship, not a romance, during the contract. But if you have issues with Gunner, we have a few others to consider*—even more painful. She'd tried to negotiate with Jewel, but Jewel had been in the industry long enough to know what was negotiable and what wasn't. Apparently, swapping Gunner for Cash wasn't a viable option.

She hadn't told Cash about the offer, and she didn't plan to until she saw him again in person. And now, as she stood beside Brianna, one of Savannah's sisters-in-law, watching the sun set along the mountains beyond the Braden ranch, and her mother put her hand on her shoulder, she wished once again that she could cry. But apparently, only her brothers could make tears come from Siena's eyes.

"You okay, honey? You've been so quiet all day." Her mother wore her hair loose, and as Lacy, Savannah's brother Dane's girlfriend, approached, she dropped her hand from Siena's shoulder.

"I'm fine, Mom. This is so beautiful. I was just taking it in."

"You girls okay?" Lacy's blond corkscrew curls framed her tanned face. She and Dane lived on a boat off the coast of Florida. He owned the Brave Foundation and worked as a marine researcher and shark tagger, and Lacy worked remotely for World Geographic, developing and managing marketing programs for nonprofit organizations.

"Yeah, perfect," Siena said. "What can we help with?"

"We were just admiring the view. Of course, this side of the yard is my favorite, because that's where we said our vows," Brianna said with a smile.

"A night we'll never forget." Lacy put her arm around Brianna. "So, Hugh's at home with Layla?"

"Yeah. He's got a whole weekend of father-daughter time planned. Layla's excited." Hugh had adopted Layla, Brianna's six-year-old daughter, when they married. "I'm sorry he missed Jack's quasi bachelor party, but he refused to let me hire a sitter, and my mom was booked. He's really particular about who watches Layla."

"Jack doesn't mind. He's like Treat. Family comes first, and Layla is family. You probably should have just brought her," Savannah said.

"As much as she would have loved it, I kinda wanted some girl time with you guys." Brianna shrugged.

"I don't blame you, dear." Siena's mother patted Brianna on the back.

Ellie, Kate, and Riley, Savannah's brother Josh's fiancée who was a fashion designer like Josh and lived in Manhattan not far from Savannah, carried big boxes into the living room and set them down on the table.

"We've got goodies!" Riley's brown hair was pulled back in a ponytail, and she placed her hands on her hips with a sigh, looking great in her skinny jeans and sweater. Riley was a curvy, beautiful woman, and Siena admired how comfortable she was in her own skin.

"Fun bridal shower games," Ellie added.

Siena loved that Savannah had invited Ellie and Kate, and she loved knowing that Savannah's brothers and Jack would be with Cash tonight. Somehow that made him feel even more a part of the family.

The front door opened and closed. Treat helped Max take off her coat and boots. Then they came into the living room hand in hand in their stockinged feet. He hugged Savannah, then greeted Siena's mom. Even in his stockinged feet, Levi's, and rugged leather coat, Treat looked regal.

"I can't believe you drove her over," Savannah chided him. "Max is a capable woman and Rex plowed the road between your driveway and Dad's perfectly."

"You don't take chances with the people you love," Treat said.

Siena's heart melted a little. She remembered how each of Savannah's brothers had fawned over their significant others at Hugh's wedding. That's what she wanted, to be loved like that. *That's what I have with Cash.*

Treat leaned against the wall with his long legs crossed in

front of him. "I still can't believe my baby sister's getting married."

Max went to his side and hugged him. "I love you, but you see how you're the only male in the room?"

Treat looked at the others and lifted a brow.

"You are banished from the house." She kissed him, consumed by his large frame as he wrapped his arms around her and deepened the kiss.

"Am I allowed to go see Dad?" Treat rose and patted Max's butt as she walked by him.

"He's in the barn." Savannah locked eyes with him. "Rex is with him. I think he's missing Mom."

Treat nodded. "You guys have fun. Hey, sweetness, do you want me to come back and get you?"

Max blew him a kiss. "I'm staying with the girls tonight."

Savannah wrapped her arm around her. "It's only one night."

"One night without my wife—that's what my little sister getting married costs me?" Treat smiled. "Totally worth it. Have fun. I'm going to spend some time with Dad. Then we're heading over to Gage's." He kissed Max on the top of her head before heading to the door, where he hesitated and turned back. "If you guys need anything tonight, call me. I don't mind coming back, but I don't want you guys on the roads at night. They freeze over here really quickly. It's different than in the city."

Savannah rolled her eyes. "Yes, Dad."

As soon as he was out the door, Siena moved closer to Max. "You're so lucky."

So am I.

Max smiled. "Braden men definitely know how to treat

their women."

Jade filled wineglasses for each of them and handed Max a glass of ice water, then clinked her glass with Max's. "Hear, hear."

Siena smiled. "Cash is that type of man."

"So are your brothers," Savannah said.

"Not all of them are like that." Siena sat back, thinking of her brothers. "Look at Rush. He's as cocky as they come. I'm not sure how he gets the women he does. They must have a thing for Olympic skiers, because he's not the fawning type. Now, Dex and Sage, they're fawners, and I have no idea what Kurt is like with women. He's so glued to his desk that I wonder if he even dates."

"Oh, honey. I'm sure Kurt dates," her mother said. "He's just very focused on his career right now."

"It's the quiet ones that are animals in the bedroom." Jade leaned forward as if sharing a secret. "Rex." She nodded.

Siena's mom, Joanie, shook her head.

Savannah covered her ears and closed her eyes. "Please. *Ugh*, that's my brother."

"Speaking of brothers. Savannah, Mom and I made something for you, and if you don't mind, I'd like to give it to you now, before you drink too much to really enjoy it."

Savannah looked between Siena and her mother. "You made me something? Wow. Of course I'd love to see it."

Siena retrieved the gift-wrapped box from the room where she was staying and brought it to Savannah. "We wanted to give you something you couldn't buy yourself."

Savannah settled onto the couch with the others surrounding her. Siena and her mother stood behind her. "Thank you." She unwrapped the box and withdrew the wooden photo album, tastefully painted with a mountainous landscape. Savannah looked at Joanie. "You painted this?"

Joanie nodded, smiled.

"It reminds me of when Jack and I met." She ran her fingers over the image of trees and the sunset blooming over the mountaintops. "It's gorgeous. Thank you."

Savannah opened the album. The first page announced their wedding date in silver calligraphy. She turned the pages, lingering over every one. "You've got our whole lives in here. Look how cute Jack was at six." She pointed to a picture of Jack holding a shovel, a wide smile on his lips.

"We even included those awkward years that you'd rather forget. Wait until you see the pictures from when you guys were teenagers." Siena looked at her mom and smiled.

Savannah flipped forward. "Oh my God. Look at those bangs! I can't believe I ever wore my hair like that."

"We all did," Jade reminded her.

Savannah flipped forward and slowed as she came to the years when Jack was with Linda. *The In-Between Years.* Joanie placed her hand on Savannah's shoulder, and Savannah patted it with her own.

"I'm glad you included this," Savannah said. She looked up at Joanie. "I don't want to pretend Jack didn't have a life, and a wife, before me. I've always felt that Jack is who he is because of all he'd gone through." She looked at Siena. "Thank you for doing this." She had tears in her eyes. She set the album on the table and stood to embrace each of them.

"I never thought I'd meet anyone like Jack," Savannah admitted. "And I can't imagine how I ever went so many years without him."

"Jack is a very special man," Joanie said, brushing Savannah's hair from her shoulder. "I think all of you ladies have found very special men."

"All I can say is, I never thought I'd meet a guy like Cash, and I'm so glad I did." Siena saw Jade, her mother, and Savannah exchange a knowing look. Siena wished they could turn their attention back to the album. It had been a nice distraction from thinking about the predicament she was in.

"Let's all sit down and relax." Savannah settled back on the couch.

Siena reached for her wine and took a gulp. The uncomfortable wave of tension she'd felt when she'd walked into NightCaps and found she was in the middle of some type of intervention returned. The room went deathly silent. She finished her wine and set her glass on the table.

"So, Siena. Let's talk about your smart-ass-turned-romantic fireman that you adore so much you're willing to throw him away." Jade refilled her glass.

"Why do I feel like I've been set up…again?"

"Maybe because you have," Savannah answered.

"Why does everyone feel like I need an intervention? I love Cash and he loves me. That's the bottom line and the only thing that matters." Siena sat on the couch and was immediately flanked by her mother on one side and Savannah on the other. Ellie and Kate sat in the recliners facing them, and Max settled into Hal's favorite leather recliner beside the couch. Brianna sat on the floor by Ellie's chair. Riley carried one of the boxes into the room, and Jade carried the wine to the coffee table; then they sat on the floor facing Siena.

"Honey, you can't cut and run from this hen party." Her mother patted her leg. "So you might as well forget that wall you're putting up and settle in, or it's going to be a long night.

Now, these women just want to share their thoughts with you. They care about you."

Riley pulled out the magazines that had pictures of Siena and Gunner together and spread them across the living room floor in front of her and Kate. "There are ten here," Riley said.

"And probably about fifty more pictures online, at least from what I saw," Ellie said.

"And I told you that Gunner was Aida's client, so I know the *whole* story." Savannah glared at Siena.

Gulp!

"And all I want to know is, are you really considering the Track Sports contract with Gunner attached to it?" Savannah crossed her arms and tilted her head, her eyes locked on Siena.

"No." She looked around the room. "Yes. I don't know." She leaned forward and buried her face in her hands, then felt her mother stroking her back. "When you say you know the whole story, exactly what does that mean?"

"What I know, and what these girls know, isn't the same thing. Suffice it to say that I know everything, and they just know what they've seen in the magazines." Savannah looked at Jade, who nodded.

"I've only seen the magazines," Jade confirmed.

"Well, not exactly only that," Max added. She looked at Siena with a wrinkled brow. "I'm sorry, Siena. I know this feels wrong. But do you really love Cash?"

"Yes, with all my heart and soul."

"And does he love you back?" Max asked.

"Yes." She wasn't sure where Max was going with this conversation, but her stomach clenched.

"Well, you're going to hate him, but Treat did some checking on him, because that's just what he does." Max shook her head. "I'm so sorry. I know he shouldn't have."

"I don't understand. Why would he do that?"

Savannah sighed. "Because my brother checks out everyone who's affiliated to those he loves. He checked up on Jack, and I'm sure he checked up on all of you, too, when you hooked up with my brothers." She ran her eyes over Lacy, Jade, Max, Riley, and Bree. "He worries about stuff. It's just who he is. I can't make up excuses for him. He just…cares too much."

"I'm still really lost here." Siena's voice began to rise, and she felt her mother's hand on her back again.

"Honey, he was being helpful," her mother said.

"So, what did he find? Because I don't care if he has skeletons in his closet. I love him for who he is now, not for whatever he might have done in his past." *Oh my God. What could he have done to warrant the worried look in Max's eyes?*

Max rolled her eyes. "Nothing. He couldn't find a damn bit of dirt on him."

Siena breathed a sigh of relief. "You guys must think I'm crazy. Especially all of you." She looked at the others. "I'm not a slut, and I'm not someone who hurts other people for the fun of it, either."

"We all know that," Savannah said. "But I have to admit, I'm really confused. You talked about wanting a strong romantic man who will treat you well and love you for you, and it seems like you found him, unless maybe you didn't and we're not seeing that?"

"No. I definitely did. Cash is"—she sighed—"everything. He's more than everything."

"So why date this goof?" Bree held up *Us Daily*.

Shame brought a flush to Siena's neck and cheeks. Everyone was staring at her. She felt like she was in a pressure cooker, and the worst part was, she knew she was in the wrong. She'd known it since she first accepted the date with Gunner. "Aren't we supposed to be celebrating Savannah's engagement?"

"How can we when we know you're hurting?" Savannah asked.

"Well, why don't I leave so I don't ruin the party?" She pushed off the couch, and Savannah pulled her back down.

"I know you don't have any sisters," Savannah began. "And neither did I until I met these girls, who are now my best friends. This, I found out, is what sisters do."

"Yeah, well, I have five brothers who are really good at making me feel like shit, thank you very much."

Her mother gasped. "Siena."

"Sorry, Mom. But don't you think I'm not already ashamed by those stupid pictures? By accepting the stupid dates in the first place?" She ran her eyes over the others. "Okay, fine. I hate myself for agreeing to it in the first place, and now Jewel, my agent, has secured an almost ten-million-dollar contract because I was willing to dirty my goody-goody image. And I hate myself for it. I hate those stupid pictures." She kicked the magazines out of the way and felt her eyes well with tears. The need to tell them the truth she'd been holding in for so long burned in her chest. Her body began to tremble, and the words tumbled out, pulling tears from her eyes. "I can't stand to look in the mirror, and every time I look at Cash, I know how much it hurt him to see them, even though he knew the truth behind them before they came out."

"Siena." Savannah touched her back.

Siena shrugged her off. "No. You're right. You're all right. And you're all better people than me, because I was too weak to stand up to my agent and tell her to fuck off. I was afraid of losing my other contracts, when—" She spun around and faced her mother with tears streaking her cheeks. "Oh God, Mom. I didn't mean to say *fuck*. Shit. Oh God. I'm sorry."

Her mother shook her head. "Finish your damn story."

When her mother smiled, she knew she understood, and it made her laugh through her tears.

"Well, I don't know about the others, but I'm no better than you. When Rex and I were first dating, I put him through hell to get me," Jade said.

"But I'm not doing it to get Cash's attention. I'm just weak." She covered her face with her hands again.

"I don't buy it," her mother said. "You're one of the strongest women I know."

"Oh, really? I compromised my own values for a potential contract so Dad could look at me and go, *That's my girl.*"

The room went silent, save for her beating heart. "Holy shit. Oh my God." Siena pushed to her feet. "Where the fuck did that come from?" She paced the floor as her mother rose to her feet. "Shit. Shit. Shit. I have more money than I could ever spend. I have security for my kids."

"Kids?" her mother asked.

Siena was too wrapped up in her own head to answer. "I don't need that stupid contract, and I don't need an agent who would ask me to do it, either. What the fuck was I thinking?" She gathered her hair in one hand and pulled it over her shoulder. "Oh my God. Cash. Jesus. What must he think of me?" She looked at Savannah. "I know exactly what he thinks. The same thing I think when I look in the mirror. Holy shit. I have to fix this." She looked around the room, not knowing what in the hell she was looking for.

"Siena? Honey?" Her mother stood, and Siena wrenched

herself away from her as she dialed the phone and left a message for Jewel. "Jewel, it's Siena Remington. Turn it down. I don't want Track Sports, and we need to have a talk. I refuse to make my personal life part of any deal. If that means I lose contracts, then it does. Sorry. I'll be back in town Monday. Please don't call this weekend, because I'm with my family." She ended the call and punched the road Gage lived on into the GPS on her phone.

"Siena, are you okay? We didn't mean to make you hate yourself," Savannah said.

"I owe you so much, Savannah. I hated myself for even considering the contract. I love you for making me realize why I was doing it." She spun around and looked at her mother's furrowed brow, her loving gaze. "Mom, I'm so sorry. I love Dad; you know I do. And I never realized I might be doing any part of what I do with my life because of him. When that came out just now? That was news to me. Maybe it's an excuse. I have no idea, but I know something compelled me to be weak in a time when I should have been strong, and whether that was the need to impress Dad or something else, I have no clue. But I do know this. I want to be with Cash Ryder more than I want anything in this world—including modeling, which you know I live and breathe."

"Yes, honey. I know you do." Her mother hugged her. "It would have been odd for you to grow up unscathed by being pushed so hard. I'm not saying that the pressure to keep doing more and being more is because of your father. I think that drive is internal, too, but all things happen for a reason."

"What did you say?"

"All things happen for a reason," her mother repeated.

"That's what Vetta said, too. I'm starting to think she's

right." Siena headed for the front door.

"Where are you going?" Savannah called after her.

"I have to go see Cash." She stopped in front of the door. "I don't have a car. Can I borrow a car?" She looked frantically from Jade to Savannah. Her entire body was shaking. She had to get to him.

"Yes, of course." Savannah grabbed the keys to her rental car from the kitchen counter and threw them to Siena. "But I'm going, too."

"Me too," her mother said.

"Wait. I can't miss this." Ellie said, running toward the door with Kate right behind her.

"As much as I want to see this, and trust me I do," Jade began, "I'll stay with Max, because you might think Treat is a full-on gentleman, but if Max were left alone or put in a car after dark on a night when it had been flurrying all day, he'd string me up like a kite."

"Thanks, Jade," Max said.

Brianna and Lacy said they were staying, too, but Riley followed the others out to the car.

Snow flurries dampened Siena's hair as she climbed into the driver's seat. As her socks hit the gas pedal, she realized she hadn't put on her shoes. Or her coat. Her mother joined her in the front, and Siena decided not to tell anyone of her idiocy. Savannah, Riley, Ellie, and Kate piled into the back. Siena drove fast along the dark rural roads and headed toward the mountain, following the voice on her GPS, which directed her perfectly to Mount Grail Road.

"Siena, slow down." Her mother grasped the door as the SUV whipped around the bend and onto Mount Grail Road.

Her mother's warning brought a flashback to the night she

met Cash and had her accident. She pushed it away. "I can't believe I almost let anything come between me and Cash. I'm an idiot. He might not even want to be with me anymore." The road was almost pitch-black, illuminated only by the headlights of the SUV. Siena looked into the rearview mirror as the car hit a pothole, sending everyone forward, then slamming back against their seats. "Sorry." The road became very steep as it wound around the mountain. "Who would live up here?"

"Jack would," Savannah said as they hit a gully in the road, and Siena fought to keep the vehicle on the road. The snow began falling harder, and she turned on the wipers to clear it from her field of vision.

The tires spun on a patch of ice and careened to the right. Kate and Ellie screamed.

"I've got it. Turn into the spin. Dad taught me." She straightened the vehicle and eased off the gas a little, wondering why she hadn't done that the night she drove off the embankment and met Cash. *Fate. It had to be fate.* "See, Dad taught me that. Oh God. Mom, I have no idea what to think. What if Cash doesn't want to be with me?"

"Then he's a fool," Ellie said.

"Sage said he could tell Cash loved you by the look in his eye," Kate said.

Siena turned toward Kate, and the SUV swerved with her. "Shit." She wrestled it back on the road as they hit another pothole, and it bottomed out with a loud *clunk*. "Holy crap. This road is crazy." She locked her eyes on the road. "Sage said that?"

"Yeah. I saw it, too. Watch the road or you'll be dead and it won't matter," Kate warned her.

She turned up her windshield wipers to combat the heavier

snowfall. "I thought we weren't supposed to get snow."

"The mountains are always different." Savannah set her hand on Siena's shoulder from the backseat. "Keep your eyes on the road and stop worrying about Cash."

"Oh, right. The only man I ever loved might hate me as much as I hate myself, and I'm not supposed to worry about it?" She shook her head. "Not happening. Look, I see a light up ahead. That must be it."

"I don't see a light," Ellie said.

Siena took her hand off the wheel and pointed just as she hit another pothole. The SUV jolted right, and then there was a loud *pop!* Siena yelled, "Hang on," as she used all her strength to try and straighten the tires. It was no use. They'd hit a patch of ice, and the SUV slid off the road and into a ditch. All of them screamed as they jarred to a halt.

"Holy shit. Mom? Are you okay?"

"Yes. Fine. Ellie? Kate? Savannah? Riley?" her mother asked.

"Yes," Ellie said with a shaky voice.

"I'm okay," Riley said quickly.

Kate clung to Savannah's arm. "Uh-huh."

"Fine here, too," Savannah said.

Siena jumped out of the truck and promptly slipped and fell on her ass. Her feet were soaking wet.

"Are you okay?" Her mother stuck her head out of the driver's side door.

"Fine." She pushed herself up and began running up the road.

"Siena!" Savannah called after her. "Wait. Take my coat."

Siena waved her off. *Fuck the coat. Fuck the shoes.* She had to get to Cash. Her body shook, and by the time she reached the illuminated driveway, her feet and fingers were numb. Her cell phone rang and she pulled it out, saw her mother's name, and shoved it back in her pocket. She had to get to Cash. She pounded on the front door of the little cabin.

"Cash?" She shivered as she crossed the porch and peered into the window.

The front door opened and an old man came out on the porch. He looked her up and down. "Can I help you?"

Through chattering teeth, she said, "C-cash. I'm looking for Cash Ryder."

"Ryder? You mean Gage's place? Why, he's a mile farther up the road."

Siena ran down the porch steps and through the freezing snow toward the road again.

"Wait. You can't get there without shoes and a coat. You'll catch your death of cold."

She kept running. She might be frozen or dead when she reached him. She could barely feel her feet, and she was beginning to think the old man was right, which is why, when he pulled out of his driveway riding a snowmobile and told her to put on his coat and climb on, she did just that.

Chapter Thirty-One

BEING WITH JACK and the other men should have been just what Cash needed. They were boisterous, intelligent, and easy to be with, but what Cash needed was Siena.

"So, you're in love with my sister and she's driving you crazy," Jack said.

"I'm in love with her, but she's not driving me crazy." *I'm driving me crazy.*

"That's a load of shit," Rex said. "I saw the pictures of her in the paper. I didn't want to say anything, but Jack said you knew. Man, if Jade pulled that shit, I'd—"

Treat slapped Rex's arm. They were sitting around the table drinking, having abandoned the poker game an hour before in lieu of discussions about fires and the wilderness, the resorts Treat owned, and now the women in their lives.

"Don't listen to Rex. Jade has him wrapped around her little finger, and if she said she wanted to go on a date with some guy for the press—"

Cash leaned forward. "What did you say?"

"Don't listen to Rex?" Treat looked away.

Cash's heart slammed against his ribs. "No, you said for the press. How do you know that?"

Treat crossed his arms and lowered his chin. "I'm pretty well connected."

Josh, another of Savannah's older brothers, who lived in Manhattan said, "He heard it from me."

"And you heard it from?"

"Savannah, I'm sure," Jack said.

"Shit. Do you know what that could do to Siena's contract? To her press?" Cash's stomach burned. "Does Siena know you all know?"

"No way. But, Cash, what the hell, dude?" Rex asked. "No offense, Jack, but what about your pride, man?"

"Hey, careful," Gage said to Rex.

"No, he's right." Cash heard a rumbling of engines in the distance. "That's why I'm not making her choose. If I make her feel like she needs to choose, and she chooses me, she'll forever hold it against me."

"So what's the plan?" Jack asked.

Cash looked down at the table. "Look, your sister has a chance at a multimillion-dollar contract. The only thing holding her back is me. The way I see it, I need to get out of the equation for her to be the best she can be."

"And she knows this?" Jack pinned him to his chair with a heated stare and his deep voice.

"No. I'll…Look, I love her, Jack. I don't want to spend a minute without her, much less a lifetime. But I can't hold her back."

Gage got up from the table and went to the window.

"She loves you." Jack leaned across the table. "She's never loved a man before that I know of. That means something."

"No, Jack. That means everything, not something." He shrugged. "Would you rather I make her choose, and then maybe she regrets it down the line?" He rose to his feet to see what the noise outside was. "I love her, Jack. I don't want to do either. I don't want to end it and I don't want to make her choose between me and the goddamn Track Sports contract." He didn't mean to yell, but the truth of his words burned his tongue.

"Holy fuck. Cash? Does Siena have long hair?" Gage turned to him and went to the door. "Because I think she's here."

"No way. She's with the girls at Hal's." Cash grabbed his parka and headed out front just in time to see a snowmobile come to a stop and Siena push herself off of the back and fall facefirst into the snow. The man on the snowmobile rose to help her, and Cash and Jack ran toward them. She got to her feet and stumbled forward, her arms flailing in a giant coat, her hair covered with snow, her face bright red. She ran to Cash and clung to his arms. Her body shook so hard her lips were blue. He looked down at her stocking feet.

"You're barefoot," Cash and Jack said in unison. Cash shot him a look and Jack took a step backward.

Fear ripped through Cash as he scooped her into his arms, assessing her blue lips, the look of her skin, her breathing. "What the hell are you doing out here? Where are your shoes? Whose coat are you wearing?" He carried her inside, followed by the man on the snowmobile, Savannah's brothers, and Gage. He grabbed a blanket from the back of the couch he passed on his way to the hearth, where he sat down with her on his lap. "You're so…"

Her teeth clanked together. "Un—un—unprep—unprepared."

He took her face in his hands, the other men forgotten, and stared into her beautiful pool-blue eyes, then kissed her lips.

"Unprepared." He kissed her again, knowing there was no way in hell he was going to ever walk out of her life. He took her feet in his hands, pulled off her wet socks, and exchanged them for a pair of dry, thick woolen socks Gage handed to him.

"What are you doing out here like this? You could have died of hypothermia. You could get frostbite. You could have—"

She lowered her cold lips to his again and kissed him. He held her so tight in the bulky coat that he could feel her body trembling. He tightened his grip until her shaking slowed and her lips began to return to their normal pinkish color. "Gage, hot chocolate, please."

Siena's lips lifted to a crooked smile.

"Your face is numb, isn't it?"

She nodded.

"Damn it, Siena." He cupped the back of her head and drew her cheek against his. God, he loved the feel of her, and the fear of seeing her wet and freezing with some stranger—*Oh God*. He lifted his eyes to the old man, who was watching them with concern in his hooded eyes. "Thank you, sir. I can't thank you enough."

Siena leaned her forehead against his. "I told…Jewel to…kiss off. I don't want…anything to…do with that contract."

"Shh." *Holy shit. Did I hear you right?* He grabbed the warm mug from Gage and brought it to her lips. She closed her eyes as she took a sip.

"Cash, I'm…ashamed of what I did."

"Shh. It's okay."

She shook her head, and he carefully brushed wet strands of hair from her cheeks.

"No. No, it's not. I was ashamed before we started going

out. That I accepted the date with Gunner in the first place."

Jack came and stood beside them. Siena looked up at him, then back at Cash.

"I…I never wanted to do it. I was scared not to. But I don't ever…" Her teeth chattered again, and Cash helped her take another sip of the warm drink. "I will never compromise my beliefs again. I won't compromise us again."

"Babe, it's okay." He knew in his heart their love meant as much to her as it did to him. He'd known in his heart she'd do the right thing, and hearing it come from her lips brought goddamn tears to his eyes.

She shook her head again. "No. It's not okay." She spun around. "Oh, shit. Jack. Savannah, Mom, Ellie, Riley, and Kate are in the SUV on Mount Grail Road. I drove off the road and ran to that man's house."

"I'm on it." Jack grabbed Rex and headed out the door.

"Right behind you with my tow chain on the truck," Gage said.

Treat patted the old man's shoulder. "Give me a ride down the mountain? You'll be faster than them. Josh—"

"On my way," Josh followed Gage outside.

"Cash, I love you. I'm never prepared. I suck. I know. I wasn't prepared when Jewel told me what she wanted me to do, and I went into her office earlier this week ready to tell her I was done. I swear I did, but then the Track Sports thing threw me off. I started thinking about kids, and family, and…There's no excuse. I suck at being prepared, but I don't suck at loving you. I love you with all my heart and soul. I want you. I want us."

Cash could hardly believe what he was hearing. Every part of him wanted to hold her and tell her how much he loved her, but he didn't want to gloss over the reality of the last few days.

"Siena, they're going to offer you a boatload of money. You might regret it. You might end up hating me because of it. Every time you see someone else's face on a Track Sports ad, you might think, *If only...*"

She shook her head. "No. I won't. You know how I know?"

"How?"

"Because the only other time I've felt what I feel when I'm modeling is when I'm with you." She touched his cheek with her chilly hand. "Remember the look in my eyes when I was leaving the restaurant with Gunner?"

That was a look he'd never forget. It was the look he saw in her eyes every time they made love. He nodded.

"What I told you was the truth." Siena took his hand in hers. "The only way to get that look was to think of you, and I don't ever want people to think it's because of some other man. I want you, Cash. Only you. If you'll forgive me."

Cash pulled her close and kissed her again. "Forgive you? You're the most beautiful, frustrating, stubborn, and unprepared woman I've ever met. And you're the only woman I'll ever want. I love you, Siena."

"See? Everything in life does happen for a reason."

"What could you possibly mean? The others are stuck on that dangerous road." Cash kissed her again before she could answer.

"I can't remember what I meant. Kiss me again." She wiggled her toes. "I'm getting warmer. Try that again." She lowered her lips to his and he deepened the kiss.

When they parted, he felt her fingers, then her toes. "You're okay?"

"Yeah. I'm fine now that I know we're okay. But I think the girls are going to hate me. I left them in the car and ran to find you."

"That's my girl. Unprepared and willing to risk the lives of others."

"But I won't risk your heart. Not ever again."

The sound of trucks out front brought a serious look to Siena's eyes. She took his cheeks in her hands and said, "They're going to kill me. Save me."

"Always and forever."

He rose to his feet with her in his arms as the others burst through the door.

"Siena Remington!" Her mother crossed the floor, and Cash turned sideways with Siena clinging to his neck. "Oh, don't think that I won't give you my two cents just because your big handsome fireman is rescuing you yet again."

"Mom, I'm sorry. I had to find him."

"Did you, now?"

Siena faced her mother and saw that she had a broad smile across her face.

"What am I going to do with you? This poor man will spend his life rescuing you from snow, wind, ice cream on your clothes, and God knows what else." Joanie leaned in close to Cash. "You've got your hands full with this one." Then she looked at Siena and said, "It's about damn time you came to your senses. Do you know how hard it was for me to bite my tongue when you first told me about that Gibson man?" She shook her head and pointed to Jack. "Your brother had to talk me off that ledge. And another thing, young lady, get on the phone with your father and tell him what you told me. No need to carry that stuff around in your belly."

Savannah came at her next. "You left us there. Just left us. We could have been hit by a car or died of hypothermia. And you left us to proclaim your love for Cash, and I didn't even get to see it." She shook her head.

Cash set Siena down on her feet, and she clung to him wearing the old man's coat and his brother's socks.

She opened her arms to Savannah and flapped the six inches of extra coat sleeves at her. "Come here."

Savannah hugged her.

"I'm sorry I ruined your bridal shower. And thank you for pissing me off enough to make me see clearly."

"I'm telling you, that's what sisters are for."

"Oh God. They've bonded," Jack said as he draped an arm over Cash's shoulder. "Welcome to the family. Crazy shit and all." Then he leaned down and whispered, "I'm glad it worked out. I was starting to feel bad about having to kill you if you hurt my sister."

"I have a feeling that I'd have more than you to wrestle with if I hurt Siena." He nodded toward the women, who were embracing her in a group hug. "Your sister holds my heart in the palm of her hand. I'll never be the one doing the hurting."

"Dude, that's what they do. They make you crazy; then they make you love them. Then they make you crazy again, but by then you're in too deep to do anything but love them more." Rex nodded at Cash.

"That is true," Jack said.

Savannah broke free from the group hug and said to the other women, "Aren't they cute? They think they have women all figured out."

The men held up their hands in surrender.

"So," Gage whispered to Cash. "Who's gonna clue Gunner in on the end of his love affair?"

In one swift move, Cash elbowed him in the gut.

Siena wrapped her arms around Cash and kissed him. "Sliding off the road that night was the best thing that ever happened to me."

Cash pulled her close and leaned his forehead against hers. "No, babe. The best is yet to come."

Ready for more Remingtons?

Fall in love with Rush Remington and Jayla Stone in SLOPE OF LOVE

Chapter One

THE MUSCLE ON the side of Rush Remington's jaw bunched as he glanced out the window at the snow that had been falling since the plane touched down in Colorado. Rush didn't need much to be happy—a snowy slope, a set of skis, a daily dose or two of protein powder, and a little time with his best friend. The ski team equipment had been shipped separately and had already arrived at the Colorado Ski Center, where he and a few other Olympic ski team members were teaching ski workshops this week. Rush pulled two duffel bags from beneath his seat. One was packed tight with protein powder, movies, and gummy bears—his best friend's go-to snack—the other stuffed to the hilt with his clothes.

He dug his vibrating cell phone from his pocket—another text from Jayla. He and Jayla Stone been best friends for more than fifteen years, and this was supposed to be *their* week to hang out. He eyed the reporters waiting by the entrance of the lodge before stealing a look toward the back of the van, where Jayla sat beside Marcus White, pretending to rummage through her purse for something. Rush knew that she was really avoiding making eye contact with him because of Marcus. The only thing in that damn purse was a man's wallet—because *women's wallets are too bulky*—her keys, personal products (wrapped in tissues and hidden in a zippered pouch because *they're embarrassing*), and probably a few empty bags of gummy bears.

He read the text from Jayla. *Cute reporter. Blonde. Red coat.*

At six foot two, with a shock of dark brown hair, an ever-present tan, perfect teeth, and an insatiable appetite for exercise, the media—and women—loved Rush, but today he was in no mood to smile for the camera.

He laughed under his breath and shook his head. A year ago he'd have scoped out the hot blonde, scored by midnight, then forgotten her name by the next morning when he and Jayla met for breakfast. She'd have teased him about adding a notch to his belt or some other random shit, and then they'd have hit the slopes. A year ago he was a totally different guy.

He texted her back. *If she's not made of powder, I'm not interested. Just wanna ski.*

In a week, the competitive ski season would be over, and Rush could have all the women he wanted without worrying about them messing with his head and, in turn, screwing with his ability to win. But getting laid by some random woman wasn't anywhere on Rush's agenda. Rush had planned on revealing to Jayla that he finally realized he was truly, madly, and infuriatingly in love with her. Now his plan was shot to hell, and he had no interest in doing anything other than making it through the week and coming out on top of the North Face Competition, the last race of the season.

He didn't have to look at Jayla to know that her eyebrows were drawn together and she was reaching for that empty bag of gummy bears, hoping to find just one more to calm her nerves. Or to know that Marcus fucking White was eyeing every move she made.

Rush followed the other members of the ski team who had volunteered to teach the ski workshops off of the van. Cliff Bail and Patrick Staller looked like they had just walked out of *Skier* magazine with their strong physiques and dirty-blond, sun-streaked hair. They checked out the female reporters as they headed for the resort with Kia Lyle and Teri Martin on their heels. Rush hung back, hoping the reporters would get their fill of interviews with his teammates and give him a break. He inhaled the crisp, cold mountain air, kicked the blanket of fresh snow with the toe of his boot, and surveyed the grounds of the place that he'd call home for the next week. The majestic three-story stone and cedar lodge was set against the backdrop of snowcapped mountains. Curvy slopes carved wide white paths through the trees, snaking from the mountain peaks to the valleys below, and it took his breath away.

Reporters and cameramen were on him seconds later, shoving microphones in his face and snapping photos.

"Rush, do you have anything you'd like to say to your fans?"

Rush answered the male reporter without breaking stride on his way into the lobby, with a serious look in his eyes and a practiced media-worthy smile. "I appreciate their support, and they can count on me to be ready for the next Olympics."

He wondered if they'd even caught his last words as Jayla stepped from the van and every camera turned in her direction. Since winning two Olympic gold medals, Jayla had been hounded by the press even more than he had. Nothing beat a hot female Olympic medalist. Having been friends with her for years, he was thrilled for her success, though he couldn't ignore the ego slap at being cast aside by the press. He didn't blame them really. Jayla was America's sweetheart, the new face of Dove, and the best damn role model young girls could ask for.

The Olympic ski team had been sponsored by leading ski manufacturers and clothing manufacturers. After winning his Olympic golds, Rush had secured several of his own sponsors, ranging from sunscreen manufacturers to energy drink manufacturers, and since winning her Olympic gold medal for the downhill event, Jayla had also received sponsorships from hair care and beauty product manufacturers.

"Dude, you a statue? Let's go." Marcus pushed past Rush, carrying a leather bag thrown over his shoulder.

America's sweetheart and the new girlfriend of this asshole.

"Three bags. Over there," Marcus snapped at the twenty-something bellboy who looked like he'd just come from at a day at the beach, with his long sun-streaked bangs covering his eyes and tanned face.

Rush gritted his teeth to keep from giving him a two-fisted lesson in manners. *Asshole.* He and Marcus had trained together for the last three years. At the Olympics two years earlier, Marcus failed to qualify to compete in the medal rounds while Rush had gone on to become one of the few men to win Olympic medals in all five disciplines: gold in the slalom and giant slalom, and silver in the Super-G, downhill, and combined. Marcus had been a prick before Rush won, and he'd turned into a prick extraordinaire ever since. And for the last three weeks, he'd monopolized every second of Jayla's time—a harsh reminder that Rush had waited too long already, and he needed to tell Jayla how he felt about her before she and Marcus got in any deeper.

Rush watched him barge through the glass doors with his chin held high. He'd like to knock that pointy chin into tomorrow.

Marcus shouldn't even be there. He hadn't volunteered like Rush and a few of the other team members had to help his buddy Blake Carter's wife, Danica, teach a ski workshop for kids from her youth center, No Limitz. Community outreach was important for Rush's and his teammates' images, but Rush hadn't volunteered for that reason. Blake was his buddy, and he liked to promote the sport to youth. Hell, if it were up to Rush, he'd teach kids to ski the minute they could walk.

Rush held the door open as the volunteers from the women's ski team filed through, listening as Jayla tried to disengage from the press.

"Any messages for your fans?" The red-coated reporter shoved a microphone in her face.

Since winning her gold, Jayla had been all over television and radio commercials as well as print ads for Dove and a few of her other sponsors, and young girls from all over had emailed her in support, many thanking her for inspiring them. Jayla wasn't the type to get an inflated ego. Prior to Marcus consuming Jayla's personal life, Rush had been by her side when she personally answered many of those emails, and her genuine gratitude had reeled his heart in even more. Then again, gratitude and sincerity were integral parts of Jayla's sweet nature.

"Yes. I appreciate their support. I love hearing from them, and I hope to make them proud next weekend."

"Any plans for the next Olympics?" a different female reporter asked.

The next Olympics might be two years away, but Rush, Jayla, and the rest of the team practiced as if it were right around the corner.

"Train and win." Jayla slung a bag over her shoulder and waved as she walked away. A reporter hurried beside her, and Jayla slowed just long enough to say a gracious thank you before catching up to Rush.

"Thanks, Rush," she said as she came through the door.

Rush leaned in close and tried to mask the storm brewing in his gut. "Thought you were coming alone."

She narrowed her eyes. "So did I."

He'd seen her flinch when she lifted her bag, and since she'd had two previous shoulder injuries, Rush did what he'd always done. He reached for her bag.

She glared at him. "I'm fine."

He held up his hands in surrender.

Most women were needy, clingy, and while Rush was all too happy to spend a few hours getting his groove on and pleasuring them, he wasn't the type to listen to bitching and moaning and to answer questions like, *Do these jeans make me look fat?* He'd learned this lesson early in life, when he'd answered honestly on more than one occasion. *No, the lard in that cake you just downed makes you look fat.* Jayla wasn't like most women. She was intense, competitive, strong. Those were just a few of the many qualities he loved about her. She was a freaking bulldog when she wanted to be, and she was also stubborn as a goddamn mule.

He tried to ignore the clutch in his chest as she flipped her long brown hair over her shoulder and flashed a smile at Marcus. Rush and Jayla had met at ski camp as teenagers, and they'd quickly become as close as two friends could be. He trusted Jayla with his dirtiest secrets, and he knew her deepest fears. He was surprised that after all these years she still put up with him and that he hadn't fucked up their friendship, especially now that he realized—or rather, *accepted*—what a womanizing douche he'd been for all those years, something he'd never tried to hide from her. He had his eldest brother, Jack, and a comment from Jayla to thank for that little eye-opening nugget of truth. Although they'd shared the details of their personal lives, they'd never judged each other, and for the first time ever, he was having a hard time keeping his mouth shut. In order to make it through this messed-up week, he pushed aside thoughts of Jayla and Marcus and focused on the upcoming North Face Competition, the last race of the season.

"Ow!"

Rush turned and caught a glimpse of Jayla rubbing her arm. He clenched his jaw and narrowed his eyes, locking a heated stare on Marcus. He could hardly believe she'd gone out with him once, much less that they were still together after three weeks. It made no sense at all. Marcus was a total controlling prick, and Jayla was…He wouldn't allow himself to think of the litany of qualities he loved about her or how long it had taken him to finally open his eyes and realize just how much he loved them.

Jayla was facing the opposite direction, and without walking over, he'd have no way of knowing if Marcus had hurt her or if she was bitching about breaking a nail. Then again, Jayla didn't give a shit about her nails. Never had.

Marcus slung his arm around Jayla's shoulder and turned away with a smirk. Rush didn't miss the way Jayla's body went rigid beneath his touch.

Not my problem.

To continue reading, please buy
SLOPE OF LOVE

New to the Love in Bloom big-family romance collection? Start at the beginning of the big-family romance collection with Treat and Max in LOVERS AT HEART, REIMAGINED.

Treat Braden wasn't looking for love when Max Armstrong walked into his Nassau resort, but he saw right through the efficient and capable facade she wore like a shield to the sweet, sensual woman beneath. One magnificent evening together sparked an intense connection, and for the first time in his life Treat wanted more than a casual affair. But something caused Max to turn away, and now, after weeks of unanswered phone calls and longing for the one woman he cannot have, Treat is going back to his family's ranch to try to finally move on.

A chance encounter brings Treat and Max together again, and it turns into a night of intense passion and honesty. When Max reveals her secret, painful past, Treat vows to do everything within his power to win Max's heart forever—including helping her finally face her demons head-on.

Buy **LOVERS AT HEART, REIMAGINED**

For free Love in Bloom family trees, publication schedules, series checklists, and more, please visit the special Reader Goodies page that I've set up for you.
www.MelissaFoster.com/Reader-Goodies

Sign up for my newsletter to keep up to date with new releases and to receive free short story featuring Jack Remington and Savannah Braden.
www.MelissaFoster.com/Newsletter

Join my Facebook Fan Club to chat with me about current and upcoming books. You never know when you'll inspire a story or character and end up in one of my books, as several fan club members have already discovered.
www.Facebook.com/groups/MelissaFosterFans

Remember to like and follow my Facebook fan page to stay abreast of what's going on in our fictional boyfriends' worlds.
www.Facebook.com/MelissaFosterAuthor

More Books By Melissa Foster

LOVE IN BLOOM SERIES

SNOW SISTERS
Sisters in Love
Sisters in Bloom
Sisters in White

THE BRADENS at Weston
Lovers at Heart, Reimagined
Destined for Love
Friendship on Fire
Sea of Love
Bursting with Love
Hearts at Play

THE BRADENS at Trusty
Taken by Love
Fated for Love
Romancing My Love
Flirting with Love
Dreaming of Love
Crashing into Love

THE BRADENS at Peaceful Harbor
Healed by Love
Surrender My Love
River of Love
Crushing on Love
Whisper of Love
Thrill of Love

THE BRADENS & MONTGOMERYS at Pleasant Hill – Oak Falls
Embracing Her Heart
Anything For Love
Trails of Love
Wild, Crazy Hearts
Making You Mine

THE BRADEN NOVELLAS
Promise My Love
Our New Love
Daring Her Love
Story of Love
Love at Last

THE REMINGTONS
Game of Love
Stroke of Love
Flames of Love
Slope of Love
Read, Write, Love
Touched by Love

SEASIDE SUMMERS
Seaside Dreams
Seaside Hearts
Seaside Sunsets
Seaside Secrets
Seaside Nights
Seaside Embrace
Seaside Lovers
Seaside Whispers

BAYSIDE SUMMERS
Bayside Desires
Bayside Passions
Bayside Heat
Bayside Escape
Bayside Romance

THE RYDERS
Seized by Love
Claimed by Love
Chased by Love
Rescued by Love
Swept Into Love

SUGAR LAKE
The Real Thing
Only for You
Love Like Ours
Finding My Girl

SEXY STANDALONE ROMANCE
Tru Blue
Truly, Madly, Whiskey
Driving Whiskey Wild
Wicked Whiskey Love
Mad About Moon
Taming My Whiskey

<u>BILLIONAIRES AFTER DARK SERIES</u>

WILD BOYS AFTER DARK
Logan
Heath
Jackson
Cooper

BAD BOYS AFTER DARK
Mick
Dylan
Carson
Brett

HARBORSIDE NIGHTS SERIES
Includes characters from the Love in Bloom series
Catching Cassidy
Discovering Delilah
Tempting Tristan

More Books by Melissa
Chasing Amanda (mystery/suspense)
Come Back to Me (mystery/suspense)
Have No Shame (historical fiction/romance)
Love, Lies & Mystery (3-book bundle)
Megan's Way (literary fiction)
Traces of Kara (psychological thriller)
Where Petals Fall (suspense)

Acknowledgments

My readers are a constant source of inspiration and support. I enjoy hearing from you, and I hope you will continue to reach out to me on social media and through emails. Thank you for connecting with my stories and with me.

I would like to thank all of the firefighters who risk their lives on a daily basis to keep us safe. I think many people don't fully recognize the fear and risk they face when they're on the job. I know I didn't before speaking with Gary Hoffman, paramedic firefighter with the Williamsport Company 2, VFD-EMS. Thank you for taking the time to answer my questions, Gary. I have taken many creative liberties, and all errors are my own.

Many thanks to all of my friends and family who have reached out in support of my writing, read through my various scenes, and talked me off the ledge on a few occasions when perfecting scenes. My editorial team continues to amaze me on a daily basis with their patience, persistence, and meticulous attention to detail. Tremendous gratitude goes to Kristen Weber, Penina Lopez, Jenna Bagnini, Juliette Hill, Marlene Engel, and Lynn Mullan.

Last, but never, ever least, Les, thank you for supporting me while I fall in love over and over again with fictional men. I adore you.

~Meet Melissa~

www.MelissaFoster.com

Having sold more than three million books, Melissa Foster is a *New York Times* and *USA Today* bestselling and award-winning author. Her books have been recommended by *USA Today's* book blog, *Hagerstown* magazine, *The Patriot*, and several other print venues. Melissa has painted and donated several murals to the Hospital for Sick Children in Washington, DC.

Visit Melissa on her website or chat with her on social media. Melissa enjoys discussing her books with book clubs and reader groups and welcomes an invitation to your event.

Melissa's books are available through most online retailers in paperback, digital, and audio formats.

Printed in Great Britain
by Amazon